THE FORGOTTEN

By Bishop O'Connell

The Forgotten
The Stolen

THE FORGOTTEN

An American Faerie Tale

BISHOP O'CONNELL

HARPER

VOYAGER
IMPULSE

An Imprint of HarperCollins Publishers

7/20/15

THE FORGOTTEN

This is a work of fiction. Names, characters, places, and incidents are products of the author's imagination or are used fictitiously and are not to be construed as real. Any resemblance to actual events, locales, organizations, or persons, living or dead, is entirely coincidental.

EPub Edition MARCH 2015 ISBN: 9780062358783

Print Edition ISBN: 9780062358806

10 9 8 7 6 5 4 3 2 1

For *"The Boot"* and Dennis Morgan.

CHAPTER ONE

Dante glanced around the office, noting how little it had changed over the years. The room was large, but Spartan in its furnishings; just a few club chairs and rows of bookshelves covering three of the four walls. He ran his fingers along the intricately carved desk and smiled, remembering the craftsman who made it, and how angry John Adams had been when Dante had bought it out from under him. Of course, it'd been nothing compared to Abigail's fury. But it would've been a shame if it had burned with the White House in 1814.

So much history, he thought.

He looked at the computer and three monitors that now sat upon it. Then he turned his gaze to the sprawling Boston cityscape beyond the windows. He was going to miss this office almost as much as his position as magister, but then, he could never have passed up a promotion like the one he'd been given.

"And so much change," he said quietly.

"What?" Faolan asked, looking up from the massive table in the middle of the room.

"Nothing," Dante said, looking at the new magister and content at least that this region was going to be in good hands.

He joined Faolan and looked down at the large touchscreen that made up the table's surface. He studied the map on display. The western two-thirds were littered with a rainbow of virtual pushpins. "What do the colors mean?"

"Yellow means confirmed reports of more than a hundred," Faolan said, tapping the pins over Los Angeles, Las Vegas, New Orleans, Houston, Dallas, Kansas City, and Chicago. With each tap, a different number displayed briefly next to the pin.

Dante swallowed back the taste of bile.

"Blue is more than fifty." Faolan tapped the pins over Minneapolis, St. Louis, Nashville, and Indianapolis.

Dante shook his head, his shoulder-length hair falling around his face. "All changelings?"

"Yes, and more than ninety-five percent are kids."

Dante's stomach knotted as his luminescent green eyes swept over the mass of black pins scattered across the map—there had to be hundreds of them. "Do I even want to ask what black means?"

Faolan let out a breath. "Unconfirmed by Rogue Court sources and being investigated further."

Dante looked up. "How many before you note it worth investigation?"

"Fifty."

"So many?"

Faolan ran a hand through his short auburn hair and his blue eyes dimmed to gray. "We're getting reports from everywhere. Even after pooling resources with Brigid in the Middle Region, we don't have enough marshals to investigate everything. The threshold started at a dozen, but we had to raise it when we reached two hundred cities."

"And the mortal authorities aren't looking into it?" Dante asked.

Faolan grimaced. "There's not a big demand to investigate missing street kids. Not only are they usually transient, but most people don't like to think about them." He shook his head. "I'm not making excuses, but it's a matter of limited resources. It's just as likely a kid or group of kids packed up and went to a different city. It isn't that they don't care—"

"There's only so much they can do," Dante said.

Faolan nodded.

Dante let out a long sigh. "I was so focused on the Eastern Region—"

"And look," Faolan said, gesturing to the east coast, "just four black pins from Canada to Cuba. You had a third of the country under your purview, and there are fewer missing changelings than in any single state."

Dante patted Faolan's shoulder. "I appreciate the thought, but that's not much comfort to those—" He winced. "At least two hundred and fifty missing kids." He took a deep breath and his eyes drifted to a yellow pin in Seattle. "What about the magister of the New Western Region? Still no word?"

Faolan made a disgusted face. "No. I've tried repeatedly to see if Donovan could spare some marshals." He looked away. "I've had to rely on, um, local sources."

Dante's eyebrows rose.

Faolan didn't say anything, but the ghost of a smile appeared at one corner of his thin lips.

Dante chuckled a little. "Well, I suppose you're entitled to your secrets."

"Thank you, Magis—" Faolan winced. "Sorry, Regent, I—"

Dante shrugged. "It's okay, I'm still getting used to it myself." He turned his attention back to the map, noting several white pins were almost hidden from view by the mass of black, green, and yellow. "What do those represent?"

Faolan straightened up and crossed his arms. "That's the really odd thing. They mark reports of wizards."

Dante looked at Faolan with wide eyes. "Wizards? In all those cities?"

Faolan nodded. "And not just one in each. From most cities, we're receiving reports of dozens."

Dante's mouth fell open. "Dozens?"

"At least." Faolan pursed his lips. "And almost without exception, they're also homeless kids."

"That can't be a coincidence."

"I don't think so either," Faolan said. "But I have no idea how someone could start spawning wizards."

"I don't either," Dante said. "Any idea where this all began?"

"The reports are so scattered, it's hard to pin down a timeline."

Dante arched an eyebrow. "You're saying you don't know? I'm not sure I've ever heard you say those words before."

Faolan chuckled. "I don't know yet, but I will. We're trying to work backwards, but like I said, our information isn't good."

"I'll start looking into it."

Faolan opened his mouth to object.

"I have some, um, free time on my hands recently, what with someone else managing the day-to-day business." Dante forced a smile. "Besides, I'm responsible for all three regions now. And didn't you say we're stretched thin?"

"Well, yes, but—"

"I'm open to other ideas if you have any."

Faolan thought for a moment, then closed his mouth and shook his head.

"I know I don't need to ask—" Dante started.

"I'll make sure the queen mother and her family are well looked after," Faolan said.

"Thank you."

"Should I make you some road-trip playlists?" Faolan asked through a smile.

Dante shook his head. "No, but I'll take some weapons." He thought for a moment, then added, "and some tokens of favor."

"Really?"

Dante nodded at the map. "If your reports are even just half right, that's more than a thousand changeling kids missing. Combine that with the sudden explosion of mortals skilled in the craft, and we have something potentially world changing going on."

"That's why I called you in," Faolan said.

Dante sighed and ran his fingers through his long blond hair. "I'm sorry it took me so long to get here."

"You were otherwise occupied." Faolan patted his shoulder. "It's been a hard six months for all of us. Besides, when I first mentioned it, I only knew Donovan wasn't responding to any court messages. The time gave me a chance to collect what you're looking at now."

Dante looked at the map, imaging the faces of the countless children who were lost and forgotten. "Even so, how many of these disappearances could we have prevented if I'd become involved sooner?"

"With all due respect," Faolan said, "this isn't your fault or responsibility. You had your hands more than full with the Cruinnigh and the aftermath of a failed insurrection. On top of that, we just didn't know."

Dante could see the weight of responsibility settling in behind Faolan's blue eyes. "No, but we should have."

Faolan sighed. "Well, I can't argue with that."

"So let's make sure there are no more pins."

CHAPTER TWO

Jane's mind was fuzzy. Her eyes opened, but the colors and lines wouldn't coalesce. She wasn't even sure if she was awake or dreaming. Somewhere in the distance were vaguely familiar voices, but something about the tone was . . . disconcerting. She tried to focus.

"Mom? Dad?" Her mouth was dry.

The voices stopped and a long silence followed.

"I'm sorry, but you've left us no choice, Janey," her father said.

"What?" Jane tried to rub her eyes, but something around her wrists kept her arms above her head. "What the—?" She yanked against the bindings.

Panic made her vision narrow, but finally everything came into focus. She was in her room, lying on her bed with her wrists and ankles tied to the frame. Her parents stood over her with grim expressions. Her mother's eyes were red and puffy, as though she'd been crying.

"What are you doing?" Jane resumed her struggle, but her wrists were already raw.

Her mother winced. "Please stop, honey. Don't make it worse." She reached out, but Jane's father caught her hand and whispered something. Neither of them would meet Jane's eyes.

"Pleas—"

Her father lifted a hand. "Don't." He sighed and shook his head. "What happened to our little girl?" When he finally looked at her, his blue eyes were hard and cold. "You were such a sweet child."

Jane swallowed. "Nothing. Nothing happened to me. I'm still me—"

"Don't speak to me! I won't hear your lies, Satan!" her father screamed.

Jane flinched, a fresh wave of bone-numbing fear rushing through her.

Her father took a deep breath and closed his eyes. When he opened them, his voice was calm and soft. "We only asked you to abandon the lies of men and science." His eyes were wet. "Janey, we begged you to return to God and the path of righteousness."

"But, I did—"

"Lies!" he roared.

The room fell into a frightened silence. But it almost sounded like someone was chuckling.

"I told you, Mary," her father said, "it's up to us. We must remain strong. Our child needs our strength and our faith. We must bring her, willing or other-wise, back to the light of God. Only he can cast away the evil that has tainted her. Only he can save her soul now."

"Daddy, please," was all Jane could choke out. She shook her head, tears running down her cheeks. This had to be a dream. Any minute she'd wake up.

Her father stared at her, his blue eyes as cold as a winter sky. "Lord, hear us as we pray for this wayward child."

"Why are you doing this? I didn't do anything!" Jane screamed.

"Then explain these." Her father held up a battered composition book.

Sobbing now racked Jane's body so hard she couldn't speak. She just kept shaking her head. It's not supposed to be like this, it's wrong. Everything around her was wrong, somehow.

Her father opened one of the books and showed her the scribbled calculations, the obscenely complex equations and formulas. "You lied to us. You lied again, and again."

"I told you," Jane said between sobs. "It's just math!"

He held up the book. "No. These are lies created by Satan, meant to turn us away from God and his truth. They lead us astray! It is a sin to presume to understand the mind of God! Seek not the answers in science. Seek it in the Word of the Lord." His voice was calm now, flat and devoid of any emotion. "This is not *just* math." His face twisted. "It's witchcraft."

"Richard, it's time to begin." A remarkably unremarkable man in his late forties stepped forward, a small leather-bound book held tightly to his black shirt. The white of his Roman collar was stained and yellowed.

Jane blinked at the priest. "Father Williams?"

"Peace, child. Fear not, we will drive the devil and his darkness from you," he said. His voice had as much emotion as most people would use to recite a grocery list.

"Drive out . . ." Jane's whisper died and her heart fell through the floor. She struggled anew at her bindings. "No! No way! I don't need an exorcism! Are you insane?"

Father Williams opened the book. The hand holding it was wrapped in a chain from which a small crucifix dangled. His other hand drew a clear glass vial emblazoned with a gold cross from his pocket.

Jane turned to her mother, mouthing silently, "Mommy?"

Her mother clenched her jaw tight as tears spilled down her cheeks. It looked as though she was about to speak when her father wrapped his arm around her. She turned from Jane and buried her face in his shoulder.

It was then that Jane noticed him.

A tall, thin man stood in the corner. Drenched in heavy shadow, he defied the bright lighting of the room. His black suit and tie were rumpled, and he wore a flat wide-brimmed hat. The only contrast was white—the cuffs of his shirt, the accents of his two-toned wingtip shoes, and the lenses of his round, curiously opaque spectacles. He looked like something out of a comic book.

He chuckled. The sound was like the mix of a diesel engine, a cat's purr, and a psychotic version of the Cookie Monster.

Pain tore through Jane's head.

"That which does not kill you, only makes you stronger," Nightstick said. His gravelly voice was almost singsong. "Usually."

Jane knew that was the shadow man's name, but couldn't explain how any more than she could say why no one else noticed him.

"Hear me, Satan," Father Williams said.

Jane looked at Nightstick.

He laughed. "Sorry, kid. Afraid he's talking to you."

"Leave this child," Father Williams continued. "Remove your black stain from her soul! The power of Christ compels you!"

"But I'm not possessed!" Jane screamed. Then the absurdity of it all crashed down on her, and she began laughing uncontrollably.

"See how she mocks our lord!" Father Williams cried.

For a moment, Jane could've sworn the priest was actually smiling, which only made her laugh harder.

He slapped her face, hard.

The sharp sting of pain and the coppery taste of blood brought the laughter to a stop. Jane glared at the priest and a rush of anger replaced fear as she jerked at her bonds. She imagined herself in a movie, and this was the part where she'd give some bad one-liner, her theme music would start, and then she'd break free and kill this bastard.

"Go to hell, you son of a—"

Numbers and symbols swam through the air, nearly translucent, and though Jane hadn't noticed them before, she knew they'd always been there. Like a swarm of insects, they converged upon the stereo sitting on her desk.

Loud, thumping techno music filled the room, and a synthesized voice spoke between the heavy beats. "The transfiguration process has begun."

The room jolted.

Everyone, including Jane, froze and stared with wide eyes at the stereo.

"This is murder," the digitized voice said.

Father Williams crossed himself.

"Well now, this is really getting entertaining," Nightstick said.

"It wasn't me!" Jane yelled.

"Actually, it was, my dear," Nightstick said and chuckled.

Numbers and symbols continued to dance in the air. Those closest to the stereo joined the others, forming long and intricate calculations.

The volume increased.

"By the power of Jesus Christ, I command you to leave this child!" Father Williams bellowed, though his voice lacked conviction. "The power of Christ compels you!" Using the vial, he cast a watery cross over Jane.

There was a visceral sense of relief in finding that the water didn't burn. She really wasn't possessed. However, there was a growing pressure in the spot between her eyes.

The numbers and symbols grew more frenetic in their movements.

Amid the minutia of seemingly endless equations, everything froze as she had a realization. Even her heart seemed to hold still in reverence to the magnitude of her moment of clarity. It was the missing piece of a grand unifying theory, something no one else had been able to see, ever.

"Will," Jane whispered. "The will of a sentient consciousness."

Time resumed, and Jane sighed at the rush of adrenaline that poured through her.

Her father was jabbing at buttons, trying to turn off the stereo. In response to each attempt, the floating equations moved into a different sequence, allowing the flow of electrons to bypass his latest effort. His face red, he finally tore the plug from the wall and tossed the stereo across her room, music still blasting.

Just before the stereo hit the wall, the numbers and symbols leapt to the small TV on her chest of drawers. It turned on to show an actor portraying Jesus stepping between an angry mob and a young girl, hands raised. "Let he among you who is without sin cast the first stone."

Her mother crossed herself and took a step back, whispering something under her breath.

"Oh, nicely done," Nightstick said. "Very dramatic touch."

The pressure in Jane's head turned to white-hot pain and a tingling began to spread over her body.

"Shut up!" she screamed.

Father Williams's words were incoherent to her now. In fact, the whole scene was slowly drowning in a sea of pain and confusion, the numbers and symbols becoming almost luminescent.

"No!" she screamed through clenched teeth and pulled at the ropes. "God, please help me!"

She screamed again as what felt like a superheated ice pick was driven into her skull. Every muscle in her body tightened at once. A torrent of wind shattered the windows, all of them, and swept through the room, hurling broken glass and debris everywhere.

"Sorry," Nightstick said. "God's away on business."

Jane's eyes snapped open and she sat up with a gasp. She put her hands to her throbbing head and took slow, deep breaths as the pain subsided. Her stomach was doing backflips.

Slowly, hesitantly, she blinked and looked at her hands. The ropes were still around her wrists, the fibers stained with blood, but the ends dangled down near her forearms, cut clean through and singed.

It took several minutes of staring at her shaking hands to get them to stop enough to untie the bindings from her wrists. She winced as the strands caught and pulled her raw flesh. She tossed the ropes away and went to work on the ones around her ankles.

She was sitting on her bedspread. It was mostly intact, embroidered angels and all. Beneath it, however, she found the sheets and just the top inch of the mattress. Like the ropes, the cut was perfectly straight and bore the faintest trace of scorching at the edges.

Her messenger bag lay at the foot of the decapitated bed. She grabbed the bag, got to her feet, slung it over her shoulder, and finally noticed her surroundings.

"Holy shit."

Trees, everywhere she looked were trees, and not the kind that grew outside her bedroom window, or anywhere else in Kansas. These were massive, the color of red clay, and stretched in every direction for as far as she could see. Her eyes moved from one to another to another until the haze in the distance swallowed them. A soft breeze blew over her, and she could hear birdsong from all around.

The canopy was hundreds of feet above her. Through the reaching branches, she could see bright blue sky and puffy white clouds. Her mind spun, trying to understand what had happened and how. "This so isn't happening. It's a really messed-up dream, and I just need to wake up—" She blinked.

Her heart thudded in her ears, and she felt cold. She shook her head and noticed the debris from her room cast about in the ferns. There were old food wrappers, empty pop cans, stray papers, window-glass shards, and even the notebook her father had used as evidence against her.

A numb feeling came over her as she lifted a corner of the cover to find it was actually half a notebook. Beneath it, she saw three fingers of a human hand neatly severed in the same manner as everything else.

She dropped the book and leapt back.

The longer she looked at the book, the more unreal the fingers beneath became. Her eyes shifted to her bag. She lifted the flap the same way someone would open a booby-trapped box. Then she opened the secret pocket and removed two other battered composition books. After a slight hesitation, she flipped through one, scanning the physics formulae, quantum theory, and various calculations. She'd jokingly thought of these books as her grimoire, and not just because of the power that the formulations in them held.

Her eyes drifted from a particular theorem to the detritus that had once been in her room and back. The equation almost seemed to move, as if trying to lift from the page. As she was remembering the equations that had floated in her room, she could just make out in her peripheral vision the same kinds of symbols and numbers joining together into equations, then disbanding and joining other symbols to make new calculations.

Again, she started laughing. This was either a vindication of her theories or the result of a complete mental breakdown. She'd snapped and was lying in a hospital bed somewhere, drooling while her family argued with the doctors over brain activity. She pondered the ludicrousness of the situation and laughed harder. If this was a delusion, where was Johnny Depp?

After several moments, she thought of Nightstick and her manic laughter subsided.

He stood twenty feet away, obscured by shadows in blatant disregard to the daylight that shone on everything around him.

"I'm really sorry to disappoint you," he said. "About not being Mr. Depp, I mean."

"Who are you?" she asked.

"Well, that's quite a question, isn't it?" Nightstick scratched at his cheek and looked around for a long moment. "I suppose the simple answer is that I'm a hallucination."

"So, I'm crazy?" It was actually a bit of a relief. Talk about mixed emotions.

"I'm not really an expert," he said. "But no, not in the way you're hoping, I'm afraid." He chuckled, and it sent a shiver down Jane's back. "Though I suppose my very existence speaks to some sort of mental disrepair."

"So this is real?"

Nightstick considered the question for a long moment. "For the sake of brevity, yes."

"What's that mean?"

"As far as you're concerned, yes, you did make the stereo play, even when it wasn't plugged in. And you did make the TV turn on to show Jesus—which was truly inspired, by the way. You did all that, in a matter of speaking." He looked around. "But, this is really and truly a redwood forest in Northern California—"

"You just qualified almost everything you said," Jane said.

Nightstick shrugged. "If you really want to have an in-depth discussion on the nature of reality with yourself . . ."

Jane looked down at the composition books and her hands started to shake, so she put the books away and clenched her hands into fists. When she looked up, Nightstick was staring at her.

"If you're not going help, get lost," she said.

It was as if he were never there.

She looked around. Crazy or not, she was alone with no idea how she'd traveled several thousand miles or how she was going to get home. A twitch of her hands brought a stab of pain from her bloodied wrists. Did she even want to go home?

The abrupt emptiness and fear caught her off guard. She'd thought about running away plenty, more so as her parents went further off the deep end of their Bibles. The bag on her shoulder had a few other hidden pouches containing cash, a couple boxes of matches, a St. Christopher medallion, a multi-tool, an eagle feather, and a few other assorted items, just in case. However, as the minutes ticked by, it was becoming quite clear that thinking about running away was very different from actually doing it. She looked down at her Chuck Taylor sneakers and was grateful she'd fallen asleep fully clothed last night.

She ran her hands through her tangled brown hair and let out a breath.

"So, what now?" she asked.

As if in answer, her stomach lurched and she fell to

her knees. Symbols, numbers, and calculations began spinning overhead, forming then disjoining, over and over. The pressure was so intense, she thought her skull might explode. She focused her gaze and concentrated on one formulation, then another. As she did, they became more opaque and less frantic in their movements. They combined into the quantum wormhole theory—the joining of two points in space—and it made sense. It was so simple. Dimensional space was an illusion, a construct, and it could be circumvented. She'd done it with the power of her mind. How else could she have gotten here?

Incoherent whispers filled the air, bringing Jane's attention back to the here and now. She focused, but couldn't make out the words. It sounded like children.

"Hello?" she shouted. "Who's there? Nightstick?"

Like a whisper, the shadow man appeared in front of her. "That's not me," he said. "And I'd love to help, but it's sort of beyond my design specs."

More whispers. They grew steadily louder, more insistent, but there were too many to make out anything. It felt like a thousand voices pulling on her sleeve, desperate to get her attention.

"Stop, please," she said.

The whispers just grew louder, more garbled as still more voices joined the cacophony.

"Shut up!" Jane closed her eyes and covered her ears with shaking hands. "Get out of my head!"

Everything was silent.

After several minutes, she dropped her hands.

Slowly, the vacuum of sound began to fill; wind, birds, and insects. Beyond that, she could just make out the sound of running water and she realized she was incredibly thirsty.

Reluctantly, she opened her eyes. The floating symbols and numbers were gone, as was Nightstick.

She stood and followed the sound, soon arriving at a clear and swift little stream. She dropped her bag, knelt down, and plunged her head into the water.

This wasn't a delusion or a dream, and she knew it. She took several swallows of the cool water and considered keeping her head there. After a while, the cold water made her ears ache.

She sat up, sucked in a deep breath of air, pushed her wet hair back, and stared at her reflection. Her eyes were red and puffy, but the irises were as soft in color and vibrant in tone as ever. She'd always liked the color; it reminded her of melted chocolate. She was taller than most of the boys in school, even the seniors; she was brushing six feet when last she checked, but was also skinny. Her build was more fitting to a boy about to start puberty, not a girl nearing the end of it. Her hair was a brown, slightly shaggy pixie cut.

She slung her bag over her shoulder, walked to a large rock, and sat down.

Would she ever see Michael and Josie again? The thought of her little brother and sister stuck with her parents, especially now that they'd completely lost their freaking minds, broke her heart. She drew her knees to her chest and began to cry. Even as she wept, her mind tried to return to the calculations. It was a subtle nagging at first, but slowly built in insistence. She fought it back, trying to cling to the image of her siblings.

The formulations won their fight, bursting into life around her.

The pain returned, searing and all-consuming, right between her eyes. She tried to scream, but her breath caught in her chest. The symbols whirled around her, little more than a blur. Soon the world spun with them, and once again everything went black.

Jane woke with her teeth chattering. She was shivering so violently that her muscles ached. With effort, she climbed out of a massive snowdrift. She hugged herself tight, wishing she was wearing more than hand-me-down jeans and a dingy brown jacket that was a couple sizes too big.

This new place was as barren and desolate as the forest had been verdant and lush. Nothing but snow and ice stretched for miles in every direction. At least the whiteout hid the persistent equations from view. Cold wind whipped at her face and froze tears to her burning cheeks. Her hands and feet were already numb, and the lack of sensation was spreading. Her body was racked by shivers so hard they were more like seizures.

The formulae surged momentarily.

She started walking but didn't make it far before

her muscles gave out and she collapsed. The only thing she could do was lie there, shivering and waiting for the end to come.

"Giving up?" Nightstick asked. "That's so very disappointing."

"Piss off," she said. Or rather, she tried to. It came out sounding more like Porky Pig's stutter.

Nightstick sighed.

She ignored him and tried to bring it all to an end through sheer force of will. Hadn't she read something about hypothermia? That it made you fall asleep? Maybe that would mean there wouldn't be any—

When the pain returned, the heat of it was almost a welcome contrast to the bitter cold. She found herself welcoming the approaching blackness. Maybe this time it would be over. Maybe this time the darkness would last forever.

It didn't.

In fact, the darkness didn't come at all. Her body felt like it was stretching and compressing a hundred times a second. The equations came into focus, swirling around her in an inescapable tornado. She studied them, but soon found her focus was needed to avoid motion sickness.

Then she saw it. They were infinite probability determinations—a mathematical formula to derive a specific outcome from the infinite possibilities that reality offered. It took focus, more than she'd ever had to summon in her life, but she didn't vomit and was able to see pieces that should go together. As she noticed them, the parts merged into longer and more complicated equations.

She didn't know how, but she knew she was causing it.

After what was probably just seconds, but felt like years, the formulation reached a zero sum and the whirling stopped.

She didn't.

She smacked face-first into a brick wall at about warp seventy and bounced off, landing flat on her back. She didn't move. There was a ringing in her ears and her left shoulder screamed in protest. Something warm and wet ran down her face, and when she touched her cheek, her fingers came away sticky with blood.

"Damn it," she screamed through gritted teeth.

She rolled over, wiping more blood from her face. At least it was warmer here. She was surrounded by skyscrapers, and the lights from bright and colorful neon signs stabbed at her vision. The smell of cooked food came to her, but she didn't recognize the dishes. She noticed then that all the words on the signs were in Japanese or Chinese, or some kind of characters that she didn't recognize. She started crying again and slid down the wall until she was sitting in the alleyway, burying her face in her arms.

Why was this happening to her? Despite what her parents might think, she did believe in God. But she couldn't imagine any God would be interested enough in the petty details of her life to punish her like this. And what other explanation was there?

She looked up at the cloudy sky, illuminated by light pollution and blurred by her tears. "I give up, all right? Whatever I did, I'm sorry!"

Eventually the headache returned, and everything repeated: the dancing numbers and symbols, the stomach-churning whirlwind, and then—she found herself in another new location.

The scenes shifted from mountains to desert to rocky coast to sandy beaches and barren flats. Mixed in were cities ranging from metropolis-like behemoths of glass and stone to modest little towns, and she even landed once in a dark and twisted forest, like something out of a child's nightmare.

Occasionally Nightstick would appear, offering snide commentary and absolutely no help. All the same, he was her only company. She didn't dare try to find help. Without any control, she didn't want to risk anyone else losing fingers, or worse. The amount of time that had passed between each shift in her location varied from a few minutes to several hours, though beyond that, time had no meaning to her.

Nothing did.

CHAPTER THREE

Dante stared at his laptop, ignoring the milling patrons in the Austin coffee shop and his salad. He read over the notes from his investigation and the meager details he'd been able to collect. Almost three months of talking to street kids and cops in cities and towns all over the Midwest, and he had just this side of nothing to show for it.

"More, um, coffee?" the waitress asked.

Dante glanced. She was maybe in her early twenties, but the way she chewed her lip as she looked at him made her appear even younger. He was used to mortals staring at him like that and normally he enjoyed the attention, but today his mind was elsewhere. It had been for the last couple of months. He really needed to keep up his glamour better.

He gave her a smile, which made her breath catch. "Actually," he said, quickly reading her name tag, "Sarah, I'm having tea."

She swallowed. "Oh, I'm sorry. Would you like—?"

"I'm fine, but thank you very much."

She nodded. "Okay, but if you need anything, just let me know."

"I certainly will."

She stopped biting her lip, but didn't move. "You know, I, um, my shift ends—"

When his phone rang, Dante gave Sarah an apologetic smile. "I'm sorry, but I need to take this."

She blinked, and her smile faltered. "Oh, right, I'm sorry." She turned and walked away, shaking her head and muttering to herself.

Dante answered his phone. "Please tell me you have something new."

"I'm fine, thanks. How are you?" Faolan asked.

Dante rubbed his temples and muttered something impolite.

"Want to visit Kansas?"

He straightened. "What do you have?"

"Well, it turns out the information you've gathered was enough to extrapolate a rough timeline."

"You're kidding."

"Someday you'll stop being surprised by my magnificence."

"Not in this lifetime," Dante said, his first genuine smile in weeks on his lips. "Tell me."

"It looks like things started small," Faolan said. "Then about nine months ago, disappearances skyrocketed. Coincidentally, that's also when we have our first report of homeless kids wielding magic."

"And you wouldn't be talking about visiting the Sunflower State if you hadn't found something more."

"There were two major events within a week of the first noticeable increase in disappearances. The first was the oíche's attempted insurrection . . ."

"I think it's safe to say that was unrelated," Dante said. "What's the other?"

"A car accident in Topeka, Kansas," Faolan said. "A fifteen-year-old girl and her parents were T-boned by a drunk driver early on a Sunday afternoon. Their car caught fire. Rescue units couldn't get there in time to save the parents."

Dante leaned forward. "And the daughter?"

"Was found in the backseat, after the fire was out," Faolan said. "Something like ten minutes later."

"And?"

"Not even a singed hair."

Dante let out a low whistle.

"Yeah, and it gets better—well, worse," Faolan said.

"Tell me."

"The fire department didn't put the fire out," Faolan said. "The car was too far gone when they arrived. Per procedure, the risk of explosion kept them back. Then reports say they heard a girl scream. A powerful wind came out of nowhere, strong enough to roll the car from its roof back onto its wheels. When it was righted, the fires just went out. First responders found the girl in a ball in the backseat, muttering to herself. The police described her as mentally unstable."

"Can't imagine why," Dante said. "Where is she now?"

"Well, she didn't have any other family, so she went into the system."

Dante winced and muttered an oath. "I can guess what happened next."

"Yep, bounced from home to home," Faolan said. "She ran away a few times, but kept getting picked up by the local police. The last report of her running was three weeks after being assigned to a new foster home. She vanished, along with three other kids." Faolan paused. "This particular foster home has had twenty-seven foster kids reported as runaways."

"So is it just a bad place?" Dante asked. "Or is something else going on?"

"I hear Kansas is lovely in the summer," Faolan said.

"Do I have a flight?"

"Sorry, cutbacks. You're walking," Faolan said.

Dante chuckled as he saw Padraig enter the shop, dressed in fashionable jeans and a fitted white button-down shirt. When he smoothed his dark red hair and scanned the room, every woman turned and stared.

"I think my guide is here. I'll call you when I land."

"I'll be here," Faolan said.

Dante hung up as Padraig made his way to the booth.

"Magis—" He winced. "Sorry—"

Dante waved it off. "Lots of that going around. Forget it." He shut down his laptop and tucked it away in his briefcase.

Then he caught a glimpse of Sarah looking at him and trying to pretend she wasn't. Dante put a twenty on the table to cover the tea and salad, then pulled out a hundred-dollar bill. With a few twists, he folded it into a rose. He set the rose on the twenty, grabbed his briefcase, and stood up.

"You're the guide," he said to Padraig. "Lead the way."

Even after all the times Dante had walked the Far Trails, their incongruent geography never ceased to amaze him. They'd stepped onto the trails through a large but parched-looking pecan tree in Zilker Park. Then Dante stood in a surreal forest of impossibly tall trees. The ground had no scrub growth, which gave it the appearance of a manicured orchard. Everywhere he looked, there was a clear path.

Padraig led him a dozen paces down a trail and opened the way back. They stepped out less than half a mile from the Country Club Plaza in the heart of Kansas City, Missouri.

"There's a car over there," Padraig said, handing Dante a set of keys. "I'll go back and take care of the one in Austin."

"This is why I never cease to be amazed by Faolan's magnificence," Dante said, accepting the keys.

Padraig grinned, then turned and stepped back into the trails.

Dante had just lifted the keys to find the car when a tall and slender woman walked toward him. Her dark green pencil skirt was slit high up one side, flashing the pale skin of her thigh as she walked. Her dark auburn hair was like living fire, and the perfection of her porcelain skin was only interrupted by a few freckles on the apples of her cheeks.

A nostalgic smile found its way across Dante's face.

The woman returned the grin. She arched an eyebrow and tucked her hair behind her pointed ear.

"It's been a long time, Brigid," Dante said. When she offered her hand, he kissed it. "Or do you prefer, *Magister*?"

"There's a mortal saying," Brigid said, her words silken and husky. "Call me anything you like, just be sure to call me."

Dante laughed. "How did you ever play the mortal nun?"

"You know full well I was canonized," Brigid said, a teasing note in her voice.

"You're not exactly what most would imagine when they hear the word *saint*."

"And at the time, my piety was sincere." Her green eyes sparkled. "But I've become worldlier since then."

"Haven't we all," Dante said. "Now, tell me what you're doing here. Not just happening by, I assume."

"*Mavourneen*," she said. "You don't think I'd let you investigate in my region without offering to help, do you?"

"So you're joining me, then," Dante said.

"Just like old times."

Dante used the key fob to find the car. His good mood vanished when he saw a black Suburban flash its lights. He stared at the black monstrosity for a long moment before letting out a long sigh and re-signing himself to his fate. Brigid shrugged, barely hiding a chuckle. He set his briefcase behind the driver's seat and they both climbed in. When the engine turned over, the touchscreen GPS was already pre-programmed with the home address of the girl's last foster parents. He had barely pulled out of the parking spot when his phone rang and Faolan's face appeared on the screen.

Dante pressed the send button. "Are you kidding me?" he asked.

"What?" Faolan's gleeful voice came through the Bluetooth system. "If you want to play like you're a federal agent bigwig, you have to drive a big black SUV."

Dante shot a glance at Brigid. "This was your idea, wasn't it?"

She gave him an innocent look, then drew from the glove box a set of authentic-looking FBI credentials.

"I miss my Mustang," Dante muttered as he merged into traffic.

"I'll get it detailed for you," Faolan said through a laugh.

"Wax, not polish," Dante said.

"But of course, *sahib*," Faolan said, the words dripping with sarcasm.

"In the meantime," Dante said. "We need some details on the girl."

"I see what you did there, very witty," Faolan said. There was the sound of computer keys clicking. "Unfortunately, there's not much else to say. The social services files say the girl's name is Jane Essex. Her parents were George and Katherine. After the accident, Jane was put under observation and was diagnosed with post-traumatic stress disorder."

"Must've been a genius doctor to figure that one out," Brigid said.

"They tried sending Jane back to school with her first foster family." There was a pause. "It, um, didn't go well."

Dante and Brigid exchanged a glance. "That's rather vague," Dante said.

"The file has some witness reports, but it also dismisses them as nonsense. They say Jane was being bullied. Some girls pushed her against the wall and she freaked out—the report's words, not mine. She went into a ball and screamed something."

"What's nonsense about that?" Brigid asked.

"The part where every window within a hundred-foot radius blew out," Faolan said.

"Okay, that sounds bad," Dante said.

"What do you know about the most recent foster family?" Brigid asked. "The one with all the runaways."

Dante gave her a questioning look.

"He filled me in while you were on your way here," she said.

"That would be Richard and Mary Fredricks," Faolan said. "They've been investigated repeatedly, but nothing was ever found to pull their foster status."

"Nothing?" Dante asked. "Really?"

"Gee, that doesn't sound suspicious at all," Brigid said.

"According to the reports, everything was done aboveboard," Faolan said. "Surprise visits, inspections, interviews with the kids still there. Nothing."

"Well, I'm sure there was nothing to find then," Brigid said, words dripping sarcasm.

"Yeah, but we'll pay them a visit anyway." Dante pressed down on the gas.

CHAPTER FOUR

Wraith had no memory of waking up one day and being confused. She was fairly sure the fateful exorcism that had started all this had been about ten months ago, give or take. Beyond that, it got murkier. The loss of her sense of time made it all the more difficult. As best she could tell, at least four months were completely blank before she had ended up in Seattle. The tattoos on her palms, the backs of her hands, and scattered over her body had never been a shock, but she couldn't remember getting them. While it was true that a sixteen-year-old—or was she fifteen?—couldn't walk into just any tattoo shop, tats weren't hard to come by.

The tattoo designs were another mystery. She couldn't recall devising the complex formulae represented in the whirling lines and shapes, the effects they were tied to, or even if she had been the one to come up with them at all. There were other details she knew but didn't remember learning. The existence of faeries, changelings (called "fifties" on the streets), shapeshifters, and the supernatural world in general, for example. Surely at some point she'd at least been a little freaked out to learn her friends were half human, half fae—or fifty-fifty—but she didn't remember it. Hell and a ham sandwich, she wasn't even sure at which point she'd stopped being Jane Essex, a relatively normal girl, and had become Wraith, a street urchin spell-slinger.

Her life had become a recurring series of the same events: avoid the police, pimps, and gangsters, then find food and a safe place to sleep. If she was lucky, she wouldn't come across any snatchers. Though the few times she had so far, she'd been able to make a clean getaway.

Any downtime was spent trying to fit together the scattered pieces of her life. She hadn't made much progress. Truth to tell, it felt as if she were actually losing ground. Nothing seemed real anymore, and she wondered more and more often if she was going insane. Nightstick told her that questioning her sanity was a sign she was still sane. It sounded like bullshit to her.

She opened her eyes, leaned her head back against the brick wall of the alley, and drew in a breath. The familiar calculations of reality drifted around her, but she hardly noticed them any longer. Well, until she needed them anyway.

Somehow, she had to figure this out on her own. No one was going to help her. She didn't have many friends, and they were all too busy just trying to survive another day. The police couldn't be bothered with her, or those like her, unless it was to hassle them for loitering. The mundane street kids avoided her like a leper. For that matter, people in general rarely even acknowledged her existence. She couldn't blame them really. To most of them, she was an unhappy reminder of what was just a pink slip or missed mortgage payment away.

Something clicked and a tattered memory started to form in her mind.

Her parents, it had to do with her parents. She could almost smell something, a light fragrance on the air. It was perfume, flowery and familiar. It made her feel safe. Her heart pounded as pieces started to fill in. There were voices, and they were talking about—

"You hungry, Stretch?" the voice was feminine and carried a faint southwestern accent.

The image crumbled and slipped through her fingers into nothingness.

"Damn it!" Wraith glared at Shadow. The girl was only a bit older than Wraith and almost a foot shorter. Her reddish brown skin, dark hair, and chiseled features left no doubt as to her Native American heritage. The swirling darkness in her eyes left no doubt that she wasn't all mortal.

"Yikes," Shadow said and took a step back. "Sorry, grump much?"

Wraith put her face in her hands. "I almost had something. I could feel it. It was right there!"

Shadow's face fell. "Oh, damn. Sorry."

Wraith got to her feet and forced a smile. "It wasn't your fault. Honestly, I don't know why I bother anymore. I think I might actually be remembering less, or remembering it wrong, or both."

Shadow furrowed her brow and opened her mouth.

Wraith lifted a hand. "Because it's like a scab or a loose tooth. You can't leave it be; you have to poke at it."

Shadow nodded. "So, you hungry?"

"One-track mind," Wraith muttered and started walking.

With effort, Shadow kept pace. "Yeah, when I'm hungry. That's what people do when they're hungry. They think about food and eating."

Wraith arched an eyebrow.

"Okay, so maybe bean poles like you don't, but the rest—"

"Not the best way to ask me to go shopping," Wraith said lightly.

"Oh? Well, what would you prefer, Your Royal Highness?"

Wraith stopped and considered for a moment and said, "Something like: Wraith, my dearest and truest friend, would you please, pretty please, with sugar and a cherry on top, get me something tasty to eat so I'll stop my whining?"

"I don't whine!" Shadow whined.

Wraith chuckled and the pair continued walking.

"Besides," Shadow said. "Who found that choice squat we're in?"

"Yes," Wraith droned. "You're amazing."

"That's right, and I don't see you—"

Wraith put her face in her hands. "Fine! Just stop talking. I need some smokes anyway."

Shadow smiled. "I win, as usual."

Making her way between the clueless shoppers, Wraith was careful that neither she, nor the messenger bag hanging at her back, bumped anyone. The hood of her jacket was up and only a few stray strands of dirty pixie-cut hair peaked out. In her left hand, she gripped a metal bottle cap, the logo of which had been painstakingly rubbed away. On the inside was a symbol made of intersecting lines, at the center of which was a small hole with a length of string looped through.

She paused and stared at the register, where a large woman in a blue apron scanned items in the usual daze of a mega-mart clerk. To her left, Shadow was trying to look casual as she flipped through a tabloid. Next to her, SK, a freckled boy with a long face, was sharing a joke with Fritz, a girl with a German accent who made Shadow look like a basketball player. Both Fritz and Shadow had faintly luminescent eyes, revealing the fae half of their heritage to anyone who could see beneath the glamour. Nightstick stood to her right, silently smoking a cigarette that never burned away.

"I can tell you're still here," Shadow whispered without looking up.

"What are you waiting for?" SK sighed. "Either go

get them or let's just get out of here, I don't care which. It's you two with the damn addiction."

Shadow shot him a murderous glare and muttered something unladylike.

Wraith let out a quiet breath, shook her head, and looked back to the only checkout lane that sold tobacco products. Of course, it just had to be the busiest one in the place. Resigning herself to inevitability, she made her way through the throng of customers, careful that her rain-soaked sneakers didn't squeak on the tile floor.

When she reached her destination, Wraith crouched and moved around the rotund clerk. A headache had started behind her eyes, but she pushed it aside and carefully grabbed several packs of cigarettes from the rack. As her long fingers touched the little boxes, she squeezed the bottle cap tighter and the sharp edges bit into her palm. The zero-sum formula, and the accompanying soft pressure that she felt over her whole body, extended past her fingers and surrounded the pilfered smokes. Like her, they were now invisible to the herd of mundane sheeple.

"Did you find everything okay?" the clerk said with a monotone voice to a guy in line, not even pretending to be interested.

Wraith smiled, tucked her prize into an inside jack pocket, and scanned the area. *Why, yes, I did,* she thought. *Thank you very—*

"Do you see this month's *Tiger Beat*?" Shadow asked SK in a nervous tone.

Wraith froze.

"Um, no," SK said. His voice was also a little shaky. "I think I see *three* copies of *Teen Cosmo* though."

Wraith turned her head very slowly. Two men in hooded trench coats were staring at her. Their hoods were up, but Wraith could see the glint of mirrored sunglasses.

Her heart leapt into her throat, and she tried to swallow it back down. It couldn't be. They'd always been safe around normals. Besides, there were only two and—

One of the men removed his shades, revealing cold, dark eyes, a faint purple glow behind them.

Wraith's stomach knotted and her blood turned to ice water.

The snatcher gave her a cold smile, then winked before replacing the glasses.

There was a flash of pain behind her eyes, like someone was reaching into her brain. For a long moment, her only thought was—Everything is fine, just as it should be. But the thought tasted of plastic, seemed false somehow. She pushed it aside, but in doing so her focus slipped and the equation shifted, no longer zeroing out. The veil around her expanded, enveloping half the rack of cigarettes.

"Holy crap!" a man in line said. His eyes looked like they were trying to leap out of his head.

"Time to fight or flee," Nightstick said, his tone bored as he leaned against the wall.

Unconcerned with the out-of-control cloaking equation, Wraith turned to flee, but her face drove hard into the jeans that strained over the clerk's prodigious backside. The impact drove Wraith into the wall of cigarettes. Her hood fell back and an avalanche of little boxes pummeled her. She felt a pop in her ears as her concentration, the equation, and the cloak collapsed.

"Oh, crap," she whispered as gasps of surprise erupted from the people in line.

The clerk blinked at her. "Where did you—" Her eyes darted from Wraith to her bag packed with stolen food. "Hey! What are—?"

Before the clerk could finish, Wraith was on her feet, sprinting for the door.

One of the snatchers moved to cut her off.

"*Ferrousan!*" SK shouted.

The snatcher's foot hit the ground and stuck, causing him to stumble.

Fritz said something Wraith didn't hear, and screeching feedback erupted from the PA system. At the same time, Shadow rushed forward, lifted her hands, and shouted something in Siouan. The fluorescent bulbs in the store didn't snuff out; rather, their light collected into Shadow's hands. The darkness left behind was complete.

Shadow shouted again, and Wraith was barely able to cover her eyes in time. Even with eyes closed and a hand over them, she still saw nothing but white for a moment after Shadow released the collected light in a sudden, intense burst.

"Wraith, go!" Shadow yelled. "Get the hell out of here!"

"I'm not leaving you guys!"

Shadow cursed. "We're right behind you. Run!"

Wraith bolted.

A third snatcher, one she hadn't seen, must have avoided the flash because he shoved past a family and reached for Wraith as she ran for the door. His hand caught the hood of her jacket.

Wraith twisted, symbols gathering around her foot, and kicked at his knee as hard as she could. She didn't weigh a lot and wasn't a Kung Fu master, but her legs were three miles long and made an excellent fulcrum. Physics could be fun, especially when supplemented by a little kinetic entropy.

There was a wet popping sound from the snatcher's knee as tendons snapped. He cried out in pain and released her as he collapsed to the ground.

Wraith turned to run but chanced a glance over her shoulder. She didn't see SK or Fritz, but Shadow was drawing in for another flash.

"Watch the birdie, bitches!" Shadow yelled.

Wraith pulled her hood over her face and turned away.

"Christ!" the snatcher at her feet bellowed.

"Move your ass!" SK yelled and a hand shoved Wraith forward.

She emerged from the sliding doors into the dreary, rainy afternoon and ran for the parking lot. There was a screech as she barely avoided a black windowless utility van. Before the vehicle had come to a full stop, a snatcher leapt from a door on the far side.

Wraith dodged him, but another flash of pain almost made her fall.

She looked back over her shoulder. The snatchers were hauling a blue-haired girl from the store. Wraith blinked, and when she opened her eyes, Shadow was kicking at the snatcher who held her fast. Wraith knew something wasn't right, but all she could think of was the color blue.

"Get out of here, you idiot!" Shadow shouted. She twisted and managed to get a leg free and kicked again at the snatcher who'd grabbed her. Another emerged from the store and put a black hood over her head.

Wraith's mind whirled, like a gear spinning free. She knew the inside of the hood. She knew that it was musty, that it smelled of bad breath, vomit, and tears.

Her knees went weak and the world seemed to shift around her as she tumbled down next to a parked car. "No . . ." She shook her head, trying to get everything to line back up. This wasn't right. None of the normals around her seemed to be reacting to what was happening, though some were staring at her with a mix of confusion and wariness.

"SK? Fritz?" Wraith yelled.

"Get her!" someone shouted.

Wraith snapped out of it just in time to see a snatcher flick his hand toward her. A thin silver cord leapt from his palm and snaked towards her. She dodged around the car, and in the blink of an eye, she was running. She wasn't overly graceful, but her long legs ate lots of ground. Unfortunately, after a dozen blocks, her lungs were burning and she gasped for breath as the pounding in her head began to settle in for a lengthy stay.

Before rounding another corner, she chanced a look behind her. The snatchers were a ways back, but she knew they were still on her tail and the snatcher-mobile couldn't be far behind them. She spotted a door just down a narrow side street and gathered a chaotic formulation into her hand. She hated taking chances like this, but she didn't have time for anything else. She did keep the spell small as she flung the equation at the door. A moment later she pulled the door open and stepped through.

She stepped out of a completely different door. A quick glance around told her she'd bought a dozen blocks or so, moving away from the Space Needle toward downtown. She took off again. None of this made any sense. Snatchers had never grabbed anyone in broad daylight and never with so many mundy witnesses.

She stayed to the alleyways, putting as many turns as she could between her and her pursuers, even chancing a few more random doors. Every so often, she'd pass Nightstick where he lounged against a wall.

Before long, she realized she had no idea where she was or where to go. The tall buildings loomed over her, and she felt like a rat searching for cheese. People walked down the streets, but no one seemed to give her a second glance. And why didn't anyone else see the snatchers? It was almost like she was the only one who could see them. But she wasn't just imagining them. Was she?

Pain lanced through her head, and the thought shattered.

"This way!" a snatcher shouted from ahead of her.

"Are these guys marathon runners or something?" Wraith said. Nightstick didn't answer.

She fled again, down yet another alley. When she passed a Dumpster, she stopped. With all the strength she could manage, she pushed it at an angle until it blocked the narrow path. But the alley was a dead end.

Nightstick stood to one side playing cat's cradle with a loop of string. "Running out of ground, rabbit."

"*Apartium!*" yelled a man from the alley entrance.

She backed away as a thin line of white heat ran up the middle of the Dumpster and cut it in half.

"*Crosian!*" another man shouted, and the two ends crumpled like pop cans against the brick walls.

"Oh, they look angry," Nightstick said, still focused on the string looped between his fingers.

Wraith looked around as the snatchers strode toward her. She spotted a weathered metal door, then flung the probability equation and reached for the handle at the same moment. An instant after the magic hit, she pulled open the door, stepped through, and slammed it shut behind her, returning it to a normal door.

She found herself on the top level of a parking garage. The door now led to the stairwell, but she thought better of using it. Stepping to the railing, she looked over. It was sixty feet down, at least. With no other option, she ran for the ramp down but froze when a van turned the corner on the level below and stopped at the far end of the ramp, less than a hundred feet away.

The nagging fear in her stomach became a meal to sharp-toothed anger and defiance.

Drawing a slow breath in through her nose, she raised her right hand, index finger pointing at the van like an imaginary gun. She planted her feet as she balled up all the fear and anger and focused on the symbol tattooed on the palm of her hand. Some of the numbers and symbols that floated around her zipped into her hands, forming an elaborate mass of equations.

The engine revved, tires squealed, and the van lurched forward.

"BANG!" Her hand came up in recoil and she slid back several feet.

An invisible ball of collected particles the size of a basketball, with the mass and speed of an armored car at a hundred miles per hour, smashed into the grill. The front of the van caved in as the rest of it came to a loud and sudden stop, the back end lifting up off the ground a couple feet.

When it came down, the crash was deafening. Then all was quiet.

Wraith's eyes went wide and she looked from her trembling hand to the wreckage. "Shadow!"

She yanked open the driver's side door and a bloody, unconscious man fell out. She stepped over the snatcher and looked inside. Shadow was suspended in a web of thin chains, a black bag over her head. Wraith knew those chains, somehow. And she knew they drained away the hope and magic of their captives in equal parts.

Tears ran down Wraith's face, and she started to climb inside to free her friend

"You little—" The snatcher on the ground grabbed her ankle.

Wraith screamed and kicked over and over. The man's nose cracked, blood sprayed, and he fell back. His head smacked the ground, and he went still.

Wraith climbed into the van, tears pouring down her face as she yanked off the hood.

A blue-haired girl flinched away. "Please, don't hurt me!"

"You're not Shadow," Wraith said.

"Who's Shadow?" the girl asked.

"Well, this is an interesting turn of events," Nightstick said from the back of the van.

Confusion and a throbbing in her brain caused Wraith to wince. Something tried to crawl from the darkness of her memories. "No, no, no," she said as she gripped her hair. "You have to be Shadow. You have to be!"

"What the hell are you doing?" Shadow asked.

Wraith opened her eyes and looked at her friend, who was staring back at her impatiently. The girl with the blue hair was gone. It was Shadow in the van, in chains. "Where—?" Wraith opened her mouth to ask a question, but the thought was pulled into the darkness of her mind.

"You need to get out of here," Shadow said.

"What? No, not without you," Wraith said.

"Time is short, kid," Nightstick said. "Best hurry."

Wraith's hands shook trying to open the locks. "Damn it, Fritz could just make them pop open."

"There's no time, you have to run, Stretch!"

Wraith clenched her jaw and ignored the nagging confusion, but it was like a splinter in her mind. "No, I'm not leaving you! Not agai—" Pain lanced through Wraith's head, and the world felt artificial. She could hear Nightstick making an unhappy sound.

The door to the stairwell opened. The two snatchers stepped out and looked around.

"I'll get away, I always do," Shadow said. "They can't hold me. Run, now!"

Reluctantly, Wraith climbed out. She gave the creep on the ground another kick to the face.

"We're not here for you," one of the snatchers said, nodding at the van. "She's the one we want."

Wraith backed away from the snatchers, but stopped when she bumped into the railing. She glanced over her shoulder at the drop, then at her shoes.

"You need to stop interfering," the other snatcher said. "You know what we're doing and how important it is."

"Heard that before, haven't we?" Nightstick asked.

Wraith closed her eyes, clenched her fists, and drew in a slow breath. "Suck on this."

Though he was silent, she could sense Nightstick's approval.

Both men sensed her drawing in power and raised their left hands, the symbols drawn on their palms glowing with a faint purple light.

"You can't have them! Leave us alone!" The floating numbers shook in anticipation and glowed brightly as she leapt up onto the metal tubing and then into empty air, slapping her left shoe, or rather the symbols drawn on it, and forcing power into them.

Then she fell, and time seemed to slow.

The symbols around her fluttered drunkenly for a long moment, then the magic sputtered and symbols streaked to her shoes, but she continued to fall. She gritted her teeth and focused harder, her shoes growing hot with the increased flow of power. She tried to steady the torrent, desperate not to blow the charm, but she continued to fall. Then more numbers joined the others, completing the formula and zeroing the sum.

The air thickened around her until it felt like she was falling through Jell-O. She hit the ground running with little more force than if she had come from a five-foot drop. Chancing a glance over her shoulder, she saw the two snatchers watching her from the railing, one speaking into a cell phone. She was glad these trained monkeys couldn't fly.

A couple miles, countless turns, and an indefinable amount of time later, she stopped and doubled over, gasping for breath. After a couple short minutes, the stitch in her side faded. She pulled a battered pair of leather-and-brass goggles from her bag and slipped them on. The left lens was red, the right green, and they were both covered with thin copper wire shaped into whirling symbols. After a moment's concentration, the color faded from the world. Traces of magic drifted almost invisibly from the mundane people passing by and the scattered plant life. She scanned all around, but didn't see the bright glow that would surround the snatchers or any sign they'd put a tracking spell on her.

"Congratulations, clean getaway," Nightstick said, a sneer behind his words.

"What's that supposed to mean?"

"You could've taken them out and you know it."

Wraith ignored the twisting in her stomach. Convinced the coast was clear, she pushed the goggles up from her eyes and walked to the condemned tenement. There, she moved a graffiti-covered sheet of plywood and slipped inside. The abandoned building was quiet. The only sound was the flapping soles of her now demolished shoes slapping the dust- and debris-strewn floor. She headed for the stairs. Seven stories later, she reached the uppermost level.

She stopped and stared.

The room was a large rectangle stretching forty feet wide by twenty feet deep. Most of the far wall was comprised of windows with square glass panes. Near a section of mostly intact windows was a single old mattress with several blankets on it. A collection of knick-knacks were scattered nearby. Other than that, and Nightstick leaning on his ever-present shillelagh, the room was empty.

"What the hell?" She looked where the other beds

should've been, were supposed to be, and, in fact, had been that morning.

"SK? Fritz?"

The silence was oppressive and seemed to swallow her small voice.

"Did the snatchers grab them after all?"

"Well, that isn't very likely, is it?" Nightstick said, chuckling.

Wraith ignored him and continued talking to herself—the self that wasn't a snarky hallucination. "And then what? They came here and took all their stuff?"

Her head throbbed, so she closed her eyes and rubbed her temples.

Nightstick made some comment, but she wasn't listening. Something moved in her peripheral vision, and she nearly jumped out of her skin. A dog the size of a small pony, but with the reddish coloring of a coyote, limped out of the darkness toward her, favoring his right front leg.

Wraith let out a nervous laugh. "Toto, you scared the Skittles out of me." She knelt down, wrapped her arms around the dog, and hugged him tightly.

Toto licked her face a few times.

"I missed you too." She ruffled the dog's fur, and didn't let go. "They got Shadow. And I don't know what happened to SK or Fritz."

Toto tilted his head to one side.

Nightstick chuckled. "What's that? Timmy's stuck in a well?"

Wraith shot him a glare, and he turned away. Though there was no way to see them behind his white glasses, she knew he rolled his eyes.

"We'll give it some time," she said to the dog. "Maybe someone just stole their stuff." It wouldn't be the first time someone picked them clean. She felt bad, though. Fritz had managed to collect some decent tools, and Shadow's sketchbook and pencils were her solace.

Toto sniffed her bag and his mouth opened into a doggy grin as his tail went into manic wagging.

Wraith sat down next to the window and opened her bag. "Yeah, I got something for you."

Toto followed her and waited patiently, sort of.

She removed the bag of treats and tossed some on the ground. As the dog munched the bacon-flavored strips, Wraith removed her destroyed sneakers and examined them. The soles were melted and flapped like a puppet's mouth. The symbols had nearly burned through the toe.

"Not exactly what I'd intended, but at least it worked," she said to Toto and tossed the shoes into a corner.

He never looked up.

"Thanks for reminding me of my place." She slid her mattress to one side, lifted a floorboard, and retrieved a pair of glittery ruby red Doc Martens boots from the stash. She'd hoped her Chucks would last longer, but it couldn't be helped. She replaced the board and the bed, then sat and pulled on the boots.

Toto put his big head in her lap and whimpered.

"Don't worry, I'm sure they'll turn up," Wraith said as she retrieved a cigarette from one of the pilfered packs, put it between her lips, and snapped her fingers a few times until the numbers fell in place. A small flame appeared from her thumb. After a long drag, she blew out the flame with the smoke, leaned back, and fed the dog another treat.

"Oh, I'm sure they will," Nightstick said.

After smoking half the cigarette, she reached into her messenger bag and drew out a giant pack of Skittles. She opened it and poured some of the colored candies into her mouth.

Toto's ears pricked up and he looked at her.

"Don't give me that," she said. "I need the sugar."

Toto snorted, then laid his head back down.

Wraith smiled and stroked the big dog. "Something's changed, buddy. They came after us in a store, in broad daylight. As soon as Fritz and SK get here, we need to find another place to stay."

"How admirable, run away yet again," Nightstick said.

Wraith scratched Toto's ear. "There's a reason we all agreed to the cut-and-run plan if anyone got snatched. Those guys are like the freaking boogeyman, only less cuddly."

"You know, I should be well offended that the dog gets more attention than I do."

"He's not as annoying as you," Wraith said.

"Oh, but your wit wounds me so."

Toto nuzzled her leg.

Wraith took another drag and tried to convince herself the tears were from the smoke getting in her eyes.

Minutes turned to hours. The sun vanished and darkness settled over the city. Nightstick grew tired of being ignored and left for wherever he went when he wasn't offering commentary. Wraith sat at the window, never moving. She watched, hoping to see her friends in the alley or hear them coming up the stairs. With each passing minute, her heart broke a little more. It was well past midnight when her eyes finally closed and she fell asleep.

CHAPTER FIVE

Dante and Brigid sat in the parked SUV, down the street from the home of Richard and Mary Fredricks. It was a large, well-kept but nondescript house. In fact, it was so innocuous that it struck Dante as unnatural.

"You getting the plastic feel too?" Brigid asked.

He nodded. It wasn't a close community, physically speaking. The houses all sat on large plots of land, perhaps a quarter mile from each other, and there weren't any cars to be seen. Upon closer inspection, no birds either. There was indeed an artificial feel to it, like a set piece done to exacting detail, but lacking any depth or warmth.

A cold dread inched up his spine, and he looked at Brigid. "You feel that?"

She reached into the glove box and pulled out two pistols, handing him one and securing the other to the waistband of her skirt.

"There's something wrong in the air," she said.

He nodded. It was something dark and vaguely familiar, but he couldn't place it. That in itself was unsettling.

"Well, won't plow a field by turning it over in your mind," Dante said and slid out.

Brigid blinked and started to say something, but he had walked around to the back of the SUV. She got out, pulled on a dark gray blazer, and ran her hands down her skirt. As she did, the color slid from dark green to a matching gray. Then she wrapped a deeper glamour around herself. The long and flowing dark auburn hair faded to plain brown that was cut in a short pageboy style. Her perfect skin shifted, the color darkening a few shades as small blemishes and fine lines appeared. When she opened her eyes, their vibrant green had faded to a more hazel tone.

Dante wrapped his own illusion around himself, then wrapped it again and again, like weaving together strips of leather for armor. The weight and solidity of it brought him comfort and eased away the lingering apprehension. After a long moment, he opened his eyes, now a plain brown on a chiseled but utterly average face.

"Nice," Brigid said as she looked from one side of him to the other. "Impressive."

Dante clipped the holstered pistol on his belt, in proper FBI fashion, and tucked the fake credentials into his back pocket. "Agent Thompson," he said, nodding at her.

"Agent Phillips," she answered.

They turned and headed for the house. It was actually a beautiful neighborhood, with lots of trees—even these felt false, as though they were growing here only under protest. It was like walking through an empty Hollywood sound stage. Neither Dante nor Brigid spoke, but they were thinking the same thing: each glad not to be making this visit alone.

"No wonder so many kids ran away from this place," Brigid said in a low whisper.

Dante opened the gate to the waist-high chain link fence that surrounded the house, relieved it was aluminum rather than iron. Brigid glided past him and together they walked up the path to the front door. The lawn on either side was almost too perfectly manicured, complete with flawlessly symmetrical flower beds, and not a single wilted blossom. The grass was devoid of any sign that children lived there: no toys, no bicycles, nothing. It didn't even have worn patches from being played on.

They walked up wooden steps to the porch. Brigid took position just behind him and to his left. He knew it was to give her a clear line of sight into the house when the door opened. Her breathing, like his, was slow and steady.

Dante rang the doorbell.

An electronic version of the first few bars of "Amazing Grace" played inside.

"You continue your studying, I'll be right back," a woman said from inside the house.

Dante heard footsteps on hardwood floors approach and saw movement through the curtains that covered the sidelights. The door opened a long moment later to reveal a middle-aged woman in a modest housedress. Her face had laugh lines and crow's feet, but apart from that, she had no wrinkles

"Can I help you?" she asked in a saccharine sweet voice, flashing a motherly smile that felt more insincere than it looked.

Dante and Brigid produced their credentials as smoothly as if they'd been doing it for years. "I'm Special Agent Drew Phillips, ma'am," he said, then motioned to Brigid. "This is Special Agent Abigale Thompson."

The woman looked at the IDs and badges, then back at them. "Oh, my goodness. The FBI?" Her eyes moved over them both, slow and deliberate. He could almost smell the hint of magic in the air, felt it probing the edges of their glamours.

"Yes, ma'am," Dante said in a firm, polite tone. "We're investigating a series of missing children that we think might be related. We were wondering if we could talk to you about a"—he pulled out his phone and glanced at a blank note—"Jane Essex?"

"Oh, of course, please come in," the woman said and stepped back to let them through.

Inwardly, Dante sighed in relief that she'd invited them in. "Thank you, Mrs. Fredricks," he said, stepping into the living room. Brigid followed him, again taking position just behind and to his left.

"It is Mrs. Fredricks, isn't it?" he asked, scanning the

house. It was immaculate with the cold feel of a model home. The furniture looked as if it were never used. The rest of the house was just as perfect, not a speck of dust anywhere. It did, however, have personal touches, or at least attempts to mimic personal touches. There were pictures of kids ranging in age from seven to their late teens, dozens and dozens of them, on every flat surface and covering the walls. He also counted no less than fourteen crosses, four pictures of Jesus, and three Bibles just in this room.

"Please call me Mary," she said. "Would either of you like some coffee?"

"Thank you, ma'am, but no," Brigid said.

Dante smiled. "We don't want to take too much of your time."

"Mary, who is it?" asked a man from upstairs.

Dante could hear soft footsteps in a room down the hall and to the right from where he and Brigid stood—children from the sound, young and in stocking feet. He glanced at Brigid.

"Six?" she mouthed silently.

Dante nodded subtly. From upstairs, he could hear heavier footsteps and the subtle creaking of the house that denoted three more children and the unknown man. He was big, but not huge.

"It's a couple of FBI agents, dear," Mary said as calm and light as if saying it was the mailman.

Dante and Brigid exchanged another imperceptible glance.

A man in his mid-fifties came down the stairs. He

didn't look the sort who smiled much. He wore a pair of jeans and a flannel shirt. His eyes were blue, pale blue, and hard as frozen granite.

"What's the FBI doing here?" he asked.

"As I was explaining to your wife—" Dante started to say.

"They're here about Jane," Mary said.

"She ran away," Richard said, his voice devoid of any care or concern. "Police came out, then the social services rep, again."

Dante nodded. "We're aware—"

"It's not our fault these kids keep running away," Richard said.

"No one is saying it was, sir," Brigid said. "As my colleague was saying, we're investigating a series of missing children reports."

"We think they might be connected," Dante said. "And if we have a serial abductor, we want to gather all we can about the victims to get a good profile."

"Victims?" Mary asked. "Goodness, are you saying you found Jane?"

Richard's expression didn't change. His face was a mask made from the same stone as his eyes. Mary looked concerned, but like her smile, it didn't reach her eyes.

"No, ma'am, nothing like that," Dante said. "The timing just makes us think she might be one of the earliest of these abductions."

"By any chance, could we see Jane's room?" Brigid asked and took a step forward.

"Not her room anymore," Richard said, moving to block her view of the hallway. "We're full up with kids and can't keep rooms open for those that choose to run away."

"I understand," Dante said. "You'll forgive me for being blunt, but you've had a number of children run away."

Mary's smile faded, and she reached up to touch a gold cross at her throat. Like everything else, the movement look rehearsed, done for Dante's and Brigid's benefit. No wonder the police and social workers didn't find anything. Most mortals wouldn't pick up on the intricate subterfuge.

"Far too many," Mary said.

"Agents," Richard said, his tone softer but resolute. "We're good Christian people. We take in children who're troubled and have problems. We try to provide them a good life, a good home, but some just run. It's how it is."

"We do what we can," Mary said. "But sometimes, too often, it isn't enough."

"We've been investigated by the police and social services more times than I can count," Richard said. "We always cooperate and we're still fostering. Are we being investigated by the FBI now?"

"Not at all," Dante said. "Like I said, we're looking into a serial abductor. But you understand why I had to ask."

"Of course," Mary said and gave Richard a reproachful glance. That at least was sincere.

Dante felt Brigid's body posture change. She'd noticed the glance too. Richard wasn't playing along as well as he should, and Mary wasn't happy about it.

"What can you tell us about Jane?" Dante asked. "What did she read? What were her interests? Did she have any friends?"

"The poor dear kept to herself," Mary said, clutching her cross a little tighter. "You know about what happened to her parents?"

Dante nodded. "We do."

"We're strict but caring," Richard said. "We try to instill good Christian values. As such, we limit what books the children read and music they listen to."

"How many children are you currently fostering?" Brigid asked as she studied a wall of framed photos.

"What has the got to do with—?"

"Richard, don't be rude," Mary said then turned to Dante. "Right now, we have ten."

"And were any of them here during the same time as Jane?" Dante asked.

"Like I said, we see a lot of kids come through here," Richard said. "It's hard to keep track of who was here when."

Dante nodded. "I apologize. We didn't want to have to wade through the reports. We thought you might spare us the trouble, but it was rude of us to presume."

Brigid nodded and pulled out her phone. "I'll have all the records relating to the Fredricks for that time period pulled."

Mary and Richard exchanged a very subtle glance.

"I believe Thomas, Michael, and Josephine were here then," Mary said just before Brigid hit the send button.

"I see," Dante said and nodded to Brigid, who put her phone away. "May we speak to them?"

There was a tense moment.

"I'll be honest, Agent," Richard said. "Thomas has been with us the longest, nearly five years. Social services have found him more permanent homes over the years, but he wanted to stay here. He's become like a son to us. The other two are eight and seven and very shy."

"We'll be brief," Brigid said.

Mary looked at Richard, who nodded after a moment.

"I'll go get them," Mary said and left the room.

Dante looked at the pictures. "Is Jane one of these kids?"

Richard shook his head. "We try to get photos of all the kids here longer than a few weeks, but some are, well, less than cooperative."

Dante watched Brigid from the corner of his eyes and saw her glance at a few. He followed her line of sight and saw a lot of changeling kids just at the edge of the Change, when a changeling's fae heritage begins to show and their powers emerge. Without exception, they were hidden in crowds of other children, each desperate not to be photographed. He noted how few of the children were smiling, and his eyes were drawn to a picture of half a dozen children of varying ages and heritages playing some board game Dante didn't recognize. At the edge of the photo, a thin girl with short brown hair sat in a chair, her legs drawn up and her face hidden behind some kind of math book. Brigid smiled very, very faintly.

"Who is that?" Dante asked, pointing to the girl.

Richard's face went a little pale, then he forced half a smile. "Well, I'll be. That's Jane, all right. I didn't think she was in any of the pictures."

"You're sure?" Dante asked.

"She's reading a math book," Richard said.

"Not a common choice for a child her age," Brigid said, nodding.

"I prefer to find my answers in the pages of the Good Book, miss," Richard said, putting emphasis on the last word. "All I need to know is there."

"Do you mind?" Dante asked, holding up his phone to take a picture of the picture.

"Not at all," Richard said.

Dante leaned in close and snapped the photo.

Mary returned with a couple of towheaded children, a boy and girl who were probably siblings. They held hands tight and stared at the floor, but Dante could see their eyes were pale blue, the shade that looks white in black and white photos.

Brigid knelt down and put on a smile that was warm and comforting.

"This is Agent Thompson," Mary said to the children. "She's here about Jane. Do you remember her?"

Both children shrugged.

"Let me guess, you're Josephine," Brigid said to the boy. "And you'd be Michael," she said to the girl.

The little boy started to giggle, but the little girl shook her head. "No, I'm Josephine."

Brigid smiled. "Of course you are, such a pretty girl would have an equally pretty name."

Josephine beamed, but Michael glanced up at Richard. Dante moved to block the little boy's view of the man without looking like he was.

"I'm trying to find Jane," Brigid said in a gentle tone. "Can either of you tell me about her? What she was like?"

"She was nice," Josephine said, eyes back down on the ground.

"She knew magic," Michael said.

The room filled with a sudden, powerful tension.

"Really? That's pretty cool," Brigid said.

"We don't approve of that kind of nonsense," Richard said, stepping around Dante.

Michael visibly withdrew and whispered. "Jesus says that magic is bad."

Brigid gave Dante a glance before turning back to the children. She asked a few other questions, but the answers were all shrugs or single words.

"Thank you both very much," Brigid said to the children. "You've both been a big help."

"Okay, back to Bible study," Mary said and ushered the kids out of the room.

Dante stepped over to Richard. "What about Thomas?"

"He's out running errands," Richard said.

Dante arched an eyebrow.

"We get so busy, and he's such a help," Mary said from the hallway, urging Michael and Josephine into a side room.

Brigid stood, smoothed out her skirt, and turned to the pictures. "Which boy is Thomas?"

"Oh, this is him right here," Mary said and reached for a photo. She tripped and fell, knocking several photos to the floor.

Glass shattered and Dante had to fight the instinct to catch the woman, lest his fae reflexes give him away. He also had to fight the urge to roll his eyes at this pathetic ruse.

"Oh heavens, what have I done?" Mary said from the floor.

Dante saw a couple drops of blood on the shining hardwood. He started to kneel down. "Let me help you—"

"I think you've done quite enough," Richard said, stepping between Dante and Mary, his boot right on the blood drops. He produced a handkerchief from his pocket and wrapped Mary's injured hand.

"I need to tend to this and clean up," Mary said as she got to her feet. "I'm very sorry."

Dante smiled and nodded. "No problem, I think we have all we need. Thank you both for your time."

"Of course," Richard said, the relief evident in his tone. He led Dante and Brigid to the door. "As we said, we want to cooperate however we can."

Of course you do, Dante thought.

Brigid stepped out first, and Dante joined her before

turning back to the open door. "Thank you again. Have a good day."

"God bless you," Mary said from inside the house.

Richard closed the door.

"Wonder why they didn't want us to see Thomas," Brigid said as they headed back to the SUV.

"And what kind of kid would choose to stay in a place like that?" Dante said.

They both climbed in and wasted no time in pulling away. He gave the house a long look before he dialed Faolan.

It rang several times, which was unusual. After the fifth ring, it picked up.

"Sorry about that," Faolan said. "Your timing is perfect, as ever."

"Oh?" Dante looked at Brigid who shrugged.

"You need to get to Seattle, right away."

Dante stepped on the gas and headed for the highway back to Kansas City.

"Donovan?" Brigid asked.

"He's still dark," Faolan said. "But I have a contact there who reached out to me."

"What is it?" Dante asked.

"More than fifty changelings and a dozen wizard kids have vanished in the last month," Faolan said. "But now twelve bodies have turned up, all changeling kids."

Dante's blood ran cold as he pulled onto the highway and gunned the SUV.

"In a month?" Brigid's voice was unsteady.

"Word is the local police have asked for help from the FBI."

Dante glanced at Brigid. "I don't suppose there's any way you could come along to help?"

Brigid shook her head. "I'm sorry."

"Don't be," Dante said. "You have your own region to take care of." He turned his attention back to his phone. "How much time do I have?"

"Two days before a team of agents is sniffing around. It's been street kids, but still kids," Faolan said. "That will cut a lot of red tape."

"Have Padraig meet me in Kansas City in an hour," Dante said.

"He'll be there," Faolan said. "What did you learn? Anything useful?"

"It's not good," Dante said. "But I don't know how useful it will be."

CHAPTER SIX

When Toto's head moved, Wraith was instantly awake. Months of living under the specter of danger breeds certain habits, one of which is staying quiet and listening when something wakes a person. A glance out the window told her it was still hours before dawn. Wraith inched away from the window and the light that came in from the streetlights outside.

Toto's ears twitched, and he lifted his head.

Wraith could just hear voices downstairs. She closed her eyes and focused on the sounds, hoping it was her friends.

"Didn't I tell you?" a voice said from the stairwell. "This place will be perfect. Cops never come out this way."

Wraith winced and bit back tears as fear replaced her dashed hopes. She made her way silently to her bed. Toto limped a step behind her and turned to watch the doorway as Wraith began collecting her more precious belongings and rolling up her blankets. She fought back the fear and noted the voices were coming closer.

"Hell, they're coming up," Wraith whispered.

Toto growled low and deep.

Once Wraith was ready to leave, she watched the doorway. It was the only exit, which led to the only staircase. There was an elevator shaft, but seven floors is quite a drop.

Wraith pulled the bottle cap from around her neck and gripped it in her hand. "Come here, boy," she whispered.

Toto walked over, then turned back to face the door. The voices were on the floor just below.

Wraith drew in a breath and focused on the cap and the calculations it encompassed. The long and complex formulations, and the accompanying familiar pressure, enveloped her and Toto.

"Don't worry, I can hold the cloak," Wraith whispered.

Assuming they don't stay for long.

"Ah yes, the ever tried and true hide-and-run," Nightstick said from the doorway.

Less than a minute later, three shadowy figures came up the stairs and into the room

"I have to say, I'm impressed," the leader said as he looked around. "You might not be completely useless after all."

One of the younger thugs bristled when the others laughed, but his ire was replaced by his own guffaw when he spotted the mattress. "Looks like this place has tenants!"

"Had tenants," the leader said. "They're about to get evicted."

Wraith could sense Toto's muscles tensing as the ruffian's gaze passed over them. Anger rose in her at this invasion. Why were people always taking from her? These thugs weren't any different than the snatchers who took Shadow and—

The room, or maybe it was reality itself, lurched and a sudden flash of pain in her head caused Wraith to wince and let out a small sound.

"What was that?" a man's voice asked.

When Wraith looked up, her stomach dropped. Three snatchers were right in front of her, looking at the spot where she was standing, their eyes narrowed.

"Do you see that?" one of them asked.

Something wasn't right, but Wraith couldn't place what it was.

"Are you just going to run again?" Nightstick asked. "They took Shadow. Then you left her with them. You need to make this right. They'll know where she is."

Guilt merged with anger in the pit of Wraith's stomach, evaporating her confusion. She could run, she always did.

"And they just keep chasing you," Nightstick said, now behind her. "Don't you think you should make them be afraid for a change?"

Wraith raised a shaking hand, took aim like she had in the parking garage, and dropped her cloak.

The snatchers stared at her with wide eyes and open mouths.

"Where's Shadow, you bastards?"

"How the—"

"I said, where's Shadow?" Wraith shouted.

The biggest of the three looked at her hand and started laughing.

Toto growled and bared his teeth.

The three looked at the big dog and took an unconscious step back.

After a moment, the lead snatcher swallowed and found his bravado. "Listen, little girl, if you don't keep that thing on a leash I'll have to put him down." He nodded at her hand as he pulled a gleaming pistol from his jacket and leveled it at her. "Except mine is real."

Wraith didn't think. "BANG!"

The snatcher took the hit square in the chest and flew backward through the air, the pistol slipping from his hand and vanishing into the shadows. He landed just before his head smacked into the far wall and he didn't move.

"Boss!" one of the others shouted as he drew a pistol of his own and started firing.

In the same instant, Wraith saw flashes of calculations and felt power focus around the tattoo on her left clavicle, just above her heart.

The numbers reached a zero sum and a hazy wall of blue mist manifested between her and the shooter. A tenth of a blink later, the bullets passed through the mist. Wraith could feel the molecular bonds holding the bullets together break. The minute remains struck Wraith's hooded jacket like puffs of air, their force dispersed.

The strength left her body and she fought to stay

on her feet as the shield equation fell apart. When she looked up, the snatchers were staring at her in silence, jaws nearly on the floor.

"You can stop acting," Wraith said, gritting her teeth against the pain in her head. "I can see you! The illusion isn't working!"

The one who had fired on her tossed his gun away. "The place is yours, all right?"

She ground her teeth and annunciated each word carefully. "Stop pretending! Tell me where you took Shadow!"

Both snatchers raised their hands and traded glances.

"We don't know anyone named Shadow. We swear!"

"He's not lying," the other said. "We just—"

Another flash of pain, this one more intense, caused Wraith to flinch. That was all they needed. Both snatchers surged forward. Toto pounced on one and brought him to the ground, the other grabbed Wraith's wrist and pointed her hand away. With his free hand, he delivered a hard punch to her face.

White light exploded in her eyes, and her head pounded so hard she thought her skull would shatter.

"Don't know what you are," her attacker said, then delivered another punch. "But I'm putting you down."

Wraith could only watch in a daze as the snatcher drew back to punch again.

Toto's jaws clamped on his forearm, and with a jerk of his head, the big dog pulled the snatcher off her.

Just beyond the sound of the struggle, Wraith heard

the other snatcher running down the stairs. Her eyes went wide in panic. It wouldn't be long before he came back with others. She had to get out—

Power surged up her spine and joined with a familiar agony, one she hadn't experienced in several months, focused right between her eyes. Equations formed around her and began to whirl, slowly at first but building in speed.

She gritted her teeth and tried to break apart the formula, but it had a life of its own.

"Toto! Stride!" Wraith shouted

The dog released the snatcher and leapt toward her.

Wraith barely felt fur under her fingers as the surge reached its crescendo, the pieces of the formula joining into a single massively complex equation. The room, the world around it, and reality itself spun. Something landed on her foot and she barely made out the shape of a hand, severed at the wrist. She kicked it away and pulled Toto tighter.

Fighting past the blinding pain and digging for reserves of strength she didn't have, she focused on the symbols tattooed on the backs of her hands and fought to shift the equations into what she wanted. She tried to fix on a destination, but her mind couldn't settle on a single place or idea. Her stomach lurched, and she grunted in a final attempt to direct the maelstrom, but it wasn't working. She couldn't explain how, but she knew it.

Everything lurched to one side, and Toto slipped from her hands.

CHAPTER SEVEN

"Are you sure she isn't dead?" a small, feminine voice asked.

"Well, I'm no doctor, mind," a boy answered in a thick Cockney accent. "But me keen observational skills tell me she ain't. What with her still breathing and all, yeah?"

"I don't know," the first voice said, unsure. "I think she's dead."

Wraith opened her eyes and regretted it. A throbbing in her head, one she hadn't noticed before, spiked when the light hit her eyes. She covered her face with her hands and let out a cry of pain.

"See there?" the boy said. "I'm sure I read somewhere that dead people don't do that."

"Maybe," the little voice said, still skeptical.

Thankfully, the lights in the room dimmed and Wraith was able to open her eyes without her head threatening to explode, though that probably would've been a relief.

"Hi," a small girl, no older than seven or eight, said and smiled down at Wraith. The girl had pale blond hair, and her eyes were so blue that Wraith half expected to see clouds in them.

A boy, maybe a year older than Wraith, stepped into view. He had tousled brown hair, bulbous dark green eyes, and a patchy goatee over a weak chin. "All right, love?"

There was something about the formulae floating around these two, something off. Wraith's brain finally engaged and panic seized her. She rolled to one side, got to her feet, and grabbed the bottle cap that hung from her neck. The equation surrounded her and the cloak came up. However, rather than settling in close, it surged and pulsed several feet around her as the sum of the equation bounced up and down. Try as she might, she couldn't get it to zero out, and every attempt caused her headache to worsen.

"Bloody hell!" the boy said.

"I told you she's a slinger," the girl said.

"Thank you, Captain Obvious." The boy stepped in front of the little girl and lifted his hands. Fire gathered into his palms. "Easy does it, love—"

She was in a large square room with five doorways, only one of which had a door. The walls, floors, and ceiling were old and battered concrete, and there were no windows. A mismatched collection of old chairs and a sofa that had seen much better days were scattered about. Through the open doorways, she saw mattresses and personal decorations. Clearly, this was a home. Her eyes came back around to the boy and girl. His eyes darted around the room, but he kept himself between the little girl and where he thought Wraith might be.

"Con," the little girl said. "Put your fire out. Can't you see she's just scared?"

The boy, Con apparently, cast an incredulous glance over his shoulder. "Well, no. As she's currently invisible, I can't see nothing, can I? So, if you don't mind, I'll just—"

"Now!" the girl said. Her arms were crossed and her face was a child's approximation of stern.

"But—"

"She's our guest."

Con let out a breath, the fire went out, and he dropped his hands. "There, you happy now?"

The little girl beamed and nodded. "Yep."

Wraith just stared for several seconds. She didn't know whether to run or laugh.

"It's okay," the girl said, looking around the room. "We're not going to hurt you."

Without meaning to, Wraith let go of the bottle cap and dropped the cloak.

"I'm sorry," Wraith said. "I just—" She swallowed and rubbed her eyes. "I'm very confused and, well—do you know how I got here?"

"We was hoping you'd illuminate us on that matter," Con said.

Wraith waited for him to expound, but he didn't.

"Well, like I said, I can't. I don't know. Can you at least tell me where am I?"

Con puffed out his chest. "Why don't you let me ask the bleeding questions?"

"Oh, okay. That's fair." Wraith nodded.

A long moment of silence passed. Con's brow furrowed and he fretted his lower lip, but he didn't say anything.

"I'm called Sprout," the little girl finally said.

"Oi!" Con protested.

"He's called Confillagation," Sprout said.

The boy sighed. "Bloody hell, it's Conflagration. Is that so difficult to remember?"

"We just call him Con." Sprout gave him a sidelong glance and whispered, "He's British," as if that explained everything.

Con opened his mouth to say something, but just shook his head instead.

"What's your name?" Sprout asked.

"Wraith." She glanced at the four bedrooms.

"Nice to meet you," Sprout said. "We live here. The others, Geek and Ovation, are out getting money and food. Con was supposed to watch me, and you, and if you woke up, he was supposed to find out how you got past our—"

"Oi! You going to tell her the color knickers I'm wearing as well, then?"

Sprout looked at him, confused. "White with little yellow duckies, but why would she care? Is it supposed to be a secret?"

Wraith stifled chuckle.

Con rubbed his temples and muttered.

Sprout turned back to Wraith. "How did you get here?"

"I—" Wraith paused. Pieces of memory drifted in her mind but were utterly incoherent. "I don't know. How long have I been here?"

Con opened his mouth, but Sprout beat him to it. "We found you three days ago, just lying there. We woke up, and there you were."

Wraith noticed the section of the floor she'd been lying on was covered in thick, soft grass. She squatted down and saw that it had actually grown out of the concrete.

"The floor is really hard and cold," Sprout said.

"Thank you."

"Brilliant," Con said. "Since I'm no longer needed, I'll just have meself a sit-down. Give us a shout when you're done, yeah?" Con fell into a chair, crossed his arms, and tried to look like he wasn't staring at Wraith.

Wraith eyed him back and couldn't shake the feeling she'd met him somewhere before. It was just beyond her fingertips.

"That's why they call me Sprout." The girl smiled. "I make things grow."

"Reckon she put that together," Con said. "I imagine she noticed the correlation."

Wraith stared harder at Con. She knew his eyes from somewhere. "Are we friends?"

"We can be!" Sprout said.

Con narrowed his eyes. "You saying you don't know if you know us?"

"No. I don't know. I'm sorry, this is all very strange."

Con leaned back in the chair. "Just for you. This kind of thing happens to us a couple times a week."

Sprout turned to him. "No it doesn't."

Con ignored her. "What do you remember last?"

Wraith opened her mouth but before the words got out, she forgot them.

Con arched an eyebrow. "You don't remember what you remember either?"

After a moment, Wraith finally said, "I remember . . . pancakes?"

"I love pancakes," Sprout said.

Wraith nodded. "I was having chocolate chip pancakes." She tapped her forehead and scattered images began to shake loose. The words escaped without her thinking about them. "And Jesus was playing a trumpet. The doctor said I should do something, but there was this tattooed woman in an evening gown— Was that before or after the funeral?"

"Doctor?" Con asked. "Well that explains a lot, doesn't it?"

"What? Sorry." She looked at him, but the thoughts and images were bouncing around, so it was hard to keep things straight. Wraith ran a hand through her short hair. "It was the bacon, I think, or the coffee. No, Shadow was having the coffee. Or was it both of us?"

"Shadow?" Con asked.

"It was important," Wraith said and brought both

hands up to her hair. Feeling the almost pixie cut, she froze, except for touching all around her head. "I think my hair is supposed to be longer."

Con blinked. "Brilliant, you're a bleeding nutter."

"Con, be nice," a strong masculine voice said.

Wraith spun and saw two boys in the now-open doorway. One was taller than Wraith and rail thin. The overlarge shirt with a Superman *S* on it only added to the effect. He wore glasses and short dreadlocks fell in all directions from his head. A large canvas bag rested on his shoulder. The other boy was closer to twenty years old, with broad shoulders and chiseled features. When he smiled, Wraith felt herself flush.

"Calling it like I see it, mate," Con said. "She's the one what mentioned a doctor."

The two boys stepped inside the room.

"Ovation!" Sprout ran to the older boy with her arms open.

He set down a guitar case, bent down, and gave her a hug. "Hey, midget."

"What took so long?" Con asked.

"The usual spots were dead," the skinny boy said. "And that dog is still circling the place. We had to take the back way to avoid him."

Wraith narrowed her eyes. "Dog?"

Ovation gave her a smile that made her heart beat a little faster. "Glad to see you're awake. You met Con and Sprout." He said the last part as he tousled the girl's hair. "I'm Ovation, and that's Geek."

The skinny boy waved.

Wraith only vaguely heard them. Her mind was struggling to put pieces together.

"You okay?" Ovation asked.

"Did I call it, or what? She came to a little bit ago and went wonky," Con said.

Wraith's brain clicked. "What did he look like?"

"What? Who?" Ovation asked.

"The dog."

"He was big," Geek said.

Ovation stood up. "He looked kind of like a big coyot—"

"Toto!" Wraith bolted for the door.

"Geek, stop her!" Con shouted.

Geek dropped the bag and grabbed her arm as she went by, but the look on his face was unsure.

Wraith tried to get loose, but his hand was like a vise. He barely even moved with her struggles. "Let me go, damn it! That's my dog!"

"Just take it easy," Ovation said. "We'll take you to him, but we can't just let you throw open the outer door."

"Please, calm down," Geek said.

Something about those words made Wraith freeze. She looked from the skinny boy to his friends. When she finally understood how absurd she was acting, she looked at the floor and a few tears fell to the concrete. That's when she saw the bag at Geek's feet was loaded with canned food. It must've weighed a hundred pounds, easy.

"You're making her cry!" Sprout said.

Geek snapped his hand back. "Oh, I'm so sorry. I didn't mean to hurt you. I just—"

"I don't think it was you." Ovation put a hand on Wraith's shoulder. "We're not going to hurt you, but I can't let you put us at risk."

Wraith stared into his eyes. Things in her head started to feel chaotic. "My friends are gone, and I have no idea what happened to them. I don't know where I am or how I got here. I just want my dog."

"You're sure I didn't hurt you?" Geek asked again.

Wraith shook her head and knelt on the floor. She just wanted to get to Toto and get gone. She knew her friends needed her, but she didn't know why or even where they were.

Ovation sat down, looked her in the eye, and spoke softly. "You're in the Emerald City."

Wraith looked at him quizzically.

"It's what they call Seattle," he said. "Because of all the plants. We're just outside downtown. Anyway, I couldn't just let you leave, because we have wards around this place. That's why we were surprised to find you in our living room without having tripped any of them."

"Then could you just take me to get Toto?" Wraith looked at each of them in turn, finally stopping on Ovation. "Please."

"Of course." He helped her to her feet, then led her and the others down a short hallway to a second door. It was old gray painted metal with signs of rust, but it looked heavy and tough.

"Cover your ears," Ovation said.

Wraith narrowed her eyes. "Why?"

"Just trust me."

Ovation stepped to the door, said something, and brought his hands together. Even with her ears covered, Wraith felt the sonic boom reverberate through her bones. The door shuddered and small symbols briefly lit around the frame.

That's when Wraith noticed the small equations that were laced together and surrounding the doorframe. It was rudimentary, and she could see the obvious holes that could be exploited to unravel the whole thing.

Ovation took Wraith's hands from her ears.

"It's tuned to our abilities, so only someone in our group can disarm it," he said.

Geek stepped up, grasped the doorknob, and pulled it open. It creaked so loud that Wraith thought it might have been rusted shut, but the skinny boy didn't even seem to strain.

"It sticks," Geek said.

"Come on," Sprout said and took Wraith's hand. "It's safe now."

They stepped through the door, and Geek pulled it closed behind them.

Stretching before them was a long hallway with dirty glass tiles in the ceiling that let in only sparse rays of dreary light.

"This way," Ovation said and began walking.

Sprout kept hold of Wraith's hand and led her right

behind him. The walls were covered in graffiti and water stains.

"Where are we?" she asked.

"Seattle Underground," Geek said. "The parts deemed not quite safe."

"The city was built on marshland, so it kept flooding," Ovation said without looking back. "Then there was a huge fire, and the city decided to rebuild the streets a couple stories higher. Some landlords didn't wait, so their first floors eventually ended up underground, but people could still access them through here." He pointed up at the ceiling. "Not much light got in, so it became a haven for criminals in hiding. The city condemned it about a hundred years ago, and people just kind of forgot about it."

"Just like us," Con said.

Ovation chuckled. "Amen, mate."

"I'm forgotten too," Wraith said, a little more eager than she'd intended. "And I forget. At the least the things I don't remember—"

Everyone except Sprout looked at her as if she was crazy. They were probably right. She really should learn to keep her mouth shut.

Sprout squeezed her hand. "Maybe we can help you remember."

"Maybe," Ovation said, "but one thing at a time. Okay, midget?"

They followed the hallway to an old spiral staircase. At the top was a weathered wooden door, which opened onto the floor of a long defunct factory. The few intact windows were small and dirty. It was an immense space, stretching over a hundred feet, and easily thirty or forty feet high.

Ovation pointed to a door halfway down the factory floor. "Normally, we'd use that one, but we didn't know the dog."

"And he's big," Geek said.

"Oi, man up, eh?" Con said.

Ovation looked at Wraith. "I don't know how much you know about things, but in Seattle, kids are going missing. Some have even turned up dead," he said. "Some slingers, like you, but mostly fifties. Fifties are—"

"I know what they are," Wraith said. "My friends are fifties. And I know about the snatchers. They took my friends."

"I'm sorry," Geek said.

Wraith shrugged. "I'm going to get Toto, and we'll be out of your hair." She reached out for the door.

Ovation put his hand over hers and shook his head. "No one goes outside alone, not now."

Wraith's hand tingled from the touch. "It's okay, I'll just—"

"I'll go with you," he said. "Geek and Con will watch our backs." He looked at Sprout. "You hang back here. Be ready in case we need to make a quick escape."

Sprout saluted. "Yes, sir."

Ovation opened the door slowly and peeked out. "Come on, it looks clear."

Wraith followed him out with Geek and Con almost on her heels.

The old factory's yard was asphalt slowly being overtaken by grass and weeds, all of which was surrounded by a rusty chain link fence with more than a few gaps. It all sat in the middle of a long abandoned industrial zone. In the distance, she could just see snow-capped mountains behind a huge skyline that wasn't more than a dozen miles away.

Wraith looked around. "Where is he?"

"I don't know," Ovation said. "He's been circling the place for a couple days. He'll probably—"

Wraith heard a bark and spun on her heel.

Toto sprinted toward her, tongue lolling out of his mouth.

Wraith went to her knees, caught the dog—though he nearly knocked her over—and hugged him tight. "I missed you!" The smell of his fur was familiar and comforting. She felt a little like she'd come home.

"Toto?" Con asked. "You named *that* Toto?"

"I told you he was big," Geek whispered.

"You said a big dog, mate," Con said. "Not a bleeding woolly mammoth."

At some point, the boys had all taken several steps away. They tried to look brave, but they kept casting glances at each other.

"He won't hurt you," Wraith said. "Will you, boy?"

In unison, they took a tentative step forward. Toto growled. They all took three steps back.

"Hey, it's okay," Wraith said. "They're friends."

Sprout stepped from behind them. "Puppy!"

"Wait!" the boys said at the same time.

The little girl ran up and Toto opened his mouth into a doggie smile.

"He's not a bleeding puppy, you daft—"

Sprout scratched behind one of Toto's ears, and his tail went into manic wagging.

"He likes you," Wraith said, then turned to the boys. "He won't hurt you. He's just protective of me."

"Aye," Con said. "You heard her, mate." He nudged Geek.

"Uh, go ahead, boss," Geek said to Ovation.

"I'm fine here, thanks," Ovation said.

Toto eyed them warily.

"You're just a big softie, aren't you, Toto?" Wraith said.

"Actually, his name is Hototo," Sprout said, still scratching his ear.

"What?" Wraith asked.

Sprout switched to the other ear. "He doesn't mind you calling him Toto though. He kind of likes it now."

Everyone stared at Sprout.

"And how do know you that?" Geek asked.

"He told me," Sprout said.

"So you're bleeding Dr. Doolittle now?" Con asked. "You never said you could talk with animals."

Sprout shrugged. "No one ever asked."

Toto eyed Geek.

Geek swallowed. "He, uh, isn't going to eat us, right?"

"If Wraith likes you, he does too," Sprout said.

The boys all traded a glance and let out a collective breath.

"Well, thanks, Toto," Ovation said in an uncertain tone.

"Mate, you're talking to the dog," Con said in a harsh whisper.

Sprout looked from Toto to Wraith, then back again. Her eyes went wide and her smile stretched from ear to ear. "Oh! This means I get a sister and a puppy!"

Wraith's eyes went wide. "Wait, I—"

The little girl threw her arms around Wraith and hugged her tight.

"What?" Geek and Ovation asked in stereo.

"Oh, well, that's just brilliant," Con said.

A chill made Wraith look up. In the distance, she could just make out what looked like a black utility van. It was the only vehicle around and it was headed her way. She stared at it for several seconds, watching it grow as it approached. All she could think about was Shadow hanging by chains.

"Wraith, you okay?" Ovation asked.

Wraith looked over at him then back. The van was gone.

Everyone followed her gaze.

"What is it?" Con asked.

Wraith narrowed her eyes, but not even a dust trail hung in the air and the van didn't reappear. After several moments, she shook her head. "Nothing, let's just go back in."

CHAPTER EIGHT

Dante knelt down and examined the first body. This mortal was the oldest, probably in his early thirties. From his clothes and tattoos, he was a small-time ruffian. That meant the police would probably dismiss his death as the result of a fight over turf. His rib cage was crushed in so far it had destroyed his heart and punctured both lungs, but they'd write that off as the result of a serious beating. Dante didn't know how they'd explain the evidence he was knocked back twenty feet and hit the wall so hard that the back of his skull shattered, but he knew they would. They always did. The most outlandish explanations always seemed preferable to the truth.

As Dante stood, he sucked in a breath through his nose and regretted it. The bodies had been here for a couple days, maybe a week, and the smell was overwhelming. There was, however, just beneath the fetid odor, the lingering smell of magic. The fact it was still present meant two possibilities. It could be recent, which would mean someone was hanging out with corpses: possible, but not likely. The bodies showed no sign of abuse, magical or otherwise. People don't keep company with the dead for no reason. So, it must have been the other possibility; that the magic used was powerful enough to leave remnants that lasted, potentially, for a week or more. Up until recently, he wouldn't have been sure any mortal possessed that kind of power anymore, but things had changed, drastically. He thought back to the van, its front end looking as if it had been hit by a wrecking ball. The magic around it was powerful too, but he'd also sensed two sources there. The one outside felt like the magic here, powerful but somehow wild. Inside the van had been another matter. He shook his head. It felt almost ancient and carried a chill. It was no wonder that van hadn't been towed or been picked clean.

He sighed, thinking of the wasted months chasing ghost stories in the towns and cities across the country. It still left a bitter taste in his mouth; how easy it was for some of the court nobles to be so ambivalent about the missing kids. Yes, they were changelings but they were still kids. How could anyone leave those most in need of help and protection out in the cold? Often literally. So few of the kids would talk to him, and when they did, he could almost taste their derision. It made him all the more grateful for Brigid and those like her.

He looked around again. "I should've started in Seattle," he said under his breath.

"Hey, this is a crime scene," said a gruff voice. "Let me see some ID, nice and slow."

Dante concentrated for just a moment on his glamour, then stood slowly and turned, hands in clear view. A uniformed cop in his twenties watched every move intently, hand resting on his holstered sidearm. Dante just stood there for a long three count before the cop blinked and relaxed.

"Oh, I'm sorry, Detective, I didn't recognize you. Wow, you homicide guys are quick."

"I was in the area when the call came in." Dante stepped close and read the name tag. "Officer Willard. Were you the first on scene?"

"Yes, sir. My partner and I got here and saw this." The cop coughed and gagged. "We secured the area and called it in. Steve, my partner, went to canvas the area."

"Good," Dante said. "Head outside and help your partner; I want to look around a bit before the lab rats get here."

"With pleasure." Willard hurried down the stairs.

Dante knelt down and looked over the second body. Something had twisted his head around nearly a full 360 degrees. His right hand was missing. The amputation had been just above the wrist, and the stump had been cauterized instantly. He also had some bite marks on his left wrist. At first glance, they looked like just a normal dog bite, albeit a big dog, but something about them was wrong.

The phone in Dante's pocket chirped. When he pulled it out and saw who was calling, he smiled despite the situation.

"Thanks for calling back so quickly," Dante said.

"Well, you said it was important," Edward said.

"Are you home?"

"No, I had an appointment with a patient. That's why I didn't answer when you called. What do you need?"

"I need you to do some research for me."

"Really?"

"Really." Dante glanced over his shoulder and listened to make sure no real detectives had arrived and his conversation was still private. "Someone has been kidnapping changelings and—"

"What!? Jesus—"

"It has nothing to do with Caitlin or Fiona. I'm almost entirely certain the culprits aren't fae."

Edward drew in a few slow breaths. When he finally spoke, his voice was tight. "You're sure they're not at risk?"

"I am. Aside from it being nowhere near you, all the victims have been homeless kids."

"Homeless?" Edward asked. "That's a fairly common early-stage victimology."

Dante was glad to get him onto a different topic. "What do you mean?"

"Lots of serial killers get their start that way. It gives them time to develop their skills without pressure from police. If you want to get away with something, prey on those that won't be missed or draw any attention."

"And that's exactly the case. For the most part, these have gone unnoticed and unreported."

"So, how did you find out?" Edward asked.

"Unreported to *mortal* authorities."

"Well, I'd suggest you start looking for bodies. It's gruesome but can provide you with a lot of information on who you're looking for. You can actually gain a lot of insight about a killer based on his victims, how he kills, and the like."

Dante made a noncommittal grunt.

"You're sure—"

"I swear to you, neither Fiona nor Caitlin are in any danger."

There was another long pause. "It's just—"

"Edward, if I thought there was any risk, any at all, I'd have wardens all over your place."

"Yes, of course. I'm sorry. I didn't mean to suggest otherwise."

"It's fine. All things considered, I understand completely."

"I'm not going to like this research, am I?" Edward asked.

"Probably not," Dante said. "See what you can find about granting normal mortals the ability to use magic, and if it has anything to do with changelings. I have some theories, but your library is the most extensive I know of. This is out of my area of expertise."

Edward let out a breath. "Okay, I'll head home now and get on it. I'm going to find some pretty horrible things, aren't I?"

"I'm afraid so. And I wouldn't speak to Caitlin about it, at least not right now. She doesn't need to know the things you're likely to find. Really, no one does."

"I tend to agree, but I'm not going to lie to her."

"Just don't mention it unless she asks. All right?"

"I'll give you a call as soon as I find anything."

"Thank you."

Dante disconnected the call and put the phone away. He felt bad keeping the details of how widespread this was from Edward. The wizard had proved himself worthy of trust a hundred times over, but then, this wasn't anything to do with trust. Dante was working with suspicions and conjecture. A fae could be responsible for all this, but it felt like a mortal; the magic was almost certainly mortal. If Edward found something in his, well, eclectic library, Dante would have some facts to share. Until then, there was no point casting any more darkness on the wizard than necessary.

Flashing lights out the window caught Dante's attention. Two unmarked police cars and a large black SUV pulled into the empty lot out front.

He turned to leave but stopped and looked back. For the first time, he noticed that all the items appeared to have been thrown out from a central point, a circle, a couple feet in diameter that was clear of anything, including dirt. He stepped into its center. The smell of magic actually overpowered the fetid rot. Someone had practically ripped reality apart here. Slowly, Dante turned and reexamined the room. He was right, everything was sent out from this spot, like an explosion. He looked down and saw the dirt extending away from the circle made a rough spiraling shape.

"And I told you," someone coming up the stairs said, "no one from homicide answered the call."

"I saw the guy's badge and ID," Officer Willard said. "If it was fake, it was the best I've ever seen."

"Well, that equals a great pile of puppy turds," the other voice said. "Next time you wonder why you're still on a beat, remember this moment."

Dante walked to the stairway and whispered a charm. His glamour drew up around him, making him, to mortal eyes, just another piece of the background. Officer Willard and two men in cheap suits came up the stairs, walked right by him, and went into the room.

"So, where is he?" one of the real detectives, a balding man in his fifties, asked as he looked around.

"He was here five minutes ago," Willard said.

"How many exits to this place?" the other detective, a younger guy with thick black hair, asked.

"Just the one," Willard said.

"Well, either you're wrong," baldy said, "you're hallucinating, or he grew wings and flew away."

Dante silently descended the stairs, ducked under the crime scene tape, and exited the building. He stepped around two more oblivious cops and headed to his car.

One of the patrolman's radios crackled, and Dante stopped.

"Any units in the vicinity of Myrtle Edwards Park, check report of 11–46, possible juvenile."

"Oh god," the cop said. "Glad we don't have to respond to that."

"No joke," the other said. "Another freaking kid? What's that make, fifteen just this month?"

"Nineteen."

Dante's stomach twisted. Nineteen just in this city. He opened the door to his rented Maserati, which, while an improvement over the SUV, still wasn't his custom Mustang. As he closed the door, his phone rang again. He glanced at the caller ID and answered.

"Not a good time, Faolan."

"Sorry, but you said to let you know if we heard anything. You'll want to head to—"

"Myrtle Edwards Park?" Dante asked as he started the engine. "I'm on my way now."

"Well, be prepared. Couple of joggers found another body. Report says it's a little girl, looks about ten. From the dirty clothes and hair, they think she's another street kid. Word is the FBI is being called in to investigate now."

"Took their sweet time, didn't they?" Dante sped down the road. "We need to figure this out and resolve it before the Feds get too deep into it. Try getting in touch with Donovan again."

"I'll see what I can do, but I'm running out of ideas."

"Don't take any of the usual crap from his underlings. He doesn't get to brush us off anymore."

"But—"

"I'll go see him in person, if I have to. If he has half a brain, he won't let it come to that."

Faolan laughed. "So, you'll want his address, then."

Dante left his car well away from the park and approached on foot. The flashing police lights, gathering news vans, and thronging joggers and bikers had made the spot easy to find. The crowd was mostly mortals who'd stopped to find out what happened or had just come to feed some morbid fascination. There were, however, several changeling kids hovering nearby, all in dirty secondhand clothes, whispering to each other.

The murmurs stopped when Dante approached. They were the only ones who would notice him, but every time he looked at one, they cast their eyes down and pretended they hadn't. Some in the Rogue Court looked down on these fringe dwellers—they were the untouchables of the fae world. Some of the nobles even debated whether these changelings should be recognized as court members at all. Dante suspected Donovan was in the camp that said no.

Dante walked up to the edge of the tape, careful to stay out of the view of the television cameras on the scene. The reporters and other mortals wouldn't see him if he didn't want them to, but cameras were unpredictable.

The police were standing around a white sheet with a tiny form underneath it. From the size, the girl couldn't be much over eight. He did a double take when he saw the wildflowers growing up just around the white sheet. Her mother must've been a dryad.

How are these kids coming into their power so young?

With effort, Dante kept from dwelling on Edward's stepdaughter, Fiona. Instead, he closed his eyes and looked away, swearing under his breath to find whoever was responsible and make them account for it. He didn't care anymore if it was a mortal, fae, or some creature from the Stygian Depths—someone would answer for these atrocities.

When he opened his eyes, he noticed a group of teenage changelings were looking at him and whispering again. From the look of them, they were on the cusp of the Choice, where they would have to choose between their mortal or fae natures.

"I'm—"

"We know who you are," a girl of perhaps fourteen said. Her hair was deep auburn and her sad eyes were a shade of green that nearly matched Dante's.

"What do you want, noble?" asked a boy who appeared to be going through the Change at that moment. He had brown hair and a rough beard. The small nubs of horns on his forehead spoke of his satyr heritage. "Since when do any of you care about us?"

"Some of us always have," Dante said. "Do any of you know who that is?" He motioned to the cloth-covered body.

"I do." This girl was probably nearing sixteen. She was short with bright eyes of deep purple. Her hair was a shade of lavender that spoke to a pixie in her family tree. "Her name was Luna."

"How long ago did she go missing?" Dante asked.

The girl shrugged. "No one's really sure. She was really a sweet kid. Way too young to be on her own. But like most of us, when it became clear she wasn't normal, her family didn't want anything to do with her." The girl paused to wipe away some tears. "When I didn't see her for a while, I kind of hoped she had moved on, maybe to someplace warm, maybe even to some kind of family that would accept her."

"I'm very sorry," Dante said.

"What are you doing looking into it? This isn't your region," the satyr boy said. "And the western nobles don't give a damn, unless we're getting in their way."

"I'm not the magister of the Eastern Region anymore," Dante said.

The group exchanged glances.

"And I do give a damn. I'll find who did this and—"

"Yeah, whatever." The boy turned and walked away.

"Fitch, wait." The auburn-haired girl followed him.

"Don't mind him, we're all kind of on edge," the remaining girl said.

"I can understand."

"No, you really can't." Her stare was granite. "The press cares only when the bodies turn up, and after a few minutes, everyone forgets about it. The cops don't investigate, not any more than they have to. They have *real* crimes to solve."

Dante opened his mouth but didn't get a chance to speak.

"We tried to report them, at first anyway, to the cops and the court." The girl clenched her jaw and spoke through her teeth. "The police told us they just went to a different city, and the court can't be bothered with fifties. No one cares." She looked Dante square in the eye. "Half mortal, half fae, and neither side wants us. We're on our own, always have been."

"You're not—"

"Yes, we are. We watch out for each other, since no one else will. If it wasn't daylight, we wouldn't have come." She looked past Dante to the body being placed in a black bag. "I just had to know if it was her."

Dante didn't say anything. There weren't any words.

"Everyone knows about what happened last year, how you helped that little girl. It's kind of become a legend." The girl turned her tear-filled gaze back to Dante. "Are you really going to find who's doing this? Or is this some Rogue Court publicity thing?"

"Oh, I'll find them. This is no stunt, I promise you that."

The girl nodded, her expression dark. "When you do, make them bleed. Make them pay, for every single kid they've hurt, here and everywhere else." She turned and followed her friends.

"I will, and then some," Dante said after she was gone.

CHAPTER NINE

Even without looking, Wraith could feel everyone's eyes on her. The furniture had been moved to provide her audience a better view. Ovation and Geek sat on the dingy sofa with Sprout between them, her legs folded beneath her. Con slouched in a broken old recliner, slightly apart from the others. Wraith was on a worn out, overstuffed chair, Toto's head in her lap. His ears twitched as she scratched one then the other—despite his ecstasy, he was keeping one eye on the boys.

"Well?" Con asked, his voice terse.

Ovation shot Con an icy look, then his eyes softened and he turned back to Wraith. "It's okay. Take your time."

"And you don't have to tell us anything you don't want to," Geek said.

"Like hell!" Con said.

Sprout glared at him.

"We need to know how you got here, if there's a hole in our protections, so we can close it. That's all." Ovation's voice was soft.

"I call it striding," Wraith answered.

"What is that?" Geek asked.

"It's kind of hard to explain," Wraith said.

"So give us the simple version," Ovation said.

"Okay. On the quantum level there are an infinite number of wormholes. They connect every point in reality with every other point at the same time. A sufficiently focused sentient will can modify the quantum information, shifting the probability of a convergence of wormholes from exponentially unlikely to one, or certain. That will allow something, or in this case someone, and all the constituent particles, to move from one point to another without crossing the space in between. That sentient will can then control, to a limited extent, the entropic principles that guide the location of the two ends of the wormhole, a point of origin and a destination." She shrugged. "Of course, once you reach that level, the very notion of a three-dimensional reality is completely irrelevant and actually illusionary—" She looked up and saw two completely blank expressions. Geek was the only one who seemed to understand, and he was grinning.

"That was the simple version?" Con asked.

Wraith nodded. "Pretty much."

"That is so cool!" Geek said, eyes wide. "You teleported!"

Wraith furrowed her brow. "Oh, well yeah, I guess that's a simpler way of putting it."

"You're like Nightcrawler, or Dr. Strange!" he said.

"What the bloody hell does that mean?" Con asked.

"Well, in the comics," Geek said, "Nightcrawler and Dr. Strange step through other dimensions to move from one point to another."

"Okay, mate," Con said to Ovation. "How are you going to close a trans-dimensional hole in our security?"

Ovation ignored him. "So why'd you teleport here?" Ovation asked.

Wraith shrugged. "I can't always control it. And the snatchers didn't exactly give me time to focus, you know?"

Everyone exchanged a nervous glance, except Sprout, who just kept smiling.

Wraith ignored the reaction. "Of course, even in the best of circumstances, I don't always have sufficient . . ." Her words died as pieces began to fall into place. "Could that be it?"

"What?" Ovation asked.

Wraith closed her eyes. Calculations and equations spun through her head and it took all her focus to keep them inside and to not stride, here and now. "I need my bag."

"Here," Geek said, handing it to her.

She dug into the main pouch, pulling out a composition book and pen, then flipped through pages until she found the right calculation. It was easy to spot—the manic writing was double underlined. Her hands began to shake, and she heard the pen hit the floor and her voice reading the notes aloud. "It could be that the effect of altering universal probabilities at this level, and controlling the requisite power, would cause a break from a singular-view reality."

Wraith stopped reading. At the bottom of the page, there was a single word written in large letters, circled and underlined. She didn't want to say it out loud.

Crazy.

Her throat felt tight and somewhere distant, Toto whimpered while voices talked over each other. She wanted to believe her life, her friends, and the few memories she retained were real, but—

"Wraith?" Ovation shouted.

Her mind went still. The notebook had joined the pen on the floor and she now held the arms of the chair in a white-knuckled death grip. She looked up. Everyone was staring at her.

"What?" she asked, her voice sounding small in her ears.

"Take a breath," Ovation said. "Freaking out won't help."

She managed to let go of the chair.

"Why don't we eat something?" Geek asked. "Are you hungry?"

Her stomach gurgled in response and she turned away.

"So that's a yes," Ovation said and smiled. "Don't jump to any conclusions. Maybe you're, I don't know, miscalculating or something?"

Wraith nodded. Eating seemed ridiculous, but she was hungry.

Geek went to the large canvas bag, near to overflowing with cans, and hefted it one-handed. She kept herself from staring. They went through the selection, and she made a noncommittal grunt when given a large can of SpaghettiOs. Con offered a flaming hand to warm it up for her, but she just ate them cold. She hadn't realized how hungry she was until she started eating, and paused only long enough to drink from a bottle of water. She tore a blank page from her composition book and poured onto it the remaining half a can, then set it on the floor for a grateful Toto.

She could feel Ovation's eyes on her. He didn't stare, but she knew he kept looking her way. She couldn't blame him. Having a crazy person around would make anyone uneasy.

Before long, Wraith couldn't stand the feel of being stared at. She drew in a deep breath and opened her mouth—

"What happened?" Ovation asked.

Wraith looked up in surprise. "What?"

"It might help," Geek said, and offered a kind smile. "If you want to tell us what happened to your friends."

She looked from one face to another. She probably owed them that much at least. So she recounted the events at the mega-mart, the chase through the streets, the snatchers in the squat, and her striding.

"You're sure they didn't get away?" Geek asked. "SK and Fritz, I mean."

Wraith shrugged. "Maybe, but I'm sure they got Shadow." She sighed and had a vague recollection of Shadow's voice, and pancakes for some reason. "Well, as sure as I am about anything."

"Maybe she did too," Con said. "And if you all agreed to leave—"

Wraith shook her head. "They wouldn't have."

"Well, I can't speak for your friends," Ovation said. "But we all know the snatchers are real."

Everyone looked sad and Sprout cuddled closer to Ovation.

"What if I am crazy?" Wraith asked.

"What if you aren't?" Geek asked.

Wraith opened her mouth, then closed it. She had never considered the question from that side. It was actually more frightening.

"Tell us about Shadow," Ovation said.

Wraith furrowed her brow. "Why?"

"Don't think about it, just tell us about her," Ovation said.

"She's Sioux, and a fifty, but not a faerie changeling. I think her father was a Native American spirit. She can collect light then release it." Wraith chuckled. "She's my smoking buddy, and she's always hungry."

"She's real." Ovation said. "If she wasn't, there would be holes in your memories of her, and you would need to stop and think about how to fill any gaps. But you didn't need to do that."

Geek nodded.

Wraith blinked. "You really think so?"

"I do. I could see it in your eyes," Ovation said. "Not to mention, you didn't talk about her in the past tense. You said she *is*, not she *was*."

Wraith thought about that and smiled.

"What about SK and Fritz?" Geek asked.

Wraith smiled more. "They're more in love than anyone I've ever seen. He's a smartass, tall and thin. Fritz is tiny and German, still has her accent."

"Are they fifties too?" Sprout asked.

Wraith nodded. "SK's mother was some kind of mountain faerie, Fritz is part tinker Kobold, kind of like a gremlin." She could see her friends, all the details, and remember their voices. She started to feel better, a little bit anyway, less disjointed, more solid and real.

"Thank you," she said after a moment.

"Well, maybe you're not a complete nutter," Con said.

Wraith let out a long breath. Hearing a declaration of sanity from someone else, such as it was, was like seeing a ship from the shores of a deserted island. She fully expected to see that ship drift away. But until it did, she enjoyed the long absent sensation of hope.

"I think you've just been through something . . . something really bad" Ovation said. "I've seen it before." He looked at the others then back to Wraith. "You don't end up on the streets because of anything good, and they're not the best place to escape the darkness in your past."

"Besides," Geek said. "We can't all be imagining the snatchers."

"Exactly," Ovations said. "Isn't there something in science about the simplest answer being the right one?"

Wraith nodded. "All things being equal, the simplest answer is typically the correct one. It's called Occam's Razor."

"So what's more likely?" Ovation asked. "You're imagining your friends, and just happen to be suffering some memory loss, or you're blocking out some terrible event in your past?"

They all ate in silence as Wraith tried to find holes in Ovation's logic. She was still trying when everyone was ready to get some sleep.

Sprout offered Wraith and Toto a spot on the floor in her room. Wraith accepted, more reluctantly than the dog.

"Don't worry," Sprout whispered as she cuddled close to Wraith. "You're not alone anymore. We'll find a way to help you. Ovation is really good at helping people."

Wraith just wiped her eyes and listened to the silence.

She sat on the ledge, not entirely sure how she'd gotten onto the roof of the old factory, took a drag of her cigarette—which she didn't remember lighting—and stared at the skyline. The buildings and Space Needle were so close, it felt like she could reach out and touch them. It was a glittering palace, right at her fingertips and a million miles away, all at the same time. She envied the people living in it, and their bliss-ful ignorance. They didn't know about snatchers, or suffer from lost memories.

"Can't sleep?" a voice asked from behind her.

Wraith barely managed to keep from flinching. "No."

"Mind if I join you?" Ovation asked.

Wraith bit her lip and shrugged. "Free country."

Ovation stepped onto the edge of the roof and lowered himself down next to her, legs dangling in the empty air. He smiled and looked out at the city. "I think it's only so beautiful when it's far away. That distance keeps you from seeing the dirt and grime; all you see is the shine and sparkle."

Wraith tried not to notice how close he was. His hand was resting on the ledge, less than an inch from hers, and their legs almost touched a few times as his swung. "I guess."

"When's the last time you slept?" he asked. "I mean really slept?"

Wraith opened her mouth to answer, but stopped and thought about it. She felt tired all the time, and had for as long as she could remember. She just sighed and shook her head.

"That long?" he asked.

"I honestly don't know. It's kind of hard to explain." Wraith took a long drag from her cigarette and savored the faint burning in her throat before blowing out the smoke. "Besides, you wouldn't understand."

Ovation chuckled. "If you explain it like you did

your teleporting, then you're probably right. But you could try."

She laughed, but there was no joy to it. "If you did understand, it would mean you were crazy too, or lying."

"I don't think you're—"

"Don't." She looked at him but avoided his eyes. Instead, she took a final drag and flicked the cigarette off into the open air. It tumbled like a red comet to the ground below. "You don't know. I don't even know anymore. Not for certain anyway."

Ovation furrowed his brow. "Know what?"

"Anything!" She ran her hands through her hair. "I have all these thoughts in my head and they all make sense to me, but I know they shouldn't." She didn't mention the quantum information, the constant floating numbers and symbols she could pull together. She assumed that all slingers saw them and she didn't want that assumption ruined. "They could be memories, or I could be quantum leaping from place to place and suffering horrible hallucinations and delusions as a side effect." She gritted her teeth and gripped her hair. "Damn it, it's like a dream within a nightmare, and I just want to wake up. I need to wake up, and I can't do that sleeping. You don't see. No one does. We're all sleeping through it and never see the forest for the dreams—"

Firm hands gripped her shoulders.

Wraith tried to slow her breathing. "See what I mean?" Her voice was barely above a whisper. "I don't know what's real, what I remember, or even what I'm saying."

"I'm real."

"You have no idea how much I want to believe that." She stood and started to walk away as she lit another cigarette.

Ovation was right behind her. "Maybe I don't understand, but that doesn't mean I can't listen." He put a hand on her shoulder again and she didn't shrug it off. It felt like centuries since anyone had touched her. Hell, as far as she knew, it might've been.

"It wouldn't be so frustrating, if I didn't know it wasn't always like this. I used to be normal. At least, I think so."

"What, you think the rest of us weren't?"

Wraith looked at him. Thinking back, she could almost remember Shadow and the others telling their stories. She fought to remember the words and found even the faces of her friends were growing distant. That really hurt.

"You can't think about how things used to be," Ovation said. "My parents freaked out when I started showing signs of my ability."

Wraith had to remind herself to breathe when he stepped closer to her. She was keenly aware of his hand still on her shoulder.

"They took me to doctors who gave me all kinds of meds. I got sick of it and left one day." He shook his head. "It wasn't long before I found my way here and met up with Con. He doesn't talk much about his time before. We found Geek and Sprout about nine months ago. He was kicked out when he started the Change, and Sprout was left at a mall for the same reason. The point is, we all have our own baggage to deal with. But for what it's worth, I just keep reminding myself that everything in the past helped to shape who we are now." He smiled. "And I think that who you are now is pretty cool."

Wraith's throat was dry, and her heart rivaled that of a startled bunny. "You don't even know me."

He reached over, took her hand in his, and squeezed it. "We'll help you find out what happened, to you and your friends."

"Sure, you and the others are going to take on the snatchers to find my friends? Risk your lives, or probably worse, for people you've never met, just for what? Charity?"

"Not Sprout, no way am I letting her get involved," Ovation said. "But I know Geek will want to help, and despite all evidence to the contrary, Con is a decent sort. He's itching to get out of the shadows and take the fight to the streets anyway."

"I don't even know for sure what's right or even real. There are things I'm convinced are right, even though they aren't, and there are so many holes—"

"Maybe you do have some holes in your memory," Ovation said. "You're clearly packing more power than any dozen slingers I've ever met, but it doesn't mean you're crazy." He squeezed her hand again. "It doesn't mean your friends aren't real."

"Come on." He pulled her toward the door leading back down into the factory. "You need to get some sleep. We'll tackle this again in the morning. Besides, if Sprout, or that bear of a dog of yours, wakes up and you're gone . . ."

Wraith chuckled and followed him.

Ovation didn't let go of her hand until they reached Sprout's room and Wraith had settled in between the little girl and Toto. "Get some rest," he whispered. "And remember, you're not alone in this. Not anymore." He smiled, then walked silently out of the room.

Sprout made a sound and Wraith wrapped her arm around the little girl, who snuggled against her in response. After a moment, Wraith closed her eyes, and for the first time that she could remember, sleep was waiting for her like a friend.

CHAPTER TEN

Even in sleep, Wraith felt something was wrong. A darkness was growing that threatened to consume her. She had to wake up, to get away. Somewhere deep inside she knew she couldn't go far enough to escape. Her only hope was to get help. Her friends could help her push the darkness back, but—

She felt reality shift around her. As if she was experiencing quantum superposition—existing in more than one place at the same time. Then, like a rubber band pulled and released, she felt her quantum state snap back, collapsing into a single—

"You can't sleep here," someone said in a low tone.

There was a nudge to her shoulder and the sound of a spinning coin settling on the table. Wraith opened her eyes and looked at the waitress for a long moment. She was young, her sandy blond hair was pulled back into a ponytail, and her name tag said Sarah. Wraith imagined she was normally pretty, but the dark circles under her pale blue eyes said she was probably working a double shift, and it wasn't the first time.

Wraith blinked and looked around the coffee shop. When had she gotten here? Hadn't she just been somewhere else? Her mind was a jumble, and she couldn't make the pieces come together.

Sarah whispered. "If my boss sees you sleeping, he'll toss you." She refilled Wraith's coffee mug. "So long as you're awake and paying, even if it's just a cup of coffee, he won't say anything."

Wraith opened her mouth, to ask where she was, but all that came out was, "Thanks." When the smell of the coffee hit her, she absently added several creams and lots of sugar to the warm liquid without ever looking at the cup.

Sarah furrowed her brow. "Are you, um, waiting for someone?"

Wraith looked up at Sarah and nodded. "Yes," she said. "That's it, thank you. I'm waiting for my friends. They're coming to help me." Something about that didn't seem right. "I think this was our backup plan." Wraith saw the quarter on the table, picked it up and without knowing why, spun it. Drifting numbers and symbols encircled the coin and revolved with it. Every second or so, a number or symbol would fly off and be replaced by another. Wraith took a large swallow of coffee, the taste of it like a lifeline to something real. Pieces began to come together. "Yes, that's it. I'm waiting for my friends."

"You look hungry. I think we have some soup left."

Wraith's mouth watered, but she shook her head. "No, thanks. I've only got a couple dollars, and I'm saving that for coffee and your tip."

"Well, the soup isn't exactly fresh, but it's warm." Sarah smiled. "We'd just throw it out."

Wraith forced a smile. "Thank you, that sounds great."

"I'll bring some extra crackers too," Sarah said, then headed off.

Wraith lit a cigarette, glad you still could in Texas, and drank more coffee, looking from the still-spinning quarter to the clock. Three thirty in the morning, and every second that passed sucked away a little more hope. The coffee shop was nearly empty, just a group of mundy street kids five booths down. They kept staring. Wraith tried to ignore the feeling, but it was hard. She knew they saw her as different, a freak among freaks.

"It's lonely at the bottom," she said to no one in particular.

Wraith rubbed at her still-healing wrists as she chain-smoked her way to her third cigarette, always one eye on the ever-spinning quarter. Sarah returned with the promised soup and crackers, refilled the coffee, and gave a wan smile. It made her tired eyes shine. Wraith's spotted an origami rose poking out of her uniform shirt pocket. It looked like it was made from a crisp bill.

"I'm sure they'll show up soon," Sarah said.

Wraith ate a couple spoonfuls of soup and looked

to the door just as Shadow, SK, and Fritz came in. The trio made a beeline for Wraith. She let out a breath, snatched the quarter from the table, and slumped back against the seat.

The trio moved around Sarah and slid into the booth, Shadow next to Wraith.

"You guys want some coffee?" Sarah asked.

"Thanks, but we're not staying long," SK said.

"Okay. Well, be safe." Sarah set a check on the table and walked away.

"Eat your soup," Shadow said. "We really do need to go."

"I'll help," SK said. He grabbed her spoon and began eating.

"Me too," Fritz said and began opening a packet of crackers, sliding another packet to Wraith.

Wraith hugged Shadow tight. "How did you slip the snatchers?"

Shadow hugged back just as tight. "After you got away, they called for another van, but didn't put the hood back on." She nodded at Fritz and SK as they devoured the soup and crackers. "I saw them before the snatchers did and made a supernova of a strobe light."

"And in the confusion," SK said, "I held them in place while Fritz, my brilliant and beloved tinker, snuck in and popped the locks."

"Holy crap," Wraith said in a whisper.

"*Ja*," Fritz said. "We're amazing, it's true."

"What happened after you got away?" Shadow asked.

"I went back to the squat and fell asleep waiting for you," Wraith said. "I woke up when—" She shook her head, trying to untangle the memories. "I'm not sure what happened after that."

"It doesn't matter." Shadow squeezed Wraith's hand. "You're safe, that's what matters."

Wraith nodded. "For now. But I can feel the darkness coming—"

Shadow touched Wraith's cheek. "We're here, Stretch, and together, and we can beat anything."

Wraith smiled and nodded. "Well, whatever happened, I do know Toto helped me get away."

"And where is Herr Mutley?" Fritz asked, her accent warping the *w* in *where* into a *v* sound.

"Under protest, he's waiting behind a Dumpster out back. I had to bribe him with extra treats to stay," Wraith said, not really remembering that, but knowing it was right.

"Sorry it took us so long to find you," Shadow said.

"We didn't want to risk going back to the squat," SK said. "We've been using doors all day, moving all over the country to make sure we didn't have a tracking spell on us."

"We waited until we were certain it was safe before we used the coins," Fritz said.

"Kudos again on that idea," SK said through a final mouthful of soup.

"The burden of a genius," Wraith said, then shoved some crackers into her mouth. She was still proud of herself thinking of the coins, mostly because it was so simple. She'd enchanted a penny, a dime, a nickel, and a quarter. Each would point to only one of the others.

"Well, genius, we need to get out of here," Shadow said.

"*Jawohl*," Fritz said. "But to where?"

"Somewhere safe?" SK dropped his spoon into the empty bowl.

"What, the moon?" Wraith asked as everyone slid out and headed for the door. "The bright side, I mean."

"I hear it's nice this time of year," SK said.

"The Underground," Wraith said, unsure where the idea came from.

Shadow narrowed her eyes. "You sure, Stretch?"

"Is Hawaii completely out?" SK asked.

Wraith nodded.

"Okay," Shadow said. "Lead the way."

"What about Bermuda?" SK asked. "Tahiti? Easter-freaking-Island?"

Wraith led them out of the coffee shop, and around to the back. Toto got to his feet as soon as he saw them, and, after a few ear scratches, they gathered their things and headed for the closest useable door. Wraith could've made one on the fly, but it was best to keep a low profile right now.

Half an hour later, they stood in front of a battered steel door with small symbols scratched into the brick beside it. Wraith focused on the tattoos above her left wrist. It was an elaborate calculation, one that skewed the probabilities that a door wouldn't open to what was on the other side but instead to another door somewhere else. The formula gathered around the doorframe. When the calculation reached a zero sum, there was a click and the door swung open. Instead of showing the interior of the building, a different alley stood on the other side.

"There's an entrance just down that way," Wraith said and pointed.

They all stepped through, crossing the nearly two thousand miles between Austin and Seattle in a single step, and headed for the battered stairs that led to an even more battered wooden door.

Wraith pulled the goggles from her pocket and put them on. After a moment, the scene faded to dull shades of gray, punctuated with faint strands of trailing magic.

"See anything?" Shadow asked.

Most of the floating numbers and symbols faded into the background. "No, it's clean."

"What about us?" SK asked.

Wraith looked her friends over one at a time. Shadow's aura was the usual purple equation, pulsing in time to her heart. A spot of bright orange light came from the nickel in her pocket. Next she looked over SK, finding the expected shifting red and blue numbers orbiting him. The only variance was the penny gleaming in his pocket. Fritz was the normal dancing strands of white, rigidly organized numbers; her dime was the only contrast.

"Well?" Fritz asked after a long moment of silence.

"You're clean," Wraith said, her attention back to the here and now.

"Fan-freaking-tastic," SK said. "Now, can we—pretty please, with sugar and a cherry on top—get out of this delightfully cheery alleyway?"

Wraith turned the knob and opened the door. Like most of the entrances to the Underground, the stairs down were was poorly maintained and lit even worse.

"Well," SK said, "this is usually the part of the movie where the dumb kids venture into the darkness and get chopped up by the masked killer while the audience screams, 'Don't do it'."

"I love you," Fritz said. "But you need to stop talking now."

They moved through the door one at a time and down the rickety stairs, Wraith taking the lead, goggles still on and Toto at her side. Through the darkness, she could make out the faint light of old glyphs and wards that marked the place as belonging to different factions. When they reached the bottom level, she looked around the hallway and saw an afterglow.

"Someone's been here, might still be," she said. "A slinger, maybe a fifty or two, if I'm reading it right."

"Well, if fifties are here," Shadow said, "the slinger isn't a snatcher."

"Unless they found some willing to help with the cause," SK said. "Or they figured out how to mask their aura."

"I just love your comforting American nature," Fritz said.

"Would you two get a room," Shadow whispered.

"We're trying," SK said.

Wraith felt a knot of fear wriggle to life in her stomach. It began to grow, quickly. She could feel it drawing on her power, and without knowing why, knew that was very, very bad.

"If we find anyone down here, we'll move along," Shadow said and urged Wraith on.

They walked down the hallway until it split. To their right was a door and to the left the hallway continued into the darkness.

Wraith fought the fear, but it exploded into a wave of naked terror. She almost went to her knees as she felt it draw a ton of power from her. Then it poured out of her like water from a ruptured dam, beyond her control and into the room.

On the other side of the door, Wraith felt the darkness coalesce.

A girl screamed.

A boy bellowed a curse, and there was the crackle of an electrical arc.

"Sounds like someone is in trouble," Nightstick said from a dark corner down the hall. "Can't just stand aside and do nothing, not considering the source of that trouble. Can you?"

Fear gave way to guilt mixed with anger, via a bit of confusion. "No, we can't."

Shadow turned to Wraith, eyes wide, "No, wait—"

There was no fear, only the desperate need to fight. "BANG!" Wraith yelled and blew the door in.

A young black man dressed in dirty clothes hurled bright blue bolts of lightning across the small room.

They struck a vaguely humanoid shape, seven feet tall and made of living shadow, in the chest and sent it convulsing to the floor.

Wraith knew these creatures of the darkness were indeed snatchers. She paused for only the briefest moment, tripping over the thought that these snatchers weren't right, that they should be different somehow. In the flash of light, the snatchers were almost translucent.

No, that didn't matter right now. People were in danger, somehow, because of her. Wraith might not know much for certain, but she did know that she had to help.

In another flash of light, Wraith saw two girls. One was so beautiful even the momentary glimpse of her was enough to recognize it. She moved her hand in an intricate motion while the other girl, a tiny thing, huddled behind her.

Wraith didn't have time to see anything else.

Eight more shadows began chanting. Symbols of deep red light appeared over their bodies and tendrils of darkness moved toward Wraith and her friends.

Wraith was frozen in a moment of déjà vu.

Toto barked and leapt into the room.

"Kaput!" Fritz shouted.

Sparks erupted from light fixtures in the ceiling and outlets on the wall. The shadows dimmed under a shower of sparks, and the room filled with the smell of burned wires and melted plastic.

"Help her," Shadow shouted.

"*Ferrousan!*" SK yelled as he stepped through the door and into the room.

Wraith felt the familiar tug of a gravity well, and three figures were pulled across the room and slammed into each other.

Toto grabbed the wrist of a snatcher with his powerful jaws, and twisted, bringing the shape to the ground with an inhuman shriek.

"Slink," said a young man's voice. "Get Mouse out of here, I'll hold them off." The order was punctuated with another bolt of electricity that arced across the room and struck another snatcher.

Wraith focused on the formula on her left bicep. Globes of blue fire filled her hands and rocketed toward a snatcher who was gesturing at Toto.

A hand grabbed her arm. In a rush of panic, an equation wrapped around her and she felt her magnetic field shift to match that of her assailant. The thing was tossed into the wall and she slid a few feet away.

Toto yelped and Wraith spun as a snatcher hurled what looked like liquid darkness at the big dog. It hit and sent him to the ground in a whimpering, convulsing ball of fur.

Rage swelled and a long calculation encircled the floor at the snatcher's feet. The molecules spread apart just enough to remove the field that made the floor solid. The snatcher dropped through. When his head vanished, Wraith pulled the equation apart and the molecules snapped back into place.

Shadow shouted from behind Wraith, and the light drew to her.

Wraith threw herself over Toto, covering his eyes and burying her face in her sleeve.

Shadow cried out again, her words urgent but musical. Intensely bright light exploded and the room filled with high, shrill screams.

Wraith's eyes were useless, but she could feel the boy and two girls in the darkness. She couldn't sense anyone else though. Ignoring the cold flutter in her stomach, she lifted her hand, pointed toward the opposite side of the room where she knew the snatchers had been, and drew as much power as she could.

"BANG!"

The recoil sent her back out the door and into Fritz. She deflected off her friend and smacked her head against something hard. There was a brief sense of nausea as stars burst into her vision.

"This still isn't working," SK said in the distance. "They're still getting out."

"We're not giving up on her," Shadow said.

"I didn't say we were," SK said. "But how many more of these nightmares can we fight off?"

"As many as it takes," Fritz said. "We owe her, *ja*?"

"We do," Shadow said. "Get those three and let's get out of here."

Then everything was darkness.

CHAPTER ELEVEN

Dante saw the Public Market Center sign long before the locals and tourists crowding the entrance. He drew in a deep breath, finding the scent of Puget Sound beneath the countless other smells, and held it. He loved the water, and even in a city where its natural beauty was often wiped away, it still brought him peace.

He glided through the tourists watching the famous fish throwing show at the Pike Place Fish Market. The men shouted to each other, tossing large fish back and forth to the delight of young and old alike. Dante was cautious where he walked, never crossing in front of the ubiquitous camera phones snapping stills and video. He stepped into the hallways lined on either side with stalls between the small shops that comprised the market.

Whispers and glances both proceeded and followed him. The number of young wizards took him aback.

They were mixed in with mortals, changelings, and fae, but it was hard not to notice them; magic fairly poured off them. It was one thing to hear about the new wizards emerging, it was quite another to see them with his own eyes. So many— and they were kids, all of them. The oldest wasn't much over twenty, but most of them, changelings and wizards alike, were scarcely into their teens. Brownies, goblins, dwarves, satyrs, even ogres and trolls stood behind rickety tables hawking their wares, or they perused the offered goods with the mortal shoppers. Though the ogres and trolls mostly just stood and glared, looking imposing. Dante watched the mortals and smiled. Even after centuries of seeing it, he was still amused by how humans could stand right next to a faerie and never know it, so long as the glamour didn't waver.

He glanced at the goods for sale; everything from hand-knitted hats and scarves to kitschy humorous magnets, flowers, and jewelry. Sprinkled amid their mortal counterparts were more than a few magical trinkets. They were typical charms, though the ones sold by the changelings and wizards were rough, to say the least. The items were shoddy, made from the detritus the crafters could put their hands on. Most were simple things: glamour-piercing glasses, protection sigils woven into hemp necklaces, beaded tracking charms, simple carved wands, and talismans that did everything from keeping the user warm to helping find food. However, every once in a while, among the simple goods, Dante could see some truly exquisite items. A particularly keen-eyed goblin caught Dante's attention, so he stepped to the table and examined the wares.

"My lord," the goblin said and bowed.

He was much the same as other goblins: green skin, large red eyes, bat-like ears, and a sunken nose. This one had a chunk missing from his left ear.

"I'm looking for information," Dante said.

"I'm but a humble peddler of goods," the goblin said, motioning to his table. "But I will do what I can. What does the noble lord wish to know?"

"Anything about the disappearances."

The goblin swallowed. "Disappearances?"

Dante narrowed his eyes.

The goblin cleared his throat and glanced around. When he spoke, it was a whisper. "I know very little, only that several changelings have gone missing, and some of them turned up dead. I think there were also some slingers—or wizards, if you prefer. But I don't concern myself as much with mortals."

"Don't suppose you know anything more than that?"

"My lord." The goblin had a barely contained sneer. "I'm but a peasant of the court. Undoubtedly, an elfin noble like yourself would know more than I."

"I never prescribed to such notions," Dante said. He bit back his frustration and fished out a silver disk from his pocket. "This is a token of favor."

The goblin's eyes went wide for just a moment.

"I'm offering it, and others like it, to anyone who

can provide information or assistance in this matter."
He spoke loud enough for the others nearby to hear
him. If he guessed right, in short order, word would
spread all over town. Tokens of favor weren't handed
out lightly, and everyone liked the idea of a court noble
owing you a favor, even if it was a minor one.

"I'd tell you where I'm staying," Dante continued,
"but I'm sure everyone knows."

Countless eyes were on him, but no one said anything. He shook his head, turned, and started back the
way he had come. The whispers and glances were still
there, but he ignored them. As he came to a trio of musicians playing an old Irish ballad, he stopped to listen.
Thoughts of a lost friend filled his mind. He could see
the big Fian lost in the music, and hear his clear bari-
tone.

"You'll have to excuse them for their whispers and
glares," a male voice said from behind him. "They're
not used to seeing nobles mingling with the dregs."

Dante smiled and opened his eyes. "It's been a very,
very long time."

"What's time really?" the man asked, the hint of
a chuckle to his words. "Even so, it's good to see you
again."

Dante turned to face Ciye. This time, he was a man
in his mid-twenties of average height, with chiseled
features and infinitely deep, dark eyes. His braided hair
was so black it had highlights of blue. He wore a bone
choker, and was dressed in jeans and boots. Beneath
his worn, brown leather coat was a tight black shirt

with a picture of a coyote howling at a full moon. A familiar, cocky, but undeniably charming, smile came to the man's face. It felt as if no time had passed at all. Dante laughed under his breath.

"You and that damn smile," Dante said. "No matter the shape, you always have that smile."

"Even I can't hide perfection." Ciye stepped close and pulled Dante into a hug.

When Dante drew in a breath, the smell of the desert at dawn mixed with the scent of ancient forests in spring washed over him. The wave of emotions threatened to draw him back to a time long ago, a time when things were very different. It took some effort, but he broke the embrace and stepped back.

"I'm glad to see you're not holding a grudge," Ciye said.

"I can't stay mad at you," Dante said. "Besides, if you'd been different, I never would've fallen for you."

Ciye smiled wider.

"What are you doing in Seattle?" Dante asked. "Aren't you a little far from home?"

"Like you, I go where I am needed. Besides, you remember the stories—I'm a familiar face to tribes across the country."

"I'm sure you'd happily retell the stories if I didn't— though as I recall, not all are flattering."

Ciye let out a breath and his mouth twisted into a grimace. "Yes, some of them still try to blame me for bringing death to the world."

Dante chuckled. "I'm afraid I'm here for more than

tourism. Do you know anything about these disappearances and killings?"

"Ever the noble looking out for his people. That is perhaps one of your most endearing qualities." Ciye looked around. "Come, I want to smoke and they don't let you do that inside anymore."

Dante followed Ciye out of the market and they found a spot away from casual view.

Ciye pulled a pack of American Spirits out of a pocket and offered one to Dante, who shook his head.

Ciye shrugged and lit up. "I know something." he said. "There are two kidnappers. One seems focused on the *wasicu* medicine children—slingers, these mortals call themselves." Ciye's face became like a stone mask. "The others are focused on taking your people's little ones, your changelings, as well as my people's spirit children. These dark ones are like shadows. They always hunt the little ones, never the warriors. They're cowards."

"Have you seen them, the hunters?"

"I don't think anyone has, least not that I can tell. They have powerful wièhó{dec63}'a{dec63}, magic, and they are dark, like I haven't seen in a long time." Ciye took a drag and shook his head, his eyes down. "She was just a child. I should've done better by her."

Dante put a hand on Ciye's shoulder. "Who?"

Ciye looked up and listened for a moment. Dante knew the look. Ciye was talking with his fellow spirits.

After a long moment, Ciye turned his gaze back to Dante. "I'm sorry, my friend, I have to go."

"Wait, what aren't you telling me?"

Ciye's eyes were hard. "I don't know what they call themselves now, but you knew them by a name we must not speak."

Dante felt a chill run down his back. "That's not possible."

Ciye tossed the butt down and crushed it out, then bent to pick it up and toss it into a trash can. "I have to go, but I'll be in touch." He drew Dante into an embrace, and kissed his cheek. "Watch yourself, old friend." With that, Ciye turned and vanished into the crowd.

Dante leaned back against the wall and took a slow breath as he considered what Ciye had said. Some things must not be spoken of; to do so would give them power.

"I sure hope you're wrong," he said.

As he strode back to his car, he fished out his phone and dialed Faolan.

"How's the investigation going?" Faolan asked.

"From what I've seen, Donovan has completely checked out. He's ignoring the fae who aren't nobles, and the changelings too. He might be ignoring the nobles for all I know." Dante thought of Ciye and what he'd said. "It sounds like he's brushing off not just the court, but our allies in the Cruinnigh. It's a disgrace. No one of rank in the court is trusted by the general populace." Dante sighed. "I can't really blame them, but it's frustrating. All I've found does nothing more than confirm what we already know."

"Do you think this could cause waves with the non-fae council members?" Faolan asked.

"He's not on the Cruinnigh, but he's still a court noble, so maybe."

"Well, I have some more bad news."

"Oh good, I was thinking I needed more of a challenge."

"Donovan has moved his court, and failed to tell the Cruinnigh where."

"Tell me that's a bad joke."

"Wish it was. He's proof the title noble isn't earned by deed. I think maybe one of his parents was an oíche."

Dante scoffed. "He's not that smart."

Faolan laughed. "I do know someone out there who might be able to help you. She's good, but I'll be polite and say her past is a little, well, shady."

"I'll take what I can get." Dante stood by his car and scanned the area.

"Okay, I sent the message. She should be in touch short— Wait a minute." Faolan was silent for moment. "Make that a couple of seconds."

Dante saw an elfin woman step out of the alley and start walking toward him. "I'm giving you a raise, Faolan."

Faolan laughed. "Just let me know if you need anything else."

"I'll probably need some wardens, when the time comes."

"They're waiting for your word."

Dante clicked off the phone as the woman crossed

the busy street and walked up to him. Her clothes were ill fitting and threadbare. She was short for an elf, barely six feet tall, and had dirty blond hair down to her shoulders. Her pale green eyes, very luminescent, sparkled as she smiled at him.

Dante opened his mouth, but she walked past him to the passenger side of the car, glanced around as she unlocked it in a manner he couldn't see, then got in.

After a moment, Dante got in, started the car, and pulled out.

"Sorry. Best if no one sees me talking to you," she said. "You are a noble after all, which makes you just this side of jackbooted Gestapo." She gave him a small smile. "Nothing personal."

"I understand."

"I'm Elaine. Faolan said you could use some help?"

Dante arched an eyebrow. "I wasn't expecting an elf."

She crossed her arms and stared straight ahead. "Well, let's just say my hobbies occasionally run afoul of the authorities, and my skill set isn't appreciated by Cruinnigh, or the moronic blowhard." She glanced at Dante. "I mean the magister and faerie godfather."

Dante rolled his eyes. "He's still playing at that?"

"Oh, you have no idea." she said. "I'm guessing you're looking for intel on the, uh, situation?"

"Anything you can give me. This region is a bit of an information black hole. The Cruinnigh didn't care so much before, but after the events of last year—"

"So it's true?" Her eyes widened. "About the oíche, and the princess?"

"Word travels fast." He gave her a quick glance. "Yes, it's true, but you'd be wise to keep that yourself."

"Of course, thrice promised. Not that it matters, everyone's heard the stories."

He ignored that. "I hope you know something. No one else seems to, or if they do, they're not sharing."

"I'm not surprised." Elaine reached up and adjusted the rearview mirror. "It's worse than you've heard or seen."

"Oh?"

"Aside from the missing changelings, it's the slingers. Spell slingers—it's what the kids call them. Wizards, though most have just a hint of power. They've started showing up in droves over the past couple of years."

Dante thought back to Pikes Place and how many he'd seen there.

"At first, it could almost be written it off as a fluke. But the odd part is, they're all street kids. Odder still, they seem to be migrating to Seattle. I know a dozen kids from as many states. Not a one can explain why they came here. Most just say it sounded like a good idea."

"What kind of numbers are we talking about here?" Dante asked.

Elaine glanced into the rearview mirror again. "At least a couple hundred and that's just in Seattle. Word is every city of decent size is seeing them at least in the dozens."

"And all street kids?" he asked. "You're sure you aren't just not hearing about the others?"

"I'm positive," she said. "They're self-taught, so their skills are pretty limited, usually focused in one area."

"Do you think the sudden explosion in the wizard population is connected to the abductions?"

"Well, they started showing up not long after the changelings started disappearing." She leaned back in the seat. "I don't know what the connection is, but there is one. It'd be too much of a coincidence otherwise."

"Reasonable conclusion."

"Nice to know my paranoia isn't unreasonable." She let out a breath. "No full fae have been taken, and only recently have the slingers started disappearing too. Problem is, none of them have turned up dead. Needless to say, the fifties are more than a little suspicious. So they're all forming factions."

"Factions?"

"The fifties and slingers have formed groups, like gangs, I suppose. They even name themselves—Ghosts are the biggest, with about twenty members, I think. Most are smaller, four or five. Magister Clueless doesn't do anything to help anyone who doesn't regularly kiss his ass, so the fifties had to start looking out for themselves."

"Why don't they leave?"

Elaine shrugged. "Not as easy as that. Most are so young that trying to get out would draw unwanted attention. Most are terrified to be out after dark, and traveling risks that. Easier to stay holed up somewhere and keep your head down."

"Are there any witnesses to the abductions or body drops?"

She shook her head. "There were whispers at first, but it's just rumor. They always happen at night, and are only individuals. Until a few days ago anyway."

"What happened?"

"First, some kids may have actually seen the abductors. They were near one of those giganto-marts when they felt a really powerful surge of magic. A slinger girl came running out of the place, chased by some mortals in dark coats, all wearing hoods. One of the goons threw an entanglement spell at her, but she teleported out of the way and took off. The creeps tossed some kid into a van and took off."

"A black van?" Dante asked.

Elaine nodded.

"I found a demolished black van a few days ago, but I hadn't heard anything about the attempted abduction."

"You really need to get used to that feeling," she said. "A lot happens that the nobles don't hear about."

He rubbed at his forehead.

"In this case though," Elaine continued in a gentler tone, "one of the witnesses said the mortals were just standing around in a daze; a hundred of them at least. It was like some mass mind fog. Five minutes after the van left, everyone collectively snapped out of it and went about their business like nothing happened."

His stomach started to twist. "That's not a minor spell."

"Not even close," she said. "And then last night, three

kids were taken, all at once. They were sheltered in a good spot in the Underground, with another faction not far away and wards all over. But, they were grabbed anyway, and without a single ward being set off."

Dante was starting to put the pieces together, and he didn't like the picture that was forming. This wasn't some minor magical talent. The question though was—Were both incidents the same group, or was Ciye right and it was two groups? And if it was two groups, were they working together or against each other? Dante parked the car in a secluded spot, then ran a hand through his hair.

"I saw you talking to Ciye," Elaine said.

Dante looked at her, eyes narrowed. "And?"

"Probably not my place, but I hope you know you can't trust what he tells you."

"You're right," Dante said, his tone sharp. "It isn't your place."

She rolled her eyes. "Oh well, I beg your pardon, your royal pompousness. Just pretend I didn't say anything, then. If you want to trust a trickster—"

"I know what he is," Dante said. "And I know his nature. That's why I wanted more help." He leaned in close and looked her in the eyes. "Faolan seems to trust you, and I trust him. So, are you someone I can rely on or not?"

Elaine stared back at him for a long moment. She never blinked or looked away, but instead seemed to size him up. "Faolan says you're a good sort and I put a lot of stock in his opinion."

"Is that a yes? If not I have work to do."

She nodded. "I suppose it is."

"Good." Dante leaned back. "Maybe it's time to call in some wardens."

"What, marshal law?" Elaine chuckled. "That'll go over well."

"It'll go over better than innocent kids being grabbed off the street."

She tucked her hair behind her ear. "I suppose there's logic to that, but you don't understand who you're dealing with."

"So help me understand."

"We're talking about kids," She said. "Most of them don't have families, and those who did were either tossed out, or it was so bad they thought the streets were a better option. Think about how bad something would have to be for a kid to reach that conclusion."

Dante considered that. "And most probably had no idea there was magic or anything else before their talents emerged."

She nodded. "There's that too. I'm just saying these are kids who've had to rely on themselves. They don't trust easily, and they don't react well to shows of authority. You bring in the troops and they'll go underground. It might do more harm than good."

"I'd keep it as discrete as possible," Dante said. "But these are unusual circumstances."

Elaine let out a breath. "Okay, fine. Then what's your plan?"

"I need you to find out everything you can. I need facts, not rumors."

She nodded. "I can do that. What about you?"

"First things first. It's long past time for Donovan to step up and take responsibility. Any chance you know where he moved his court to?"

She shook her head. "Only his inner circle is graced with that information. Tomorrow is Sunday though. You should try the Freemont Market. All the factions go there to trade. They don't stick out as much as they do at Pike. Some of Donovan's thugs are usually there to remind everyone who's in charge." She looked at him. "The troll might know something too."

Dante looked at her, eyebrows up. "Care to be more specific?"

"Sorry, the Freemont Troll. I don't know if he'll say anything, but it couldn't hurt."

"All right, I'll check it out," Dante said. "You do your digging. Do you have a phone?"

She nodded.

He handed her one of his cards. "Keep me updated. I'll see if I can find some of this inner circle and persuade them to share their information."

Elaine smiled and her eyes twinkled. "I think I'd rather see that." She reached to open the door, but Dante caught her arm.

"Wait, are you armed?"

She blinked. "I'm more the 'avoid a fight' kind of girl."

Dante opened his glove box and pulled out a holster. He glanced around, then removed a pistol made of green tinted metal and handed it to Elaine. "Sometimes it can't be helped, and I would rather you had this and not need it than the alternative."

"Good point under the circumstances." She checked the magazine, chambered a round, and checked the safety before slipping the pistol back into the holster and sticking it into her coat pocket.

"I'll wait a few days, but after that, I'm calling in the cavalry. It might not go over well, but I'd rather the kids be alive and calling me a despot than dead."

Elaine opened her door and got out. "I'll work fast." In seconds, she had vanished into the mass of people wandering the street.

CHAPTER TWELVE

"Come on, sleepy," said a small, worried voice from somewhere inside the disjointed reality around Wraith. "It's time to wake up."

Wraith tried to move, but her ears were ringing and her head throbbed. It felt like she was in a dozen places at the same time, and in all of them, she hurt. Her fear and anxiety churned, building in insistence, growing ever darker. She managed to push that darkness back, but it still lurked, almost like a living thing waiting for its chance.

"Come on, love," a boy said. "I think that's long enough."

"I'm trying," Wraith said through gritted teeth. The dream, if even was a dream, wouldn't let her go. She fought to hold her memories together, but they crumbled and slipped through her fingers. She couldn't lose these pieces, not now. She focused harder, but something was making it hard to breathe.

"They're trying to kill you," Nightstick whispered. "Fight, or die."

Wraith knew he was right, and she reached out for power in desperation.

"Look out!"

Wraith's eyes snapped open just as she released the flames that had gathered in her hands. Con dove to one side as twin columns of fire lanced straight up, hit the ceiling, and snuffed out. The only signs left were the pervasive heat in Sprout's room and the two large scorch marks on the concrete above Wraith's head.

Sprout and Con lay on the ground, the former obviously tackled by the latter, blinking and staring at her in silence.

Wraith tried to put the scattered pieces together, pulling herself back to reality. Her stomach was doing flips, and every time she moved her head, the throbbing behind her eyes increased.

Con leapt to his feet. "What the bloody hell was that about?"

Wraith winced. "I don't—"

"Are you trying to burn the place down, you nutty prat?"

"What? No! I just—" The words died as she felt memories crumble into nothingness.

"Oi! I'm talking at you! You could've killed her," Con said, motioning at Sprout. "What are you playing at?"

Wraith tried to answer but her hands started shaking. Nothing was holding together. If only Shadow were here, she could make it all calm. Make it all better.

"Con, stop it!" Sprout shouted.

"Get off. I'm done with this bollocks." Con took a step forward.

Toto growled and stepped in front of Wraith, teeth bared.

Con muttered something and fire gathered in his hands. "You best call him off, love, before I turn him into a barbecue."

"Everyone just stop!" Sprout shouted.

Dozens of thorny vines broke through the concrete floor and formed a wall between Toto and Con. At the same moment, the front door was thrown open. Geek and Ovation ran in, took one look at the scene, and froze.

"Um, did we miss something?" Geek asked.

"You did at that, mate," Con said. "She nearly fried the little one—"

Toto growled again, then barked in protest.

Wraith blinked. If she didn't know better, she'd say he was arguing the point.

"All right," Ovation said. "Everyone just take a breath. Sprout, could you prune this back a little?"

"That may not be a good idea," Geek said as he looked from Toto to Con, who still had the flames gathered in his hands.

"Con," Ovation said. "Snuff it."

Con shook his hands and the fire vanished. "Aye, aye, Captain. It's on your head, then."

Ovation turned to Wraith, then Sprout. "Could someone please ask Toto to settle down?"

"Come here, boy," Wraith said.

Toto turned and looked at her.

"It's okay," Wraith said. "Come on."

Toto relented and went to her. She wrapped her arm around him and pulled him close, gripping his fur like a life preserver.

After a skeptical look, Ovation nodded. "Okay, Sprout."

The vines drew back into the ground, leaving only spots of exposed earth where the floor had been pushed aside. Ovation sat between Con and Wraith as Geek began putting the displaced chunks of concrete back in place. From the way he did it, Wraith guessed it wasn't the first time.

"Now, tell me what happened," Ovation said.

Con, Sprout, and even Toto began talking, or barking, at the same time.

Ovation rubbed his head and raised his other hand. "One at a time, please. Sprout?"

"Well," she said. "A little bit after you left, Wraith started talking in her sleep. I went to wake her up. I thought maybe she was having a bad dream."

"What happened next?" Geek asked.

"I couldn't wake her up, and she looked scared," Sprout said. "I tried, but, well, then Con came over and when he touched her—"

"Her hands went up in flames, like mine do, but bigger," Con said. "And it didn't stop, so I pulled Sprout away just as two bleeding massive flames shot up and hit the ceiling." He pointed to the scorch marks for effect. "She never told us she was a damned pyromancer."

"I'm not," Wraith said. "I didn't, I mean, I just use it to light my cigarettes. I've never—"

"It's okay," Ovation said.

"Okay? Are you going soft, mate?" Con asked. "She could've killed us both, or lit the place up like a—"

Toto barked and growled.

Everyone looked at the dog, then at Sprout.

The little girl furrowed her brow.

The dog barked again, more insistently.

"What is it?" Geek asked.

"He said he wouldn't have let that happen," Sprout said.

"Well, if the pooch says so, that's brilliant. I feel loads better." Con nodded at Toto. "Cheers then, mate."

"She didn't mean to do it," Sprout said.

"I'm not saying she did." Con turned to Ovation. "But, mate, the best of intentions ain't going to keep this place from burning down or blowing up, is it? I mean, we both know she's packing more power than all of us put together. What if she loses it again?"

Ovation ran his hands through his hair. "I understand what you're saying, but, Con, I'm not about to send—"

"You don't have to," Wraith said and got to her feet. "I'll go. He's right, I can't control my power. It's not safe for you, and this isn't your problem."

"That's really not a good idea," Geek said.

Con looked at him. "Eh? What's happened, then?"

"Word is, two fifties and a slinger are missing," Geek said.

"We came across Fitch and the other Ghosts scrounging," Ovation said.

"Not real ghosts," Geek said to Wraith. "It's another faction."

"Who'd be crazy enough to go out alone?" Con asked. "Things haven't been—"

"They weren't alone," Ovation said. "The three of them were nabbed together, in a warded safe house."

"The Ghosts were down the hall," Geek said. "Not fifty feet away."

"Bloody hell," Con said.

"Who was it?" Sprout asked.

"Charge, Mouse, and Slink," Geek said.

From the look on everyone's faces, Wraith didn't need to ask if they knew them.

"Oh no," Sprout said.

"Charge weren't no bleeding pushover," Con said. "Lad packed a wallop with them bolts. Even Mouse and Slink were quick. Whoever is doing this, they're some serious bad."

"So you can understand why I'm not quick to send Wraith out there on her own," Ovation said.

Con nodded. "I do at that."

"Everyone is shutting down," Ovation said. "No one's to go out after dark at all now, alone or otherwise. From now on, when we go anywhere, we all go and only during daylight."

No one spoke and Wraith could practically taste the grief and fear in the air.

"So that's all we're going to do about it? Play like

scared little bunnies, and hope no one knocks the door down like they did theirs?"

"Con—"

"Well, they might not even need to," Con looked at Wraith. "They might just teleport in."

"Is that your great plan?" Ovation asked. "To take the snatchers on?"

"Too right! Beats hiding, don't it?"

"According to Fitch," Geek said, "the FBI is investigating."

Con laughed. "Oh, well then, now you and the pup got me just full of confidence."

"Some high-up in the court is in town too," Geek said. "He was out where they found Luna, asking around. He told Blue he'd find whoever is doing this. Maybe we just need to wait it out."

"No, we get in touch with him," Con said. "Whoever's behind this, they're part of our world. How else would they be able to pick out the slingers and fifties?"

"There's nothing more to discuss." Ovation looked at Wraith. "We're not putting you or anyone else out, and we're not letting you leave."

Con looked to Ovation. "All right, you don't want to fight, then why don't we leave? This place might not be safe anymore. There're plenty of other cities we can go."

"They're everywhere," Wraith said without thinking.

Everyone turned to her.

"Snatchers have been everywhere I've been."

"That's a rather unpleasant connection, ain't it?" Con said.

"I don't like what you're implying," Ovation said. "She didn't bring them here."

"Yeah, people went missing before she got here," Geek said.

"You sure?" Con asked. He turned to Wraith. "What happened to your mates? Shadow and the others?"

"Con," Ovation said. "Don't—"

Wraith thought back and her head started to pound. Pieces weren't right. They weren't fitting. "The snatchers showed up, I ran and waited, then—" The throbbing increased and she winced.

"Nothing down that path but pain," Nightstick said from a dark corner.

"Right in broad daylight, in front of loads of witnesses," Con said. "A bit odd, ain't it?"

"I—"

"And where did you say that was?" Con asked.

"He's poking and prodding," Nightstick said from behind Con. "I think it's about time you start poking back."

Wraith winced as her headache worsened. "Outside a, you know, one of those big stores."

"What city?"

"Poke, poke, poke, poke," Nightstick said. "You have the means, he's giving you the motive—"

Wraith looked at Nightstick, then at Con. That's when she noticed everyone was looking at her.

"It was—"

"The bastard is practically begging you," Nightstick said.

"Stop, just stop!" She put her face in her hands.

"Can't remember?" Con asked. "Shocking, that."

"All right, that's enough," Ovation said. "She can't remember, so let it go. Maybe it was Seattle, maybe it wasn't. That's just another piece we'll help her get back."

Nightstick began tapping his shillelagh on the floor.

A sudden flash of pain made Wraith wince. Images flashed in her mind. Children were screaming, begging for help, reaching out hands to her. Then it was all blood, pain, chanting, and cold. Wraith flinched as more images flashed in her mind like lightning. In the distance, the cries wouldn't stop. She put her hands over her ears.

"Stop it! The shadows won't stop! They just grab and take, but we don't want to go! I'm not going to give them what they want! Leave us alone!"

"Nothing but darkness down that river, and you don't have a paddle," Nightstick said.

"Wraith?" Ovation's voice was distant and echoed like he was in a cave.

She fought against the onslaught of images, her jaw clenched tight in concentration. Distorted voices sounded from an inconceivably massive distance, and yet some part of her knew they were right there.

Through the pain, Wraith could sense Nightstick doing a little jig and hear him singing a twisted lullaby. Then he fell to his knees next to her, his voice a raspy whisper in her ear. "You've got more fingers poking at you, little girl," he said. "I can give you a knife to start cutting some of those fingers off."

"What's happening to her?" Sprout asked.

"I don't know," Ovation said.

"Uh, oh," Nightstick said and looked at the door. "I hate party crashers. We need a bouncer."

Not far off, Wraith could sense people coming; a dozen or more. The world snapped into instant acuity. Her eyes opened. "We need to leave," she said.

"Technically, there is another option," Nightstick said. "Though you rarely choose it."

There was a boom so violent that it shook the room. Ovation's eyes went wide. "Crap!"

"That was the third ward," Geek said.

"How did they get through the first two?" Ovation asked. "I know we reset them."

"Me too," Geek agreed.

Wraith watched from the floor, her fingers still in Toto's fur. She had an odd sense of detachment. Con, Geek, and Ovation went to the door.

"I knew we should've installed a peephole," Geek said.

"Sorry, mate," Con said. "We never got around to the trip to Home Depot."

"Geek," Ovation said. "You get the door. I'll look out quick and see what we're up against. Con, you be ready to torch anything that's too close."

Geek and Con both nodded

Ovation drew in a breath, then nodded.

Geek pulled the door open.

Ovation stuck his head out and immediately ducked back in. "Close it!"

Geek slammed the door and leaned against it.

"Bad?" Geek asked.

"Ogres," Ovation said and slammed a bar across the door. "They're coming down the stairs."

"Oh, we're buggered," Con said. "What happened to my ward?"

"I don't know," Ovation said. "You want to go ask them?"

There was a thud against the door and a small dent emerged from the metal.

"Uh, *ocupado*!" Geek shouted through the door.

Everyone turned and looked at him.

The hallway went silent.

Geek shrugged. "Worked, didn't it?"

Something slammed against the door so hard it knocked Geek back and away from it.

He looked at the fresh dent, deeper than the first. "Any ideas? The door won't hold forever."

"Is there another way out?" Wraith asked.

"No," Ovation said. "The idea was the wards would deter anyone, or at least delay them enough to let us get out."

Toto growled and his fur bristled.

With another bang, the concrete around the door-frame cracked.

"Open up!" a gruff voice said from beyond the door. "We've got your eviction notice."

"Get bent!" Geek shouted back.

"Oi," Con said to Wraith. "Can you do that invisibility trick like you did when you first got here?"

Wraith shook her head. "Not with all of us."

Nightstick laughed again. "Oh, but you've got all kinds of tricks you haven't showed them, don't you?"

"So it's a fight, then." Con's hands went alight in flames.

Ovation, Geek, and Con traded a glance and Wraith saw them reach a silent agreement.

"Wraith, you take Sprout and hide," Ovation said. "We'll draw them away from the door and you two make a run for it."

When the answer came to her, it was so obvious. Wraith furrowed her brow. "We should just use the door and leave."

"What?" Geek asked.

"Well, love," Con said with exaggerated patience, "the problem is, just now the door is holding back a group of angry, smelly ogres."

"No, not that door," Wraith said and went to her bag. "THE door. Turn the knob, open the doors." She reached into her bag, pulled out her composition books, and began flipping through the pages.

Nightstick let out an exasperated sigh.

"She losing it again?" Con asked.

Wraith didn't hear anything else. A subtle pain between her eyes was steadily increasing, but she pushed it, and Nightstick, aside as she focused on the pages. "You can use the randomness of the universe. Harness the chaos. But I need a knob.

Con opened his mouth.

"If you say one word," Ovation said, "I swear to God, I'm tossing you to the ogres."

Con closed his mouth and looked away.

"I suppose I could just make one," Wraith said. She felt a rush of exhilaration as she came to a page covered in scribbles. The world returned through the pain, and it was like seeing the sunrise for the first time in years, or tasting water after weeks in the desert. When she looked up, everyone was staring at her.

"What do you mean?" Ovation asked.

Wraith held the page up. "It's right here. See?"

Ovation stared at the page, his brow furrowed.

"Don't you see it?" Wraith asked.

Ovation looked at her, and his eyes were sad.

Wraith dropped her arms and glared. "I'm not crazy!"

"That's not really helping your argument," Con said.

"Why don't we try it?" Sprout asked. "I mean, if it works, we get away. If not, we're in the same place." She shrugged. "Seems silly not to try."

"She's got a point," Geek said, his voice strained. Sweat beaded his brow. "I vote yes."

"Mate, you realize that you're suggesting a ten-year-old is the voice of reason here?" Con asked.

"It's a quantum calculation," Wraith said, walking to the door. "Whenever you open a door, well not a door, but a door-door, there's a chance at any moment that space time will momentarily collapse in on itself."

"Now you're just making my head hurt," Con said.

"You said we need a doorknob," Ovation said. "Any doorknob?"

Wraith winced against a flash of pain. "Yes, unless the door already has one."

Con closed his eyes and shook his head. "You've got to be taking the piss."

"Step aside," Ovation said to Geek. "Let her try."

Wraith examined the door. Numbers flashed in sequence on the frame and around the knob. "It's not right. It's not a door, but it can be. I need to fix it."

"What do you need?" Geek asked, leaning against the door over her.

Wraith pulled a Sharpie from her bag and began to draw tiny symbols along the frame, and over the knob. Each symbol encompassed a long and complex equation. The pain between her eyes intensified; the numbers not drawn into the equation began to swirl and power began to swell inside her.

"Maybe it's time to not run for a change," Nightstick said.

"No," Wraith said as she continued writing, "not this time." She focused her will and pushed power into the equation. The exhilaration didn't slow the approaching stride, and she couldn't pour power out of her fast enough until the equation was complete.

"Fine, but soon," Nightstick said.

Wraith's heart pounded and she was gasping, fighting to hold in the energy. When she was done, the metal frame and dented knob were completely covered in symbols and numbers.

"There, we'll smear the ink," she said between gasps. "But that's okay. It'll close the door behind us so no one else can use it."

Everyone took a step back. Geek and Ovation took

a ready stance, bending at the knees and ready to leap forward. Con lit his hands again and the three of them stepped in front of Sprout.

Wraith knocked on the door three times, each time redirecting the rushing tide of power building in her into the door. On the third knock, everything seemed to stop and the sudden disappearance of rising power that she'd been fighting nearly made her fall forward.

The pain vanished and she felt this door connect with all the other doors.

She knocked the bar out of place and pulled the door open.

"That's cool," Geek said.

"I'm fairly well gobsmacked," Con said.

When the last of the magic left her, Wraith sank into the warmth and slid to the floor. She didn't lose consciousness as much as her brain took a time out, though on the way, she did happen to notice the smell of dust, stale air, and a perfume that was familiar.

CHAPTER THIRTEEN

Elaine narrowed her eyes, focusing on the distant alleyway. Around her, the sound of people and cars faded to nothing. "Are you sure?" she asked and turned back to Dasher.

The dingy slinger kid arched an eyebrow and smirked. "Like anyone's certain of anything in this mess. But they should still work."

Elaine flashed a half-smile. "Fair enough." She pulled a twenty out of her pocket and pressed it into his hand. "Get some food."

Dasher pocketed the bill and offered a fist. "Thanks, and watch yourself."

Elaine bumped her knuckles against his. "Always."

Dasher nodded, then turned and walked off.

Elaine crossed the street and made for the entrance to the Underground. She stepped around tourists and locals, none of them giving her a second look. She smelled the magic almost a block before reaching the entrance.

She made her way down the alley to the old wooden stairs. They creaked as she took the first step, and that made her pause. Her footfalls were usually so light that even wood in the worst condition didn't make a sound. She glanced around, stepped close to the edge of the stairs, and reached the door in silence.

The brick around the door was etched with the marks of the various factions who'd claimed this section at different times. There were magic sigils of warding and protection that had faded. A mundane symbol was more recent, written with a felt marker. It warned any slinger or fifty that this place was no longer safe. Leaning close to the brick, she sniffed the stone.

The magic behind it was dwindling, but she could smell the potency of it. There was something else though. She licked her finger and traced it over one of the warding sigils. Then she put the finger to the tip of her tongue and blinked. It tasted of ash but was also acidic.

"That's not possible," she whispered to herself.

Leaning in close, she examined the collection of wards. They were still active, but the acidic taste told her they'd been tripped. She shook her and tried to puzzle out how that could be. Once a ward was tripped, it was spent and ceased to exist. A new ward was just that, a new ward. Even if it was laid over the previous, it was still distinct. She narrowed her eyes. The only answer that came to her was that, somehow, it had been tripped, then reformed almost instantly.

"But who could do that?" she asked. Her hand went to the pocket of her battered olive-drab jacket. She found the pistol and the weight of it gave her some comfort.

Leaving the gun where it was, she whispered softly the words Dasher had given her to unravel the dying wards. One lesson she'd learned a long time ago was—it's far better to be safe than sorry. A wisp of power drifted from the doorframe and she pulled the door open.

After a small landing, the stairs doubled back under themselves and vanished into darkness. Elaine listened for several seconds, blocking out the sounds of the world above. Water dripped somewhere, rats and other creatures skittered about, but nothing else. She inhaled deeply through her nose and smelled lingering ozone, residue from Charge's attempt to fight off the snatchers. More powerful than that was the scent of magic. It was powerful, but, well, the only word she could think of was *wild*.

She pulled the door closed behind her and the darkness gave way to shades of gray as her elfin sight kicked in. Carefully and silently, she made her way down the stairs and followed the hallway. As she walked, she traced her fingertips along the wall, and her eyes closed halfway. As she let out a slow breath, she opened her senses up to any latent impressions left behind. A series of disjointed images flashed through her mind too fast or blurry to make out.

She shook her head. This wasn't right. Nothing was speaking to her, not the stone, not the air, nothing. She couldn't imagine what could hide so well but still leave such an obvious and tenable trail. It was almost as if these snatchers, if they were the cause, had overwhelmed their surroundings, the magical equivalent of a flash-bang grenade.

She spotted the doorway ahead and moved forward, ever vigilant and very aware of how many steps to the exit. A dozen paces away, she could see there was no door in the frame. Her hand was inside her pocket, gripping the pistol when she reached the doorway. She peeked inside and saw the door, or rather shattered pieces of it, strewn about the dank, windowless room.

Standing in the entryway, she processed the details. Chunks were missing from two walls, likely where Charge's bolts had hit. Dozens of horizontal scorch lines were on all the walls. The whole room reeked of mortal and fae magic. This had been a brief, but intense, fight.

There were so many footprints on the dusty floor, and what looked like something having been dragged across it, that she couldn't make a clear count of how many people had been involved. She could see where someone had hit the ground just at the entrance and slid out of the room. In the hall, she examined the wall opposite the doorway and saw a few stray hairs on the floor. She bent down, picked them up, and placed them in a glass vial etched with a preservation spell. After capping the vial, she put it in an inside jacket pocket and moved into the room.

She stayed close to the wall as she went around the room, examining it from all angles. When the entrance was opposite her, she saw faint symbols drawn on the floor right at the edge of where the door would've been. She stepped over and, crouching down, examined them. They were simple barricading glyphs, strong ones at that. Hefty stuff for street slingers. They must've paid some serious swag for them, for all the good they did. A noise drew her eyes up to the exposed wooden beams. A rat was staring down at her.

Elaine smiled, reached into her pocket, and drew out a single M&M. She held the candy up so the rat could see it. "Interested in making a trade?"

The rat's eyes moved from the candy to Elaine and back again.

"I'll give you this if you can tell me what you, or any of your friends, saw."

The rat's whiskers twitched as it considered the offer.

Elaine wiggled the candy. "It's peanut butter. Good stuff."

The rat darted her way, and as she lifted her hand, it jumped and landed on her palm. It sat up, looked at the candy, then at Elaine.

"No way," she said, eyes narrowed. "Information first."

The rat squeaked.

"Fine." Elaine sighed and put the candy in its tiny, outstretched paws.

In short order, the rat had devoured the treat and began licking its little fingers clean.

"So, what can you tell me?"

The rat lowered its head.

Elaine placed a finger between its ears and images flowed into her mind.

The room was huge, but then, she was seeing it from a rat's eye view. Three kids—two girls and a boy—were eating and tossing bits to her, or rather to the rat. The scraps were salty and delicious. She felt contentment and happiness at their generosity. Then she felt cold, and her fur bristled as something approached. The kids felt it too and they moved to the far side of the room. Elaine ran and climbed to the rafters on some old pieces of wood leaning against the wall. She hurried to the safety of the den, and was sad the kids were too big to come with her. She poked her head out and tried to see, but she was afraid. There was the whispered chill of magic and panicked shouting, and then a crash as the door exploded in.

Elaine ducked into her den and tucked herself into a ball. She heard screaming and could see flashes of light through her eyelids.

Then, everything was quiet. When Elaine dared to peek out, she could see the kids on the ground, not moving. A single figure, tall and thin, stepped through the door and brushed itself off. Elaine focused, trying to make out details, but she couldn't perceive any. Three more figures joined the first and picked up the kids. The largest of these new figures turned to the first and said—

The shuffling of footsteps snapped Elaine out of her link.

It took a moment to readjust, and when she did, she closed her eyes and focused on the scents and sounds. She could hear heavy footsteps, and the creaking of leather shoes. Three, no, four mortals. She smelled hairspray, aftershave, and—

She opened her eyes and swore silently.

This was the last thing she needed. "You better get out of here," she whispered to the rat and set it down.

It hurried from the room as the beams from four flashlights moved along the floor and walls outside. They weren't more than fifty feet away now.

"Movement," a gruff-sounding man said.

"Jesus, it's a freaking rat," another man said.

"Please tell me I can shoot some of the damned things?" a woman asked.

Elaine gritted her teeth and fought the urge to grab the pistol. Instead, she moved to a corner, tucked herself into a ball, and drew her glamour in tight around her. She pretended to sleep, watching the doorway through not quite closed eyes.

Three men and a woman stepped to the door and moved to cast their lights around the room. It didn't take them long to find her.

"Another damned rat," the gruff-sounding one said with a chuckle.

"Wake up," the one in charge said in a calm tone. "Slowly, let me see your hands."

Elaine squinted against the bright lights as she sat up. "What the hell, man, I'm sleeping. This is my squat, find your own."

"On your feet, but keep your hands where I can see them," the leader said.

Elaine put on her best derisive look and stood. The gun oil she'd smelled before was almost overpowering now. When she got to her feet, she lifted her hands. "I didn't do nothing."

"What's your name?" a short blocky man with a balding head asked.

"Dazzler," Elaine said.

"Christ," the woman said. "Don't any of these homeless punks have real, grown-up names?" She was dressed severely in a gray pantsuit, her dark blond hair pulled into a tight ponytail.

"Sure," Elaine said. "There's Screw-You Anderson, and Go Fu—"

"You have any ID?" the lead agent asked.

Elaine eyed him, a lean but well-built man in his fifties. Something about him made Elaine uneasy. "No," she said. "Do you?"

The man arched an eyebrow, then reached into his jacket and produced his credentials. "I'm Special Agent Harris. These are Special Agents Kowalski, Stanton, and Gomez." He motioned first to baldy, then to the woman, and finally to a man in his late twenties with dark hair.

Elaine looked over the creds, then the agents. She knew right away that both were legit. "So, what do you want?" she asked.

"We're investigating the recent kidnappings," Harris said. "How long have you been here?"

Elaine sneered. "No idea, my Rolex stopped working last week."

"Punk," Kowalski muttered.

Elaine bit her tongue, careful not to let herself slip too far into her role.

"Don't suppose you have any information about these incidents?" Harris asked.

"I mind my own."

"You need to get out of here," Harris said. "We have to examine the scene."

Elaine moved slowly to the doorway. She could feel all their eyes boring into her. When she made to step through the doorway, Harris narrowed his eyes and blocked the way with his hand.

"Stanton?" he asked. "Is it me, or does she look a lot like that art thief that's supposed to be based in Seattle? What's her name?"

"The Diamond Shadow," Stanton answered and nodded. "And I think she does."

Elaine froze, barely managing to keep the sudden rush of panic at bay.

Harris met her eyes and stared hard. It wasn't possible, but somehow she knew he was testing her glamour. Impossible unless he was— She forced herself to calm. After a moment, she lifted her wrists. "Damn, you caught me. I got some Monets and a lost Van Gogh in the trunk of my Aston Martin."

The seconds slowed.

Harris held a card out, his face a stone mask. "If you think of anything, Miss Dazzler, let me know."

"Don't worry," Stanton said. Her eyes were cold. "We'll be in touch."

Elaine didn't ask how; she just took the card and left. She managed not to run, but just barely.

"We need lights down here," Harris said as Elaine headed to the stairs.

The rat sat on the railing, waiting for her. She picked him up and put him on her shoulder. When she finally reached the surface, the sun was setting and she relaxed enough to let herself shiver, though it had nothing to do with the chill.

"Since when does the FBI employ wizards?" she said to herself, but quietly.

It took her less than twenty minutes, despite the circuitous route, to reach her car. The pearl white Aston Martin Vanquish sat unmolested. She got in and closed the door, sinking into the soft seats. She considered checking the trunk, but decided it could wait. She took the rat into her hand and held him up so she could look him in the eye.

"Okay, let's go over this again, and I want details."

CHAPTER FOURTEEN

"No, Fiona, honey," Edward's voice said through the phone. "I can't play right now."

Dante smiled as he imagined the scene. Edward trying to juggle too many books and the phone while Fiona was tugging at his leg. It was a miracle he didn't—

There was a loud crash on the other end of the call and Dante pulled the phone away from his ear with a wince. Fiona said something Dante couldn't make out and then laughed.

"Sorry," Edward said a moment later. "You still there?"

"I am," Dante said through a chuckle.

"I'll play in a minute," Edward said.

"Oh?" Dante asked.

"No, not—"

Dante laughed.

Edward grumbled something and sighed. "Hold on."

Dante paced along the edge of the roof of the hotel. He scanned the street a dozen stories below again. A moment later, he heard a door close on Edward's end.

"Okay, sorry about that."

"It's fine," Dante said.

"So, I have good news and bad news. Bad news first: I haven't found anything definite. Just some enigmatic mentions and references to other books I couldn't find."

"Well, I'm not terribly surprised." Dante didn't mention he was also relieved.

"The good news is I keep coming across the same term. It's mentioned in several texts, and I guess Nghalon thinks it's important. I have no idea what it means though."

"Wait—Nghalon?"

"Oh, right," Edward said and laughed. "Nghalon is the genius loci of the house, and—"

"Your house has a guardian spirit?"

"I'm pretty sure that's what he is," Edward said. "I know he's the one who rearranges my library, and he's the source of voices I hear—"

"You hear voices?"

"Yes—well, no, not like you're thinking. It's more like—" There was a long pause. "You know what, let's have this conversation another time."

"I think that's a good idea," Dante said. "So what's the word?"

"Taleth-Sidhe."

For a moment, Dante's heart stopped.

"I presume it's some kind of fae, but I can't find a definition anywhere," Edward said.

Dante's mind whirled.

"Are you still there?" Edward asked.

"What? Yes, sorry. It's a mortal," he finally said.

"A mortal? But doesn't sidhe mean fae?"

"It's our word," Dante said. "Sidhe just means people. It's like when you use the words mankind or humanity. Daoine-sidhe means noble or high one. Oíche-sidhe means dark one."

"Okay, um, can I buy a vowel?"

Dante let out a breath. "Taleth is our language. It means magic."

"So it's a wizard?" Edward's tone was dubious.

"Something like that," Dante said. But not like you, he added silently. He ran his hand through his hair and moved away from the roof's edge. "It may be best if you weren't—"

Edward laughed. "I'm sort of already involved, aren't I?"

"It's not as simple as you think."

"Is it ever?" Edward laughed. "I still have some scars to remind me of that lesson. I appreciate that you're looking out for us, but from my experience, knowledge is never a bad thing."

"Believe me when I say you are completely wrong." Dante's tone came out colder than he intended.

"If you won't tell me, I'll find it on my own. I'm not putting Caitlin or Fiona at risk."

"They're not at risk," Dante said.

"I appreciate you think so, but I'd rather err on the side of not my fiancée and her daughter not being attacked by some evil wizard thing."

Several long, quiet seconds ticked by. Dante considered what to tell him, what he could tell him.

"I might be able to focus my search better if I knew more," Edward said. "From what you've told me, kids are being taken and killed. It hits close to home, you know?"

"I understand," Dante said. More than you know, he added to himself, then let out a sigh. "Magic always strives for balance. I won't go so far as to say it's a sentient intelligence, but close. When the balance is threatened, a Taleth-Sidhe is born. They are mortal, but born from magic."

"Wouldn't that mean they aren't mortal?" Edward asked.

"If it helps, think of them as human. They're powerful with a capital P, and born for the sole purpose of countering whatever is threatening the balance."

"How many have there been?"

"I know of two," Dante said. "The first was Merlin."

"Merlin?" Edward asked. "As in the Merlin?"

"The same, though time has altered the legend more than a little."

"What about the second," Edward asked.

Dante drew in a breath. "His name was Seanán; and before coming into his power as a Taleth-Sidhe, he trained with an ancient sect of wizards. These mages, as they called themselves, were betrayed and almost entirely wiped by one of their own. This *bhfeallaire*, betrayer, turned to a dark creature in his mad quest for power." Dante pushed back memories. "Seanán eventually defeated the *bhfeallaire*, crushed his circle of dark magi, and even defeated the creature who was their master."

"I didn't know any of that," Edward said.

"There's good reason," Dante said. "This creature is so powerful that merely speaking its name gives it power and a way into this world."

"And Seanán defeated this thing?"

"It gained a foothold here through its followers," Dante said. "Seanán defeated them, and banished their master. That's the kind of power a Taleth-Sidhe has." And—Dante wanted to say, but didn't—this one was also trained under your grandfather.

Dante started the car and headed for the pricier side of town. It was a safe bet that Donovan's goons would be there. He glanced in his rearview mirror. His tail wasn't very good, or maybe they weren't trying very hard. He was pretty sure who it was. He wasn't happy about it, but depending on who'd they'd sent, the person might be useful in what was to come.

Twenty minutes later, he parked the car and started walking. The sun was just setting, but he wasn't too worried. Whoever the snatchers were, their targets were in the rougher parts of downtown. And even if Dante was wrong, he didn't fit a snatcher's usual profile. He hated the thought that something might happen while he was out chasing Donovan down, but he'd just add that to the considerable tab the little weasel was already racking up.

Dante's notoriety had grown ever since Fiona's kidnapping last year, even with the have-nots of the Rogue Court. Hopefully Donovan and his lackeys didn't keep up on the current events. Just to be safe, Dante focused on his glamour and held the image of a tattered changeling tightly in his mind. Unlike mortals, fae weren't often fooled by glamours, but Dante knew just how good he was, so he wasn't particularly worried.

"What the hell are you doing on this side of town, trash?" asked a gruff voice tinged with a Russian accent.

Dante was impressed. He hadn't realized Donovan had brought in Slavic muscle. He stopped and tried to look timid for a moment, then he started walking again, quicker this time.

"Hey, my friend asked you a question, yes?" another asked.

Dante turned slowly and saw three chuhaister, or Russian forest giants, staring him down. The term giant was always applied rather loosely. These weren't even eight feet tall. All three were dressed in—Dante had to admit—rather stylish three-button pinstripe suits. He couldn't help but wonder where they found someone to make them in that size.

One of the chuhaister drove his meaty palm into Dante's shoulder. "Are you deaf, or stupid?"

Dante rolled with the blow, but made it look as if it staggered him. When he spoke, he laced some fear into his words. "What? No, I'm just looking—"

"You're looking in wrong place, yes?" the largest said.

"No, I'm looking for Dono—"

The second one shoved him and Dante let himself fall against a wall. Several people walking nearby crossed the street, or increased their pace as they went by.

"The Godfather doesn't see trash like you. You and those like you are meant to keep to your side—"

Dante drove the edge of his open hand into the giant's throat and felt something give. As the big fae doubled over reflexively, Dante drove his knee into the giant's nose. There was a cracking sound, like a tree snapping in two.

Before his friends could react, Dante jumped against the wall, then sprang off it, putting just enough magic behind it to get the job done without killing. The heel of his Bettanin & Venturi wingtip caught the second giant on the side of his face and sent him spinning to the ground, where he landed in an unconscious mountain of muscle.

When Dante turned to the last, he came face-to-face with a Taurus Raging Bull fifty-caliber revolver. He had to admire the way it had been modified to fit the massive hand that now held it, but he did so very slowly and allowed his glamour to evaporate.

"Who are you?" the remaining giant asked. "You're not changeling rabble."

"I want to speak to your boss. It's court business," Dante said. His eyes never wavered from the trigger finger. At the first twitch, he'd turn to the side and, hopefully, dodge the first shot or two.

The giant's beady eyes didn't go wide—Dante wasn't sure that was possible—but they became less beady. The giant looked to his fallen comrades, then back to Dante.

"You're the hired help," Dante said in perfect Russian. "This is a matter you should pass along."

"I suggest you listen to the man, yeah?" said a woman's voice, laced with a heavy Irish brogue, from behind the giant. It was followed by the sound of a hammer being pulled back on a gun. "I'd hate to ruin his nice clothes with your blood and brains. What few are rolling around in there, anyways."

"See," Dante said, "not just court, but Cruinnigh business. Even the Fianna sent an emissary."

Disproving Dante's theory, the giant's eyes did go wide. He swallowed, then set his gun on the ground slowly. "*Da*, hired help," he said. "I give you address."

As soon as the giant finished telling Dante the location of Donovan's court, he was pistol whipped from behind. He fell to the ground to join his fellows in a much-deserved nap. His collapse revealed the woman standing behind him, still holding the pistol she'd used to drop him. She was in her thirties with long straight black hair pulled into a ponytail and eyes so blue they could've been battery powered. She was wearing military-issue boots, black fatigue pants, and a knee-length black canvas coat over a tight black shirt. An intricate Celtic-knot tattoo started on her neck, just below her jaw, and disappeared beneath the collar of her shirt. On the lapel of her jacket, she wore the silver pin marking her as a Fian. It was a design Dante knew well, though it was usually worn on a kilt.

"Hello, Siobhan," Dante said. He didn't bother smiling.

"Magister," Siobhan said with small bow. "Been a long time."

"No one's up on current events," Dante said. "I'm not a magister anymore."

Her dark eyebrows knitted. "Sorry to hear that." She holstered her pistol back inside her jacket.

"What do you want?" Dante asked.

"What do you imagine?" she asked in genuine surprise. "Changelings go missing, mortals as well. The clan sent me here to make sure there're no more violations to the Oaths."

"Convenient timing," Dante said through clenched teeth. "You missed a pretty big one recently."

"I—"

"About a year ago, maybe you heard something about it back in Ireland?" He wasn't able to hold the venom back any longer.

Siobhan raised her hands. "If it'd been up to me—"

Dante stepped over the unconscious heap in front of him and closed on Siobhan, forcing her back until she was against a wall. Dante glared down at her, his eyes wet and his teeth clenched. "Missed you at the memorial service too."

Siobhan looked away. "Some of us wanted to go, but—"

"Let me guess, just following orders?" Dante turned and started to walk away before he did something he'd regret, or worse, something he wouldn't. "I have no time to pander to your politics. I have my own to deal with."

"*Damnú air*! It's not like that!"

Dante whirled and pointed a finger at the woman. "No! It's exactly like that. You banished him! You left Brendan to rot, alone, in a foreign land! He was your blood, Siobhan!"

"The Fionn thought he was dangerous," she said. "We all did."

"Oh, he was!" Dante said. "And he spent his life fighting for those who couldn't fight for themselves! Blazes, woman, he went toe to toe with the Dark King himself! He did it for a child he didn't know, and in the end he gave up his own life for that little girl." He lowered his voice. "Always hoping that maybe, just maybe, he'd make up for his past."

Siobhan wiped her eyes. "I know."

"No, you don't. Not one of you had the decency to see the man honored in death." When Siobhan started to speak, he raised a hand and she went silent. "I've had my issues with the Fianna in the past, but I've always respected your honor and courage." Dante's eyes turned cold. "No more. You're the ones with a debt to repay now. And make no mistake, it's a mighty one."

Siobhan lowered her head. "You're right, about all of it. There are those in our ranks who think we've lost our way." She inhaled sharply before continuing. "Let me help. Give me a chance to start paying on that debt, to honor the actions of a wronged brother—"

"Don't you dare call him that! Every one of you gave up the right to call him that." He drew in a breath. "But you're still a member of the Cruinnigh, so I've no right to deny you a place in resolving a dispute."

Siobhan didn't move, not even a twitch.

"I am very old," Dante said slowly. "And I have a long memory. I do not easily forgive." He leveled his gaze on her. "And I never, never forget."

Siobhan only nodded.

Dante turned and headed to his car. "Let's go."

Dante double-parked in front of the nondescript building, braking so hard Siobhan lurched forward against her seat belt.

"I understand your anger," she said as she undid her belt. "But—"

"Rest assured I have sufficient anger to spread over more than just the Fianna." Dante pulled a pistol from his jacket, checked it, and after giving Siobhan a sideways glance, replaced it. "Ours is a personal matter, one for another time. This is more pressing."

"So, it's a truce, then?"

"Follow my lead, and back my play." Dante looked at her. "Can I trust you to do that?"

She nodded. "Aye, I'm with you."

They both got out and walked to the large metal door. It was dented and dinged with no handle. There was, however, a square viewport at eye level, currently closed.

"I believe I got a key." Siobhan drew a sawed-off shotgun from her coat and racked a shell. "Shall I knock, then?"

Dante almost smiled. "Hold that thought." He withdrew a small copper disk covered in intricate script from his pocket and kicked the steel door three times, only hard enough to knock.

The viewport slid open and a pair of beady eyes the color of swamp water looked out at them. "Password?"

Dante tossed the disk through the slot, hitting right between the undersized eyes.

There was a muttering of surprise and a curse. A moment later the viewport slid closed and the door opened.

"I have a master key for places like this," Dante said and walked in.

Behind the door was an ogre in a tailored suit, fedora, and black-and-white spectator shoes. In the distance, jazz music played and a woman crooned in a sultry tone.

"Where is he?" Dante asked, eyes forward.

The ogre lowered his head, offering the copper disk back to Dante with one hand, pointing to another set of doors with the other.

Dante took the disk back and strode forward.

"Be a good lad and make sure our conversation is a private one, yeah?" Siobhan said as she followed Dante, shotgun across her shoulder.

The two of them stepped through the doors and into a 1940s-style jazz club. It looked like a speakeasy, down to the tiniest detail. High-ranking fae of all sorts milled around at the bar, danced on the expansive hardwood floor, or shared conversations in the quiet booths that lined the walls. Everyone one of them could've stepped out of a movie. There were zoot suits, military uniforms, and ladies in dresses from the forties, with hair in matching style. On the stage, the tuxedoed musicians played in perfect time. A woman in an elegant evening gown with both her arms covered in colorful tattoos was singing into an antique microphone. A satyr, who looked more than a little like Jesus, stood and began a trumpet solo.

"Bloody hell," Siobhan said. "This isn't odd at all, is it?"

Dante scanned the room.

At the opposite end of the dance floor, next to the stage, was a large booth on an elevated platform. Two trolls, in the requisite fashion, stood in front of velvet ropes. In the large circular booth, dressed in an exquisitely tailored black-and-gray suit, was an elf with amber-colored eyes. Around him were various court nobles: sylphs, nymphs, other elves, and even a dwarf.

"There." Dante motioned with his head.

"Should I stow it?" Siobhan asked, glancing at her gun.

"No."

Dante made his way through the dancers, all of them spinning or turning or performing expert aerial throws and catches. Siobhan stayed right behind him.

Half a dozen paces before Dante reached the ropes, one of the trolls raised his hand.

"Sorry, private—"

Dante drove his knee into the troll's groin and sent him to the ground.

Siobhan cracked the other across the face with the butt of her shotgun, sending him to the floor next to his whimpering associate.

The band stopped and everyone turned to look. Dante threw the rope aside and ascended the steps. The chattering group seated in the booth stared at him. The elf's face turned a shade of purple, and Dante almost expected to see steam coming out his ears. That did make him smile, but just a little.

"Those were my personal bodyguards!" Donovan said. "You seem to have adopted the Fian lack of manners from that lunatic—"

Dante drew his pistol and leveled it at Donovan's forehead, less than a foot between barrel and bone. "Shut up."

Donovan swallowed. "I'm the magister of this region, not—"

Dante pulled back the hammer. "Is there something in my countenance, or the words I used, that made my instructions unclear?"

Donovan gritted his teeth, but didn't speak.

"As your keen observational skills might have perceived," Dante said, "I'm a little perturbed. Best keep your hands in plain sight."

Dante caught movement to his left.

"Easy does it, sweetness," Siobhan said. "Why don't you join your mates there?"

The troll Dante had leveled limped by and sat at the end of the booth, splaying his massive hands on the table.

"Club's closed." Dante didn't shout, but his voice carried. "The magister will be covering your tabs."

Whispers and mutters of confusion sounded from the club.

"Are you thick?" Siobhan shouted. "Or did you not hear the man? That means get out, right fecking now!"

When no one moved, she fired a shot into the ceiling.

Patrons, band members, bartenders, and waitstaff alike bolted for the doors amid panicked cries.

Siobhan turned to the nobles seated in the booth. "Pretty sure he meant you as well," she said and worked the shotgun's pump action.

A spent shell clattered to the floor, and before it had bounced twice, the nobles were halfway to the door. The troll sat frozen, looking from Donovan to Dante.

"What about that one?" Siobhan asked.

"He's fine," Dante said, though his eyes never left Donovan. He uncocked his pistol and lowered it. "Now, I need a word with you, Magister."

"You won't shoot me," Donovan said, though his

tone lacked certainty. "You wouldn't dare. This isn't your region, Magister." The last word was laced with venom.

"You really should look over the communications from the Cruinnigh," Dante said. "I'm no longer the new-eastern magister."

Donovan laughed. "Someone finally come to their senses?"

Dante flung the copper disk onto the table in front of Donovan. "After the oíche uprising, I was made Regent of the New World."

Donovan went silent and his face fell as he looked from the coin to Dante. "What happened to Albericus?"

"He stepped aside," Dante said, then kicked the table. The bolts holding it to the floor snapped and the edge of the table slammed into Donovan's stomach.

Donovan gasped in pain.

Dante snatched the coin back. "Are you aware of what's been happening out there?" he asked.

Donovan looked up with murderous eyes and set the table back in place. "I know quite well what's going on in my region. Some urchin half-breeds went missing. Why should it concern me, or the court?"

Dante drew in a slow breath. "Consider yourself disposed of your position."

"On what grounds?" Donovan roared.

"Gross incompetence," Dante said. "You'll have your wardens and marshals report to me immediately."

Donovan sneered. "I disbanded them."

"You did what?"

"The members of my court saw to their own affairs. My bodyguards were sufficient to protect the nobles, so there was no longer a need for them."

Dante looked at the troll. "I'm declaring all court grounds a sanctuary for any and all who request it. That means fae, changeling, and mortal alike. Any who ask for sanctuary will be given it. Do you understand?"

The troll didn't even look at Donovan. "Yes, Regent, as you say."

"Go, inform the other"—Dante's mouth twisted—"bodyguards. I'm conscripting them into court service until this situation is resolved. If I hear of anyone being turned away, harassed, or so much as bumped in passing without an apology offered, they'll answer to me."

The troll bowed, then stood and cast a wary glance at Siobhan.

"Off with you now, sweetness," she said and winked.

The troll hurried away.

Dante looked back at Donovan. "Your properties and holdings are hereby seized."

Donovan's eyes went wide. "What? You can't do that to—"

Dante raised his gun again. "Would you prefer I make your dispossession more permanent?"

Donovan went silent.

"Give me your hand," Dante said.

The former magister stood and held out his right hand, an indignant sneer on his face.

Dante drew a knife from inside his coat and dragged the blade across Donovan's palm, eliciting a wince.

"I'm ordering a full inquiry into you and every decision you've made in the last century." Dante put his pistol away, withdrew a small stone, and dragged the blade of his knife across it, leaving behind Donovan's blood. "If you run, I will find you."

Donovan's face turned a little pale.

"Now, get out of my sight. I have things to do."

Donovan got to his feet and left the club.

Dante pulled his phone from his pocket and dialed Faolan.

"What's the word?" Faolan asked.

"Send everyone you can spare."

"That bad?"

"I need you here as well," Dante said. "Assuming you can get away from your duties?"

"As luck would have it," Faolan said, "the previous magister left me a pretty smooth-running organization. I think I can spare a few days."

Dante smiled. "Thank you, Magister."

"We can be there in a few hours."

Dante glanced at his watch. "That'll have to do."

"Where do you want to meet us?"

Dante gave Faolan the address of the club and ended the call. As he tucked his phone away, he turned to Siobhan. She'd stowed her shotgun and helped herself to a beer from the bar.

"Well, it is your place now, yeah?" she said. "I didn't figure you'd mind."

At that moment, Dante missed Brendan more than he had in quite some time, but he smiled at Siobhan. "I need your help. We have a hell of a task ahead of us, and not much time."

"As I said, I'm with you," Siobhan said.

When his phone rang, Dante answered it without looking at it. "Something wrong, Faolan?"

"Well, you're half right," Elaine said. "And as a hint, I'm not Faolan."

Dante closed his eyes and let out a long breath. "Can you get to me or do I need to come pick you up?"

"I managed just fine before you showed up," Elaine said. "Give me the address."

Dante narrowed his eyes at the sound of an engine starting, and his mouth turned up at the corners. "Is that a Vanquish?"

CHAPTER FIFTEEN

Wraith realized she was awake. The feel of cold wood against her back made her hesitant to open her eyes. A distant but powerful fear was coursing through her. Even if she couldn't name that fear, she knew it, and knew it was hard earned.

"What do we do if she doesn't wake up?" Geek asked.

"She will," Sprout said.

"Weren't you the one who was convinced she were dead?" Con asked.

"I still think she is, but that doesn't she mean she won't wake up."

There was a long pause.

Wraith opened her eyes and saw the boys exchanging glances.

"Um," Con began. "Actually, yeah, it kind of—"

"You're awake!" Ovation said and was immediately on his knees at her side.

"I told you so," Sprout said.

"Are you okay?" Ovation asked. "We were getting worried."

Wraith nodded. "I think so, where are we?"

"No idea," Geek said. "We assumed you could tell us."

"Seeing as you were driving, as it were," Con said.

Wraith started to get to her feet, and Ovation took her hand and helped her up slowly. His arm slid around her waist and she was keenly aware of how warm his hands where, how soft his touch.

"Easy does it," he said when she was on her feet.

"Thank you," Wraith said. She made to tuck her hair behind her ear, but felt incredibly stupid when she realized there wasn't enough to do that.

The smell hit Wraith first. It was familiar, and a flood of emotions washed over her, but she had no memories to give them context. She looked around the small room and felt that familiar pain of not recognizing a place, but knowing she should. It was thirty feet by twenty, the walls were brick, the floor was old planks, and the ceiling was crossed with exposed wooden beams. The only door was old and warped wood, and the spot where windows might have been once were now bricked over. Despite that, the room was well lit by some secret source.

Against one wall was an old sofa, much too large to have come through the door. A tattered loveseat was opposite the sofa with a battered coffee table between them. The furniture wasn't familiar, but when she touched the pieces, she remembered pushing them around the room, arranging them in the current pattern. Her fingers came away covered in thick dust. She absently wiped it on her worn, ill-fitting jeans and looked around the rest of the room. There were three bare mattresses on the floor. Next to each was a small cardboard box that seemed to serve as a nightstand. A fourth bed sat apart and perpendicular to the others, closest to the door. It didn't have a box. In far corner was what appeared to be a workbench.

"You know this place?" Ovation asked, but it wasn't really a question.

"I do, but I don't remember it," Wraith said, eyeing the bed that sat away from the others.

"From the looks of it," Con said, "no one's been here in ages. Dust is inches thick."

"And no foot prints but ours," Geek said.

Wraith felt a rush of panic and looked around for Toto. She spotted him lying on a huge doggie pillow on the far side of the couch, allowing an unobstructed view of the lonely bed and doorway. Toto watched her intently, but was somehow sad. Something in his eyes told her there was more behind his look than just a desire for treats or scratches behind the ear. Without thinking, Wraith walked to the workbench. No one said anything as she stepped past and around them.

The wooden surface was covered with tool marks and burns. An old soldering gun sat next to a spool of solder, still shining despite the coating of dust. Rolls of copper wire sat in organized rows, and mechanical hodgepodge sat in little trays: gears, magnets, springs, pieces of leather, and various metals, each in its place.

Wraith ran her hand over the wood, then the workings. Her feet kicked a small wooden box.

"Fritz," she said in a whisper when she saw the box.

"What?" the boys asked in unison.

"This was Fritz's workbench," Wraith said.

"Looks steampunk," Geek said.

Wraith didn't answer. She reached under the table and found the hidden release without consciously knowing it was there. A large section of the work surface popped up half an inch.

"A hidden compartment?" Geek asked. "Cool."

Wraith lifted the lid slowly, as if something might leap out and attack her. Inside was a single leather glove, more like a gauntlet; it would come nearly to her elbow. It was covered in armor-like brass plates, each riveted onto thick leather. Copper tubing ran along the forearm from a large opening, where something was obviously missing, to a winding mechanism at the wrist. She ran her finger over the glove hesitantly, afraid to pick it up. Without knowing, she knew it would fit her like, well, a glove. Brief memories, too quick to make sense of, flashed through her brain—though the impression she was left with, she understood. Her left hand traced over the tattoos on the back of her right hand. The glove was what had let her draw those supermassive, hyperaccelerated particles and shoot them. No. It was supposed to help her control it better, right? But it hadn't worked? Was that why she'd gotten tattooed? Or was the glove to increase the power?

"What's that?" Ovation asked from over her shoulder.

"Not sure," Wraith answered.

"Definitely steampunk," Geek said from her other shoulder. "And completely awesome!"

Wraith felt the others crowd around to look, but she ignored them. Something was on the edge of her brain; she could just touch it with her fingertips—but it was maddening that she couldn't grab a hold of it.

"What do you suppose these are for?" Con said, reaching out to pick up a couple of lenses that had camera-like apertures inside them, and several small jeweler's magnifying lenses attached.

Something inside Wraith surged to the surface. She smacked Ovation's hand and turned on him. *"Nein! Nicht berühren!"* she shouted, glaring at him.

Then it all made sense, and was so obvious she couldn't believe she hadn't seen it before. She set the lenses and glove on the surface of the bench after closing the hidden compartment. As she examined the lenses, she reached and picked up a small screwdriver. A few small adjustments and the collection of jeweler's lenses came off.

"Ich bin so ein dummkopf," she muttered, then grabbed a tray and retrieved similar lenses from inside it, but these were colored. Over one lens she attached a blue, then a red, and finally a purple jeweler's glass. Over the other, she put a dark-gray tinted glass, a yellow, and lastly an orange. When the work was done, she pulled the goggles from her bag. She screwed the new lenses into place. When it was done, she nodded.

She looked over the goggles and shook her head. "I can't believe I was so stupid before."

"So," Con said. "Spreken ze English again?"

"What?" Wraith asked absently as she looked over the glove. Something was still missing.

She spotted another tray and grabbed it. It was filled with pieces of polished glass. She selected a pale blue one, then she grabbed the soldering iron and a roll of copper wire.

"What the hell is happening, mate?" Con whispered to Ovation.

"I haven't the foggiest," Ovation said.

"Should we be worried?" Geek asked.

"I wish I knew," Ovation whispered.

Wraith heard but ignored them; she was focused on the task at hand. An equation formed in the air around her, then settled on the soldering iron and brought it to life. She attached the thin wires across the back of the piece of glass. As she worked, symbols and numbers settled into the glass itself, forming a winding and almost organic formulation that shifted, but always reached a zero sum. When the last solder was complete, she cleaned the iron and critiqued her work: an intricate weave of overlapping wires along the back of the glass, guiding and directing the formulation inside as well as keeping it stable. Wraith inserted the glass into the opening on the glove. It was loose, but she took a screwdriver and tightened the fittings until the glass was held firm, and it filled with a faint light.

"I thought you didn't know what it did," Ovation asked.

"*Es verfeinert die Manipulation von Quanten uber-exotische Teilchen,*" Wraith said.

"What?" everyone said together.

Wraith let out an exasperated sigh. For the briefest moment, she felt dizzy, like the room had abruptly stopped spinning. But she recovered quickly. "I said . . ." Her words died as the understanding slipped away. She looked from one face to another. Everyone looked at her expectantly, except Sprout. The little girl just smiled and took Wraith's hand, squeezing.

"It's okay," she said.

Wraith dropped the gauntlet onto the bench. "No, it's not. At all."

"Just sit down for a bit," Sprout said and led her to the loveseat.

Wraith fell into it. Toto came over and placed his head in her lap.

Ovation and Geek sat on the couch, Con paced the room, looking it over.

"Okay," Ovation said. "You said Fritz was German, right?"

Wraith nodded.

"You probably just learned it from her," Geek said, "and how to work on that stuff."

Wraith glanced at him. No, he didn't believe that either.

"Oi, I think something's missing over here," Con said. He was staring down at the floor next to the bed that was off on its own.

"What?" Ovation asked.

"No idea, mate," Con answered. "Four somethings actually, small and round."

When Wraith approached, Con stepped to one side, not saying anything, just gesturing to the floor.

Wraith knelt down and looked. Sure enough, amid the dust that coverd the old planks were four voids, all circles of different sizes.

Con chuckled. "Almost looks like someone's spare change might've—"

Wraith looked at him, and she felt herself smile. Con's words died, and her hands went to her pockets, searching fantically. She froze when her fingers touched the edge of the quarter. She took it out and set it slowly, almost reverently, down on the floor. It fit perfectly in the largest void.

"What's it mean?" Ovation asked.

Wraith smiled at him, tears rolling down her cheeks. "It means I can find her!"

"How's that, then?" Con asked.

Wraith held the quarter in her palm, headside up, and concentrated. Numbers and symbols drifted down, circling the coin and forming the calculation. "It's entangled, on a quantum level, to another coin Shadow keeps with her," Wraith said.

"Magical science?" Con asked.

"Any sufficiently advanced technology is indistinguishable from magic," Geek said and smiled. "Arthur C. Clarke's third law."

"No idea what you're talking about, mate," Con said.

Nothing was happening. Wraith focused harder, reaching out to find the bound coin.

"Quiet," Ovation said. "Can't you see she's—"

Then Wraith felt it take hold and she spun to stare at a bed across the room, the one furthest from her. She rushed to it, feeling the pull from the quarter in her hand. Falling to her knees, she moved the box, then pulled it open, but it was empty. She focused again, then realized it was the bed. Hesitantly, she tried to lift the mattress.

The coin fell from Wraith's hand and bounced on the floor as the entire world seemed to collapse around her.

"Let me help," Geek said. He easily lifted the mattress, setting it on its side and leaning it against the wall.

The uncovered spot almost gleamed from the lack of dust. Alone in that sea of polished hardwood sat a single penny.

"What the hell?" Con asked and knelt down.

Wraith closed her eyes. "No, this isn't right," she whispered.

Con and Ovation went to the other beds and lifted them, but Wraith knew what they'd find before they even looked.

"A dime," Ovation said.

"I got a nickel, mate," Con said.

Each boy carefully returned the beds to their original spots, then gathered around Wraith, each setting a coin down next to the quarter and penny.

After a long moment of silence, Geek looked from one person to another. "What's it mean?"

"It means I don't know what's real anymore," Wraith said through the sound of her reality shattering on the floor.

CHAPTER SIXTEEN

In her head, Wraith went over every detail of every memory she could find as she paced the room. She was more focused than she could ever remember being. No one said anything, but even if they had, she wouldn't have heard them.

Like a vision, her friends stood before her. Fritz—her small, agile form leaning against SK—him tall and lanky, their arms entangled. Her eyes a mossy green, his light brown. She could see the freckles on his cheeks and the sad look Fritz always wore. She focused on Shadow, on her face: oval in shape, strong cheekbones, piercing dark eyes, long and straight dark hair. Wraith could hear her voice, soft and almost melodic. Stepping back in her mind, Wraith could see her friend more clearly, the casual smile belying the wisdom behind it.

They were real! Weren't they?

They had to be. Didn't they?

No. Maybe she could've formed one from stereotypes she'd seen on TV or read about in books, but all three?

"It's a conundrum, to be sure," Nightstick said from a corner, leaning against the wall casually and smoking. "Some questions are better left unanswered." He turned and she felt him staring at her. "Or dug too deep into, lest you learn something you really didn't want to know."

Wraith ignored him.

Fritz's workbench, that was real. But Wraith had completed her work so effortlessly. Apparently, she'd even spoken German. Did she have split personalities? Was that it?

She began searching around the room, frantic to find something, anything, that would prove her sanity. No, it was more than that. She didn't care if she was crazy, but she did care that the people she knew and loved were real.

Wraith flipped mattresses, turned over boxes, rooted through drawers of the workbench. It wasn't until she shoved the couch to look under it that anyone said anything.

"Bloody hell, you could've just asked us to move!" Con shouted.

"Here, let me help," Geek said.

The others stood off to one side and Geek lifted the couch with one hand.

Nothing.

He set it down and lifted the loveseat. Wraith fell to her knees and ran her fingers through the dust, ignoring the teardrops that fell.

"There has to be something," she said through clenched teeth. "I know they're real!"

A gentle hand rested on her shoulder. She didn't pull away.

"We'll help," Ovation said, his voice soft.

"Mate, there's nothing—"

"We'll help," Ovation said again, though not to her, his voice stern.

"Right, then," Con said. "Come on, there's a wild goose waiting."

Wraith just sat there on her knees, head bowed, as the others began searching the room. Sprout turned over the cushions and Geek knocked on the wall, presumably listening for a hollow spot. Ovation stepped onto the couch and pulled himself up to look at the tops of the beams.

"Oi, hello there," Con said.

Everyone stopped and turned, including Wraith.

Her tears evaporated and hope swelled in her heart when she saw him over a spot on the floor away from everything. He was dragging his fingertips around a floorboard.

"What is it?" Ovation asked, leaping down from the beam and stepping to Con.

"This board is loose, I think," Con said.

Wraith was on her feet and across the room before she was even aware of what she was doing. Con moved aside for her as she knelt down and examined the board.

"I can't get it to budge," Con said. "But it's definitely not like the others around it. You got anything to pry it up with?"

Wraith saw the faint traces of an equation drifting around the edges of the board, binding it to those around it. It wouldn't come up without the others. Not until it let go.

Floorboards creaked behind Wraith and she heard Nightstick sigh. "Careful, kid," he said. "Better make sure you really want to know."

Wraith carefully unraveled the binding. The last number drifted away and the board shifted. With a shaking hand, she pressed on one end, raising the opposite end so she could lift it. In the space beneath was a gray metal strong box with a hinged handle on top and a simple combination lock on the face. Wraith drew it out and, at first touch, she knew this was what she was looking for.

But then why was she overwhelmed with dread?

She set the box before her, turned the wheels of the lock until it read 3143, and pressed the release.

The lid popped free.

Wraith drew in a breath, steeled her heart, and opened the lid.

"Well, I'll be buggered," Con said.

Tears poured down Wraith's cheeks, not all sad and not all happy.

Inside the box sat an eagle feather, the quill end wrapped with threads of different colors. It was like finding a long-lost favorite childhood toy. Wraith picked up Shadow's feather and the power of the fetish washed over her. She could feel Shadow's very essence in that moment and knew, without a doubt, her friend was real. She kissed the feather then pressed it to her cheek. After a long moment, she looked back into the box. There was a multitool with so many tools built in that it could give the best Swiss Army Knife an inferiority complex. As Wraith ran her fingers over it, she felt Fritz's magic soaked into it and saw it in Fritz's small hands, working deftly on some device or another. Wraith picked it up and set it reverently next to the feather. All that remained in the box was a pendant on a black cord. Wraith picked up SK's necklace by the thong. The pendent itself was a worn silvery metal, pewter she thought, but wasn't sure. The engraving was worn, and she could see SK worrying it between his fingers before dropping it back under his shirt. On one side was a line of text she couldn't read, surrounded by more text in a circle. On the opposing side was an intricate design; four triangles overlapping into a star. It was circled with still more script. Wraith could feel the protective powers of the symbol. Even though she couldn't read any of the text, it didn't matter. She knew who it belonged to and as she ran her fingers over the smooth metal, she felt SK's residual emotional impression.

She swallowed and closed her eyes, letting a few more tears escape. Yes, she knew for sure all her friends were real, but she also knew they never went anywhere without these prized possessions.

Her legs had begun to fall asleep when she finally blinked, but she still kept staring at the things in front of her, the most treasured belongings of her friends, and the coins that were supposed to make sure they could always find each other. After a long moment, she kissed the pendant, slipped it over her head, and tucked it beneath her shirt. Next, she kissed the multitool and stuck it in the cargo pocket of her jeans. Lastly, she picked up the feather and more tears came as she kissed it. She was about to put it in her bag, but she hesitated. She didn't want to break or crush it.

"I think I can tie it into your hair," Sprout said. "If you want."

Wraith turned at the beaming girl, blue eyes almost aglow. Despite all that weighed on Wraith, she couldn't help but smile back. "That would be nice," she said, then kissed the girl's cheek. "Thank you."

"You sit here," Sprout said from the loveseat.

Wraith joined her, and after a few minutes, Sprout asked for the feather, which Wraith surrendered reluctantly. She managed to resist telling the girl to be careful.

"I'm, uh," Con started. "Hell, I owe you an apology, don't I?"

"No, you don't," Wraith said. "I probably am half crazy, but I think I have a firm grip on the half that isn't."

"Well, I'm sorry all the same," Con said, finally looking up at her, then around the room. "For this whole giant ball of shite."

It was like someone opened a window and all the tension just flowed out.

"So, what do we do now?" Geek asked.

"You're asking the wrong person," Ovation said, looking at Wraith.

Wraith shrugged. "I'm still not sure of a lot of things, but at least I know my friends are real." She closed her eyes. "Or they were. I'm going to find out what happened to them, and that means I need to figure out what happened to me."

"It's done," Sprout said.

"Thank you," Wraith said, then wrapped her arm around the little girl, who snuggled close. Toto, unhappy at being left out, came over and dropped his head on her lap.

There was a long moment of silence as everyone traded glances.

"The snatchers, they did this to me," Wraith said. "I know they did, somehow."

"Why?" Sprout asked.

"They're psychotic boogeymen?" Con asked.

Wraith's soft chuckle was weary. "They want me for something. Before you ask, I don't know what, not yet anyway." She took a deep breath and braced herself for the impact of what she was about to say. "So I'm going to give them what they want. Maybe it'll stop the snatchings, and the . . ." She couldn't say the word. Saying it would make her think about what might have happened to her friends, and she couldn't do that.

The boys traded glances.

Sprout furrowed her brow. "It's not your fault."

Wraith managed a smile. "Thank you, Sprout, but Con was right."

"Again?" Ovation asked.

"I was?"

"Mark the calendar," Geek said to Ovation, who chuckled but didn't look away from Wraith.

She nodded. "I'm done running, of being hunted. They had me once and I got away. I know lots of others didn't, maybe all of the others didn't. I don't know exactly what they want, but I'm going to stop them, or die trying. I can't let this continue while I hide in the shadows."

"That's brilliant!" Con said with a fierce smile. "I take back nearly everything I said about you. You're still a nutter, mind, but you're all right."

"Thanks," Wraith said. "But I'm doing this alone—"

"Look, I'm not so much concerned for myself," Ovation said and looked at everyone, but his gaze lingered on Wraith. "I just don't want anything to happen to the rest of you."

"No," Wraith said, shaking her head. "You don't under—"

"Well that's not your call, mate," Con said. "I for one am plenty tired of playing the hare in this game of coursing. I say we give a little back. If I go down, I'm taking some of those buggers and a bleeding city block with me."

"No!" Wraith shouted and everyone turned to her. "Not you! Me!"

"Sure," Con said. "We'll just sit here then, shall we? Have a nice cuppa?"

"Well, yes," Wraith said. "Whatever a cuppa is."

"Doesn't this seem convenient?" Geek asked. "I mean, you've been struggling for however long, and now all of a sudden, poof?"

Wraith stared at Geek.

"That didn't come out right," he said. "But what if this is part of their plan? What if this is their way of getting you to come back on your own?"

"So we're going to second-guess decisions we haven't made yet?" Con asked.

"You're not listening to me," Wraith said. "None of this matters. I'm doing it alone!"

Ovation looked her in the eye. "No, you're not."

Wraith fretted her lower lip.

"Too right," Con said.

Sprout squeezed Wraith's hand. "Yeah, I'm with you too."

"So," Geek said, "if there are answers in your head, how do we go about plumbing the depths of your mind? Don't suppose anyone here is secretly a Vulcan who's mastered the mind meld?"

"I'll figure it out," Wraith said. Her conviction was starting to waver. She didn't have time to stumble in the dark while people were dying, or worse.

Ovation began pacing. "There's got to be something we can do," he said.

"Oi, what about the wizard?" Con asked.

Everyone traded glances.

Ovation nodded. "I hadn't thought of that. But it's a good idea. That old charm seller at the market has all kinds of stuff, powerful too."

"Charms! You're a genius!" Wraith turned, still smiling. "Information, like energy, can't be destroyed. I just need the proper charm to find the information."

"I don't imagine they sell that at the Freemont Market. Kind of a specialized thing, yeah?" Con asked.

Wraith glanced at the workbench, to her goggles and the glove, and then back to Con. "Then I'll find the pieces and make it myself."

Con chuckled and smiled. "Well then, guess we're off to see the wizard."

There was a groan and several eyes rolled.

"Market isn't until tomorrow, Scarecrow," Ovation said to Con. "That means we can all take a breath and rest." He turned to Wraith. "Is it safe here?"

"I thought lions were supposed to be brave," Con said.

Wraith shrugged. "Should be okay for tonight."

"Since I'm clearly the level-headed Tin Man," Geek said, "I'll be the one to ask: Do we even know where we are? I mean, if we teleported, couldn't we be in China or something?"

Wraith shrugged again. "I'm not sure, but it doesn't matter."

"Here it comes," Con said, pinching the spot between his eyes.

Wraith motioned to the door. "It's a door."

Con nodded. "Right, not a door, but a door-door."

Wraith nodded. "Exactly."

"Can you lock them?" Geek asked. "The doors, I mean."

After a moment of consideration, she leapt up, almost pulling Sprout off the couch, and rushed to the door. She ran her fingers along the doorframe.

"Do you think that's a yes?" Geek asked.

"Not even gonna guess," Con said, and started to lie down on the bed under which they'd found the penny. "I'm going to rest. I get the feeling we've got a bloody long day ahead of us."

Wraith didn't hear anything else, she was focused on the formulations that circled the door—the ones that made it a door-door, not just a door. She didn't see how she could lock just that one, but maybe . . . She looked back to the workbench and the gauntlet, then retrieved it. As anticipated, it fit her perfectly. She returned to the door and concentrated, pressing the palm of her gloved hand to the dented surface. The blue glass embedded in the glove glowed brighter. All around her, numbers and symbols appeared, more than she'd ever seen. The room was so full, it made Ovation and the others blurry. Her head started to throb as she figured the calculation, focused on keeping every number in its place. When the formula was together, she willed it into the door.

"Bloody hell, would you look at her eyes!" someone said behind her.

"Look at her tattoos!" someone else said. "They're glowing too!"

The voices were familiar, but all she could see was the doorway and all the potential doors that connected to it. Her head began to swim, then she felt the doors all lock as the power flooded out of her and she fell into darkness.

CHAPTER SEVENTEEN

Dante stopped his pacing across the dance floor. "What did you say?" He kept from dropping the phone.

"They're closed," Faolan said, the disbelief in his voice palpable.

"The Far Trails are closed?" Dante asked, hoping perhaps the third time would make it untrue. He should've known better.

"That's the only way I can describe it," Faolan said.

Dante swallowed and pushed down the growing knot in his stomach.

"This has only happened once before when the Taleth—"

"I know," Dante said. "I was there too." He exhaled. From the beginning, he added to himself. His mind began to race. Seanán wouldn't have come out of retirement without coming to the court first. There couldn't be another Taleth-Sidhe. Could there? The pieces of the puzzle were starting to fall into place, and Dante didn't like the picture.

"I had Padraig try as well, just in case it was something to do with me. I'll spare you his exact comments. Suffice it to say, he was mildly flustered."

Dante resumed pacing and chanced a glance at Siobhan. The Fian was listening, taking small sips from her bottle of beer. She didn't say anything, but she obviously understood.

"Okay, what are our contingencies?" Dante said.

Faolan laughed. "Contingences? For this? None of us thought it would ever come up again." There was a moment of silence. "Our only options are mortal modes of travel."

"It's too far to drive, and too risky," Dante said.

"We have access to private planes, but it isn't like we have a troop transport on standby."

Dante made a mental note to address that problem at some point in the future.

"And it's not like we'll be discreet," Faolan said. "We're talking a few dozen armed and armored wardens, and all their gear. Even if we crated the stuff, we're talking a lot of bodies and equipment. That means a big aircraft. It's going to take time to arrange it all so we don't run into issues with the mortal authorities."

"This is a bit beyond just a glamour."

"A bit."

"How long?" Dante asked.

Faolan paused. "Right now, I'd say a couple of days."

Dante winced. Just because he was expecting that answer didn't make it any easier. "You know I have to ask if you can shave that down."

"I'll have a better idea once I get on it, but I'd be amazed if I can be there in less than twenty-four hours. I'm sorry."

"Don't apologize," Dante said. "I'm sure anyone else would take a week to pull it off. Do what you can, but keep in mind that minutes matter."

"Understood."

Dante ended the call, put his phone in his pocket, and walked to the nearest wall. Once there, he counted to ten in a slow whisper. Then he put his right fist through the brick and let fly a curse that would've made the Dusk Court king himself raise his eyebrows.

"Well, that's colorful," Elaine said as she began walking across the club.

Dante withdrew his hand from the wall and brushed off the brick dust. "Had a bit of an off-putting phone call."

Elaine fretted her lower lip. "I doubt this will help your mood, but I'm mystified as to what it means."

"I need a drink," he said and walked to the bar. "What about you?"

"Vodka?" Elaine asked.

"How do you take it?" Dante asked as he began mixing himself a martini.

"The bottle and a straw would be good," Elaine said as she approached the bar.

She and Siobhan exchanged nods.

"Don't like barstools?" Elaine asked.

"I prefer to keep me back to the wall," Siobhan said.

"I've always wondered," Elaine said, "are you a Fian as well, or a Fianette?"

Siobhan smiled and slid her shotgun around so Elaine could see it. "We could discuss it if you like." Siobhan winked.

Elaine chuckled softly.

Dante came around the bar and set a fresh bottle of beer next to Siobhan, a glass with ice, a wedge of lemon, and vodka in front of Elaine. Then he took a large swallow from his martini glass before sitting at a nearby table.

"*Sláinte,*" Siobhan said, lifting the offered beer in a salute after joining Dante at the table.

"What've you found?" Dante asked Elaine as she sat.

"It's strange," Elaine said and drew a glass tube with a cork stopper from an inside pocket.

"That's about right for the night, aye?" Siobhan asked.

Elaine looked at Dante from under a furrowed brow.

"I'll explain in a minute," he said. "I'd say your news isn't going to be the strangest thing I've heard today, but I'm afraid to make that bet."

Elaine handed Dante the glass tube.

He examined it, holding it so Siobhan could see it when she leaned close. Inside was a long, straight, black hair.

"A hair?" Siobhan asked, looking from one elf to the other.

"Look close," Elaine said.

Dante's eyes went wide. "It's conjured."

"What?" Siobhan asked.

Elaine nodded. "My source says it's from a changeling girl."

"Who the bloody hell conjures a changeling?" Siobhan asked.

Elaine shrugged.

"How old is this?" Dante asked.

"Closing in on twenty-four hours," Elaine said.

"Like hell," Siobhan said. "No bloody wizard can summon up that kind of power. And this ain't what was conjured, it's just a piece of it. Damn thing should've gone to nothing in minutes after it came loose."

Elaine nodded. "I agree with you completely." She motioned to the hair. "And yet."

Dante set the tube down, then looked at Elaine. "You're sure about its age?"

She nodded. "Give or take a couple hours, but I got it from a reliable source who also happened to be a witness."

"How reliable?" Dante asked.

"Witness to what?" Siobhan asked.

"Very reliable. He's a rat that was in the rafters when the slinger and fifties were snatched last night," Elaine said to Dante, then turned to Siobhan. "The rat was a witness to the conjuring, but not like one I've ever heard of before."

Dante took another drink, finishing the martini, then he let out a long breath. "Let me have it."

"The rat said the three kids, two changelings and a slinger, came in just before nightfall," Elaine said. "He said they've been staying there for a few days, and they were always nice to him. A few hours before dawn, the rat said the temperature in the room dropped significantly and he felt more afraid than he could remember. The kids must've felt it too because they woke up and began whispering and crying."

"Magical fear?" Dante asked.

Elaine nodded. "I think so. A minute or so after the fear and cold arrived, a massive flood of magic poured into the room and these giant shadowy-like things appeared out of nowhere. The slinger set to fighting them off."

"Brave," Siobhan said with a nod of approval.

"Charge is an electromancer, and pretty skilled," Elaine said. "But he didn't get more than a couple shots out before the door blew open and these four kids and a huge dog rushed in and started attacking the shadows. Three kids were changelings, and the fourth was a slinger that apparently was tossing around some very serious magic." Elaine looked at each of them in turn. "The changelings were all conjured. The rat said he could smell it on them."

Dante clenched the empty martini glass stem, but eased up when he felt it might crack.

"The rat said the dog wasn't a normal dog, but he couldn't explain it in a way I could understand," Elaine continued. "Anyway, the new arrivals took down the shadows, who I'm fairly sure are the snatchers we've been hearing about. But the slinger, a girl, got hurt and was knocked out or something."

"What do you mean or something?" Siobhan asked.

Elaine shrugged. "It's not like we had a conversation in English. He gave me visions and impressions which I have to interpret. He kept thinking of falling asleep, so I can only assume she was knocked out." Elaine took a drink. "And when the fight was done, the kids, the three in the room to start, and the four who showed up, had a brief conversation and they all just vanished. Poof."

"What do you mean vanished?" Dante asked.

Elaine took another drink, this one longer, and shook her head. "One minute they were there, the next they were gone. Not so much as a whisper of magic. But the rat thinks Charge and his friends went willingly."

"That don't make no bleeding sense," Siobhan said.

"I didn't say it would," Elaine said. "I know Charge. I'm guessing it was Slink and Mouse with him. They usually ran together. They are real."

Dante looked at the hair, turning the glass tube in his fingers.

"All I can think is that those four kids who came to save them might've been conjured, but if they were it's not like any conjuring I've ever encountered. The rat swears they were though."

"Well, this hair is conjured," Dante said. "But it's

almost an insult to use that term. This is master-level stuff."

"And you're sure they were just bleeding kids?" Siobhan asked.

Elaine nodded. "The rat had no doubt on that point. Age is sort of a bizarre concept, but he spends enough time around people to know the difference between kids and adults."

"*Dia ár gcumhdach*," Siobhan said and crossed herself.

"Yeah," Elaine said, lifting her glass. "What she said."

"What if," Dante said, slowly, eyes still on the hair, "we're talking about a slinger powerful enough to not just conjure a form, but create an actual, real living body? Not just a vessel. Some shape that looks like a body, but really is one: blood, sweat"—he held up the tube—"hair."

"I don't have to tell you the amount of power required to pull something like that off," Elaine said. "Or how absolutely terrifying that idea is."

Dante shook his head. "No, you don't."

Siobhan laughed and both the elves looked at her.

"Sorry," Siobhan said. "I was just thinking it was like them transporter things in *Star Trek*, yeah?"

Dante and Elaine exchanged long looks.

"What did I say, then?" Siobhan asked.

"Maybe we're thinking of this the wrong way," Dante said. "Maybe it's a sort of quantum magic."

Elaine nodded. "A type of teleportation where you break down a body and reform it somewhere else?"

"No less complicated," Dante said. "But it would explain things, like how the kids vanished, but this hair is still around."

"Scotty missed the hair when he beamed them up, yeah?" Siobhan asked.

"So," Dante said, "somewhere out there is a kid wielding Taleth-Sidhe–level power, fighting off snatchers and then stealing the kids away herself?"

"Maybe she's taking them to safety," Elaine said.

"It's a theory," Dante said. "Wish we had more, but it's a start."

Siobhan leaned back into her chair and ran a hand through her hair. "Fair play there," she said to Elaine. "That beats the news he's got for you."

Dante went back to the bar and made himself another martini.

"Well, despite my fear of being disappointed," Elaine said. "I have to ask—"

"The trails are closed," Dante said as he finished making his drink.

"What?" Elaine laughed. "No, really, what is it?"

Dante walked back to the table and sat down. He took a sip and just looked at her.

"You're serious?" Elaine's smile vanished. "Holy—"

"Aye, that was about my thoughts on it as well," Siobhan said.

"But," Elaine said, "the trails have only ever been closed . . ."

"Yeah," Dante said.

"But that's impossible, right?" Elaine asked. "I mean, wouldn't we, all of us, know about it if Seanán was back?" Her eyes went to the hair. "*Mon Dieu.*"

Dante studied them each in turn. "I need you to swear an oath of secrecy," he said at last. "Both of you."

"What—" Elaine started to ask.

"Thrice promised," Dante said to her. Then he turned to Siobhan. "Bound by your honor never to speak of what I tell you to another being unless I release you to do so. That includes the Fionn."

"*Dar fia*, man, do you know what you're asking of me?" Siobhan said.

"I'm in," Elaine said. She drew a small knife of greenish metal from her pocket, dragged the blade over her palm, and let a drop of blood fall onto the table. "By my blood and all I am, I promise that I shall never reveal, through any means, any of what you tell me." She let a second drop join the first. "I swear to you, by the power of my blood and magic, I'll keep whatever you reveal through pain or death." A third drop joined the other two. "I give you to my solemn oath, never to share the secrets you impart to me, in any means or method, come pain, death, or geas."

At her final word, the three droplets drew tight and solidified into a dark ruby.

Dante withdrew a small wooden box inlaid with complex knot work from an inside jacket pocket, then set the stone inside and nodded. Elaine's eyes were fierce.

After half a heartbeat, he turned to Siobhan. "I need you to swear, or leave. This is beyond Cruinnigh business, and not open for discussion."

They looked at each other for a long while, and he could see the hesitation in her eyes. You aren't half the warrior he was, Dante thought. Brendan wouldn't have let me finish my sentence before promising.

"Aye," Siobhan said and nodded. She drew her own knife—nearly ten inches long—from behind her back and cut a lock of her long hair from her ponytail. Then she looked at Elaine. "Cover your ears, this part ain't for you to hear."

Elaine turned away and did as she was asked.

Siobhan offered Dante the hair. "I, Siobhan Aoife O'Riordan, do swear onto you by my honor and all I am, to keep your secret, through pain, death or worse, so help me."

Dante accepted the hair, added it to the box, and then closed it before returning it to his jacket. He knew it was customary to burn the hair when the oath was made, as a sign of mutual trust, but he just didn't have it in him to trust the Fianna again, not yet. Siobhan must have picked up on it, because she didn't protest.

"It's done," he said and tapped Elaine's shoulder.

Elaine looked at Siobhan, and then both women turned to Dante.

"You've both heard about Fiona Brady?" Dante asked.

They nodded.

"The wizard who helped me bring down the oíche is her soon to be stepfather. He has the most extensive library I've ever seen outside of the Acadamh. I sent him to research what could be behind the kidnappings, the murders, and the sudden explosion of wizards."

"What did he find, then?" Siobhan asked.

"Nothing definite. But this library has some specific eccentricities, and he kept coming across the same phrase: Taleth-Sidhe."

"But it's done," Elaine said. "That battle was won. The dark magi were defeated."

Siobhan nodded. "Aye, not a pretty ending to be sure, but it's done all the same."

Dante let out a breath. "I know. But that doesn't change what's happening around us. We're seeing evidence of magic that is beyond what the next hundred most powerful mortal wizards can manage working together. I'm seeing changelings coming into the powers several years before they should." He pointed at the glass tube holding the hair. "And there's that."

Elaine nodded. "Then there's the mortal wizards sprouting up like weeds, and always street kids."

"This goes well past just chance," Dante said. "I'm not certain, but neither am I foolish enough to completely dismiss this. There are just too many things that point that way. The closing of the trails is just the latest."

"I still don't understand how we couldn't have known," Elaine said. "Why we didn't sense it."

"I don't know," Dante said. That drew nervous

glances from both women. "But now you're both in this up to your chins. It wouldn't be right for me to keep you involved and not be forthcoming."

Elaine swallowed. "You do realize if the trails are closed, that means that in all likelihood, so are the gateways to the Tír."

"Bloody hell," Siobhan said. "This is a serious mess here. I have to get word to—"

Dante glared at her.

"Apologies," Siobhan said. "Me mouth went off without consulting me brain."

"So what do we do?" Elaine asked.

"Dig in," Dante said. "We open the doors and give shelter to any and all who need it: mortal, fae, changeling, everyone."

"If you're right, shouldn't we get word to the other Cruinnigh members?" Siobhan asked. "And before you say it, I'm not just talking about the Fianna."

"I think they know," Dante said. "I can't be sure, but I think this is being done by the remnants of the dark magi we thought Seanán wiped out. They're calling themselves something different now, but if they're serving the same master, it could explain the Taleth-Sidhe connection."

"Like fecking cockroaches, they are," Siobhan said.

"I think that's an insult to roaches," Dante said. "But if this is them, this is a group that just knowing about is dangerous, let alone actually speaking of. Besides, and I don't like it, but I don't have the resources to spare even a courier."

"So we bar the doors and hope tonight is quiet?" Elaine asked.

Dante gave her a look. "Don't think it's a choice I make lightly, but there's little the three of us can do tonight."

"You're right," Elaine said. "But it sucks."

"Agreed," Dante said. "Tomorrow, we'll go to the market. We'll see if the troll knows anything, and you can start spreading the word to the factions. It's time for them to end their rivalries and come in, get behind some serious walls. I have wardens coming, but they're a day away at best, maybe two."

Elaine let out a breath. "I don't think—"

"I'm going to take them with me when I go," Dante said. "I'm not looking to occupy the city. I'm just tired of children going missing."

Elaine eyed him.

"I'm not some corrupt politician looking to become dictator, and I'm not Donovan."

Elaine didn't say anything, but it felt like she was looking through him. Dante wondered what ghosts were hidden behind those eyes.

After a long moment, she nodded. "Fair enough, if you say I have your word."

"You do," Dante said.

"Well, I'm bloody well with you, ain't I?" Siobhan said.

"We'll hole up here tonight and start in the morning," Dante said. "Get some rest if you can."

"After I say a few prayers for the little ones," Siobhan said.

Dante almost considered burning the hair she'd given him. Almost. He opened his mouth to say something, but his phone rang. He glanced at the screen, then stood and stepped away from the table before answering.

"That was quick, even for you, Faolan, what have you got?"

"Another complication," Faolan said.

"May I please speak to him?" Dante heard Caitlin ask.

Dante closed his eyes and took a long breath. "Give her the phone."

"So, I'm guessing you don't know about the strange guys who've been watching Eddy, Fiona, and me?"

"What?" Dante asked, almost dropping the phone.

"Let me explain," Edward said, his voice distant, as if from behind Caitlin.

"Hold on," Caitlin said.

"Can you hear me?" Edward asked.

"I can."

"We put you on speaker, seemed easier."

"What do you mean you're being watched?" Dante asked.

"I've been adding wards and magical trip wires around the house," Edward said. "It's been good practice for me, and seemed like a good idea, all things considered. About a week ago, someone set them off. I set it up so any one who isn't a neighbor picks up a little tag every time they drive by."

Dante raised his eyebrows. "That's rather brilliant actually."

"Thanks," Edward said. "Anyway, I started getting lots of hits. Half a dozen people were showing up with dozens of tags on them. Now it's hundreds of tags. Much more than they'd get from just commuting to work this way."

"Faolan," Dante said. "Please tell me you didn't know about this. And then tell me how you didn't know about this."

"You were otherwise occupied," Faolan said. "So I detailed more marshals around the area to keep an eye on things."

"What do you mean, *more* marshals?" Edward asked.

Dante opened his mouth.

"Let me guess," Caitlin said. "Fiona was given protection."

"Oh," Edward said.

"Am I right?" Caitlin asked.

"Yes," Dante said.

"Thank you," Caitlin said and then added wryly, "and you still should've told us."

Dante could only smile. "Well, I knew you'd figure it out."

"Uh, huh," Caitlin said. "So what now?"

"We'll find out what's going on," Dante said.

"Yes, we will," Faolan said.

"Good enough," Caitlin said. "Eddy has something to tell you."

There was the sound of the phone being picked up and the speakerphone being turned off, but Dante could hear footsteps fade away.

"She saw me working," Edward said. "And I told you I wouldn't lie to her."

"I told you I wouldn't ask you to," Dante said. "But why didn't you tell me about being watched?"

"I told Faolan and he said he'd handle it," Edward said, his words unsure. "I'm sorry, should I have told you too?"

Dante scrunched up his face and shook his head. "No, Faolan can, and should, handle it." He reminded himself he wasn't magister anymore.

"Okay, so what I wanted to tell you," Edward said. "I came across something else, and thought it might be important. I keep seeing mentions of 'The Forgotten Order.'"

Dante's stomach twisted into knot and he mouthed a few choice expletives.

"I have no idea who it is," Edward said. "I can't find anything that explains who, or what it is. The really odd part is the way the term is used. I could be mistranslating it, but it doesn't sound like it's so much a proper name or title as an instruction. Like they should be forgotten."

Dante let out a silent sigh of relief. He was thankful he'd convinced Edward's grandfather not to keep any written details. It was worth the eight-hundred-plus years of grumbling Morgan had done after reluctantly agreeing.

"But it keeps coming up and I thought you should know," Edward said.

"Thanks, that helps. I have to go."

"Oh, sure, no problem. Let me know if you need anything—"

Dante ended the call, and put his phone in his pocket, face grim.

"Another complication?" Elaine asked.

"And then some," Dante said. "It's a sort of confirmation."

CHAPTER EIGHTEEN

Wraith stood in the middle of a ruined gothic church. Around her lay battered pews, tossed like some giant kid's Lincoln Logs set after a particularly nasty tantrum. She turned slowly, taking in the place. Not one stained glass window was intact, and huge sections of the roof were missing, allowing her to see the storm raging outside. Lightning flashed over a leaden sky, but even those bursts of light couldn't penetrate the gloom of this place. It was cold, dark, and incredibly familiar. The wind that howled through the holes sounded like the cries and moans of countless tortured souls.

Wraith saw movement in the shadows past the pulpit and altar. No, it was the shadows that were moving, and the whole building seemed to lurch as if they were chained to it. Wraith stumbled and took an unconscious step back, but paused when she heard voices. They were familiar but hard to make out over the wind. She crept forward until she could see Shadow and Nightstick facing each other in front of the altar.

"You know what my purpose is," Nightstick said in a low, harsh tone.

Shadow motioned to the churning darkness that filled the far reaches of the church. "It keeps getting out. We're doing our best to stop it, but it's getting stronger. It's almost like it has a mind of its own."

Wraith stared, dumbstruck.

Nightstick clenched his fists, then kicked a pew. "I can control it!"

"Really?" Shadow asked. "Because from where I'm standing—"

"Don't lecture me, little girl. I've allowed you and the others to leave—"

"You've *allowed* us?" Shadow asked.

"That's right," Nightstick said. "You wander because of my largess, and it's a gift that can be taken away."

"Just try and see what happens," Shadow said.

"Don't tempt me."

Anger began to stir inside Wraith.

As if in response, the roiling shadows seemed to grow more frenetic and the wind outside responded in kind.

"Don't forget that I'm not alone," Shadow said.

Wraith felt a pervasive sensation of being watched. She glanced around nervously, and that's when she noticed the carved angels all around her. Every one of them was staring at her.

"You think the lot of you can stand against me?" Nightstick asked.

"If need be," Shadow said. "You're just the steward of power, a caretaker. And you know, she'll never let you—"

"She has what I allow her to have," he said. "And this is my domain, not hers. She doesn't want to know. Or have you forgotten as well?"

"You're wrong," Shadow said. "Maybe she didn't, but she does now. You're just afraid of what that means for you."

"I'm afraid of nothing!" he bellowed and raised a hand. "I hold power beyond imagining!"

"Leave her alone!" Wraith shouted and rushed forward.

Both figures turned to her and stared. Nightstick's face was the usual mask of shadow, but Wraith could sense the surprise on his face.

Wraith stepped in front of Shadow and glared at Nightstick. "Don't you touch her."

Nightstick looked between the two girls. "You brought her here?"

"No," Shadow said, shaking her head. "I don't know how—"

"No one likes trespassers," Nightstick said, turning his attention back to Wraith.

"Interesting way to word it," Shadow said.

"I'm just the steward, right? A guard dog," Nightstick said. "Any issues with the arrangements need to be taken up with management."

"What the hell are you talking about?" Wraith asked.

She couldn't say how, but Wraith knew Nightstick smiled. "Unfortunately, management isn't available just now."

Something about his voice and the way it echoed here made Wraith more than a little uneasy, but she didn't move. Nightstick stepped forward. Wraith took a step back and felt Shadow behind her. Somehow knowing her friend was there pushed back at the fear.

"I won't let you take her," Wraith said. "I won't let you hurt her, not again."

Nightstick froze in place. "What? No—"

Formulations appeared in the air around Wraith and she drew them to her. More calculations began flowing down from the carved angels around her, and without looking, Wraith knew they had followed her movements and were watching her still.

"No," Nightstick said looking around. "You're confused, I'm not—"

As her rage began to build, the shadows churned and began whispering in a thousand voices.

"It's going to get loose again!" Shadow said.

"Get out! Get her out of here!" Nightstick shouted, then turned to the shadows, lifting his shillelagh. "That's enough from you!"

"Time to go, Stretch," Shadow said and pulled at Wraith's shoulder.

Wraith had taken half a dozen steps before she'd even realized she was moving.

Nightstick swung his shillelagh at the darkness, shouting curses. It recoiled from the blows and retreated.

"What is this place?" Wraith said, turning to her friend.

Shadow looked at her with sad eyes, ageless wisdom in those dark pools. "You know it, but you've forgotten."

"What does that mean?"

The building shook around them and the crucifix that hung above the altar fell with a crash.

"Soon," Shadow said and cupped Wraith's face in her hands.

Wraith wanted to ask more, but Shadow kissed her forehead and everything went away.

Wraith opened her eyes. She was back in the safe house, lying in bed, her bed. Toto lay next to her, still and sleeping but warm against her side. She didn't move, just stared at the ceiling, following the lines in the wooden beams, and she knew she'd done this countless times before. She also knew that she'd done it while feeling this same sense of loss weighing on her heart.

But it had been just a dream. Hadn't it?

She turned her head and saw Ovation, Geek, Con, and Sprout were asleep on the other beds, away from her. That was why the beds had been arrange this way, so she could look over her friends as they rested, even if these were different friends.

She closed her eyes and drew in a deep breath, taking in all the familiar scents, letting them wrap around her like a soft blanket. She went back to the dream, or not-dream, and tried to figure out what it all meant. After a few minutes she let it go, tiring of chasing her proverbial tail. Instead, she decided on a course of action.

She moved carefully, but Toto woke immediately.

"Shh," she said.

When he cocked his head, she leaned in close.

"I'm going without them, boy," she said. "They have their own fight, and this one is mine." She looked around. "They'll be safe here, no one can get in. Besides, it's me they're after."

Toto looked at her for a long moment, then he rose and stretched.

"No, boy," she said and glanced at Sprout. "You stay here and watch over them for me."

Toto whimpered a little and buried his face into Wraith's neck.

"I want you to come too, buddy," she said, hugging the big dog. "But I need you here to keep Sprout from getting scared. I promise I'll come back as soon as I can."

Toto looked at her then licked her face a few times.

She hugged the dog again, petting him as she did. "Thanks, boy."

Toto gave her a doggy grin, then he went and settled back on the bed, facing the sleeping quartet.

Wraith got to her feet and gathered her belongings, including the gauntlet and goggles, careful not to make a sound. As she stepped around the room, she instinctively knew which boards creaked and avoided them. When she was ready, she stepped to the door, set the goggles on top of her head, then slipped on the glove and ran her fingers over the doorframe. It was a slow process, gently unweaving the seemingly infinite threads that locked this door, and perhaps every other door as well.

When it was done, she wrapped the door in another calculation and opened it. On the other side she could see a neighborhood just waking up. Before stepping through, she glanced back at her friends. They were her friends, weren't they? She looked at her bed, where Toto was watching her. She realized she didn't remember going to it after locking the door, so someone had put her to bed.

"Thank you," she whispered.

Steeling her will, she drew a breath, and stepped through the door. She closed it slowly and softly, then pulled the equation from it. She couldn't risk them following her, so she let the door close. She'd come back as soon as she could, probably before they even woke. Then she'd find someplace for them.

CHAPTER NINETEEN

"Trust me," Elaine said into her phone from the passenger seat. "This is a legit offer." She shook her head. "No, Donovan's gone. In fact, his club is sanctuary central." She smiled and nodded at Dante. "Good, I'll see you there later. Tell everyone, and I mean everyone."

Dante made a turn, then cast a glance back at Siobhan in the rearview mirror. The Fian was scanning the area, her right index finger tapping the handle of her gun.

"Park up here," Elaine said and gestured.

Dante found a spot and pulled in, then turned to Elaine. "So what's the word?"

She smiled. "No one heard about any snatchings last night," Elaine said. "And the word is being spread to come in."

"I can see how much they mean to you," Dante said. "We'll do all we can to keep them safe."

Elaine looked at him for a long moment, then

frowned a little. "I really misjudged you," she said. "I'm sorry."

Siobhan sighed then slid out of the car, muttering in Irish.

"That legendary Fian patience," Elaine said.

The three of them walked up the hill in silence, past the houses just beginning to stir on a quiet Sunday morning. Dante led the way, grateful the street was lined with, and well covered by, trees. He and Elaine might have the benefit of glamour to blend in, but Siobhan was anything but inconspicuous. Dante inhaled deeply as they walked. The faint scent of brewing coffee poured from most of the houses, and he smiled.

Dante focused on the overpass ahead, or rather the spot beneath it. He'd heard stories of the Freemont Troll. Mortals thought it a curious piece of art, but the fae delighted in the fact that one of their own was able to hide in plain sight. When Dante finally caught a glimpse of the troll, he stopped and stared. He hadn't been expecting it to be such an old troll, or to have grown so large. It appeared to mortal eyes as a large monstrosity of concrete, buried to his waist, one massive hand resting over a VW Beetle. If he were to rise from the ground, he'd be near forty feet tall. The sculpture only had one visible eye, but the actual troll had two. Aside from that, there was no glamour to him.

"Bloody hell," Siobhan said as she came up behind Dante.

"Hey, Freemont," Elaine said and waved as she stepped past both Dante and Siobhan.

The troll turned his massive head and his exaggerated frown eased, becoming a gentle smile. "Hello, Elaine," he said, his voice low and rumbling. It would be easy to confuse his speech for especially heavy road noise from the overpass. "I haven't seen you in quite a while."

"Sorry about that," Elaine said as she stood in front of the huge troll.

Dante and Siobhan exchanged a glance, a silent agreement not to be shown up, and then both joined Elaine.

"I've brought some, um, friends," Elaine said.

"Oh, I like new faces," Freemont said. "I see so many, but I always like to see more."

"This is Siobhan, of the Fianna," Elaine said.

"Been a long time since I've seen a Fian," Freemont said. "Pleasure to meet you, Lady Siobhan."

Siobhan swallowed as she eyed the massive hands. After less than a second, she bowed. "Aye, and you. May I call you Freemont?"

"Of course," Freemont said. Then he smiled more and chuckled, a low rumbling sound not entirely unlike a rock slide. "I don't remember the Fianna being so polite in my youth."

"On behalf of my clan," Siobhan said, "I do apologize and hope you'll find us fairer company now."

Dante arched an eyebrow.

Siobhan didn't look at him, but she did smile, just a little.

Freemont smiled more. "So I do."

Elaine gestured to Dante, and he stepped forward. "And this is—"

"Oh, I know who you are, Regent," Freemont said and bowed, lower than Dante would've thought possible for being half buried.

Dante bowed in reply. "I'm impressed, Freemont. You honor me."

"No less than you deserve," Freemont said. "I might not wander like I once did, but I still listen when something is worth hearing, and I've heard much of you through the years."

"I know leprechauns who'd envy that kind of information flow," Dante said.

Freemont laughed again. "As do I, though truth be told, I hear more than a little from them."

"That's actually what brings us here," Dante said. "Not leprechauns, but—"

"The missing changelings," Freemont said.

Dante nodded.

Freemont's infectious smile faded back to a heavy frown. "Sad business, that is."

"I'm here to see if I can stop it," Dante said. "If there's anything you can tell me to help, I'd be in your debt." Dante felt Elaine and Siobhan both look at him.

"I have no need of debts or favors anymore, Regent," Freemont said. "I live for the magic in the laughter and smiles of children. The joy of mortal lovers stealing kisses when they think no one is looking."

"Then help me," Dante said.

Freemont sighed. "It's an old evil that gathers these

children. An evil best forgotten and not spoken of, but I think you know this."

"I do."

"I know little else, except to say that shadows are not always to be feared," Freemont said. "Sometimes there is safety in the shadows. Not all who come are there to steal, some are to save."

Dante looked from Elaine to Siobhan and back, but they both just shrugged.

"I've seen the true evil," Freemont said. "Weeks ago four changeling children came to me, desperate for my protection." Freemont's face turned hard. "I gave it, destroying two who'd come to take what was not theirs. Now that darkness stays well away from here and many more children find safety instead."

"On behalf of the court and the Cruinnigh, I thank you," Dante said. "Though I know you don't need or want thanks, I offer it all the same."

Freemont gestured with his massive hand for Dante to come closer.

Dante did, well aware that hand could swallow him whole, leaving nothing visible beyond its stony grasp.

"I tell you true," Freemont said in a low whisper. "Your fears are founded, but incomplete. There are more players at this game than you're aware."

"What do you mean?" Dante asked.

"The mortals have learned that we and our world, the world they thought existed only stories and legends, is real. They have found power once more, hoping to regain past glories, I think," Freemont said. "Though as ever, their actions are cloaked in magnanimity."

The sound of laughter brought Dante's next question up short. He turned, but the source of the laughter was still out of sight. When he looked back at Freemont, the troll had resumed his long-held pose. A moment later, a small mob of laughing children, the oldest perhaps nine, came running up and began climbing on Freemont. A group of adults stepped past Dante, not noticing him, but giving Siobhan a wide berth, and began taking pictures of the children.

Dante saw the corners of Freemont's mouth turn up into a small smile, and Dante smiled too before turning to Elaine and Siobhan and gesturing for them to go.

"Any idea what any of that meant?" Siobhan asked when they were well away.

"I'm not sure," Dante said. "He confirmed who was responsible, though I'm still unsure as to the motives. The short-term motives, I mean."

"What do you suppose he meant about the mortals learning of us?" Elaine asked. "The Fianna are mortal, and they're involved in fae matters."

Dante glanced at Siobhan. "But they're not mortal, technically speaking."

"We ain't bleeding immortals," Siobhan said.

"No," Dante agreed. "But neither are you mundane, and I think that's what he meant. I'm more interested that he mentioned saving four changeling children from being kidnapped."

"What's our next move, then?" Siobhan asked.

"We need to find those kids," Dante said.

"The market," Elaine said. "It's where they're most likely to be. Although we may have trouble finding them. I doubt they're advertising that they escaped."

"I noticed Freemont didn't mention any names," Dante said.

"Even so," Elaine said. "It'll be good for you get out there, let them see your face and show them things really have changed, that someone does care and is offering to protect them."

"A goodwill mission, then?" Siobhan asked.

"Don't get carried away," Elaine said. "Most of them still won't trust you, and I'm sure I've lost some credibility by helping you. I'll accept that if it saves lives, but it will still sound better coming from me than you."

"Lead the way," Dante said. "And I'll try to hang back so the kids still think you're cool."

Elaine rolled her eyes and started walking.

Siobhan didn't succeed in containing a chuckle, but she didn't really try either.

CHAPTER TWENTY

In typical Seattle fashion, the gray skies gave way to a drizzle. Wraith pulled up her hood and continued to stare. Despite the early hour, the market was filling with people. She pulled her oversized jacket tight around her, pushed the goggles down over her eyes, and stepped into the chaos. Her stomach rumbled at the scents wafting from the food vendors: coffee, bacon, crepes, and waffles. Hood pulled low, she kept walking, scanning the booths for an old man selling charms, and hoping there really was a wizard. People avoided her, most doing so unconsciously. She knew they weren't bad people; they just didn't like being reminded of how hard life could be. But that didn't make her feel any better.

It seemed that everything was available for sale. There were vendors selling furniture, clothes, jewelry, books, music, crafts of all kinds, and bicycles. It wasn't long before Wraith saw not everyone was ignoring her. In fact, several people were staring at her so hard she could feel it without even looking. A quick glance showed her fifties of all kinds. Most were buskers— kids playing music, singing, juggling, or the like, for money. A few were selling various pieces of detritus from the "normal" world that had been refashioned into art, jewelry, or the like. Wraith kept moving but scanned the items, some of which had traces of magic drifting off of them.

Halfway down the tent-lined street, Wraith spotted two large, gruff-looking fae talking with some street kids. One fae handed the kids a piece of paper with what might have been an address written on it. When one of the kids glanced her way, she turned her head and kept moving.

"You there," another of the big fae said to her in a thick Russian accent.

Wraith pretended she didn't hear him.

"Do you know that one?" the Russian fae asked someone.

"Nah, never seen her before," said one of the teen boys.

Wraith could feel the dismissal in his words, but knew he was watching her. She kept searching for the wizard. Of course, she'd be having an easier time if she'd brought Ovation and the others along, but she couldn't. Guilt ate at her, and she briefly considered going back to check on them, but she reminded herself that Toto would look after them.

"I'll have your answer now," one of the big, gruff fae said.

"Beat it, Ivan," the boy said. "I told you where you could stick your sanctuary."

"*Da*," the big fae said. "It's your ass. *Kher s nim*."

Wraith just moved away quickly, head down, not wanting to be around if a fight broke out. The market stretched on, more of the same. Then she spotted three people who might as well have been wearing signs that said "cops." A short, blocky man with a balding head and a woman in her thirties with a severe blond ponytail were shooing people away as a lean man in his fifties, apparently the boss, talked to a group of street kids.

"We're here to help," he said.

The kids laughed. "Of course you are, man," one of them said.

"We're trying to catch the people who've been taking your friends," the cop said in a frosty tone.

"You know about anyone getting taken, Dash?" a dark-haired boy near Wraith's age asked a thin blond teen.

"Nah, I don't know anything about that."

Wraith moved past them, making sure to keep plenty of people around her, and trying desperately to blend into the background. No one said anything, but she could feel eyes watching her. When she was well away, she ducked behind a stall and looked back. A faint stream of equations drifted around the woman. It was complex, and despite how meager it appeared, Wraith knew there was power behind it. The woman wasn't just a mundane with some latent talent, she was skilled enough to hide what she had.

"You've forgotten your way," someone said.

Wraith nearly jumped out of her skin.

"I can see it," the voice said. From the sound of it, he was really old. "It's a terrible thing to walk alone down a dark path for which the maps have been forgotten and lost. Makes you feel rather forgotten and lost as well, yes?"

Wraith turned and looked at the speaker. A man with a lined, weather-worn face sat behind a table. If his shabby clothes and beard were any clue, he was homeless.

Wraith's eyes widened and her jaw fell open. The glow of magic from the items on his table was an intense, shifting spectrum. It was like a two-million-candle-power spotlight compared to the dim glow of the minor charms and miscellany the fifties, slingers, and even some of the fae were selling. When she looked back at the man, his smile—despite missing some teeth—was gentle and patient. Magic poured off of him too, but it was kept close, as if carefully controlled. She couldn't help it, she envied that kind of control.

"Are you the wizard?" Wraith asked, barely above a whisper. It didn't matter, as soon as she said the words, she felt like an idiot.

"That's what the kids call me," the old man said. "Of course in my day, they called us mages, or magi." He gazed off, as if back in time. "I always liked that term, mage."

Wraith watched in rapt fascination as a seemingly endless formulation circled around him. It wasn't overly complicated—quite the opposite, in fact. It was elegant in its simplicity.

"But there I go, rambling again," the old man said.

The shift in the equations around him was so abrupt, Wraith flinched.

It was almost like she'd seen him in his underwear and he'd pulled a robe around himself at noticing. "I'm sorry, I didn't mean to . . ." She looked away, pushing the goggles up on her head.

"Lots of people have eyes, but not many really see," he said.

"No, they don't."

The old man leaned forward and looked around before focusing his gaze on Wraith.

Wraith leaned forward.

"It's because they don't want to," he said.

Wraith swallowed at the intensity of his gaze.

"And they're smart," he said.

"What?" Wraith asked, the uncomfortable feeling vanishing.

"Do you want to see the train coming at you if there's no time to jump out of the way?"

Wraith eyed the old man, noticing for the first time that one of his eyes was blue and the other brown. The corner of his mouth turned up and she knew there was more to his question than the obvious.

"Yes," she said, "I would."

The old man narrowed his eyes. "Why?"

Wraith shrugged. "Because I'm tired of being willfully ignorant."

"Despite the cost?"

"Ignorance isn't free either; it costs more," she said. "It just doesn't cost all at once."

The old man smiled, but it was sad. "You have far too much wisdom for one so young. Wisdom like that doesn't come easy."

Wraith let out a breath. "I wouldn't know."

He reached into a bag at his feet and came out with an odd clockwork device. He held it out in his hand and Wraith looked it over. It looked like a gyroscope inside rings of copper sitting on four spindly legs. A single needle pointed down from the base of the gyro at his hand. There were various cogs and springs around the copper rings that might power it.

"What is that?" Wraith asked, her hand reaching out to touch it.

"It's a drill," the old man said.

Wraith snatched her hand back and looked at him. "A what?"

"A drill," he said. "When things are forgotten, sometimes you have to dig deep."

Wraith swallowed, but managed not to turn and run.

The old man just stared at her. "Choo-choo, girl."

Wraith glanced at the old man's mismatched eyes, then back to the drill. "How much? I don't have—"

"I'll sell it for a song," he said.

Wraith blinked. "A song?"

He nodded.

"What song?"

"Your mother's favorite song," he said.

Wraith's stomach twisted and she pushed her hands into her pocket. "I don't know what her favorite song was."

"You will," he said. "When you remember, you can give it to me."

Wraith looked from the old man's wrinkled face to the drill, still held out for her, and back. "You're crazy."

"Look around, girl," he said.

When he didn't continue, she did. No one was paying them the least bit of attention, not even the fifties and slingers. People were just going about their day, not seeing her or the old man.

"I'd be crazy to be sane," he said and laughed.

Wraith turned back to him. "Deal."

The old man held the drill up. "On your word. For a song."

Wraith took the drill gingerly, making sure to keep the needle away from her skin. "On my word."

"Pleasure doing business with you," he said and smiled as if he'd just sold her a used car.

Wraith looked at the drill, holding it at almost arm's length. "How do I use it?"

"Wind the dial, set it in your palm, then hold on," he said.

It wasn't the words but the tone that sent a shiver down Wraith's spine.

"Just remember, Dorothy, Kansas might not be like you remember," he said.

She gave him a questioning look, but he just chuckled and adjusted himself on the upturned bucket that served as his seat. He resumed staring into space as if she wasn't there.

Wraith turned to leave, opening her bag to put the drill away. A hand grabbed her shoulder and spun her around. The drill fell to the ground.

"What faction are you with?" a tough-looking boy asked her.

Wraith jerked away from him, causing the goggles to fall down over her eyes.

"What's this?" the boy asked and picked up the drill.

"It's mine," Wraith said.

"Are you sure?" he asked.

Wraith stared at him through the colored lenses of her goggles. She could see the ripples of magic that flowed over him, hiding his true appearance. To her, though, he sported a long goatee, frizzy hair, and a pair of small horns on his forehead.

"Give it back," Wraith said, her voice barely above a whisper. She slipped her hand inside her bag and into the glove.

"And what if I don't?" the boy asked. "I'm a Ghost and we control this section of town. Do you know what that means?"

"No, and I don't care," Wraith said. "Give it back."

"It means you pay us a toll, slinger," the boy said, the last word coming out like a curse. "And this will cover enough for you to get the hell out of here." He pushed her shoulder and she stumbled back a step before catching herself.

Something snapped inside her. Wraith drew her gloved hand out of the bag and, with barely a thought, an equation formed in her hand.

"BANG!" she yelled.

The fifty was hit in the chest by an invisible wrecking ball and went flying through a stall across the street, then bounced off the chain link fence several feet behind the stall.

"Fitch!" a girl screamed.

"Don't touch me," Wraith said through clenched teeth.

Everything went completely still and quiet for a long second. The only sound was Wraith's heart as she looked down the long street lined with shoppers and sellers, none of them moving, all of them staring. Then the whispers and murmurs began.

Several mundanes had phones out and were recording. Wraith clenched shaking fists, and that's when she saw the drill. It was floating in midair right where the boy, Fitch, had been holding it.

"It's some kind of publicity thing, I bet," someone said.

"It looks so real!" someone else said.

Wraith looked around at the growing mass of people. Her head swam and she wobbled on her feet as a cold and vile fear rose up inside her. Power poured into her, feeding the fear and her vision began to grow dark. Then the fear fled from her, taking the power with it. Wraith shook her head, then snatched the drill from the air and stuck it in her bag. As she latched it shut, she heard a bloodcurdling scream. People started running in all directions, shoving each other aside and even trampling stalls in their desperate attempt to flee. But still, no one even brushed against her. They parted around her like a boulder in a stream. She craned her neck trying to see, but it turned out she needn't have bothered.

Visible above the crowd were a dozen snatchers making their way up through the market. They were roughly humanoid shape, a wispy, living darkness. As they moved, the shadows seemed to cling to them. Her stomach dropped and her blood ran cold.

"No," Wraith whispered. "This is wrong."

Someone touched her shoulder. "We've got to go, Stretch, right now."

Wraith spun, gloved hand lifted and ready to un-leash—

Her mouth fell open and her eyes went wide.

Shadow stared back at her, and it really was Shadow, but she looked so tired. Her skin was pale, and her eyes were sunken.

"No," Wraith said. "You were taken. I was coming to find you."

"I can explain, later," Shadow said. "We have to go."

"*Ferrousan!*" a familiar voice shouted.

Wraith turned. SK and Fritz were holding back the snatchers while everyone else ran. SK was using well-placed gravity to hurl items—ranging from chairs to cement Jersey barriers—at the snatchers. Fritz reached into her jacket and drew a pistol with a giant vacuum tube where the barrel should be. Countless arcs of electricity danced inside the glass tube as she took aim and fired. A bright flash of lightning leapt forth and hit one of the snatchers, sending it convulsing to the ground.

Wraith turned back to Shadow. "No! I saw the coins! This isn't right!"

"Wraith, please—" Shadow reached out to touch Wraith's shoulder.

She recoiled. "Don't touch me!"

The world twisted and spun around her. Everywhere she looked, Wraith saw nothing but lies. The fae and fifties, the mundanes, even the snatchers! It was all lies, and she could see them, the twisting equation that surrounded them all. She looked at Shadow, and she saw it there too.

"No more lies," she whispered as she felt power rush into her.

Shadow lifted her hands. "No, don't—"

Wraith reached out with the gloved hand, seizing the quantum thread that ran through the false world.

"NO. MORE. LIES!" she yelled, and tore it all away.

CHAPTER TWENTY-ONE

Dante stopped a hundred feet short of the market's entrance.

"What is it, then?" Siobhan asked.

"There are a lot of people here," Dante said. "Keep that sawed-off cannon out of view."

"And here I was planning on using it to point out attractions," Siobhan said.

"He's asking you to button your coat," Elaine said.

"And what will I do when trouble breaks out?" Siobhan asked them both.

"I don't intend for any trouble—" Dante words were cut off by a shout.

A mass of people were making a hasty exit from the market, but more were converging around something further in.

Dante looked at Siobhan, who just shrugged and smiled.

"Come on," Dante said and walked quickly into the market.

It didn't take long before the press of people made progress impossible.

"Damn," Elaine said and ducked behind some spectators.

Dante looked at her, eyes narrowed.

Elaine nodded behind him.

"Out of the way, please. FBI," someone said with authority.

Dante turned with everyone else as a stern man in his fifties flashed credentials and the crowd opened a path for him. He was followed by two others, one looked like a bald human fire hydrant, the other was a striking woman. Something about her didn't feel right.

"I ran into them earlier," Elaine said when the agents vanished into the throng.

"That's fecking perfect," Siobhan said. "Bleeding feds, just what we need."

A cold shiver ran down Dante's spine, then he felt a surge of power, like the pull of the ocean as a big wave approaches in the distance.

"That's a lot of magic," Elaine said, looking from Dante to Siobhan.

"And I think I know who," Dante said, trying to see.

Siobhan reached into her coat and gripped her shotgun. "I could clear this place out pretty quick," she said.

"I'm sure the FBI agents would like to have a word with you if you did," Dante said. "Something is about to happen, something—"

Twelve nightmarish creatures, formed of nothing but darkness, appeared from nowhere. They were tall, almost two feet taller than Dante and three times his width. Their shadowy forms swirled around them like robes, and they reached out with ghostly hands.

"The snatchers," Elaine whispered, disbelief heavy in her voice.

For a moment, time froze.

Then it was bedlam.

People screamed and stampeded out of the market, trampling stalls and other people with equal abandon. Dante grabbed Siobhan and Elaine, tossing them against the wall and out of the path. He leapt after them, barely avoiding the panicked rush. In moments, the previously packed market was empty enough to allow them to move.

Dante pointed at the people who lay on the ground, moaning in pain after being crushed. "Get them out of here!" he shouted to Elaine, then turned to Siobhan. "You're with me."

Siobhan already had her shotgun out.

"How am I supposed—" Elaine started to ask.

"Drag them!" Dante snarled as he drew a pistol.

He and Siobhan moved forward after the snatchers. When he saw one reach for a changeling street kid, he fired twice, aiming high to make sure he didn't hit the kid.

The hits were like splashes on inky water. The snatcher lurched like someone had bumped against it accidently, not like it had been hit with two forty-five-caliber rounds.

"Get off 'im, you *mac mallachta!*" Siobhan shouted and fired.

She was apparently firing slugs. Her shot hit the snatcher on the shoulder and it exploded like a water balloon. The shade started to turn, but Dante and Siobhan fired together. They both came up empty at the same time, but the creature fell to the ground and evaporated into nothing.

"What the bloody hell are those things?" Siobhan asked.

"Conjurings," Dante said, shaking his head. "Powerful ones."

"You don't say?" Siobhan asked as they both reloaded.

At that moment, two changeling kids appeared, quite literally out of thin air, and began fighting the remaining snatchers.

Dante could do nothing but stare for a long moment. One, a boy in his late teens who was clearly of mountain fae parentage, used his earth magic to hurl cement barriers, and anything else he could think of, at the conjured monsters. The other was a diminutive teenage girl, with tinker blood. She wore a belt of tools and drew an odd-looking gun from her jacket. It looked like something out of a Jules Verne steampunk mashup novel. She leveled it and fired bolts of lightning, swearing in German the whole time.

"*Dia ár réiteach,*" Siobhan said softly. "What's going on?"

Dante opened his mouth to answer but was brought up short.

Magic washed over them, like the pressure wave of an explosion. Both he and Siobhan were knocked off their feet and onto their backs, but the snatchers and two changelings vanished like smoke in a strong wind.

Dante's head spun, his mind struggling to put a coherent thought together as he looked around and fought to get to his feet. He saw a girl standing alone in the market. She was young, probably in her midteens, but tall and thin. She wore an oversized hooded jacket, strange goggles, and an even stranger leather gauntlet on her right hand.

Dante looked at Siobhan, who was staring at him with wide eyes and open mouth.

His glamour was gone.

"FBI!" a man shouted.

Dante looked up to see the agents pointing their pistols at the girl.

"Hands where I can see them," the lead agent said. The other two men were on either side, the woman was to the right and just behind.

"Why won't you just leave us all alone?" the girl shouted. "Stop sending your damned snatchers after us!"

"That's not us," the bald agent said. "We're the ones trying to stop the Theurg—"

"*In nomine domine mi*," the woman agent said, then shot her partners in the back of the head.

Dante watched in shock as the three men fell to the ground.

"*Aetate legenda revertetur*," the woman said.

The girl lifted her gloved hand and shouted, "BANG!"

The agent flew back, then tumbled to a stop, not moving.

The girl ran toward Dante.

Siobhan lifted her shotgun and took aim.

"No!" Dante shouted and tackled the Fian.

Her shot went wide, blowing apart an already mangled stall.

The girl glanced at Dante as she ran by. He saw markings over one side of her face, not the magical symbols of the Taleth-Sidhe but complex mathematical formulae. Her eyes were another matter. They were brown and sad, but behind them burned the blue fire of raw magic.

Then she grabbed something around her neck and vanished.

"What the bloody hell are you thinking?" Siobhan asked, shoving Dante away from her. "You let her get away!"

"No," Dante said. "I saved your life. Didn't you see what she did to that agent?"

Siobhan didn't answer; she just got to her feet and offered Dante her hand.

He took it and was pulled roughly to a standing position. He stumbled past the three dead men to their traitorous companion. The woman lay limp but still breathing.

"My glamour is gone!" Elaine shouted as she came

running up. "We have to go, the police are coming and we can't let them see us like this!"

"Too right, that," Siobhan said.

Dante knelt over the unconscious agent and drew a pinch of sand from inside his coat. *"Codail,"* he whispered and sprinkled the sand in her eyes.

"What are you doing with her?" Elaine asked. "Who is she?"

"Someone I hope can answer some questions," Dante said, lifting the lifeless woman and throwing her over his shoulder in a fireman's carry.

"You're putting her under a slumber?" Elaine asked.

Sirens filled the air from several directions.

"We leave now," Siobhan said. "Or some nice fellas in blue with guns are going to be giving us ride."

They ran as fast as they could.

CHAPTER TWENTY-TWO

Everything was madness and the pandemonium reached well past the market. Mundanes were running and screaming or cowering and whimpering, while fae and fifties tried to cover themselves as they fled for some place to hide. Wraith didn't run, she walked through the insanity wrapped in the cloak, an unseen witness to the havoc she'd created. Despite being invisible to the world, no one came near her. It was surreal; people came running at her full speed, but swerved around her without seeming to notice. Sometimes Wraith would see someone pull out a phone to record the mayhem.

"*Kaput*," she would whisper absently, waving her hand toward the device. Then the phones would die. Some sprayed sparks, others caught fire.

Her mind raced and she fought to fit lucid pieces together. That had been Shadow, SK, and Fritz, but how?

She hadn't even really been surprised when they'd vanished, but the snatchers disappearing had caught her off guard. As had the bald man's final words. She'd come to a few conclusions as to why it had happened that way, but she kept returning to one in particular, and it made her stomach twist. And her anger rise.

Police cars, as well as unmarked black SUVs, raced by with lights and sirens going, but she didn't hear anything.

"They tried to warn me," she said to herself. She stopped walking and leaned against the wall as the world spun around her. After several long, slow breaths, everything settled and she opened her eyes.

She turned down an alley toward an old steel door, a door-door; the tumult of the world around her faded further into the background, growing more and more distant.

She focused on the equations, gathering them around her, and grabbed the knob—

Her breath caught and the formulation fell apart as she yanked her hand back.

It was open!

But how?

Her heart began to race and she struggled to put the calculation together again, but her concentration kept slipping. She'd closed it behind her; she knew she had. Her hands started to shake. She didn't even notice when her cloak collapsed around her. Somewhere deep inside, something whispered that the door had been opened from the inside.

She fell to her knees, tears running down her face.

Then it dawned on her and a sense of betrayal chilled her. Her friends, she'd called them her friends. And weren't they? No, it couldn't have been them. None of them could've opened the door. Someone had gotten in and made it look like it was opened from the inside, right? That had to be it.

She'd thought Shadow and the others were her friends, but they'd known all along and kept it from her. Why would friends do that? She sobbed harder, not knowing what to believe anymore. She closed her eyes and drew in one slow breath after another until her sobbing eased, then stopped. It didn't matter. Ovation and his group were trapped in that room because of her. She'd left them there with no way out; her, no one else. Even so, she couldn't shake the feeling that she was being played, and had been for quite a while.

"Okay then," she said through gritted teeth as she got to her feet. "It's time I got into the game."

The equation snapped back into place, then wove into the doorframe with little more than a thought from her. Wraith grabbed the knob and turned it. She had to pull hard, but when the open door-door and physical door aligned, the latter flew open and she stepped through.

Her breath caught and she stopped just inside the room.

The place had been turned upside down, maybe literally. The furniture was reduced to splintered pieces, most with burn marks, a few still smoldering. The workbench lay broken in the corner opposite where it had been; the beds had been tossed against a wall. A hole had been knocked through the bricks, and smoke drifted out from a few small fires that still burned. Wraith lifted her gloved hand, formed a thread formulation, and snapped it like a whip. It tore pieces from the fire's quantum information and they all died.

She swallowed and looked around again. No one was here. She was too late. She noticed roughly fist-sized holes in spots along the wall, and more than a few scorch marks. Geek and Con had put up a fight. She swallowed when she saw the blood. Not pools of it, but spattered on the walls and floors.

Her heart turned to lead and she leaned against the wall to keep from collapsing.

She heard a soft whimper.

Her head snapped up. "Toto?"

Another quiet whimper, muffled. She turned to source of the sound and saw a couple of mattresses lay atop each other and they were moving, barely.

She was there instantly, tossing the beds aside.

Underneath she found Toto, crouched in front of an unconscious Con and Sprout. Con held Sprout in one arm, her face buried in his chest. Wraith could see one of Con's arms was broken and Toto had taken a serious beating.

Wraith extended a shaking hand and touched Sprout's cheek. Relief flooded her when she felt warmth and life. Toto whimpered louder and tried to press his head to Wraith's leg.

"Easy, boy," she said and stroked the dog. "I'm sorry. I shouldn't have left you."

"Not your fault," Con said, eyes still closed and not moving.

Wraith looked at him. His face was bruised and he had scrapes and cuts. Someone had tossed him like one of the mattresses, probably a few times.

"Snatchers?" Wraith asked.

Con shrugged. "Don't know, didn't get to ask. Buggers came in fast and hard like bloody SEAL Team Six. Dressed for the part too."

Wraith blinked. "What?"

Con turned and groaned, wincing. "Half a dozen blokes, dressed in camouflage, like something out of a bleeding movie, and tossing magic like it was nothing. Serious heavyweights."

Something tugged at Wraith's memory, but she couldn't get a hold of it and it was infuriating.

"We gave nearly as good as we got," Con said. "Nearly. Ovation and Geek took them head on, told me to watch the little one." His expression turned grim as he looked around the room. "The bastards got them both." He stroked Sprout's hair, then petted Toto. "If it weren't for your pup . . ."

The way Con looked at Sprout tore at Wraith's heart, and she fought back tears as she hugged the big dog, careful it wasn't too tight.

"We shouldn't take any chances," Wraith said. "Not with Sprout or with your arm."

"My arm?" Con said and tried lifting it, but grimaced and stifled a groan.

"Don't move it, you idiot," Wraith said.

"Bleeding thing's broken," he said after getting his breath back.

"Can you walk?"

"I can bloody well walk out of here," Con said. "But I can't carry Sprout with one arm."

"I'll take her." Wraith turned to Toto. "What about you, can you walk?"

The big dog got to his feet. He staggered, but didn't fall. When he seemed sure, he licked Wraith's hand.

"Did you find what you were looking for?" Con asked.

She swallowed back a tide of guilt. "I think so, but things went, um, badly."

Con nodded. "Seems to be a lot of that going around. Here, take her."

Wraith gingerly took Sprout into her arms. She was surprised how light the little girl was, and how small she felt.

Con pushed himself up, grunting through clenched teeth. Watching it made Wraith wince; but after a long moment he straightened, holding his broken arm close to his side, and nodded.

Wraith started toward the door, Toto limping behind her.

"We can't go to a hospital," Con said. "So where are we going?"

Wraith stopped midstep and turned around. "Why not?"

He nodded at Sprout. "At her age, she'll be in a foster home before you can blink, likely me as well." He shook his head. "She hasn't talked about it, but I got enough from Geek to know things were bad and she wouldn't want to go back."

Wraith looked down at the girl. It was disconcerting how limp she was, and black circles were appearing around her eyes.

"No, I won't let them—"

"What?" Con asked. "Take her? You going to take on the police and the hospital staff?"

"I don't know," Wraith said.

"We've got to find someplace safe," Con said. "A sanctuary."

Wraith blinked. "What did you say?"

"Sanctuary?"

She tried to remember. That big Russian fae had said something about sanctuary, hadn't he? No, it was the street kid, he'd used the word, but she'd come in the middle of the conversation. She closed her eyes and focused harder.

"What are—" Con asked, but when Wraith shook her head, he went silent.

The fae had handed the kids a piece of paper and—

She opened her eyes. "I know where we're going."

"Okay," Con said and nodded. "Where's that, then?"

"I don't know."

Con sighed.

"But I think we'll be safe there," she added

Con gave her a weary smile. "Your skill at building confidence is truly astounding." Wraith made to apologize, but Con shook his head. "Lead on."

Wraith went to the door and shifted Sprout so she could hold the girl with one arm. Still wearing the glove, Wraith reached out to the door. She began reworking the equation, shifting the variables to try and find a door close to the address she had seen. It was more complicated than anything she'd ever done before. As the formulation neared completion, it felt oddly familiar to her and Wraith felt a twinge of apprehension. Eventually, the formulation reached a zero sum. Wraith opened the door, cautiously.

"Stay close and be ready," she said. "It might be some kind of lure or trap."

Con nodded, wincing as he let go of his broken arm. After a moment's effort, he lifted his good right hand, and with a muttered word, it became wreathed in fire.

Wraith stepped through the door, Con and Toto close behind her.

CHAPTER TWENTY-THREE

Dante led the way. They ran through yards and narrow alleyways, desperate not to be seen. Despite the glamour being gone, there was also the unconscious murderer Dante had slung over his shoulder.

The sound of sirens and helicopters overhead brought Dante up short. He stopped near a fence under the cover of tress, and crouched down, Elaine and Siobhan following his lead.

"We're never going to make it back to the car," Dante said.

"We can't walk back to the club," Elaine said.

"Aye," Siobhan agreed. "Not with the baggage and your arse showing, as it were."

Both elves gave her a disapproving look.

"You two stay here," she said, ignoring their withering stares. "I'll find us a ride."

"Wait—" Dante started to say.

"You two keep your heads, and ears, down," Siobhan said. "I'll be back."

Before either could protest, Siobhan was running down the street.

"What happened?" Elaine asked.

Dante could hear the fear in her words. He also knew what she was really asking: Was it permanent?

"I don't know," he said and put his hand on her shoulder. "We have to deal with one problem at a time."

Elaine looked up at him. Her luminescent eyes were a couple shades paler green than he'd remembered, but there was a strength and determination behind them. They looked at each other for a long, silent moment.

"I mean we need to deal with the more immediate and urgent problems first," he said, slowly withdrawing his hand.

She smiled, just a little. "That's not very comforting."

His mouth turned up at the corners. "Best I can do on short notice."

A screeching of tires made them both look up to see a fairly new minivan skid to a stop. Dante exchanged a look with Elaine. The side door slid open and Siobhan leaned over.

"This ain't a house," she said. "You don't need a fecking invitation."

"After you," Dante said and motioned to Elaine, who climbed into the backseat.

Dante laid the still-unconscious woman across the

bench seat in the third row and climbed in, shutting the door.

"Interesting choice of vehicles," he said when they started moving.

"Get on the floor," Siobhan said. "Keep out of sight."

Dante and Elaine did, but both of them had to tuck their legs up to fit.

"What do you think the odds are that the guard will stop the family football coach?" Siobhan said.

"That's good thinking," Dante conceded. "You know the way back?"

"Aye, just keep down," Siobhan said. "If something happens, I'll let you know. I don't want someone spotting your glowing eyes and pointy ears."

Dante let out a breath. He wasn't exactly comfortable, but his metaphorical position was exceedingly less so than his actual one.

What felt like hours later, the minivan came to a stop.

"Tell me you didn't—"

"I parked down the alley," Siobhan said. "Let me make sure the way is clear."

Dante waited, then waited some more.

The door slid open. "Aye, no one around, let's go."

Dante got out, threw the prisoner over his shoulder, and made his way to the side entrance of the club. When he reached the door, he realized Siobhan was heading back to the minivan.

"Where are you going?" he asked.

"It's a stolen vehicle, isn't it?" she said. "I'll park it a ways off and come back."

Dante didn't have time to reply before the minivan was gone.

"I'll give it to her," Elaine said. "She's not stupid. Uncouth and short tempered, but not stupid."

Dante nodded. "Well, we shouldn't continue standing in broad daylight with an unconscious body," he said. "Come on."

He reached out, but before his fingers touched the door, it opened, and Dante's mouth dropped open.

"Regent," Faolan said smiling. He was dressed in a dark green military-style uniform with a slender sword on one hip and a compact assault rifle in one hand. Then his eyes narrowed as he looked Dante over. Half a second later, his eyes went wide. "Your glamour!"

"We'll get to that," Dante said.

Faolan stepped back to let them inside.

"How did you get here?" Dante asked.

"Trails opened back up," Faolan said as they walked to the main room of the club. "I kept Padraig posted near an entrance and had him checking it every hour, just in case."

Dante stepped onto the dance floor and smiled as a wave of relief washed over him. Three dozen elves, all dressed in marshal combat gear, were gathered around various crates and boxes. Some were checking weapons, some were working on laptops, and others were talking into radios.

Dante gripped Faolan's shoulder. "I'm glad to see you."

Faolan smiled, but it was tempered. "And I you, but, um . . ."

Dante nodded. "Our missing glamour is a complicated story, and we're on a tight schedule."

"Okay," Faolan said, then pointed to the form over Dante's shoulder. "Who's that?"

"Someone I hope will make it less confusing, if not less complicated," Dante said.

Faolan whistled and waved over a couple marshals.

"Secure her," Faolan said. "Ready her for interrogation."

"I think she might be a wizard," Dante said.

Everyone stared and the marshals took a step back.

"Get her inside a circle," Dante said.

"You heard him," Faolan said. "Move."

The marshals straightened, then took the woman and carried her off.

When they were gone, Dante turned back to Faolan. "Sorry, I didn't mean to step on your toes. Old habits die hard."

"You didn't," Faolan said. "We're here to support you."

Dante noticed Faolan glance at Elaine. "You two know each other, right?"

Faolan smirked and his eyes almost twinkled. "We do. Nice to see you again."

"And you," Elaine said. "Especially without the cuffs."

Dante glanced at Elaine and arched an eyebrow.

"It's a long story," she said.

"Another time, then," Dante said and turned back to Faolan. "What's the situation?"

"We arrived a little over an hour ago," Faolan said and gestured to a forest giant talking to some marshals. "The chuhaister said you'd gone to follow a lead, so we set up a command center. Not long after, kids started streaming in, changelings of every court, and wizards too." He shook his head. "I didn't know there were so many."

"How many are here?"

"Twenty-nine so far," Faolan said. "Twelve wizards, seventeen changelings. We have them all upstairs in the rather lavish living quarters there. They were less than thrilled about it, but I assured them they were free to come and go as they wish."

"I'm going talk to them," Elaine said. "See if I can put them at ease."

"Thank you," Dante said.

"Stairway is over there," Faolan said.

Elaine gave Dante a hug. "Thank you." She kissed his cheek. "And I'm sorry for misjudging you."

Dante hugged her back. Her hair brushed his cheek, like a whisper, carrying the smell of honeysuckle. He broke the hug and cleared his throat. "It's forgotten."

Elaine hurried toward the stairs.

Faolan was smiling.

"Don't even—"

"I didn't say a word, Regent," Faolan said, smiling more.

"So, you arrived a little over an hour ago . . ." Dante said.

Faolan's smile vanished and his tone was all business. "We tried calling you, but you didn't answer. Then we saw the news report and started putting together a retrieval team—"

Dante took out his phone, pressed a button, and sighed. "It's dead; must've have happened when she stripped the glamour."

"Who?" Faolan asked.

"Later," Dante said. "What's the story the mortals are running with?"

"Terrorist attack," Faolan said. "Some kind of hallucinogenic gas is the initial report from the officials."

"More and more complicated."

"They're calling in Homeland Security."

"And I thought it couldn't get any better," Dante said.

"They're reporting a dozen casualties, most from cardiac arrest."

Dante furrowed his brow.

"Scared to death by what they saw, I'd say," Faolan said. "But there's a report of FBI agents who were shot."

Dante nodded. "Courtesy of our guest—she was their partner."

Faolan's face paled. "She's an agent? A real agent?"

"I think they were all real agents," Dante said. "But I think she's a mole working for the—" He shrugged. "I don't know what they're calling themselves now, but I'm almost certain it's the remnants of the dark magi."

Faolan swallowed, then muttered a curse.

"My thoughts exactly," Dante said. "I have no idea how we can do anything now." He ran a hand through his hair. "Especially not looking like this."

A female marshal with short dark-brown hair and keen lavender eyes approached, and Faolan nodded at her.

"The prisoner is secured," the marshal said. "The wizard says the circle is solid and should keep her—"

"The wizard?" Dante asked, looking at Faolan.

"We'll be right there," Faolan told the marshal, who then hurried off.

"Don't tell me you brought him here," Dante said.

Faolan shrugged. "Okay, but that's the good news."

Dante's stomach twisted. "Do I want to know the bad news?"

"The queen mother is here," Faolan said.

"What? Are you out of your mind?"

Faolan opened his mouth to speak.

"Where's Fiona?" Dante asked.

Faolan looked down and bit his lip.

"You brought her too?"

"She's upstairs playing Angry Birds," said Caitlin in a calm voice from behind Dante.

Dante studied Caitlin for a moment, hardly able to believe she was the same woman who had stepped into a mysterious world to go after her stolen child. Had it really only been ten months? She still was the picture of Celtic womanhood: bright green eyes, red curly hair, and pale skin sprinkled with freckles. But she stood a little taller, more confident and sure of herself.

No, she wasn't the same. None of them were. Caitlin had been thrown into a world she didn't imagine could exist. Not to mention finding out she was a changeling, her father once the consort to the queen of The Dawn Court. And learning that the father of her daughter was the king of the Dusk Court. Those kinds of revelations can have a lasting impact.

"Eddy is watching her and helping with your guests," Caitlin said. "Most haven't seen a doctor in years, so we've been treating their various ailments."

Dante nodded. "Thank you. Now you need to tell me what you're doing here, all of you."

Faolan started to open his mouth, but Caitlin cut him off.

"He didn't have a choice. Eddy and I talked about it and figured something was happening. So when Faolan swapped out some of the marshals watching over us—"

Dante turned to Faolan.

"I wanted to make sure I left some of my best people with them," Faolan said.

"We explained to Faolan that we weren't going to just sit on the sidelines if there was something we could do to help," Caitlin said, then smiled softly. "Sort of like others did for me."

Dante sighed and rubbed his forehead.

"They're safer here than just about anywhere else in the world," Faolan said.

Dante nodded. "I know. I'm growing tired of constant complications."

A door at the back of the club shook, then opened.

Everyone stared as a young girl in a long, over-sized, hooded jacket walked in. She carried a young changeling girl and was followed by a young man with one hand covered in flames. His other arm, obviously broken, was held close to his body.

Dante's breath caught when he recognized the girl. Then he saw a large coyote limp into the room and look around. His eyes went immediately to Dante.

"Ciye?" Dante said in disbelief.

"Please," the girl said between labored breaths. "We need help."

CHAPTER TWENTY-FOUR

No one spoke or moved. Wraith stared at the elves, all of whom looked ready to invade a small country, except for one. He was eyeing her intently.

"Bugger me," Con said softly behind her.

"Please," Wraith said, pulling Sprout closer. "She's hurt and I don't know how bad. And my friend has a broken arm."

A short woman with curly red hair and kind eyes started to move forward, but the elf caught her shoulder.

"What are you doing?" the woman asked, pulling herself free. "Those are hurt kids and I'm a nurse."

"You don't know—" the elf started to say.

"And I don't care," she said and walked slowly toward Wraith, hands up. "My name is Caitlin, honey, what's yours?"

"Wraith."

"Con."

"I'm a nurse, and I'm going to help, okay?"

Wraith swallowed, then looked at Con. After moment they reached a silent agreement. Wraith turned back to Caitlin and nodded.

"What happened?" she asked, nodding to Sprout.

"Got tossed and hit her head," Con said.

Caitlin eyed them both.

"Weren't us, mum," Con said. "Snatchers broke in and took our friends."

Caitlin held her arms out. "Let me take her. I promise I'll take care of her."

Wraith looked at her. "Do you swear?"

Caitlin smiled, and it brought a sense of comfort to Wraith she'd almost forgotten. "Yes, I swear I'm going to help her however I can."

"No hospitals," Con said.

"I can't promise that," Caitlin said. "That might be the only way to help her—"

Wraith drew Sprout back.

"Okay," Caitlin said. "No hospitals, I promise."

Wraith reluctantly passed Sprout to her.

"Her name is Sprout," Wraith said.

Caitlin looked down at Sprout with genuine concern.

"I need to take her upstairs," Caitlin said. "Why don't you two come along?"

"Go ahead," Wraith said to Con. "Let her take care of your arm."

"What about you?" Con asked.

Wraith looked at the elf. He was looking from her to Toto and back. "I don't think I'm welcome here."

"Don't be ridiculous," Caitlin said, then cast a glance back over her shoulder.

"You were at the market, weren't you?" Wraith asked the elf.

He nodded.

"You saved me," Wraith said. "She was going to shoot me, but you stopped her?"

Caitlin's eyes went wide, and she looked from Wraith to the elf but didn't say anything.

"I did," the elf said.

"Thank you."

"I don't know what's going on," Caitlin said. "And I get the feeling we're going to have a long talk when this is done—but right now, these two need medical attention." She glanced at Wraith. "You probably do as well."

"I'm fine," Wraith said, then shook her head. "Well, relatively speaking."

"You sure you're okay, love?" Con asked.

Wraith nodded. "Go with her; stay with Sprout."

Con nodded then opened his mouth as if to speak, but just shook his head instead, let the fire in his hand go out, and followed Caitlin.

"I'm sorry," she said, too softly for anyone to hear.

When Caitlin and Con were gone, Wraith looked at Dante.

"I'll go. I'm sorry for what I did." She shook her head. "It wasn't on purpose, I mean it." She let out a breath. "Before I go, I need you to promise me you'll take care of my friends, and my dog."

Dante blinked. "Your dog?"

Wraith nodded and scratched Toto behind the ears. "His name is Toto."

A tall, powerfully built woman all in black with tattoos on her neck stepped out from a hallway and into the room. Wraith recognized her immediately. The woman had tried to shoot her. Panic seized Wraith, and power rose up inside her.

"*M'anam!*" the woman said and reached into her coat.

"No!" Wraith lashed out with her gloved hand, entangling the weapon's quantum information and increasing its mass exponentially.

There was a loud thunk as the gun tore from its holster and fell to the floor.

"*Mo mhallacht ort,*" the woman said, and reached around to her back.

Toto growled louder than Wraith had ever heard and stepped in front of her, teeth bared.

"Stop it!" Dante shouted.

Wraith noticed then that everyone in the room had drawn a weapon, but they were apparently unsure where to aim.

"She's the *girseach* from the market," the woman said.

"I know," Dante said. "And she's here on an invitation I made, offering sanctuary. And that," he motioned to Toto, "is a member of the Cruinnigh."

The contingent of elves exchanged glances then lowered their weapons.

Dante turned back to Wraith and approached slowly, hands out. "I'm sorry about that. This is a sanctuary, you're safe here."

Wraith shrugged. "It's okay, all things considered. I'm just glad no one opened fire."

He closed to within a few feet, giving a long look at Toto. "You said your name is Wraith?"

She nodded.

"It's nice to meet you. I'm Dante." He offered his hand.

She looked from it to him and back. Finally, she looked down at Toto. He was staring at Dante, almost longingly. "I think he really likes you," she said and took his hand.

Dante shook her hand. "We're actually old friends."

Wraith looked at Toto and could've sworn he smiled. Not a doggie grin, but a real smile.

Dante knelt down and gently ran his hands over Toto's flank and right front leg. "Someone beat the hell out of you, *a rún*," Dante said.

"The snatchers," Wraith said. "He helped save Sprout and Con."

Dante smiled and spoke to Toto in a language she didn't know. Then she recognized it as the same language Shadow spoke. Siouan, she'd said, right?

Toto looked into Dante's eyes. Then, after a while, shook his head.

"You're sure?" Dante asked.

Toto looked down almost as if in shame.

Dante kissed the top of his head and ran his hands along his back. "It's okay, my friend. I'll help however I can."

Wraith stared. "You can talk to him?"

Dante smiled at her. "Sort of."

"So you'll help him?" Wraith asked.

"Of course," Dante said, then carefully lifted Toto into his arms. "Come on, let's go upstairs. We have food."

Wraith shook her head. "I should leave."

"It's not safe out there," Dante said. "Even for you."

"I'll manage."

"My point is you don't have to. You're safe here."

"It's not about safe. I'm not safe anywhere."

"Where will you go?"

Wraith opened her mouth but realized she had no idea. When she remembered the drill, she stared at Dante. He looked back and she knew, somehow, that he could be trusted. "Is there some place I can go? I need to do something, and I need to do it alone."

Dante looked from her to Toto. Wraith was amazed he didn't seem to have any trouble holding him all this time.

The big dog looked at him, then huffed loudly.

"Okay, if you say so," Dante said to Toto, then turned to another elf, who still had a hand resting casually on the hilt of a sword. "Faolan, is there a basement?"

"Not exactly, but there is the old first floor of the building," Faolan said.

"The Underground?" Wraith asked. "That's good."

"Would you show our guest the way, please?" Dante said, emphasizing the word *guest*.

Faolan nodded, but shared a long look with Dante.

"I get it," Wraith said. "You don't trust me, and I don't blame you."

Both elves looked at her.

"It's not about trust," Dante said.

"Yes it is," Wraith said. "I'm dangerous, unpredictable, and not completely sure of much of anything. But I plan to do something about that. I have friends that've been taken, at least two, maybe more. I'm going to get them out, but there's something I need to do to find them. Once I do that, I'll be gone and you'll never see me again."

"It's not like that," Dante said.

"Come on," Faolan said and led her to a set of stairs.

Before descending, Wraith looked back at Toto. She couldn't shake the feeling she'd never see him again. It was probably for the best. If she left him here, he'd be safe and with friends. That was better than with her. It still made a few tears slip from her eyes though.

"You coming?" Faolan asked from several steps ahead.

Wraith followed him down.

CHAPTER TWENTY-FIVE

Dante found a private office and carried Ciye inside. He cast a quick glance into the residence and saw kids of all ages, none of whom were acting like kids. They were clustered in small groups, whispering and pointing to the large couch where Sprout lay. Edward and Caitlin knelt, examining the small girl's injuries.

Dante closed the office door behind him. The room was large, replete with a couple of sofas, a couple of armchairs, and an intricately carved wooden desk that was several miles past ostentatious. He laid Ciye on a sofa and the large coyote shimmered, resolving into the familiar form of his former love.

"Thank you," Ciye said with sadness in his eyes.

"Toto?" Dante asked, smiling.

Ciye smiled. "Hototo, actually. She misheard the first time my daughter told her. Shadow found it so funny, she adopted it."

"Are you going to tell me what's going on?" Dante asked.

Ciye drew in a long breath, but winced.

"Here, let me see." Dante knelt down and moved to lift Ciye's shirt.

Ciye caught his hand. "I'll be fine, it's nothing serious. I've taken worse from Badger many times."

Dante looked into his dark eyes. "You always excelled at finding trouble."

"No, old friend, trouble never leaves my side." Ciye's smile faded a little. "And it seems I passed that on to my daughter."

Dante took Ciye's hand in his and kissed it. "Tell me."

"The shadows aren't the snatchers everyone is speaking of," Ciye began. "Wraith is carrying a dark power inside her, and it feeds on fear and anger. Those shadows are her fears come to life."

"She's conjuring them?" Dante asked.

Ciye nodded. "And fighting them as well," he said. "The survivors of the dark magi, they're the ones who collect our children, the spirit children and the changelings. They torture and kill them. But before their tortured souls can find peace, the dark ones bind them to mortal children."

"But why?" Dante asked.

"To give them more power," Ciye said. "They give the children power, then turn them loose so the other mortals will see and remember the past they've chosen to forget." Ciye swallowed. "They took my daughter and her friends, along with Wraith. She was powerful even before they got to her."

Dante just listened.

"I don't know how many they tied to her," he said. "Hundreds at least, the last of which were my daughter and her friends." He looked at Dante, fear in his eyes. "They wanted to make her into a Taleth-Sidhe, or perhaps force another to emerge, I'm not sure. She escaped, and chose to lock away her power." He shook his head. "But like the ocean against cliffs, it wears away at the cage. I would've told you sooner, but I couldn't leave that child alone. I was only able to come to you that first time when she and I were separated. I was trying to find her, and as soon as I did, I had to leave."

Dante stroked Ciye's dark hair. "I understand."

"I did everything I could to help that girl," Ciye said. "What I thought Shadow would want. I couldn't save my daughter, and it seems I couldn't save her friend either."

"She's not lost yet," Dante said.

Ciye gripped Dante's hand tight as he looked into his eyes. "I can't finish this, but I can't ask—"

"You don't have to," Dante said. "You rest, sleep, heal. I'll find peace for your child, and maybe some for that lost girl."

"Thank you," Ciye said, tears welling in his eyes.

Dante bent down and kissed Ciye's forehead. When he lifted his lips, Ciye was sleeping.

Quietly, Dante stepped out of the office and closed the door.

"Got a second?" Elaine asked from behind him.

Dante turned. "Just."

Elaine nodded to a group of kids in the far corner. "That's Charge, the girls with him are Mouse and Slink. They're the ones that rat saw that night."

"So they did escape?" Dante asked.

Elaine nodded. "They said these four kids showed up and teleported them to a squat somewhere in Kansas, they think."

"That's an interesting coincidence," Dante said.

"Yeah, and other kids are telling similar stories," Elaine said. "But the really strange part is, when they opened the door to leave their respective safe houses, they didn't step outside. They stepped into this club."

Dante narrowed his eyes. "Just like Wraith."

"Who?"

"Later," Dante said. "Are they all okay?"

"Well enough," Elaine said.

"Good," Dante said. "If you need anything just ask."

Elaine nodded, then turned and went back to the kids.

Dante headed downstairs and found a marshal.

"I want a sentry on the office upstairs. No one goes in without my leave," Dante said.

"Yes, Regent," the marshal said, then called another over and the two went upstairs.

Faolan walked over. "Learn anything useful?"

Dante nodded. "I'm afraid so."

"How bad is it?"

Dante told him.

Faolan's face twisted in a blend of rage and disgust, his hands clenched into fists. "I think it's time we had a talk with that FBI agent."

Dante ground his teeth. "Oh yes, let's talk."

Dante examined the circle, checking for any flaws. He trusted Edward, but there was no harm in being safe, especially now. The circle was almost perfectly spherical, as was the inner circle. Each symbol between the two was precise and clear. When he was certain it was adequate, he stood and looked at Faolan.

"When I break the slumber," Dante said. "You close the circle."

Faolan nodded.

Dante stepped over the circle and Faolan knelt down, his fingers resting just above the outer edge of it. Focusing, Dante unwove the slumber, letting the charm evaporate. Just before stepping out of the circle, he slapped the agent across the face.

The moment he stepped out, Faolan closed it.

The woman blinked and slowly lifted her head. It took a moment for her to realize she was bound to a chair. When she did, her eyes opened wide and she began struggling.

"There's no point," Dante said. "Those cords were made for holding things much stronger and more powerful than you."

The woman looked at him with hate in her eyes. She tried to tip her chair back, but found it secured to the floor.

"We thought of that too," Dante said.

"*Dominum invocant te tenebras,*" the woman said.

The circle flared bright with blue light and she cried out in pain.

Dante looked at Faolan.

"I used a silence charm," he said. "So we're good."

When the woman recovered, she examined the circle, then looked up again. "*Tu ausus ad me?*"

Dante rolled his eyes. "Yes, we're all impressed you speak fluent Latin."

The woman snarled. "What have you done with the Taleth—"

"She is not a Taleth-Sidhe!" Dante roared. "She is a child you tormented and twisted!"

The woman smiled. "She was a child, but now she is the dark light that will cast away the false shadows."

"Where are your compatriots?" Dante asked.

The woman spit at him, but it hit an invisible wall and hung in midair. "You think you can defeat us? Kill me, kill a dozen others, or a hundred, it doesn't matter." She leaned forward. "We are countless."

"If you were so many," Dante said, "you wouldn't have to resort to petty intrigues. I was there. I fought alongside the true Taleth-Sidhe when he killed your leaders. Even your master's power couldn't stop him." Dante leaned in close, though still conscious of the circle. "You and the rabble that remain are nothing. You will fall much easier this time."

The woman started laughing. "The all-knowing fae; how you love to dabble in the affairs of mortals."

Dante felt a chill run down his spine.

"The Theurgic Order was born from the ashes of that eons-long war," she said. "We are everywhere, faerie. Even a magister of your own court chose to serve at our side rather than lay in our wake."

"Donovan?" Dante whispered.

"When faced with our power, our mission, all will fall," she said. "Either they will fall before us, or in line with us. With every whisper, every mention of our master's name, we grow in strength!"

Dante looked at Faolan. "She's right."

"You'll have nothing more from me, elf, so you may as well kill—"

Her words were cut off by a single gunshot. It echoed in the small room, but the silence charm dampened it significantly.

Faolan lowered the gun.

Dante sighed. "That was a good silence charm."

"I did it myself," Faolan said.

"You know I normally deplore executions—"

"Good thing I'm the one who shot her, then," Faolan said, then looked down. "Oh, and this is her own weapon."

"We'll need to make sure she's found," Dante said. "She might've been a dark magi sleeper, but she was also an agent. The FBI doesn't know what happened, and they'll want to find out. They won't stop looking for her."

"When night falls," Faolan said, "I'll take care of it."

Dante glanced at the body slumped in the chair and gritted his teeth. He reached into his pocket and drew out a small stone engraved with a single symbol, over which was a smear of dried blood.

He handed the stone to Faolan. "Bring Donovan to me, alive."

"You don't really believe he had a hand in this, do you?" Faolan asked, accepting the stone. "He was Dawn Court!"

"Have you ever read Nietzsche?"

"That's a little, well, dreary for me," Faolan said.

Dante nodded. "For the most part, but in *Beyond Good and Evil* there's an aphorism. Mortals never seem to remember the whole thing: 'Whoever fights with monsters should see to it that he does not become a monster in the process. And when you gaze long into an abyss, the abyss also gazes into you.'"

Faolan nodded. "I know that one."

"Well, it seems some of us are more diligent in our fight against monsters." Dante glanced at the body in the chair. "We need to remind ourselves how easy it is to let that diligence slip. Damnation is a journey of a million small steps."

Faolan looked from the body to Dante. "You're right, but I took no joy in it."

Dante's smile faltered. "Really? I did, a little."

"That it bothers you should be reassuring."

Dante sighed. "Bring Donovan in. I want to know what's going on. If he had any part in this—"

"Justice, not vengeance," Faolan said.

"Sometimes they can be hard to differentiate," Dante said.

"No," Faolan said. "Sometimes they just walk the same path."

CHAPTER TWENTY-SIX

Wraith heard the door close. She lowered the goggles and looked around, making sure she was alone. The room was empty except for cases of liquor and beer. It was a dark and dusty room, maybe twenty feet square in total. There was the cold, clammy chill that seemed to fill all underground spaces. Satisfied it was just her, some spiders, and rats, she sat on the cold floor cross-legged. Slowly, almost reverently, she removed first the goggles, then the glove, and set them down beside her. The silence was heavy, and it hadn't occurred to her before this moment just how long it'd been since she knew silence so complete. She pulled her bag off and removed the drill, trying to pretend her hands weren't shaking.

"I'm already on the tracks," she said softly. "All I'm doing is turning to see the train."

Her fingers found the dial in the dim light and turned it until it would turn no more.

She held out her right hand, palm up. It was still trembling.

"Just get on with it, already," she told herself.

Hesitantly, she set the drill on her palm.

There was a sudden whirring sound, the drill clamped tight, and she felt the spinning needle bite into her hand. No, it was more than just her hand. Blinding pain surged through her and everything went, blessedly, black.

Wraith opened her eyes.

The whole world was swirling gray mist, like a black-and-white painting that had once been a picture, but someone had smeared. Only the ghosts of details remained and the harder she looked, the more obscure they became. She looked down and could see her feet, but the ground beneath them was the same smeared gray.

Choosing a direction at random, she began walking. After a dozen steps of nothing changing, she gasped.

A massive cathedral appeared out of nowhere. The stained glass windows were smashed, and the stone walls were crumbling. It looked like something left behind after a carpet bombing. It was a disquieting sight, all the more so for its familiarity.

She walked around it, which took much longer than she would've thought. There was no sense of time, but it felt like it took days. When she finally reached the front, there was an archway that should've been an entrance. Instead of doors, however, there was a wall of mortared stone. She touched the barrier and found it to be made of the same stone as the church itself, but the mortar was of a different shade. This was done recently.

Wraith turned and looked around, keenly aware someone was watching her, and she knew just who it was.

"Nightstick," she yelled. "Open the door."

Silence.

She pushed on the makeshift wall, but it wouldn't give. She tried wiggling stones free, but they all were held tight. She even tried breaking off the mortar, but it didn't give.

"You want to play it this way?" she asked. "Fine with me." She took a few steps back and lifted her right hand, aiming her fingers and drawing in power.

Nothing happened.

She looked around, realizing for the first time that no numbers or symbols hung in the air. Anger flared and she began punching and kicking the stones, but they didn't budge. As she ran her fingers through her hair, she spotted her wrist and blinked. She pushed the sleeves of her jacket up to her elbows and stared in shock. Her tattoos were gone!

She drew in a slow breath and began thinking. "This is my head, right? I'm supposed to be the one who makes the rules—" Realization hit her like a runaway truck.

"I did, didn't I? I made this place." She turned and looked around. "And I meant to keep myself out."

No one answered, but no one had to. She knew she was right. She'd always assumed it was the snatchers who'd done this to her, but was she wrong? Had this all been her doing? The memory loss, the confusion, the hallucinations, all of it something she did to herself? Why?

"I told you, kid," Nightstick said from the other side of the wall. "Don't ask questions you don't want to know the answers to."

Wraith shook her head. No, there was no way she'd wanted this outcome: to be stumbling around in the dark, lost and filled with doubt. Whatever the answer was, she had to know.

Slowly, she drew in a breath and stepped up to the door.

"Let me in," she said, her tone calm and even.

"Not by the hair of my chiny-chin-chin," Nightstick said.

Wraith lifted her right hand and looked at the palm. Without the formulations on it she'd grown used to, it didn't look like hers. She placed her palm against the stones and closed her eyes. She focused, and one by one all her fears and apprehension melted away.

"Let me in," she whispered. "Or I'll huff and I'll puff."

There was a cracking sound and, when she opened her eyes, stones fell away, dissolving into a gray haze when they hit the ground. In the archway now were two massive wooden doors, each open and barely hanging by a single hinge.

She remembered the place, but it was different now. There were no shadows, no oppressive sense to it. She walked slowly down the aisle, stepping over splintered pieces of the pews. Sitting at the far end was Nightstick. He was slumped, back against the altar, smoking.

"Who are you?" she asked.

He didn't look at her, he just took another drag and blew out smoke. "I failed you, kid."

"You failed me? So I made you too," she said, more to herself than to him.

Nightstick didn't look up.

"What is this place?" she asked.

"Turn on the lights," he said. "It's your place, after all."

Wraith was about to ask how when thousands upon thousands of candles lit all at once. The light wasn't bright, but it was complete, lighting every corner. Her mouth fell open as she turned slowly. Books, millions of them, lined every wall. Most sat in plain wooden bookcases that reached the vaulted ceiling. Some of the shelves had collapsed, or been destroyed, and their books lay haphazard on the floor. Other books were stacked on the marble tiles.

"It was so beautiful here," Nightstick said. "Before the storm came, it was truly beautiful. You did a fine job."

"What storm—?" Wraith turned to him and gasped when she saw his face, no longer hidden by darkness. He was older than she'd imagined; his face lined from years of smiling and frowning too much. The small patch of hair under his lip was gray; and his brown hair, the same plain shade as her own, was sprinkled with white. His eyes were lined, but inside they sparkled and shined, vivid and intense and the color of melted chocolate. He looked so familiar, but—

He smiled. "You had so much light in you, so much joy." His smile faded and he shook his head. "You asked me to keep it safe, to lock the darkness away." He looked up at her. "You trusted me, and look what happened."

He stood and walked through the piled, broken pews to one book-covered wall. Wraith followed silently.

"You found some peace, or a piece of peace perhaps," he said and scratched his head, which pushed his hat back. "For a while anyway, but the darkness was too much. It started at the edges, subtle and small." He gestured around the church, then at himself. "But it wasn't long before it did this, and broke me."

"Broke you?" Wraith asked. "What do you mean? Why did I make you? Why did I lock this place away and leave you to guard it?"

Nightstick sighed and shook his head. "No one could handle something like that alone, how could a child?" He looked at her, his eyes pleading. "I tried the best I could, but I was broken, you see? Tainted by the same darkness I tried to hold back."

"What are you talking about?" Wraith asked.

"I'm sorry," he said. "It did so much damage, and I think I might've done some myself, but I can't remember." He bent down and picked up a book, but when he opened it, the pages fell to dust.

Something drove her to reach out and take a book herself. She picked one off the shelf and examined it. It had a brown leather cover but no title. She opened it and words were overwritten, as if the pages of a different book were printed over them. She flipped through it slowly and carefully. Some pages were missing, in part or in whole, while others had been inserted. Some pages had been written over so heavily she couldn't read anything at all. On one page, the text was merely faded and a clean replacement was written above each line. She read the page, and a memory flooded over her.

She was twelve. Billy, the most handsome boy she'd ever seen, was leading her behind the old barn. She couldn't believe he was really going to kiss her! When they were out of sight of anyone who might wander by, he turned her so her back was to the barn and stepped close.

"Close your eyes," he whispered.

She did, alight with anticipation.

Then the first handful of manure hit her, right in the face.

She opened her eyes and saw Billy and his friends laughing.

"Why—"

They all began pelting her with clumps of wet, foul-smelling muck. She fell to her knees, hand covering her face and eyes as tears poured down her cheeks. The onslaught *didn't slow, and soon they were throwing rocks too. She cried out, pleading with them to stop, to let her go.*

They just kept laughing and taunting her.

"Please," she begged. "Just—"

Wraith tore her eyes from the book.

"No, that's wrong," she said and looked at Nightstick. "It felt wrong, like it belonged to someone else."

Nightstick nodded at the book.

She looked back at the page, but this time carefully ignored the notes, lines, and additions. She read only the printed words. Another memory washed her away.

She was eight, and the sun was shining. She could smell fresh-cut grass and hear children laughing. Her father was pushing her on a swing.

"Higher, Daddy," she said, gripping the chains as tight as she could.

"Okay!" he said. "Hang on!" He heaved and she soared up higher and higher.

It felt like she was flying. In that brief moment when she reached the top of the arc and hung in the air, she saw her mother. She was beautiful, and she was smiling.

The world lurched, like she'd hit a wall, and Wraith was back in the church. She looked up from the book, tears running down her cheeks.

"These are my memories," she said softly, looking from one book to another.

Nightstick nodded solemnly. "But not just your memories anymore. The others' too."

"Others?" Wraith asked. "What others? What are you talking about?"

"The whispers and screams of the shades in your head," Nightstick said. "But the trust is still locked away, and you can't have it without the key. That's the rules."

She looked from book to Nightstick. "What are you talking about? Who did this? Was it me?"

"I can't tell you," he said. "I made a pinky swear, and you can't break that. But I can say, it's all part of the same corruption you see around you." He looked away from her. "So many memories from so many scared children; they all began to blend together. I tried to save them, to save yours, but there was just too much, you see."

When he looked up, her knees went weak and a heavy sob racked her body.

He nodded again, smiling sadly. "Yeah, you wanted me to look like your father."

Wraith swallowed. "But you're not him."

Nightstick shook his head. "No. I'm sure there's part of him in here, but I'm not him."

Wraith looked back to the books, and she had to lean on what was left of a pew to keep standing. So many books had crumbled to dust, been burned, ripped to pieces, or just had their pages torn out and thrown about. She wiped her eyes and looked at Nightstick.

"These memories" she said, gesturing to the ruined books. "Are they—?"

He swallowed. "They're gone."

Wraith clenched her fists and screamed. The sound of it echoed through the church, shattering the silence that had permeated it.

When she'd gotten her rage under control, she looked at him. "Why would I make you and tell you to lock all my memories up?"

"You didn't want me to lock up the memories," he said. "But to lock up what you wanted me to, they had to come too. Unfortunately, that kept the memories close to the dark power. That made them easier to destroy and corrupt."

"Where did that dark power come from?" Wraith asked. "It wasn't always there, was it?"

At that moment, the church began to rumble and she saw shadows begin to emerge from the cracks in the stone floor.

Wraith's blood ran cold and she took an unconscious step back. "The snatchers?"

"No," Shadow said from behind her. "Not really."

Wraith turned to see SK, Fritz, and Shadow standing beside her.

"These are shades born from fear, anger," Shadow said, "and the power that feeds on them." She shook her head. "A side effect of everything that's gone so terribly wrong."

"I'm tired of riddles and half-truths," Wraith said. "Can't you just tell me?"

"No," SK said.

"It's in here," Nightstick said, tapping his chest.

"What is?" Wraith asked.

"The answer," Nightstick said. "The truth, kept as safe as I could make it."

Wraith looked from him to her friends and back. "Then give it to me."

He sighed. "I can't."

"Why not?" Wraith asked, her patience faltering.

"I don't have the key," Nightstick said. "I'm just the lock."

Wraith opened her mouth, but then she figured it out. "There is no key, is there?"

He shook his head.

"I have to destroy you if I want to know," she said. "I made it so it wouldn't be easy."

"We tried to talk you out of doing it that way," Shadow said.

"You were quite stubborn about it," Fritz said. "As you were about a great many things."

"It's okay, kid," Nightstick said. "It's time to put this old dog down. You're ready to know. You deserve to know."

Wraith looked at her friends, but none of them would look at her. She turned back to Nightstick. He took off his jacket and unbuttoned his shirt, then pulled it open to expose a chest covered in horrible burns and scars.

She flinched away.

Nightstick glanced down, then nodded at the writhing shades. "Yeah, they worked me over pretty good," he said, then smiled. "But I gave right back. You'd be proud." He draped his jacked over the pew, then his shirt, smoothing them out. He drew in a slow breath, then turned to face Wraith. "Now, let's do what needs doing."

Wraith lifted her shaking hand, and without knowing how, the drill appeared in her palm. Only now it was clutched in her hand and the needle was facing out. She turned the drill to point at Nightstick.

No one moved. Even the motes of dust hung still in the air.

Wraith closed her eyes. "I'm sorry, I can't—"

"It's okay," Nightstick said, smiling sadly. "I understand." Then he grabbed her wrist and pulled her forward.

"No!" Wraith shouted and tried to pull back, but Nightstick held her fast.

The drill whirred and bit into him, but instead of blood, gray mist poured from him.

He didn't make a sound, but Wraith shook with sobs as tears ran from her eyes.

"I'm sorry, doodle-bug," Nightstick said in a voice that wasn't quite his, and evaporated.

"Daddy!" Wraith yelled and fell to her knees.

Around her, the world shifted and the books began to shake on their walls. A large book, bound in black leather, sat before her, right where Nightstick had been standing. She stared at it through tear-filled eyes, terrified to touch it, terrified of what lay inside.

CHAPTER TWENTY-SEVEN

The book sat still, and after what felt like ages, Wraith reached a hand out. The cover flew open and the pages flipped to the middle, all on their own.

Memories rose up around Wraith, surrounding and enveloping her, then pulling her into them.

Wraith was cold, and the stone floor she sat on only served to drain the remaining warmth from her. She was hurting all over, and so hungry.

"Slipped away again?" Shadow asked.

Wraith blinked, pulling herself from the memories of the tormented dead that now resided in her head. She pushed the insistent voices back with gentle reassurances. She couldn't speak, so she just nodded.

"Were you someplace nice?" SK asked. "Warm sandy

beaches, all of us enjoying umbrella drinks and all you can eat buffets?"

Wraith shook her head. "No."

When she opened her eyes, Wraith and her friends were still in their cage. The prison cell was little more than a spot carved from the stone all around them. The opening was a wall of bars and a door. She lifted her head, which was filled with lead, both from exhaustion and from the drugs the Order kept her on. She looked at her friends. Shadow, SK, and Fritz were pale, dirty, and wasting away from hunger. Toto's emaciated form lay across Shadow's lap, and she absently stroked his head.

Her stomach convulsed with a racking hunger. How many days had it been since she'd eaten? She could hear the screams, those outside her head, but she'd grown so used to them that their terrified cries of pain and desperation were just white noise. So many crying out, some inside her head, some outside; it was getting hard to tell them apart. And with every child the Order killed, the screams became worse.

"How long was I out this time?" Wraith asked, her tongue thick and unwilling to form words.

"Not long," Fritz said. "Couple hours maybe."

"Sorry," SK said. "I forgot to wind my watch."

Despite it all, when Fritz smacked SK's head, Wraith smiled. A little.

"After everything they've done, you're still a smartass," Shadow said.

"It's my indomitable spirit," SK said. He lifted Fritz's hand and kissed it.

Wraith fought to quiet the cries of the dead. It grew worse

every time she passed out, not least because she always woke with more ghosts in her head.

"What did I miss this time?" Wraith asked, fighting back the nausea. She could hear new voices in her head, all of them confused, hurting, and terrified.

"Three more," Shadow said sadly.

"Three?" Wraith would've cried if she'd had any tears left. Three more rituals performed. That meant thirty-nine more kids tortured and killed. Thirty-nine new souls inside her, not including her own. Part of her was glad to not remember.

"They'll be back soon," Shadow said. "I can hear them preparing the ritual room again."

Wraith closed her eyes against the fear, and pain, and grief of so many, forever lost. But closing her eyes just made the screams louder and harder to block out.

"We have to get away," Wraith said. She put her hands to her head to try and keep her skull from exploding. "It's so crowded. I can't take anymore."

"That's a novel idea," SK said. "I hadn't thought about leaving—"

Wraith winced as power surged through her, twisting her insides. Around her, the numbers and symbols churned in a frantic pace. She tried to form a coherent formulation, but the numbers couldn't hear her through the screams and haze that filled her brain.

The heavy metal door at the end of the prison chamber opened and closed. In answer, hundreds of desperate voices cried out from the other cells. Most were small, calling for their mothers. The older kids had learned to keep quiet, but the little ones were always overcome by fear.

"They're coming," SK said and hugged Fritz tight.

"No," Wraith said, her heart breaking at the fear on her friends' faces. "I've got to get you out of here—" Her eyes drifted closed and she slipped into unconsciousness.

She woke to a slap.

"Not much time now," Shadow said and slapped Wraith's cheek again, staring hard into her eyes. "You've got to push past whatever they've got you on. You can do it."

The door to their cage opened.

Wraith tried to push past the cold, the exhaustion, and the fear. She reached out for the formulations, clenching her jaw. One by one, the symbols began to move into place. Agonizingly slowly, the spell took shape and power trickled through the drug-induced fog.

"Nein!" Fritz yelled.

"Get off her!" SK shouted.

"Wraith!" Shadow said. "Wake up!"

Wraith looked up to see her friends being seized by figures in dark robes. There was a growl and Toto snapped at one that went for Shadow. The robed figure sent the big dog across the cell and into a stone wall. He hit with a whimper and fell to the ground.

"No!" Wraith yelled, or tried to, but no sound came. She groped again for her magic, but it slipped through her fingers.

The robed figures wrapped thin chains around the wrists of her friends, who were too weak and beaten to resist. It was up to her; Wraith was their only hope. But she couldn't find the strength to even speak. Her body hurt everywhere and her head felt like a thousand spikes were piercing it. Reaching through the pain, ignoring the overwhelming sense

*of futility, she channeled the fear and desperation. She man-
aged a meager formulation, drawing the symbols and numbers together.*

"BANG!" she said.

*The blow hit the lead figure in the shoulder, but he only
staggered and stumbled into the cage door.*

*Someone backhanded her and sent her to the ground
with the taste of blood in her mouth.*

*She was overwhelmed by flashes of other children's
memories: playing hide-and-seek, getting a new puppy,
being shoved by a bully, police taking her parents away, her
big brother being gunned down as a car sped away. These
weren't her memories, but she was the keeper of them now.*

*Wraith pulled herself back to the present. She was being
carried down the long hallway of carved stone, as she had
been so many times before. She saw her friends being dragged
along by the chains around their wrists. The cells were quiet
now. The countless cages filled with terrified and dirty kids,
all of them staring at her with pity and relief that it wasn't
them. No one made a sound, lest they draw attention to
themselves. Wraith closed her eyes.*

*"Please," she whispered. "Not again." How many of these
rituals had they put her through? She remembered dozens.
But how many had she forgotten, or blocked out?*

*A familiar fear welled inside her as somewhere in the dis-
tance, she heard the voices of the Order members in their prepa-
rations. Beneath that, she heard the muffled sobs of her friends.*

*Wraith went still. "Shadow?" Her voice was slurred, her
mouth dry.*

The voices stopped and she sensed movement around her.

She remembered where she was, what was going to happen. A sob seized her. "Why are you doing this? Not them, please." She begged. It wouldn't do any good, but she tried anyway.

There was a long silence.

"I won't fight you," she said. "I promise. Just let them go, please."

"This is a gift, not a punishment," the ritual master said.

His face was shadowed by his hood, but she could see the hard line of his jaw and feel his cold, dark gaze boring into her. A faint purple glow burned from his eyes.

"You will be the first of many," he said. "You will bring back the past humanity has chosen to forget. The age of magic will return, thanks to you." He smiled. "And with the return of magic, our master can claim this world as his own."

Wraith tried to rub her eyes but something around her wrists kept her arms above her head. It was cold, and it bit into her soul. Panic, anger, and fear fought for dominance inside her. She was so tired. She wanted nothing so much as for the darkness to swallow her up for good.

Then she heard her friends crying.

She reached out for the magic. Not for her, but for them. She tried to pull against the bindings, but a sharp pain tore her from the haze and the calculations around her fell apart. Reluctantly, her eyes opened and her vision came into focus.

It was the same room—a huge cave actually—the same as so many times before. She was bound to the same stone table in the center of the same massive circle, sixty feet across. She turned her head one way, then the other, to the tables that were set around the outside edge of the circle. She saw her friends bound to three of them, and others, more changeling kids she didn't know, chained to the other ten.

Voices cried out inside her, feeding her strength and power.

Her mind reeled, remembering the previous rituals, both from her own eyes, and from the eyes of the tormented hundreds who were now inside her. She didn't have the strength to fight anymore. But others did.

"Mihi," she said in a voice that wasn't hers, and one of the robed figures flew up into the air, striking the ceiling of the cave with so much force that pieces of rock fell down with his limp, dead form.

"Stop her!" the ritual master yelled.

"That's right, fight them!" Shadow yelled, but her voice was weak and heavy with tears.

Chanting filled the room, the chains drew tight, and Wraith screamed as pain tore through her.

The crumpled body on the ground was taken away and the ritual master loomed over Wraith.

"Not again," Wraith screamed. "Please, no more!" Numbers and symbols flashed in the air around her and she tried hopelessly to bring them into something that could help. But like every time before, the pain fought her. She pushed back with all she had, pulled at her bindings with all the strength she could find.

"She's fighting it," a calm voice said.

"Of course she is," the ritual master said. Then he began whispering something in a language she didn't know. The chains bit into the already raw flesh of her wrists and drew her thrashing body hard against the stone.

She screamed again. The formulations fell apart, then vanished from view entirely.

Then the circle closed.

The ritual master smiled and touched Wraith's cheek. "This will go so much easier if you just accept it. You're destined to be much more than just the child of respectable talent. You will be the dawn of a new age!"

Shadow shrieked in pain.

"No!" Wraith screamed.

Power lashed out from her, shaking the chamber.

"The circle is faltering," the ritual master said. "She's breaking through."

Voices rose and Wraith smelled the ritual master's rancid breath as he leaned down, one of his hands resting on her stomach.

"We've grand designs for you," he said, his fingertips reaching past flesh into her soul, twisting it, rending it, and feeding dark power into it.

Wraith could only sob. Inside her head, hundreds upon hundreds of lost souls screamed for her.

"Fight them," Shadow said from somewhere in the distance. Her voice was hoarse, as if she'd been screaming for a long time.

Wraith screamed. "Please, I can't, not you! Make it stop!"

Chanting echoed off the stone walls, sounding like a chorus of hundreds.

Wraith closed her eyes at what she knew was coming. Tears rolled down her cheeks.

"Fight—" Shadow's words were lost in a cry that tore at

Wraith's soul. Then SK was screaming, then Fritz, then the others, one by one.

Then her own torment began; dark and twisted magic boring into her, rending her soul. She convulsed at the pain, biting her tongue and tasting blood. The chains held her fast, tearing her raw flesh as she writhed. She tried to scream, wanted to, but there wasn't enough left of her. Her senses were dull, her hands and feet numb from the prolonged restraint.

She wanted for it all to be over, but she knew it wouldn't be.

"I won't help you," Wraith said. "You can go to hell—"A lance of white hot pain between her eyes stopped her words.

"Now we bring them a light that they cannot turn away!" the ritual master said. "We bring the light of truth! We bring the Taleth-Sidhe, wrapped in shadows!"

The chanting around her grew louder, and she heard the first scream stop. Wraith felt the heat and rush of power fill her as another whimpering, crying soul took up residence inside her.

"I'll kill you all," was all Wraith could say between gasps, her body shaking. "I'll tear you from existence!"

Another scream stopped and she felt the surge of power, and then another, and another, and another, and another. They came so fast, so quickly, she couldn't even breathe. Inside her, the confused souls of the tormented cried out in desperation.

"I'm sorry," Wraith whispered to them, and to her friends.

"I love you!" Fritz yelled.

"I love you too!" SK answered.

Both their screams died together, and the wave of power that filled Wraith felt like her soul was being torn to shreds.

"It's not your fault," Shadow said, then she screamed and it went on longer than any should've been able to. When it finally stopped, the abruptness was more unsettling than the scream itself had been.

Then the room was quiet and still.

Power churned through Wraith. "You killed them!" she roared and the cave shook.

"Yes!" the ritual master said through a smile. "And now their power is yours. Every soul, its power heightened by fear and pain at the moment of death, torn away and bound to you. Feel that dark power, the gift of our Master."

Wraith's tears slowed when she felt not darkness but the familiar warmth and comfort of her friends. Then the screams, cries, and pleas inside her went quiet, their pain soothed by three so full of love and kindness.

"It's time to leave, Stretch," Shadow said from inside Wraith, her voice calm and reassuring. "We'll help you, all of us."

Wraith nodded, drew in a breath, and opened her eyes. She spoke to the power churning around her. The magic answered her summons. Formulations lashed out. The chains holding her shattered, as did the stone table she lay upon. With borrowed strength, Wraith got to her feet.

Robed figures began running.

"There's no light here," Wraith said. "If you want darkness, I'll bring it to you."

She reached out to one of fleeing figures. She closed her power around his quantum information. Then she tore it away.

He vanished entirely from existence.

She rent another from reality, and another, and another. Then she turned on the ritual master. He wasn't running. He was standing, smiling at her with pride. She knew her hold on the immense power running through her was slipping. Around her, the cavern was shuddering, reality itself buckling. Wraith looked from the ritual master to the bodies of her friends and knew she couldn't both get them out and kill him.

"I won't let you win," she said.

He looked around and smiled more. "You already have."

"Desaparecer," she said, waving a hand at him, sending a trickle of her power. He was sent flying across the room. His leg caught one of the stone tables and sent him flailing amid the sound of breaking bones.

Wraith moved to the bodies of her friends, her strength fading. The terrible wounds that had tortured them before death were almost too much to look at. Each fought to keep the memories of receiving them hidden from her. Through tears, Wraith reached out around her with her magic, finding the other ten who'd been tortured, killed, and then had their souls bound to her. She wrapped her power around them, holding them gently as if in loving arms. Then she stepped through time and space, taking their broken bodies from this terrible place.

Sometime later, Wraith woke. She tried opening her eyes but found them crusted over. Her head was swimming as she wiped at her eyes until her vision cleared. Birds were singing and a cool breeze brought fresh air tinged with the smell of damp earth and moss.

She sat up, and regretted it. The world spun around her

and she put her hands to her head. Closing her eyes again, she focused on the ground beneath her, how it was solid and still. After a few slow breaths the spinning stopped. She licked her dry lips and swallowed. When she opened her eyes, she shivered, but it had nothing to do with the cold. The remnants of the chains were still around her wrists, the metal stained with blood where it had cut her flesh. She tore at the chains with shaking hands. When she finally got them undone, she winced as the links caught and pulled the raw flesh. She hurled the chains away and noticed her surroundings.

Redwoods and sequoia trees stretched in every direction, until the haze in the distance swallowed them. Slowly, Wraith got to her feet and looked up, almost tripping over a large chunk of the stone table she'd been chained too.

The canopy was hundreds of feet above her. Through the reaching branches, she could see bright blue sky and puffy white clouds. Over everything were long, intricate calculations, the numbers and symbols weaving through every tree, branch, and leaf. Even the clouds and the sky were filled with formulations. When she looked down, the ferns and the ground itself were living equations, and she could read them all. She knew the tree in front of her was exactly 241 feet, 8 3/4 inches tall. It had been alive for 674,616 days, 7 hours, and 16 minutes. In those churning numbers and symbols, she could read the history of the tree, the centuries it had seen pass. Her head started to hurt from the sheer amount of information. She looked away and saw the ferns and other ground growth. Still the endless stream of information flowed into her.

She closed her eyes, truly understanding the phrase "Drinking from a fire hose." It took several minutes before she was able push the influx of data aside, let it pass through her without noting every piece of it. Soon it felt more like paddling along the river instead of being washed away by it. Then came the memories. She doubled over, gripping her stomach where hundreds of knives had cut and killed all those now inside her.

She opened her eyes, pushing away the torrent of recollections, and looked to her left. Toto lay nearby. His very presence, and the subtle rise and fall of his chest, brought her an overwhelming sense of relief. She'd nearly forgotten the big dog when she'd taken them all from that terrible place. Her magic must've found him and brought him, or maybe Shadow—what was left of her—wouldn't leave him behind. Shadow had always had a strong bond with Toto, but Wraith never knew why or how. Maybe that connection was what had done it. She knelt down and scratched behind his ear as he slept and his back leg jerked. She saw the fur of his right front leg was matted with blood.

She stood, numb to her very soul, staring at the bodies of her friends and the ten strangers she'd taken from that nightmarish place. They lay on the forest floor, and Wraith's heart broke again as she looked at their faces, still twisted in pain, their tattered clothes stained with blood. She forced herself to look at them, each of them, and memorize their faces. She made herself listen to the cries of the voices that recognized their own corpse. It tore her up inside, but she didn't turn away.

"They can't hurt you anymore," she said to them. Tears

flowed freely when Wraith saw the formulae that ran through the twisted, broken bodies. The coursing power spoke only of the physical bodies, nothing of the people they had been. Everything that had made them who they were was gone and—

"No, not forgotten," she said.

Wraith knew she couldn't leave them like this. She had to bury them somehow.

As if in answer to her thoughts, the ground lifted from twelve different spots and settled back down next to the open graves. Wraith reached out, adjusting flow of gravity. The bodies, one by one, lifted from the ground and were set, gently and reverently, to rest. She placed her friends last, SK and Fritz sharing a grave so they could be together in death as they always were in life. Then Wraith moved the earth back to cover them all. When it was done, only small mounds of raised earth, still covered in ferns, marked the place for what it was: a graveyard of the lost and forgotten.

"The world might forget," Wraith whispered, "but I'll remember." She knelt down between her friends' two graves and wept without shame. "I'm sorry," she said through sobs. "I'm sorry I wasn't strong enough to save you."

"It wasn't your fault," Shadow said from behind her.

Wraith spun and stared with wide, wet eyes. She grasped for words, but none came.

Shadow smiled, as did Fritz and SK, who were standing behind her, hand in hand as ever. Gone were the sunken eyes and thin bodies eaten away by starvation. They were healthy, smiling, and very alive.

Wraith stood, looking from the graves to her friends. She

opened her mouth, but stopped when saw the pulsing equations coursing through her friends, holding them together. Her breath came up short. It was her. She was, well, she didn't know what. Conjuring bodies for their souls? Was that even possible?

"You're not real," Wraith said.

"Ouch," SK said. "That's just mean."

Wraith blinked.

"We're real, Stretch," Shadow said, smiling. "We're just not alive." She shook her head. "I have no idea how you did it, but you created these forms for us."

"You don't know?" Wraith asked.

"We kind of got gypped on the whole universal-wisdom-when-you-die thing," SK said. After a moment he looked at Fritz and Shadow. "Or is it just me?"

"Whatever comes next," Shadow said to Wraith, "you're not going to be alone."

"You made sure we were together," Fritz said and pressed herself against SK. "We're not leaving you alone."

"Yeah, what she said." SK smiled as he squeezed Fritz.

Wraith threw her arms around Shadow and was beyond relieved when she felt her friend hug back. Wraith held as tight as she dared, then she beckoned SK and Fritz to join. There was a whimper and they all turned to see Toto limp over and press himself into the group hug. It was a balm to her tattered heart.

CHAPTER TWENTY-EIGHT

Wraith was on her hands and knees, back in the church of her mind. Power, pure and intense, coursed through her like a raging river. With it came more threads of memories, snippets and pieces.

She remembered leaving the forest. In a matter of weeks, she'd mastered striding, moving effortlessly from one door-door to another, then surpassing the need for physical doors at all. That's how they had found their sanctuary—the safe house with the workbench—a place with no way in but striding. From there, the four of them had begun hunting the hunters, saving as many kids as they could and killing every member of the Theurgic Order they found. But for every kid they saved, dozens, maybe hundreds more were taken. And it was happening all over the world. They saved some, but mostly just found stories of missing kids. The real snatchers, the Order, were like shadows. They left no trace, just emptiness in the lives of those closest to the taken. Through it all, Wraith's power grew, becoming more unpredictable and uncontrollable.

Then came the explosion.

Why it happened, she couldn't remember, but the entire front of the supermarket had been blown out, and the roof had collapsed. She didn't know how many people, innocent people, had died, but it was too many.

They'd gone looking for help, for anyone who could help bring Wraith's increasing power under control, or even take it away. No one would, or could. So Wraith figured out how to do it herself. But there would be a cost. Her power and her sense of self were so closely tied that one couldn't be locked away without the other; if her magic went, most of her memories would go too. That was how Nightstick was born. A sentient hallucination to help her, and keep the power locked away. Shadow, SK, and Fritz had all helped, and then begged her to create a back door, a key to undo it. She'd agreed reluctantly.

But her plan hadn't worked. The darkness the Order had put in her had been too much for Nightstick. Power had begun to escape, and pieces of memories with it, though twisted and inaccurate. There had never been an exorcism at Richard and Mary's house. Though considering all those two had done—funneling children to the Order—they could justifiably be called devils. No, the exorcism had been her escape from the Order. Her brain had taken remnant pieces of her foster parents, and the rituals, then filled in the gaps. Thankfully, Richard and Mary weren't her parents; and Josie and Michael weren't her siblings—she was sad about that. All those early memories had just been her brain trying to make sense of the holes.

Wraith struggled for a long while before getting the upper hand on the flow of power. But she knew it was going to keep growing, and before long, it would be too much again.

"You okay?" Shadow asked.

Wraith rested her head on a broken pew. There were a lot of memories missing, and a lot of them always would be, but she had so much more than before. True, she might not know a lot about who she'd been, but she knew who she was now.

She lifted her head and looked at her friends. "I remember," she said in a whisper. "Not everything, but enough."

"I'm sorry," Shadow said, placing a hand on Wraith's shoulder.

Wraith wept. "I made a terrible mistake."

"*Nein*," Fritz said. "You couldn't keep living the way you were."

Wraith shook her head. "I know why I did it, and I shouldn't have unlocked it. It's too much power. I won't be able to control it for long. I can barely hold it now, and it's growing with every breath."

Shadow swallowed. "You could, um, lock it away again."

Wraith looked at her.

"You could do it," Shadow said.

Wraith shook her head. "Keep hiding? Pretending that there aren't kids being tortured and killed? That the Order isn't doing to others what they did to me?"

"You wouldn't remember that," SK said.

Wraith finally understood the sadness in her friends' eyes and that it came from the heavy burden she'd placed on them. "No, but you would."

None of them said anything, Fritz was the only one who moved, and she just pressed herself against SK.

"But if this power consumes me," Wraith said. "It won't just be me who's lost."

SK chortled. "We died once already. After the first time, it's really not a big deal."

Shadow wiped the tears from Wraith's eyes. "Whatever you do, we'll be with you." She placed her hand over Wraith's heart. "No one but you can remove us from there."

Wraith wiped her tears away, took a deep breath, and stood up straight. "No more hiding," she said to her friends. "No more running scared. No more standing aside and letting things happen."

The four of them hugged.

"We're with you till the very end," Shadow said.

"I love you," Wraith said. "All of you."

CHAPTER TWENTY-NINE

Dante sighed. "So, is he dead?"

Faolan shook his head. "I don't think so. The tracking spell didn't fail right away. It started, then hit a wall. I think he crossed into the Tír."

Dante looked at a TV displaying the latest breaking news, then to the door leading to the underground room. "We'll deal with him later; we have more pressing issues just now."

"Yes, you do," Caitlin said.

Dante and Faolan turned to look at her.

"We need to talk," Caitlin said to Dante, then turned to Faolan. "Could you give us a minute?"

Faolan looked to Dante, who nodded.

"I'll go check in on the Fian and Elaine," Faolan said, bowing to Caitlin before leaving to join the two women at the bar.

Dante looked to the TV, to the continuing snippets

of videos that witnesses were sending to the news stations. The videos were all short. Most of the devices had been destroyed, and only fragments of video could be recovered. Thankfully, those that had been were jumpy and of poor quality—but every time he saw an elf, goblin, satyr, or other fae appearing without glamour, Dante felt it like a physical blow.

"What happens now?" Caitlin asked, her voice tinged with concern.

Dante turned to her. "I'm sorry, what?"

Caitlin looked at him, her look one of hardened determination. It was the same look he'd seen when she'd decided to go into Tír na nÓg and rescue Fiona.

"I asked what happens now."

Dante shook his head. "Honestly, I have no idea." He looked at the marshals around the room, then up at the stairs that led to the room full of changeling and wizard children.

"I've never seen you like this," Caitlin said, stroking his arm.

Dante put his hand over hers. "It's never been like this. We've never really had to hide; the glamour did most of the work." He looked at the TV again where they'd frozen a video that clearly showed the glowing eyes of a dryad running in a panic. "Now there's Twitter and YouTube, and phones capable of recording HD video in every pocket."

Caitlin followed his gaze. "You know, generally speaking, mortals don't like our views of the world challenged. We'll do some pretty remarkable things to keep that worldview intact. I see it in the hospital all the time. As a species, we have a remarkable gift for denial and self-delusion."

"The world might not have a choice anymore," Wraith said from the doorway.

Dante and Caitlin both turned.

Then Dante blinked, his mouth fell open, and time stopped.

Wraith stood just in front of three kids. One was a small, mousy girl, probably a tinker kobold, or gremlin, changeling. She had one arm and hand entwined with a tall, thin boy who was just as clearly a coblynau, a Welsh mountain fae, changeling. The third was a Native American girl who could only be Ciye's daughter, his dead daughter. Despite all this, it was Wraith who made Dante's blood run cold. Her eyes had a burning blue fire behind them, and the mathematical equations on her hands, arms, and neck could no longer be confused for tattoos. They pulsed with blue light just under the surface, and there were more of them. He could feel the magic coursing through and around her. If Edward and other mortal wizards were like candles, she was a supermassive star. No, she wasn't a Taleth-Sidhe. She had the power of one, but she wasn't born to handle it.

"That power is going to destroy you," he said too quiet for anyone to hear.

The room was silent, and everyone was staring at Wraith. Looking from one face to another, she was

inundated with all the details their quantum information held: how long they'd lived, what they'd seen, who
they'd loved, everything that made them, well, them.
It was staggering, and she was fighting to keep from
passing out. Her brain couldn't process all the information. Even the number of particles was beyond the
scope of most to grasp. She could see the position, direction, and speed—in flagrant opposition to Heisen-
berg's uncertainty principle—of each one and how it
translated into history and personality.

She gritted her teeth, pushing aside the flood of
information that threatened to drown her. It was
like having the entire population of a million earths
screaming at her at the same time.

Wraith drew long, slow breaths, wrestling back the
power and flow of information. "I don't have much
time," she said between breaths, "but—"

"Your father thinks you're dead," Dante said to
Shadow.

Wraith turned to look at her friend, who winced.

"I am," Shadow said after a long moment.

"There isn't time to explain it," Wraith said. "And
I'm not sure I could put it in terms you'd understand."

"What did you mean when you said the world
might not have a choice?" asked Caitlin.

Wraith looked at her and in a moment knew her.
Her life, so much shorter than the elf's, was still overwhelming, but Wraith could see pieces. There was
loss, the kind Wraith knew all too well, and something
deeper—

"Are you okay?" Caitlin asked.

Wraith shook her head and looked away. "No, I'm not, but there isn't time for that either." She looked back to the room, trying not to focus on anyone. "What I meant was that when the streets of every city are filled with kids who can throw fire, teleport, change shape, or any number of other things, it's hard to deny or delude away."

"Touché," Dante said. "But you forgot about the fae that don't have a glamour anymore."

Wraith narrowed her eyes and looked from Dante to the other elves, including a blonde named Elaine. Only she and Dante were missing the equation all the others had, a slender lie that wove through their information. That's when Wraith remembered the market, and realized she stripped away their glamour and probably countless others' as well.

She drew a breath, intending to focus on building the equation to restore the glamour—and it was already done for every single fae affected, everywhere, before her breath was complete.

Dante shivered, looked around then back at Wraith.

Several hands moved to guns.

Wraith clenched her hands into fists, biting back her impatience. "You shouldn't bother," she said to the room. "You have no idea what I'm capable of. I could remove you all from existence before you even finished the thought to shoot me."

"Actually," Dante said. "I do know what you're capable of. And I think I know what they did to you."

Wraith glared at him. "You think you know what the Order did to me?" She motioned to her friends. "To them and countless others?"

"No," Dante said. "I can't even begin to understand what you all must have been put through. But I know the Theurgic Order did those gruesome things hoping to make you into a—"

"A Taleth-Sidhe?" Wraith shook her head. "Even they don't know how well they succeeded. I may not be a true Taleth-Sidhe, but I won't be the twisted abomination they hoped for either."

There was an exchange of nervous and skeptical looks

Wraith fought back more tears. "I'm not going to hurt anyone," she said, her heart breaking at the fear she saw in everyone's eyes.

"Um," SK said in a whisper. "Isn't that kind of exactly what we plan to do?"

"*Halt dein Mund, Dummkopfe,*" Fritz said in a hard whisper, followed by a smack to the back of SK's head.

"Not anyone here," Wraith said. She focused on Siobhan, who was just outside Wraith's peripheral vision, lifting her shotgun casually. Wraith sighed and reached out into the room, twisting the relevant information. A large collection of bullets and shells of every size appeared in thin air and fell to the floor ten feet away from her.

"There, now you can put the guns away," Wraith said. "They're all empty."

"Um, did I miss something?" A bespectacled man

asked as he descended the stairs and looked around. When he saw Wraith, he stopped and his eyes went wide.

Wraith looked away as Edward's information—she knew him now from that information—threatened to overwhelm her.

"You're going after them," Dante said.

Wraith didn't look at him. "You bet I am. It's time for the monster to return to its creator."

"Do you know where they are?" Dante asked.

"No," Wraith admitted. "But I won't find them standing here." She looked at Caitlin. "I just wanted to make sure Sprout and Con are going to be okay."

"The boy, Con, has a broken arm," Caitlin said.

Edward nodded. "I was able to set it. Sprout and he were both banged up, but nothing serious." He smiled at Wraith, a genuine smile filled with genuine kindness. "They'll be okay."

Wraith turned to Dante. "You'll look after them, right?"

"I will," Dante said.

"Thank you," Wraith whispered.

"Actually, there is something else," Edward said. "Sprout had something in her hand. She dropped it when she fell asleep."

Wraith had been intentionally keeping her distance from everyone, so when Edward took a step forward, she took one back.

"Sorry," he said and held out his hand. "I know it's magic, but I don't know how."

Wraith's eyes went wide, and before she was aware she was doing it, the battered quarter had vanished from Edward's hand and appeared in her own. She smiled fiercely when she saw the equations crisscrossing the quarter's surface like streets in a miniature city.

"Thank you," she said to Edward, who was staring at her with wide eyes and an open mouth.

"Um, sure," he said. "Say, how did—"

"Not now, Eddy," Caitlin said.

Wraith turned to her friends, all of whom were smiling.

"Awesome, let's go kick some ass," SK said.

"I'd like to come with you," Dante said. "If you'll permit it."

"Regent, no!" Faolan said.

"Aye, and me as well," Siobhan said.

"Not without me," Elaine said.

"I appreciate the gesture," Wraith said. "But—"

"May I explain why?" Dante said, his tone polite but firm.

Wraith was about to say there was no point, but something in his tone kept her silent and made her nod.

"Thank you," Dante said and bowed slightly. "For too long the court has ignored those who most need our help and protection." He looked to Faolan. "One may even have actively helped those who would use the lost and forgotten for truly vile purposes." He turned back to Wraith. "I want to set things right, or at least try."

"I—" Wraith started to say.

Dante went to one knee and bowed his head. Every elf, with the exception of Elaine, did the same. "On behalf of the Rogue Court of the fae and the Cruinnigh of the five houses, I offer our humblest and most sincere apologies," he said. "Give me the chance to restore the honor of my court."

Wraith was struck speechless. Who were these people? No one was like this! She turned to her friends.

"Say yes," SK said in a loud whisper. "They have lots of guns."

"You'll need to let them have the bullets back," Shadow said through a smile.

"Can we trust them?" Wraith asked in a whisper.

"By my name, I swear it," Dante said.

Wraith turned and studied Dante for a long time. The story that was written onto his quanta began flooding into her again. She struggled to push it aside, fighting through the memories that ran through her mind like a runaway train. He was sincere, she knew that much.

She closed her eyes, fighting back the information overload and spoke with effort. "Thank you, Regent Shaleez-Naran."

Dante's head snapped up and he looked at her with wide eyes. "How . . . ?"

Everyone in the room, including Edward and Caitlin, stared in shock.

The flow stopped and Wraith's mind was back to the here and now. She drew in a deep breath and shook her head, realizing she'd just used his true name, pulled from the torrent of information. "I'm sorry. There's just so much, too much." She tapped at her forehead. "Things are getting jumbled in here. It's hard for me to know what's now, and what was. Or even what's mine."

Dante rose, as did the other elves. "I, um, understand." He glanced around the room, his gaze lingering on Edward and Caitlin.

"You should let me go in your stead," Faolan said to Dante.

"No," Dante said, turning to Faolan. "I need you to stay here and try to sort this mess out." Dante glanced at Caitlin, and Edward then continued in a whisper. "And keep them safe. I've worked too hard to ensure they have a normal mortal life."

"If you leave it to me," Faolan said. "I'm going to evacuate as many as I can to other cities. Staying here isn't the smart choice."

"I defer to your judgment, Magister," Dante said. "Just be sure to let me know where to find you."

"Aye, and what about us, then?" Siobhan said.

Wraith looked at Shadow, unsure.

"When the cause is just," Shadow said, "the just will flock to the cause."

"And, just cause," SK said.

Fritz rolled her eyes. "*Meine Liebe*, you really need to learn when to stop talking."

Wraith turned back to the room, briefly glancing down at the quarter. "Okay—" She opened her hand

and looked at the quarter again. She looked at Edward. "Did you say Sprout was holding this?"

Edward nodded.

Why did Sprout have a coin? Wraith wondered. It was possible the little girl had picked it up as a keepsake, but that just didn't seem right. Then she smiled and squeezed the quarter tight.

"They gave it to her," Wraith said.

Her friends exchanged a glance, clearly not following.

"That's why Geek and Ovation charged the snatchers! They each took one of the other coins, knowing if they got taken that I could find them!" She turned to Dante. "I want to see her before we go."

CHAPTER THIRTY

When Wraith stepped into the room with SK, Fritz, and Shadow in tow, the fifties looked up at them and went silent. No one moved for a long second. Then the whispers began; first one, then more. Some of the kids pointed at Shadow and her friends, muttering something about them being the ones who rescued them.

Wraith ignored them, her eyes locked on Con and Sprout. Con was sleeping on a couch, sitting up with one arm in a pale greenish cast, not quite fiberglass but similar. Sprout was curled up next to him, nuzzled close. Wraith walked over to them.

Everyone moved as far away from her as they could.

Wraith knelt down and gently brushed Sprout's hair from her face. "I'll get them back, I promise."

No one said anything.

She looked at Con and smiled. "That was really smart, dividing the coins up," she said, her voice just above a whisper. She leaned forward and kissed Con's cheek, then Sprout's forehead. "Thank you for taking me in, for being so kind to me. I'm sorry you got caught in the middle of this. I know it's my fault. But I'll make it right. I'll use the coins to find Geek and Ovation, and I'll make the Order pay for what they did"—she glanced around the room at the scared kids, then to her friends—"to all of us."

"We'll make sure they're safe," Caitlin said. "You get your friends back."

Wraith smiled and nodded at Caitlin. Then she looked at Dante. "It's time to go."

Everyone nodded.

Wraith turned back, knelt down, and softly kissed Sprout's forehead again.

"I'll be back," Wraith said.

A tear broke loose when Sprout made a soft sound of contentment and smiled. Wraith stood, wiped her eyes, then turned around and led the way back downstairs.

The pile of ammunition was collected, and now four marshals stood ready, as did Elaine and Siobhan. Wraith noticed in the corner of her eye how Edward went to Caitlin, who was carrying a little girl that could only be her daughter, and pulled them close. Wraith felt a twinge of envy at the little girl, being in a place surrounded by love. But it was quickly replaced by a comforting feeling. There was still love, kindness, and caring in the world. All was not darkness and pain.

"So, what's the plan, Stretch?" Shadow asked.

Wraith opened her mouth, but nothing came out. She hadn't realized until that moment that she didn't have a plan, or anything even resembling one. She just shrugged.

"I sort of figured we were going to free the kids and put down those robed bastards," SK said.

Wraith exchanged glances with Shadow, who shrugged.

"I guess that's our plan," Wraith said.

Wraith noticed the uncertain looks the elves and Siobhan gave Dante. "You can change your mind," she said to him. "You've made up for—"

"With all due respect," Dante said. "I haven't." He turned to his cadre. "None of you have to come."

Siobhan answered by racking a shell into her shotgun.

Elaine rolled her eyes. "You've been watching too many movies."

The marshals just stood at attention.

Dante turned back to Wraith and gave a slight bow. "You lead the way."

Wraith nodded. "Step close, you don't want to be caught on the edges of the striding." She wasn't sure, but she thought Dante shuddered a little.

When the group had gathered close, Wraith ran her thumb over the quarter, following the entangled threads of information to the dime. She felt it instantly, a comforting weight on the end of a long strand of information. She drew in a breath, letting the power build inside her. It rose, slow and deliberate, easy to manage. Unable to resist, she clicked the heels of her glittering ruby red Doc Martens three times, and the world spun around them.

Wraith focused, the woven lines that tied the quarter to the dime pulling them along effortlessly, like a spring-loaded winder. Reality itself spun around them.

As it turned out, striding wasn't a problem. Stopping was.

When the stride ended, it was instant. Everyone was sent tumbling through plants and soft dirt. Wraith felt a twinge of déjà vu, but before she went far, she reached out and shifted the energy of her momentum into the trillion-trillion particles that made up the air. She alone remained standing as a mild wind blew out from around her in a circle.

Siobhan rolled until she stuck a massive tree and came to a stop with a grunt. The elves tumbled like circus acrobats performing a trick they'd done a thousand times. With a few tight somersaults they shed their momentum, using the last of it to come to their feet, weapons at the ready. Elaine came to a crouch, her face a shade of green to match the ground growth around them.

As if stepping out of a whisper, Wraith felt Shadow, SK, and Fritz appear behind her.

"Gently apply the brakes," SK said over her shoulder.

"Aye, he's got the right of it," Siobhan said as she got to her feet.

Wraith didn't hear them. She was busy fighting the twisting in her stomach as she scanned her surroundings. The redwoods loomed over them and a breeze that did not come from Wraith rustled the ferns. She didn't see any of that though. Her eyes were locked on the twelve mounds of earth, settled almost to the point of being invisible. But she knew each one. Her heart filled with sorrow and it seemed a struggle to make it keep beating.

"Where are we?" Elaine asked as she looked around, her color starting to return to normal. Wraith thought she could faintly smell vomit coming from Elaine's direction.

"Did we take a wrong turn, then?" Siobhan asked.

"I don't think so," Dante said and pushed moss from a stone slab that lay on the ground.

It was an odd sensation for Wraith. She was lost in the memories of this place, of burying her friends and the fifties who now resided in her. However, she was also keenly aware of everything happening around her. It was like experiencing the world from her eyes, and at the same time from a spot above everything.

"Spread out," Dante said. "Search the area."

"Stop!" Wraith said. Her voice was so loud, so firm, that everyone froze. She turned her gaze on Siobhan, who was standing with one foot in the air, inches above the spot where Shadow was buried. "Do not step there."

Siobhan blinked, then took a hesitant step back. She looked down, and after a moment, clearly saw the outline of the grave. Her eyes darted around, spotting the other burial spots quickly.

She crossed herself. "Bloody hell, it's a graveyard."

The elves stopped in their tracks and looked around. Their expressions grew darker as they saw more and more rectangles of settled earth.

"You okay?" Shadow whispered and placed a hand on Wraith's shoulder.

"Not even a little," Wraith said. She almost longed for the cold numbness that had filled her last time she was here. Now it was all grief, sadness, and guilt. Lots of guilt.

"Others have passed through here," said one of the marshals as she crouched low. "Not long ago either."

Dante and the others moved to join her, careful to step well clear of the graves.

"What do you see, Maeve?" Dante asked.

Wraith and her friends walked over, also mindful of where they stepped.

"Six came through here," Maeve said, her fingertips pressing a spot on the ground. "All mortals: five men, one woman. All were average height, but two of the men were carrying something heavy."

Wraith's attention focused tightly on the spot Maeve was examining, and she could just see the faint outline of heel prints. "Ovation and Geek," she whispered.

Maeve looked at Wraith, her dark eyebrows drawn together.

"My friends," Wraith said. "The ones who were taken."

Maeve nodded. "That would fit." She pointed. "They appeared there and walked through here." She turned and pointed in the other direction. "Tracks vanish off that way. I'm guessing they've got a trick similar to Wraith's."

"But why stop here?" Dante asked.

Maeve smiled and gestured to some flattened ferns. "Looks like their arrival was as rough as our own." The elf shot Wraith an apologetic glance. "No offense."

"It's harder than it looks," Wraith said, looking away.

"Maybe they put up a fight," Elaine said. "Fouled up the spell?"

Dante shook his head. "And they just happened to stop here?"

Wraith didn't believe that, not for a second. She looked around, trying to figure out why they'd stop here. She paused, finally noticing something, or rather a lack of something.

"The table!" she said and rushed to where she'd arrived after her escape, unconsciously giving the graves a wide berth.

"Table?" Dante asked, following her.

Wraith stood over the spot that had been hidden behind a tree from where they'd arrived. There lay a huge rectangular impression, all the plants flat and dead.

"When I got away, I took part of the table they had me tied to," she said, then a shiver that had nothing to do with the chill wind ran over her. "Ovation, he's a slinger. Maybe they plan to do to him what they did to me and they need that table?"

"A ritual foci?" Elaine asked.

Dante nodded. "That fits."

Wraith ground her teeth, remembering all the horrors that she'd gone through, and all those who had died along the way.

"I won't let them do that to Ovation," she said, power building inside her.

"Rage won't help," Dante said, his voice calm.

Wraith looked at him, then she noticed her tattoos, or whatever they were, had begun to glow with blue light.

"Save it for when it counts," Dante said. "If you can't keep it under control, just save it for later."

Wraith clenched her fists tight, feeling her nails bite into her palms, and took one slow breath after another. The power was building steadily, getting harder and harder to keep under control. Past her fury was a tugging in her heart. Glancing down, she noticed the fingers of her right hand had found their way into her pocket and were rubbing the quarter. She withdrew the weathered coin then turned and walked back to where she'd arrived. Kneeling down, she pushed her fingers into the dirt. The dime's rough edges brushed against her fingertips, sending a rush of familiar comfort through her. Closing her fingers over the coin, the retrieved it and set it in her palm, next to the quarter. Realization welled up inside her, like the rising sun, filling her mind with light. Anger rose with it. The coins in her hand vibrated, dancing over her dirty, calloused skin. So did the earth around her, a slow rumble that gradually grew.

"Wraith," Dante said.

His words were soft, and Wraith imaged it was how someone would talk to a feral, perhaps rabid, dog.

"Trust me when I say that anger will make your power harder to control," he continued.

"I don't care," she said. "I just need to hold it together long enough to get there." She turned to him, then to the others. "You shouldn't have come."

"That was our choice—"

"It doesn't matter," Wraith said. "We're leaving."

She took the dime between thumb and forefinger, turning it back and forth as she focused on the threads connecting it to the nickel. The others rushed to close in as the wind started swirling around her.

"You know he's right," Shadow said.

"I do," Wraith said. "But it doesn't matter."

Again they were all pulled along the quantum zip line.

CHAPTER THIRTY-ONE

This time Wraith channeled her anger, guilt, fear, and sorrow into willpower, wrestling the wild power flowing through her into submission. When they approached the location of the nickel, she slowed the striding, but it took all her concentration. As the power dissipated, the group slipped back into the common reality.

The elves had weapons raised before the wind had stopped, aimed in all directions.

"I knew it," Dante whispered.

Wraith stared at the too-perfect house with the perfect lawn. A fresh collection of memories rose up from the souls inside her. Countless times she remembered meeting the kindly-looking couple for the first time. She also remembered, just as many times, being taken in the night, dragged away screaming as the "kindly" couple looked on with smiles.

"Even dead, this place gives me the creeps," SK said.

Wraith stepped forward. Fear died a quiet death at the hands of the fiery storm building inside her. With each defiant step, she formed calculations.

"Regent," a marshal, this one male, said, "we can't enter without permission."

Wraith stepped up to the porch, the wooden steps cracking under the roiling power that surrounded her. She reached out and willed the formulation around and through the screen door, then through the steel one behind it, manipulating their mass.

"Open sesame," Wraith said flatly.

Both doors, the frame, and large sections of the surrounding wall, tore from the house. They flew into the yard, chewing up the manicured grass and demolishing a flower bed.

"Please, come inside," Wraith said as she walked in. The exhilaration of letting the power loose was like the best drug imaginable.

"Easy does it, Stretch," Shadow said, close on Wraith's heels. "There could be kids here."

"She's right," SK agreed.

"Then let's get them out of here," Wraith said to her friends and turned to the house at large shouting, "Richard! Mary! I'm home!"

Her voice carried through the house, shaking and then cracking the windows.

There was only silence. Even the elves standing at the door, hesitant to step past the threshold, made no sound.

"I used to live here," Wraith said. "I invited you in."

"Oh, for the love of—" Elaine pushed past the marshals and strode into the house.

When the others saw her pass safely, they followed.

No one moved or spoke for a long while. It was absolutely silent, unreal in its completeness; the floors didn't creak, the wind didn't blow, no cars went by, no birds chirped in the trees.

Wraith looked around the living room, her eyes settling on the photographs of the other kids. More memories surfaced. She could remember being in many of them, having the pictures taken and being delighted. The joy of belonging, having a place where she was wanted. It was so vivid, it banished her anger. It's impossible to describe what it's like to be alone as a child, or the joy of finding, or believing, you weren't anymore. The warmth of those memories was driven away by cold terror as she remembered, on behalf of all the souls she carried, innumerable times waking to see robed figures surrounding her bed. The smell of burning wood filled her nose and she remembered someone fighting back. Burned clothing, hair, and flesh soon joined it.

Then came the screams.

Wraith turned and fell to her knees as she remembered the punches, the kicks, and then the injections to stop their fighting. She struggled against the strong arms holding her down, but they were too many, too strong. Around her children wept quietly, their bodies and minds frozen with terror.

No, she wouldn't let them take her! Not this time!

"Get away from me!" she shouted.

The sound of splintering wood and panicked cries around her brought Wraith back to the here and now. She stood in the living room, alone. Everyone, even her friends, had fled outside. Around her was utter destruction. Walls torn apart, flooring splintered, windows shattered. The floor was covered by debris of all kinds, except a perfect circle around her that didn't even have a speck of dust on it.

"Wraith, can you hear me?" Dante shouted from outside.

The tone and desperation in his words led her to believe this wasn't the first time he was asking this question.

She swallowed as fear and panic surged through her, the power draining away. "Oh, God! Did I hurt anyone?" she asked.

"We're fine," SK said as he peeked around the tattered hole that once held the front door. "Next time though, you might try counting to ten."

Wraith put her hands to her face and sobbed. "It's growing so quickly. It's so hard to control. It's making the memories so vivid, driving my emotions."

She didn't hear his footsteps, but she knew Dante had stepped inside and was walking toward her.

"Regent, I don't think—" Maeve's words stopped abruptly.

Wraith couldn't see the gesture, but she knew Dante had silenced her.

The tall, graceful elf stepped up to her, not making a sound as he crossed the floor, now littered with splintered wood, broken glass, and chunks of drywall. He knelt down and gently put his hands on her shoulders.

"It's okay," he said. His words were gentle, but there was sincerity in them, so profound that Wraith couldn't disbelieve. "I don't claim to know what you're struggling with, but I've seen it before, in another."

Wraith looked at him, into his luminous green eyes. This time, there was no flood of information. She just saw him, the calm serenity of his face and the concern in his eyes.

"His name was Seanán," Dante said. "He was a Taleth-Sidhe. He struggled for a long time to get his power under control too."

"Did he do it?" Wraith asked. Her voice sounded desperate and small in her ears. For the first time in a very long time, she felt like a child. She hated the way it felt.

"He did, in a fashion," Dante said, smiling a little. "With help from friends, he learned to use his emotions to control the power. Anger, hate, fear—they only made him reckless."

Wraith stared, desperate to be told that she too would be okay.

"He focused on his friends, on the ones he loved," Dante said. "He used those emotions—loyalty, love, kindness, compassion—to keep the power under control."

"It's so hard," Wraith said. Her hands were shaking

as even now the power was rising up again, as unstoppable as the tide.

Dante wiped a stray tear from her cheek. "I know, *cailin caillte*. It was for him too. He came to us younger than you, a very, very long time ago. His parents were killed when his village was raided and destroyed."

Wraith felt her heart twinge in sympathetic pain and closed her eyes, clinging to what memories she could find. "I can barely remember mine."

Dante touched her forehead. "What they did happened here." He moved his hand and put two fingers to her heart. "No one can touch who you are here, unless you let them. Nothing, no matter how terrible, can destroy who you are if you choose not to let it."

Wraith looked at him, desperately wanting those words to be true.

"I can't even begin to imagine what it was like, or is like for you now," Dante continued. "But I swear when this over, I'll do everything I can to help you."

"Why?" Wraith asked, more tears coming. "You don't know me, or owe me anything. I've done nothing but cause trouble for you. For everyone."

Wraith watched him and saw the hint of sadness come over his face, as if he were remembering something that still hurt.

"Because it's the right thing," Dante finally said. "But you're wrong. I do owe you. We let you down, and that's why you are where you are. I'm going to set things right."

"Thank you," Wraith said and before she knew

what she was doing, she threw her arms around him and hugged him as tight as she could.

Dante sighed and wrapped his arms around the child. She was, after all, still a child. He stroked her hair and held her. As he did, he thought back a long, long time ago, to a lost and scared little boy in Ireland who was running from loss, wielding power he couldn't imagine. That story had taken over a thousand years to finish. He dreaded what was to come. He knew what Wraith was going to have to do, the darkness she would have to walk through and the shadows she would carry for the rest of her life as a result

What a piece of work is a man, Dante thought.

"Come on," he said. "Let's end this."

Wraith inhaled, the smell of meadow grass grown wild filled her nose, and she realized in that moment that everything was quiet. The voices whispering and screaming inside were blessedly still, the memories weren't assaulting her senses, even the massive power in her seemed to be holding steady.

"I'm okay," she said to Dante, breaking the embrace. Then she nodded to her friends behind him.

Dante smiled, as did Shadow. Looking at her friend, her best friend, Wraith began to understand what Dante meant about using the positive emotions. He stood and helped her to her feet. She looked around the destroyed room and saw pictures scattered everywhere. Some lay loose, their frames in pieces, others still in their frames were scratched or covered in piles of broken glass. Wraith looked from one smiling face to another. As she did, there were soft whispers inside, sad but strong.

That's me, said one.

I remember that day, said another.

She collected the pictures and was soon joined by her friends, then by everyone. When all the photos had been recovered, she carefully, reverently, tucked them into her messenger bag.

"Wait here," she said to the group.

On just about every face was a look of apprehension.

"I'm not sure that's a good idea," Shadow said.

"It's fine," Wraith said. "I'm fine, or as close as I'll ever get." She turned and climbed the stairs.

She wasn't surprised when the gentle pull of the nickel lead her into the room she'd lived in. It was still furnished the same way: three sets of bunk beds, two tall dressers, two desks. On each bed sat a Bible, the props for anyone who came looking. Her eyes went up to the same crucifix still on the wall, then to the bed that had been hers.

With slow breaths, her head bowed, Wraith pushed away the memories of cold, lonely nights, crying and no one caring. When the shadows in her mind receded, she opened her eyes.

The hint of something under the bed was just visible. She swallowed, almost certain what was there.

She didn't kneel down—it was the principle. No more kneeling. Instead, she wove a calculation into the information of the beds. Then she tore it apart, ripping the bed from existence, hoping it would take the memories with it.

There on the polished floor, close to the wall, sat the nickel. She tried to picture how it had gotten here. The Order had likely brought Geek and Ovation here to—she swallowed—collect more kids for the ritual. She closed her eyes and imagined Ovation or Geek on the bed, and through a drugged haze, dropping the nickel between the bed and the wall.

She ran her fingers over the feather that was woven into her hair. "No more," she whispered, not to the empty room but to the countless tortured souls inside her. "I'm going to end this." She bent down, picked up the nickel, and closed her hand over it. She turned to leave the room but paused as her eyes passed over the top bunk against the far wall. A memory sat just at the edge of her mind. She reached for them, and snippets came to her. A little boy and girl sat on the bunk together, asking for a story. But the memories felt wrong, tangled and confusing. Wraith wasn't sure what was real. She was certain Josephine and Michael were her brother and sister, but she was also certain they weren't.

Then her eyes drifted down to the bottom bunk and her mouth went dry as more memories drifted past the far reaches of her mind. She reached into the bag, withdrawing the pictures. She began flipping through them, scanning each face for one she recognized. She stopped and smiled when she saw and recognized Josephine and Michael. They were clearing the table after a dinner, each carrying plates to the kitchen, smiling as sweetly as Wraith could ever remember. But they weren't her brother and sister, were they? She pinched the bridge of her nose, trying to untangle the corrupted memories. No, of course they weren't, it was just the lingering effects of the corruption. But then her confusion increased. There in the kitchen, doing dishes and turned just enough to see his face, was Con.

Had he been here at one time too? Or was she just imagining it?

Then she found saw more faces that she recognized.

"What the hell," she said to herself.

In this picture was a group of six kids, two girls and four boys. They were all looking up from bowls of ice cream with wide smiles. Among them were Sprout and Geek.

She winced, head throbbing with the power still building inside her. When she opened her eyes, she looked at the pictures, but the faces she'd recognized were just nameless kids now.

"You don't have time for this," she told herself. "You know what's happening, let it go. You don't have time for this."

As if in response to her words, the power inside surged and it took a focused effort for her to bring it under control.

"It's building too fast," she said. "No time."

She picked up the picture and returned them all to her bag, then headed for the stairs. Con might be safe, but Geek and Ovation weren't. They needed her, and she was going to do for them what she wasn't able to do for so many others.

"Come on, we're leaving," Wraith said as she came down the stairs, walking passed everyone and out the front door.

They followed, everyone giving her a quizzical look as they gathered around her.

"You okay, Stretch?" Shadow asked, placing a hand on her shoulder.

"Third time's the charm," Wraith said, holding out the nickel. "We've wasted enough time. I'm going to end this; I'm tired of playing this game."

"Aye, let's give the bastards a right proper arse kicking, then," Siobhan said, hefting her shotgun.

"It's rather telling that the most butch person here is you," Elaine said to Siobhan with a smile.

"Hey!" SK said.

Both women laughed and Siobhan winked at SK.

"When you're ready," Dante said to Wraith.

"Almost," Wraith said, turning back to the house. She drew in a deep breath, formed a long and intricate formulation. As it grew, she wove it through and around the house, each room, every piece of furniture. "Just need to tidy up."

The equation reached a zero sum, and its mass increased exponentially. There was a tremendous crash as the house collapsed in on itself, like a sudden vacuum had appeared inside. Wraith ground her teeth and increased the mass more and more. More cracks, crashes, crunches—and soon the entire structure was a tight pile the size of a small car.

"Efficient and dramatic," Fritz said. "I approve."

Wraith smiled, but it was borrowed from a wolf. "Let's go."

CHAPTER THIRTY-TWO

Reality turned around her. Wraith and her passengers didn't move, rather everything else did. Unimaginable amounts of information flowed through her, but all she saw was a single point in the limitlessness, a single penny calling to her like a beacon. The clarity and precision was surprising. It felt wrong, it felt—

Like bait!

Her heart froze as realization dawned on her, and then she tripped midstride.

Everyone was sent tumbling as if flung by the hand of God. Wraith reacted on instinct, reaching out and driving formulations into the fabric of reality itself, stopping herself and everyone else instantly, sending their inertia out in an unfocused wave of energy pointed straight down.

There was an earthshaking boom and a massive

cloud of dust filled the air. When it cleared, Wraith hovered twenty feet above a perfectly smooth and rounded inverted dome-shaped impression in the ground. Around Wraith, hanging in various positions, were the elves, Siobhan, and her friends.

"Um, wow?" Elaine said as she hung motionless, forty feet above the crater.

"Please don't talk," Wraith said. The power surged through her now, a constant shudder, intoxicating and threatening to consume her. She focused with all she had on slowly unwinding the formulations, easing everyone to the ground, one by one.

Last was Siobhan. When her feet touched the earth a few feet from the crater's edge, she looked down at the trees, earth, and stones crushed flat, then at Wraith.

"Thanks for that one," she said.

"You wouldn't have survived at the speed we were moving," Wraith said, eyes closed to everything but the flow of information and her manipulations of it. Of course, that didn't mean she didn't know exactly what everyone was doing.

The winding formulae carried her across the open air and set her down gently next to Elaine and Dante. Letting out a slow breath, and fighting against the shaking that raked her body, Wraith opened her eyes.

They were in the middle of a small wood, one of the rare patches in Kansas not being used for as farmland, with a small creek running just a few hundred feet away. The elves and Siobhan were in a circle around Dante, Elaine, Wraith, and her friends, maybe thirty feet in diameter, wide enough that they were all hidden among the trees.

"What happened?" Dante asked Wraith.

"And where are we?" Elaine asked.

Wraith felt the penny and every inch between her and it; she also felt the lingering darkness of the house she'd destroyed. "We're 21.06 miles from the house," Wraith said.

Elaine blinked. "You couldn't get it any closer than that?"

Wraith gave her a level look. "21.067328473—"

"Okay, that's good, thanks," Elaine said, hands up.

"Wraith, what happened?" Dante asked again.

"It's a trap," Wraith said as she turned to the northwest, where the penny still called to her like a sad and mournful child. "The Order has the penny in a circle."

Dante and Elaine exchanged a glance.

Wraith shook her head. "They must've found it on one of the boys, figured out what it was and knew I'd come for them." She drew in a slow breath. "So they set a trap."

"That's fairly brilliant tactics," Elaine said. "Trap us all in the circle," she nodded to Wraith. "Strip you of your power and kill us off at their leisure."

"Let me guess," Siobhan said as she joined the group. "Them coins will only take you to one other, right?"

Wraith blinked. "How did you—?"

Siobhan shrugged. "You're a smart one; that's just

good planning. The question though is, what do we do now?"

"You know where the penny is," Elaine said. "Can't you just have us appear outside of the circle?"

Wraith shook her head. "No, I can feel it drawing me to it. If I get close, the entanglement will pull us to it and into the circle."

Siobhan nodded at the woods. "We could just walk to the bleeding place."

"And knock on the front door?" Elaine asked. "Ask nicely for them to give all the kids back?"

Siobhan shrugged. "I'm just throwing out ideas."

"A frontal assault on what must be a protected location is never a good idea," Dante said. "Even if we had enough bodies and guns, which we don't."

Wraith ran her hands through her hair and considered her next move, ignoring the debate happening next to her. When she came to the only conclusion there was, she looked around at those gathered with her. Her eyes met Shadow's. In that silent moment, there was an entire conversation spoken only with their eyes.

"Don't even think about it," Shadow's eyes said. "Don't you dare leave us behind."

"I can't risk losing you," Wraith replied. "Not again."

"Back at you, Stretch."

Wraith looked away, her attention drawn to the northwest again and the penny calling to her.

"Is it nearby?" Elaine asked.

Wraith glanced over. The three had stopped talking and were watching her now. She just nodded to the northwest.

"You look like you've got yourself a plan," Siobhan said.

"I do," Wraith said. "I'm going to get them out. I'm going to get everyone out." Then she drew in a slow breath, turned, and took several steps back. Right away, Shadow, SK, and Fritz went to her side. "Alone."

Before anyone could move, Wraith reached out and grabbed the thread of information that entangled the penny, and reality turned around her.

"NO!" Dante yelled and rushed forward.

Siobhan caught his shoulder inches from the edge of Wraith's teleportation. The ends of a few strands of hair were cut and vanished with the girl and her friends.

"Are you out of your bleeding mind?" Siobhan shouted, shoving him back from the whirlwind.

Dante wheeled on her, rage burning in him.

Siobhan didn't back down. In fact, she stood straighter and her eyes went hard. In that moment, Dante could see the ghost of her cousin Brendan. Dante glanced at Elaine, who was looking dumbfounded at the spot the four kids had just been.

"Regent?" Maeve asked. "What happened?"

Dante let out a sigh. "We were left behind." At that moment, he understood more acutely than ever before what he was doing to Caitlin and Edward by trying to keep them safe and away from the realities of the world. He'd need to reconsider his thinking when this was done.

"I'm too old to be relearning these lessons," he said to himself.

"We're going after them, yeah?" Siobhan asked.

"Right now," Dante said, his eyes going to the northwest.

In a moment, the marshals were around them and they were all moving quickly through the woods. To his surprise, Siobhan took point. Despite being at nearly a full run, she was making as little sound as the elves, wasn't leaving any tracks, and didn't knock a single leaf from the trees and bushes. Apparently, the Fianna still had the same training requirements. Though that gave him confidence, it didn't quash the feeling inside that him that he and his group were about to step into something they were terribly unprepared for.

As if tempted by fate, that thought came into stark reality.

"*Luíochán!*" Siobhan shouted as she leapt over a trip wire, bounded off a nearby tree and into a bush.

As one, the elves sprang up into the trees.

Dante vaulted himself up, landed on the branch, and drew his pistol at the same time. He scanned the area, looking for the ambush Siobhan had spotted. All he could see was the magical trip wire and the ward connected to it. At first glance, it looked like a solitary entanglement spell, but a closer look showed the lines of magic stretching from the ward up into the trees. The same trees all the elves were now hiding in.

"Down!" Dante shouted.

There was a grunt and a black-clad form was sent flying from the bush Siobhan had leapt into. The Theurgic Order sentry, dressed in surplus military camouflage, hit the ground, rolled, and tried to get to his feet. Before he could, Siobhan sprang from the brush, landing astride the dazed man. He struggled briefly but stopped when Siobhan shoved the barrel of her sawed-off shotgun into the underside of his chin, forcing his head back. She wiped blood from her face with her free hand as the elves landed in a circle around them both, weapons raised. Dante stepped in front of Elaine, and the circle closed to include her.

"Where are you mates?" Siobhan demanded.

Four more figures popped up from behind cover and took aim with small military-style rifles.

Dante pulled Elaine down as he tumbled, taking aim and firing as he covered Elaine with his body. At almost the same instant, gunshots rang out from the marshals as they rolled to one side.

The four would-be attackers jerked and dropped without firing a shot.

Siobhan glared at the man still pinned below her and shoved the shotgun barrel harder into his neck.

"You got any more fecking friends out there, sweetness?"

The loud crack of a rifle shot rang out in answer, and a split second later a bullet struck a tree behind Siobhan.

"Sniper!" Maeve shouted.

Siobhan rolled off her captive and swung her shotgun down across his stomach. The man gasped and started to sit up. The Fian twisted, bringing her leg up high before driving it down hard onto the man's throat. He fell back, slamming his head against the ground. There were a few wet gasps then he went silent.

"Anyone see where the shot came from?" Dante asked.

"Somewhere from the west," Maeve said from behind a rock.

"Keep your heads down," Dante said.

"Glad you told me," Siobhan said from behind a tree. "I was about to get up and do a little dance number, I was."

"Keep clear of that entanglement trap," Dante said, ignoring the Fian.

Elaine reached into a pocket and drew out a length of chain with half a dozen disks of different metals attached to it.

"What are you doing?" Dante asked.

"You focus on finding the snipers," Elaine said.

She pulled a brass disk from the chain and tossed it toward the trip wire. There was a series of popping sounds all around them, followed by flashes.

Everyone glanced at Elaine.

"It's a sort of hexing charm for traps and wards," Elaine said.

Dante opened his mouth.

"I like to be prepared," Elaine said, tucking the chain back into her pocket.

Dante couldn't help but smile a little as he scanned the immediate vicinity. They were near the edge of the woods, and there didn't appear to be anymore traps.

Four more loud cracks of gunfire sounded, and everyone ducked lower as the shots bounced off the rock Maeve was using for cover.

"I counted four," Maeve said. "Bastards saw through my glamour."

Dante lay down flat and moved so he could see around the tree he was hidden behind. He moved slow, calling up a concealment charm to augment his glamour. When no shots came, he surveyed the area beyond the woods. It was a flat and open area that should be used for farming, but was apparently sitting this season out. It didn't take him long to see the snipers, four of them. They were well camouflaged, but only to mortal eyes. Each was wearing a ghillie suit and was behind a very, very large caliber rifle.

Just as slowly, he moved back behind the tree.

Everyone looked at him expectantly.

"I counted four as well," Dante said. "They've got us pinned down."

"Retreat?" Maeve asked.

"We'd never make it," Dante said. "There isn't enough cover and they've got a wide field of fire."

"On the bright side," Siobhan said. "At least it's not raining, yeah?"

CHAPTER THIRTY-THREE

It happened in an instant, or would've appeared to be an instant to anyone outside the stride. Time being relative and Wraith's mind spinning very nearly the speed of light—or so it felt—the instant seemed to drag on for days. She felt the circle well before reaching it. It was incredibly powerful, focused, and worst of all, felt well and truly perfect.

She could be making a terrible mistake, but no matter what her friends said, it was hers alone to make.

"I'm not letting you go down with me," Wraith said.

"What—" Shadow started to ask.

Wraith halted the stride, for a moment so brief it could hardly be said to have existed, and shoved her friends back into reality, praying their souls wouldn't die just because Wraith was trapped in the circle and her power couldn't get out. She had no idea if her desperate plan for escape would work. And if it did, would it be quick enough to do any good?

In a frozen, stolen moment of time, in the instant between the stride ending and the trap springing, Wraith saw the familiar cave. It had been restored to the way it had looked before she'd made her escapes all those months ago. In the center a dozen or so robed figures stood around the circle, chanting and focusing power through it. A hundred or more of the robed Order members stood back from the circle, all of them channeling power into the thirteen around the circle.

Wraith drew in a breath, and then opened herself up to the power and information around her. In that flash of an instant, she drew in and held more power than she'd even known.

The trap sprung, and it was like a thousand red-hot needles being inserted all over her body. She fell to the ground, writhing, desperate to scream but unable to draw in enough breath.

Through blinding pain, and intense focus to keep her very existence from exploding from all the power she held, she was dimly aware of a robed figure limping toward the circle. Through the shadows of his hood, she saw faint purple light burning behind dark eyes.

"And we had such high hopes for you," the ritual master said. He drew back his hood, revealing a hard-edged face marked with lines and scars. His thin lips twisted into a sneer, and the purple fire burning behind his eyes grew brighter. "Such a waste."

"Happy to disappoint," Wraith said through a grunt of pain. All her muscles were tightened like an electric charge was coursing through her.

Then she let all of the power she'd drawn in loose at once.

She didn't try and form any coherent formulation, just let it loose as raw entropy. It hit the circle like ocean waves against a massive cliff. And like water, the disorder she released found its way into the structure trying to hold it back. Nothing is truly perfect, not even this masterfully crafted circle. Chaos slipped into the fabric of the circle and began unraveling the weak points on the quantum level. Each crack in the circle was infinitely small, but there were an unimaginable number of them. They grew and met, then increased again, exponentially expanding through the spell. Wraith kept pouring power, and she could feel the circle slowing giving way, but she didn't know if it would give enough before she ran out of power. She also didn't know what would happen when she released all she had. Would her own quantum information pour out of her? Would she cease to exist?

"Even you can't break this circle," the ritual master said, then leaned in close. "You think you and the other street trash are the only ones we blessed with this immense power?"

Wraith opened her eyes and saw the ritual master's hands, held up for her to see. They were covered in intricate designs of dark power, and they all seemed to glow with a dark purple light. Beneath his heavy hood, filled with shadows even when light should've banished them, two bright, deep purple fires burned.

Time, relative and imagined though it may be, seemed to drag.

Her heart sank into the floor when she saw the thirteen around the circle had similar fires burning behind their eyes. It didn't matter. At the least, maybe she could give her friends enough time to free the others—

The ritual master stepped to one side and she saw Ovation and Geek, both unconscious and bound with thin silver chains inside a circle on the stone floor.

"Now we take this faerie abomination and mortal touched by magic and use their power to add to our own," the ritual master said, then turned back to Wraith. "And when it's done, we'll tear your soul loose, and I'll have your power for my own."

Wraith was as good as dead anyway. If the Order didn't do her in, the intense power would destroy her. But she couldn't let them kill anyone else.

Before she could do anything, even piece together a coherent thought in the haze of pain and intense focus, the ritual master drew a silver knife and walked to Ovation.

Wraith tried to scream, to shatter the circle with her will alone, but the cracks and chaos were still not enough. She watched in horror as the ritual master's hand— covered in sigils not unlike her own markings, but pulsing with purple light— grabbed Ovation's hair and pulled his head back. His eyes met hers just as the blade was drawn across his throat. She saw the light of life leave him and the circle activate to capture that light.

Something inside Wraith broke.

"Can you shoot them?" Elaine asked.

"If they were in range," Maeve said. "From what I could see, they're nearly half a mile away."

"So we just sit here?" Elaine asked.

"I'm thinking," Dante said. He blinked and looked around. "Where's Siobhan?"

More shots rang out, these coming in rapid succession.

Everyone turned to look.

"Holy crap!" Maeve said.

Siobhan was sprinting across the field toward one of the hidden snipers. She was moving erratically, giving the other sharpshooters as hard a target to hit as possible. There were several loud cracks as the high-caliber rifles turned and fired at the sprinting Fian.

"I'm not mourning another one," Dante said. "Go!"

The marshals took off, following Siobhan's lead and juking randomly. Dante turned to Elaine. "Stay—"

Elaine was crouched low, whispering something into a stone in her palm, then she stomped down with a foot. Dante felt the magic immediately, a massive thrum that radiated through the earth itself, emanating from Elaine. Dante stared at her in a combination of amazement, shock, and newfound respect.

"An elemental stone?" he asked.

"I'm a woman of mystery," Elaine said with a wry smile. "I've been saving it for a special occasion; and since you wouldn't get off your ass, it seems it's up to us ladies to resolve this standoff."

The earth shook so hard, Dante had to grab a nearby tree to keep from falling over. He turned to the field just as a massive arm, six feet long and made of stone, erupted from earth not fifty feet from one of the snipers. It was soon followed by another arm, then a massive stone-and-earthen creature hauled itself up from the ground. It stood over fifteen feet tall, its eyes and mouth were openings to a glowing light inside that burned like a furnace. It turned to the sniper and bellowed with a sound like an earthquake.

"Don't worry," Elaine said. "He's on our side."

Dante turned wide eyes to her. "Where did you—"

"I told you," Elaine said, "I'm a woman of mystery."

Shots rang out and large clouds of dust erupted from the elemental, leaving large divots in its earthen body. Those, however, were soon refilled.

"Elementals aren't well known for their obedience," Dante said and broke into a run, pulling Elaine behind him.

She didn't need much encouragement before she was running alongside him. As they ran, they saw Siobhan tackle one sniper. The ground shook as the elemental pounded the ground with its huge fists. Dante and Elaine both leapt into the air to avoid the tremor, landing just as the shockwave passed, and kept running.

The marshals closed in, laying down suppressive fire. The Order snipers drew back from their positions, their cover now gone. One by one, each drew out an amulet of black stone. Dante felt a shiver as they spoke their master's name aloud, broke the amulet, and vanished.

Dante leapt at one, but the gunman vanished while Dante was in midair. He tumbled and rolled, coming back to his feet. As quick as that, it was over. The marshals closed in on Dante and took up positions around him.

"They're gone," Maeve said. "Where the hell did the elemental come from?"

Dante nodded at Elaine. "Ask the woman of mystery."

"Not all gone," one of the marshals, Simon, said.

Everyone turned to see Siobhan marching a man in a ghillie suit, his painted face looking toward the gathered elves.

There was a roar and pounding footsteps as the elemental saw the remaining soldier and rushed forward.

"Stop!" Elaine said, hand extended to the elemental.

It froze instantly, but its eyes tracked the soldier.

Dante saw, and smelled, that the soldier had wet himself and now stood staring with wide eyes. He couldn't really blame the man, not many saw an elemental and lived to tell about it.

"That your pet?" Siobhan asked Elaine as she pushed the soldier forward again.

"I call him Rolf," Elaine said, smiling.

"We'll talk about Rolf later," Dante said.

Elaine gave him a level stare. "No, we won't."

Dante smiled despite himself, but it was gone when he turned to the soldier. "How many more of you are there?"

The man just stared at the elemental, looming but still as a mountain.

"He asked you a question," Siobhan said and smacked the back of the man's head.

The sniper recovered his senses, glared at Dante and spat, "*Servio, domino meo!*"

"I'm really starting not to like this," Maeve said.

"We are standing in the open with a mountain to one side of us," Siobhan said. "I'm guessing if there were more of them, they'd be shooting by now, yeah?"

The sniper tore his own black stone amulet from his shirt and shouted, "*Audite me, dominus, Zyth—*"

Everyone raised their weapons, but Dante got the first shot off. The man's head snapped back from a single shot to his forehead, and he fell to the ground.

"Well," Elaine said, "that confirms your suspicions about who the Theurgic Order is. Not many names start that way."

Dante nodded. "Agreed." He nodded back to the woods. "We've wasted enough time. Let's go."

"What about Rolf?" Siobhan said.

"He'll keep up," Elaine said.

"I think she meant the possible attention a fifteen-foot-tall walking mountain might draw," Dante said.

Elaine rolled her eyes, then let out a high whistle before breaking into a run.

Rolf leapt and vanished into the ground like it was a pool of water.

"Woman of mystery," Maeve said.

"So it seems," Dante said, smiling more than a little, then he began his pursuit of Elaine.

THE INFORNAUT

CHAPTER THIRTY-FOUR

Time slowed. Each millisecond was like a century. Wraith watched in horror as the ritual master released Ovation's hair and his lifeless body fell forward. In that moment, the universe seemed to shrink so that nothing and no one existed but her and Ovation. She thought of all that might've been, the life he was supposed have lived, and she found herself calculating the probabilities that she could've been part of it. There was no rage or anger, which surprised her. There was only righteous indignation and mourning for the lost life that could've been.

In that moment of grief, understanding unfolded in her mind. It was as if she'd spent her life inches away from a massive painting, and now she was stepping back and seeing it all for the first time. The pain vanished as she realized that it was part of her physical body, and that her physical body was just a vessel. She was more than that. The information and power she'd been using wasn't something separate, she was part of it all, part of everything. Even the circle that was crafted to hold her was part of her. In that moment of realization, she was closer and more intimate with Ovation than any physical touch could ever have achieved.

She reached out to the circle, the billions of frayed threads in the infinite weaving that made up the circle. It didn't become unmade, or change at all. She changed. Turning, she saw her body on the ground, and looked at it as if it were a house she'd once lived in. There was a distant nostalgia when she looked at it, but it was just a house. She changed, all right. She was now, well and truly, homeless.

Looking at the Order members, she saw the other homeless, the kids who had suffered and had been forcibly bound to their hosts; those who now wore the lost and forgotten like macabre clothing. It was all so simple. No wonder she'd never seen it before. The pain that was visited on them was to disorient them, leave them lost and confused. Wraith whispered to them, all of them, even those that were bound to her. She told them a great and powerful secret, a truth so simple it was like the utterance of God.

"You are free," she said. With those words, power flowed not from her but through her. Belief could, and did, shape reality. Those tormented souls had been bound because the magic had convinced them that they were. It wasn't a lie, but the belief of the captured was stronger than the belief of their captors. Wraith would make sure of it.

Thousands of souls turned to her, their pain and confusion halted. The power that drifted through them was like a balm to their tattered essences.

"You are free," she said again, gifting to them still more understanding and power.

Then a number of things happened all at once.

Time returned to normal.

Wraith felt several strong hands grab her and pull her back into her body. It was like falling into icy water.

The circle didn't vanish, it just no longer held her. The information that formed it was rewritten, making it as impotent and useless as a paper door.

Lastly, every single captured soul was released, freed from their captive hosts. Every one of those lost and tormented children turned on their former tormenters and captors. Dozens of glowing forms of every shape and size pulled themselves from each Order member; and then proceeded to tear at them.

Shrieks of pain and panic filled and echoed through the cave, but unlike every other time, these were not the lamentations of the lost and forgotten, the tortured and terrified. It was instead the sound of balance being restored.

The ritual master's screams joined the chorus around him as hundreds, perhaps thousands, of ghostly shapes began attacking him as well.

Wraith got to her feet, her body weak and racked with pain and cold, and watched the wronged collect their justice.

"There is no safe haven for you tonight," she whispered. "Not from a debt so great."

She walked, slowly and unsteady, through the useless circle and toward the ritual master. Only the power that still flowed through her kept Wraith on her feet, but she could feel her understanding of it waver. All the wisdom and truth that was so simple moments before was now slipping away like a dream after waking.

As she passed the Order members, they hurled darkness and tainted magic at Wraith and the freed dead alike. But against the furious horde of vengeful souls, the attacks were like handfuls of dust thrown at a tornado. One by one, the Order members began to fall, their own black souls lifting away only to be torn at and ripped apart by the righteous hands of their victims.

Through the winding formulation that made up the quantum information of the Order members, Wraith saw dark threads that stretched out, reaching beyond this reality like the strings of a psychotic puppet. Though it was beyond her present understanding, she knew there was indeed a puppet master on the other side of those strings; something vast, powerful, and terribly dark. She even saw a name, one that she knew not to utter. Zythtraxion.

The ritual master raged and fought. His own power wasn't insignificant, and the threads that connected him to his master were countless. Even with all that, it wasn't enough to keep the horde at bay. They tore at him, and at the cords that made him dance. The ritual master stopped when he saw Wraith and gnashed his teeth, seemingly unconcerned about the dead still slashing at him. To Wraith, it was like something else was looking at her through those eyes.

Wraith watched in a strange, objective horror as she saw the broken filaments from the fallen Order members attach themselves to the ritual master. The puppet master would not let his toy fall so easily.

"This will not stop us," the ritual master said through grunts as the onslaught against him continued. "We are everywhere, in each shadow and darkened corner. We are the dread that fills nightmares."

"I'm the dawn that turns nightmares to empty dreams, soon forgotten," Wraith said without fear or anger. There was no reason for either. What she'd said was just simple fact. With that, she reached out to tear away the connection to his master.

"Then you will all be forgotten with us!" he screamed and dark purple fire surged down those puppet strings and filled him until it erupted from his hands. Massive tendrils of blackish-purple flame grew and spread through the cavern, consuming the bodies of the dead and those still fighting.

Wraith drew back in pain from the flames, so cold they burned. She saw the formulation of the fire, but couldn't make sense of it. It wasn't right. It was an abomination of magic, twisted and perverse. It flatly defied everything she knew and understood. She reached out to draw an equation to counter it, to cut the ties, but the power was too much for her to control. She struggled, trying to force the formulation into a zero sum, but searing agony bore into her head. She screamed and turned away. She saw Geek, unconscious but alive in his circle. The fire was closing in around him.

She looked from him to Ovation's body and back. Tears ran down her cheeks. She had power, she *was* power, but her body wasn't strong enough to control it; it never had been. She couldn't save them both. Just like before—like every time it seemed—it wasn't her power that was lacking, it was her. She might be able to quash the fire. Of course it would likely be at the cost of all that made her who she is, which she would do, but the time required would cost more. She couldn't do it fast enough to save Geek and any others who might be held in the cages beyond this cave.

She cursed her own weakness and frailty for a brief moment. Then she made her choice. She gave a last look to Ovation's body, already unrecognizable in death, and said a silent good-bye and thank-you.

"BANG!" she shouted, and sent a ball of hypermassive particles at the ritual master. It struck him hard in the chest and sent him across the room, fire still pouring from him. Wraith fought through the hurt and wove an equation around herself that would negate the heat of the flames. She ran to Geek and pulled him close, wrapping the formulation around them both.

Her mind shifted and she made to stride. It was like trying to direct the Mississippi River with her hands. Pain spread from her head to her whole body, the power slipped, and the world around her just shuddered before it settled back into its normal state. She coughed and realized for the first time she'd fallen to the ground. Her head swam and she knew it was because the oxygen in the cave was being consumed by the fire that now seemed a living thing. She fought to her feet, grabbed Geek's shoulders, and was thankful he was so slight of build. She dragged him as quickly as she could to the only doorway she knew, the one that led back to the cells.

She slipped and fell over and over, but each time she got back up and pulled Geek along with her. She was still a fifty feet from the tunnel leading to the cells when a scream from the roiling pyre of purple flame drew her up short. She turned, instinctively covering Geek's body with her own and the formulation she was barely holding together.

The ritual master, now a burned mass of skin and bone, walked through the flames toward Wraith. She could see the same twisted, unnatural equations that fueled the dark flames now winding through him entirely. The remaining souls that had not fled to find peace lashed at him, but when they touched that tainted formulae, they reeled back. Wraith could see flaming darkness begin to eat away at the souls. She closed her eyes, and instead of fighting the agony and fear, she channeled it. She used all she had left to wipe the fire from the burning spirits, and urged them to flee, to find the peace they deserved. When they did, she drew Geek closer.

"I won't leave you," she said to him. "I promise."

"And we won't leave you," Shadow's voice said.

Wraith saw three radiant, ghostly forms appear in front of her, two of them holding hands.

"No," Wraith said, fighting to stay conscious from exhaustion and the lack of oxygen. "Not you. You have to go. I don't know what he is, but he'll destroy you!"

"We'll be okay," SK said.

"Ja," Fritz said. "We're together."

"All of us," Shadow said to Wraith.

Tears blurred Wraith's vision, already fading to black, but she saw her friends lunge toward the ritual master.

She made to scream for them to stop, but a rumble shook the cave, causing sections of it to collapse. A moment later, a massive creature formed of earth and stone, eyes and mouth burning with an internal fire, sped past Wraith and hurled itself at the ritual master. It brought its colossal fists down on the burned form, smashing it to the ground, and snapping some of the black threads. The creature didn't stop, but began pounding down again and again like a manic child. Fire lashed at the stone, but even the dark and unnatural flames did nothing to slow the behemoth. Distantly, Wraith understood that the earthen nature of the being was allowing it to ground out the magic, like lightning.

Strong hands grabbed Wraith's shoulders.

She turned, ready to unleash a blast of force at her attacker, unsure one would answer.

"Easy, girl," Siobhan said, lifting her hands. "It's us."

"Come on," Dante said, offering his hand to Wraith. "Let's get you out of here."

"I'll get this one," Siobhan said and crouched down to take Geek into her arms.

Wraith gave her a skeptical look.

"It's okay, love," Siobhan said. "Let me have him."

Wraith didn't need to be convinced; there was no another option. She released Geek and took Dante's hand. He pulled her to her feet as Siobhan lifted Geek into her arms and ran for the cave entrance. Wraith nearly collapsed, but Dante scooped her up and followed the Fian.

Wraith looked back, but didn't see her friends. She could only see the vague outline of the stone creature still battering the ritual master, the few remaining threads connecting him to his master snapping with each blow. The world and time itself seemed to waver. She saw the familiar cells, all empty, doors torn off.

"You got them out?" Wraith asked in an exhausted whisper.

"Every single one of them," Dante said.

Wraith tried to smile, but the anguish from the uncertainty of her friend's fate still ate at her heart.

She felt so tired, and she hurt from her soul to her

skin. Maybe this was it, her time to go and be with her friends. That wouldn't be so bad. Maybe her parents were waiting for her too. Tears rolled down her cheeks as she slipped into darkness, whispering a silent prayer that she'd wake to see her friends, safe and intact, finally at peace.

CHAPTER THIRTY-FIVE

Wraith didn't remember waking up. One moment she
was being carried out of the Order's stronghold, the
next she was here. Where here was, she didn't know.
Everything around her was white, stark, and perfect,
save for the rolling hill she stood at the center of. The
hill was covered in grass so green it might've been colored by a child. Scattered about the grass were gleaming white tombstones, hundreds of them, reaching to
the very edge of this reality. It was as if someone had
started to create a new universe from nothingness, and
started by pulling up a section of Arlington or some
other military cemetery.

As she looked around, children began to appear,
standing behind the markers and smiling serenely.
There were so many, maybe as many as a thousand.
They looked to range in age from as young as ten to as
old as seventeen, and all of them were fifties, the vari-

ous aspects of their fae side now obvious; luminescent eyes, pointed ears, small horns, gills, with skin colors of ebony, pale blue, dark brown, or alabaster. She knew them all, and they knew her. She was them, and they were her. Or rather they had been. They weren't scared, confused, or crying out anymore. In fact, the look of serenity on their faces made Wraith realize she felt the same way. She didn't feel any pain or sadness, though the whisper of grief and regret was in the corner of her mind.

"Where am I?" she asked herself.

"It's a sort of way point," Shadow said from behind her. "A crossroads."

Wraith turned and saw her three friends, intact and smiling. She threw her arms around them, hugging them all as tight as she could. When they hugged her back, she never wanted it to end. At the conclusion, it felt as if it hadn't even been seconds. She smiled at how alive her friends looked, and then her smile faltered. She looked from them to the host of souls watching them, and understood. Her smile returned, born of both great sadness and joy together.

"It's okay, I'm ready," she said.

Now it was the smile of her friends that wavered.

"Um," Shadow began.

"No!" Wraith said. "You're not going on without me. There's nothing left for me!"

Shadow touched Wraith's cheek and smiled. "Oh, there is so much left for you, more than you can imagine."

"I don't understand," Wraith said.

SK chuckled. "Yeah, ain't it a bitch?"

Fritz poked him in the ribs.

Shadow wrapped Wraith in a hug. "We didn't want to leave without saying good-bye."

"Or saying thanks," SK said as he joined Shadow in the hug.

"*Ja*, and that we love you," Fritz added.

Wraith was going to protest, to say she couldn't go on without them, to beg them to come back with her, but she stopped when she realized just how selfish that was. Instead, she just hugged tighter and whispered, "I love you too."

A long moment later, the embrace broke again.

"Look," Shadow said and nodded behind Wraith.

She turned and saw a brilliant and beautiful light appear in the sky. In fact, to call it beautiful was so insufficient, it was an insult. It was sublime. Music began to play from everywhere, but like the light, words failed to capture the sheer magnificence of it.

"Thank you," a young Japanese boy with fox-like features said. "Thank you for setting us free." Then he looked up to the light and began to drift up to and into it.

"Thank you," whispered a girl dark brown skin and hair the color of summer grass, before floating up to the light.

"Thank you," said another, then another and another. Each so sincere and heartfelt, Wraith knew the only proper response was to cry. One by one, all the lost and forgotten thanked her, then made their way to the light. As Wraith watched, a chorus of a thousand words of thanks, in as many languages, came from the nothingness around her. She saw for the first time the countless others—those she didn't know— emerging from the white and gliding up to and into the light. It was like the most beautiful ballet imaginable.

Time had no meaning here, so Wraith didn't know how much had passed, but eventually she turned back to her friends and felt sadness finding its way into her heart, even here.

"You have to go," she said in a whisper.

Shadow nodded.

"But we'll be right here," SK said and touched Wraith's heart.

Everyone looked at him.

"What?" SK asked. "I can't be serious sometimes?"

Shadow smiled. "It's cliché but true—they'll always be a piece of us in your heart."

"And here as well," Fritz said, tapping the side of Wraith's head. "So work on your *Deutsche, ja?*"

"You German minx," SK said, turning to Fritz. "Did you just make a joke? That is so hot!" SK pulled her close and kissed her.

"You still want to come along?" Shadow dead-panned.

"Coincidently, I am rethinking that." Then Wraith hugged her again. "See you later?"

"Don't rush," Shadow said. "But we'll be waiting."

Wraith let go, reluctantly, then turned to SK. She cupped his face in her hands, kissed his cheek, then looked him in the eyes. "Thank you for always making me laugh."

"Thank you for always laughing," SK said.

Wraith hugged Fritz. "You take care of him."

"*Ja*, like anyone else would put up with him," Fritz said.

"Baby, you cut me so," SK said.

Wraith let go and stepped back. She clenched her jaw, fighting tears as her friends rose into the air. In a moment, they were gone.

Wraith closed her eyes and waited to return to the world.

Nothing happened.

She opened her eyes to find the light still shone and the music still played. She began to fear that maybe she was stuck between worlds. She imagined Dante or Caitlin giving her CPR and trying to bring her back. Thoughts of what an eternity here would be like had just started when she smelled something familiar, a woman's perfume. It was faint, but it tugged at a memory she'd thought was lost. It brought feelings of comfort, security, and the taste of grilled cheese sandwiches.

She spun to see a middle-aged couple standing in front of her. Both were tall: the woman brushing six feet, the man a few inches taller. His face lined from years of smiling and laughing. The small patch of hair under his lip was gray; and his brown hair, the same plain shade as her own, was sprinkled with white. His eyes were lined, but inside they sparkled and shined, vivid and intense; they were a match for Wraith in both color and shape. When he smiled, it reached to his eyes, and brought the same feelings of comfort to Wraith as did the perfume.

The woman was built much like Wraith, tall and slender. Her hair was the color of chestnuts, and her eyes a pale blue. Her nose and fine eyebrows were the same Wraith saw whenever she looked into a mirror. When the woman smiled, it caused her eyes to light up. Wraith knew that smile as her own.

"Mom? Dad?" Wraith barely managed to get out.

"Oh, baby," her mother said and took Wraith into her arms.

The smell of her mother's perfume was like someone turned the light on in a darkened room. Memories began to come to the surface. Wraith could remember skinned knees and the fizzing of hydrogen peroxide and birthday parties with homemade *tres leches* cake, her favorite; coming in from cold days to find grilled cheese and tomato soup waiting and working with her dad in the garage on the car, the smell of oil and gas featuring prominently; working with her father and mother on math homework. All this and so much more.

Her dad looked her in the eyes. "We don't have much time, Janey," he said.

Wraith blinked and could see both her parents were growing transparent. She looked up at the light. "No! You can't take them too! Not yet!"

"Shh, honey, listen to your father," her mother said. "Time is short, and these moments are a gift."

Wraith looked at her father, and tried not to remember what happened with Nightstick in the church.

"It wasn't an accident," her father said.

"What wasn't?" Wraith asked.

"What happened to us," her mother said.

"What? Who?"

"They did it to get to you, baby," her mother said as she stroked Wraith's hair. "To awaken your magic before we could teach you anything and make you into—" Her mother wiped tears away.

Wraith's eyes went wide. "Wait. You're both wizards?"

Her father nodded. "We were. And there are others. You need to find them, honey. They can help you."

"How do I find them?" Wraith asked.

"Go home," her mother said. "You'll find it in the secret place that opens with a magic number."

Wraith desperately racked her brain. "I don't know what that means. I don't remember everything."

Both her parents began to look nervous.

Wraith could now see through them.

"Find them, Janey," her father said. "You'll need all the help you can get, so reach out to others. But be careful who you trust."

"I know you can do it." Her mother smiled at her with pride. "You were always a remarkable child."

"Please, don't go," Wraith said.

"It's not up to us," her mother said and reached out to touch Wraith's cheek, but her hand passed through it.

Both her parents' mouths were moving, but the

only sound was the music that had been so beautiful just moments before.

"I can't hear you," Wraith said and reached out for them, but her hands passed through them both.

They began to rise up and drift toward the light.

"No! Not yet!" Wraith screamed at the light. She scrambled to think of an equation, some formulation that would give them mass, bring them back into reality, but there was nothing here for her to form it with. She pushed her desperation into a ball deep inside and tried to wish it so with her willpower.

Her father waved his arms to get Wraith's attention.

Wraith looked and watched as he pointed to his eye and mouthed "I," then he crossed his arms over his chest, "love," and pointed to her, "you."

Her mother repeated the gesture.

"I love you," Wraith said to them. "I'll find them, I promise! I won't let you down!"

Then they were gone and Wraith was alone. That once beautiful music was empty, and the light felt cold.

CHAPTER THIRTY-SIX

Wraith didn't open her eyes. If she did, it would mean she was back, and everyone that mattered to her was well and truly gone. That was when she noticed the silence. Not around her, she could hear voices as if in another room. The truly startling silence was in her head. It had been so long since she'd been alone there that she'd almost forgotten what it felt like. She even found herself missing it. Not the screams and desperate cries, of course, just the presence, the feeling of not being alone. Right now, she felt incredibly alone, more so than she could ever remember being.

Her wallowing was so consuming, she hadn't noticed her magic had returned. When she focused on it, she was confused. It was still powerful, incredibly so; the calculations and formulae drifted through her head, calm and serene now. But it felt different. The power flowed through her, not like the raging force of a flash flood but like a strong, deep, and calm river. No, it was nowhere near the levels it had been after she'd unlocked it, but it was orders of magnitude more than she'd wielded before the Order had gotten their claws into her.

She opened her eyes slowly and found herself in a rather large, nicely furnished but dimly lit bedroom. There were a pair of windows that had the curtains drawn, and while the lamp on the nightstand was on, it wasn't a bright bulb. Wraith was in a rather plush king-sized bed. The walls were a soft blue, like a summer sky, and all the furnishings looked nice. But she really wasn't sure; she just knew they were pretty. In fact, the whole room was pretty. There was a definite feminine sense to it; nothing overt, or stereotypical, just a subtlety to it. She could see three doors, one of which was open to reveal a bathroom. There was an odd-looking desk, on which sat a bundle of folded clothing, her boots, and her bag. Glancing down, she noticed for the first time that she was wearing a man's T-shirt—long on her, but not big—and her underthings. But nothing else. She briefly wondered who'd undressed her.

Pushing that thought aside, she looked back to the room. Beyond all she could see, or rather as part of it, she saw the quantum information as before. It danced through the air and everything that made up reality. It was different somehow. No, it wasn't. She was different—or how she observed it all was different. It wasn't like she was outside looking in, or even that she was inside looking out. She *was* the inside, and the outside. If before she was a conductor for the orchestra, now she was the orchestra, the instruments, the concert hall, the air that filled it, and the music that drifted through that.

Her body still ached, though only a little. Her mind was clear. Actually, it felt empty—like a house after all the kids and furniture are taken out. Mostly, she just felt really hungry and numb inside. The numbness was similar to losing her parents for the first time. She knew the pain and tears would come in time. The hunger was something she was used to and could ignore. What she couldn't ignore were the new equations drifting through her mind. She sat up and crossed her legs, then reached out with her consciousness. A calculation formed easily, as if she'd done it a thousand times before. Holding out her hand, palm up, all the light in the room—what little there was—collected in her hand. It was like a miniature sun. She could see the swirling light waves circling the infinitely small singularity that existed in this dimension in such a way that it only affected the wave form of the light, not any of the mass in the room.

She thought of Shadow, SK, and Fritz, and her heart began to ache. Actually, it began to break. The light was released in a flash like a mini supernova. But the tears that began to run down her cheeks had nothing to do with the burst of light. She turned to the lamp, now shining light as normal. Another formulation assembled and surrounded her fingers. She moved them, wrapping lines of magical code around them, and pulled. There was a pop and the light bulb went dark. She smiled and laughed a little, then looked at the desk chair. She compiled the next equation in her head. Gravitons pooled under the chair in response. There was the creaking of stressed wood, then a crash as the chair collapsed. Its splinters and broken pieces further compressing from the gravity well she'd formed.

The door flew open.

"Wraith, are you okay?" Dante asked.

Behind Dante stood a very tall woman; she was a couple inches over six feet. Her eyes were luminescent green like Dante's and her long dark-auburn hair was pulled back from her face, revealing pointed ears and gracefully curved features. She wore an expression of concern to match Dante's.

"Yeah, sorry," Wraith said, then shook her head. "I'm fine. Well, as fine as I can be."

"What happened?" Dante asked, looking at the chair, then around the dark room.

Wraith turned to the lamp and reached out to touch the bulb. Instinctively, she restored the information for the bulb back to what it had been before she hexed it. It came on and lit the room.

"Nice trick," the woman said with wide eyes. "Are you part tinker or something?"

Wraith swallowed back the stab to her heart. "Actually, I think I am now."

The elves exchanged a look, but Wraith ignored it.

"How long was I out?" she asked.

"About"—Dante glanced at his watch—"forty hours. We were starting to worry about you."

Wraith suddenly felt hungrier.

"He was worried," the woman said and smiled. "I knew you'd be fine."

"Sorry, this is Brigid," Dante said. "She's the magister of the New Middle Region." He turned to Brigid and gestured to Wraith. "Magister, this is Wraith."

"Please tell me you're the one who put me in this," Wraith said, motioning to the shirt, which on her was practically a nightgown.

Brigid nodded. "It was. Dante is too much the gentleman."

Wraith looked down at the T-shirt, noticing for the first time there was a graphic on it. It was a picture of Dr. Strange, the comic book character. His hands were surrounded by blue magic.

"Where did I get this?" Wraith asked.

"It was a gift," Dante said. "From a very grateful young man."

Wraith looked at him. Her concern must've been obvious.

"There's a lot to fill you in on," Dante said.

Wraith opened her mouth to ask one of the millions of questions forming.

"There will be time for that in a bit," Brigid said and stepped over to Wraith. She sat on the edge of the bed and looked her over. "How are you feeling? Physically, I mean."

"What about the others?" Wraith asked. "Sprout and Con." Her heart dropped and she almost didn't ask, certain she knew the answer. But she gave in. "What about Toto?"

Dante expression grew pained. "Toto wasn't just a dog. You know that, right?"

Wraith nodded, though she still wasn't sure exactly what that meant.

"Well, he went home," Dante said. "Back to his people, to rest and heal."

Wraith nodded. "That's for the best. He was never really mine. I think he just stuck around to watch out for me because of Shadow." She looked from Brigid to Dante. "What about the others?"

Dante paused, obviously considering his words. "They're fine. Healing."

Wraith narrowed her eyes. "That's not everything, is it?"

Dante smiled and opened his mouth.

"It can wait," Brigid said, turning Wraith's attention back to her. "I've looked them over and they'll be healed in no time." She gave Wraith a look that was filled with compassion but not with room for debate. "I haven't had a chance to look you over yet, since you went unconscious."

Wraith ran a hand through her hair and shrugged. "I'm sore, but I've been worse."

"Any headaches, nausea, light-headedness?" Brigid asked as she ran fingertips over Wraith's brow, brushing her hair aside.

It brought memories of her mother to mind, but Wraith pushed the emotions down and just shook her head. "Not really. I'm pretty sure it's just being hungry."

"Well then," Dante said. "You get dressed; we'll get you some food and I'll tell you—"

"Everything," Wraith supplied.

Dante smiled. "I don't know everything, but I'll tell you what I do know."

Wraith nodded and carefully got to her feet. Brigid stayed close. Wraith didn't protest. After she was sure she wouldn't collapse, Wraith nodded at Brigid. "I'm okay, thanks."

Brigid walked back to the door. "I took the liberty of washing your things. I hope you don't mind."

Wraith couldn't remember the last time she'd worn clean clothes. Then she shuddered. Actually, she did know. It was the night the Order had come and taken her and the others. She pushed the memory away. "Thank you, I appreciate it."

"The bathroom is right there if you want to wash up," Brigid said. "I'll bring some food for you."

"Take your time," Dante said and Brigid stepped out. "Eat, and when you're ready we'll talk."

Wraith nodded. As the door started to close, she asked, "Wait, where are we?"

"In my home in Kansas City," Brigid said.

Wraith glanced at the ruined chair. "Oh, sorry about that."

Brigid smiled, then she winked. "I'll just add it to your bill."

Alone in the room, Wraith started to feel her sadness and grief rise up. She wiped away the few tears that escaped, and pushed the emotions down deep. After a moment, she collected her clothes and boots, and went into the bathroom. It was huge, at least compared to Wraith's experiences, and covered in light-colored marble tile. There was a glass-walled shower in the corner and a large bathtub against one wall. Two sinks were against the wall opposite the tub and a small wall separated the toilet from the rest of the bathroom. On that wall was a rack of fluffy white towels. She didn't want to touch anything, it was all so beautiful and clean. However, the thought of a hot shower won out, so she set her clothes on the counter next to a small basket that held a toothbrush and toothpaste, a hairbrush and deodorant.

I feel like I'm in the presidential suite, she thought. She closed the door to the bedroom, turned on the shower, and got undressed.

After a long and luxuriant shower, complete with nice-smelling shampoo and fancy soap, she turned off the water, stepped out, and grabbed a towel. They were even softer than they looked. She felt clean and more than a little refreshed. Her clothes felt strange when she put them on, softer than she was used to, aside from being clean. They also had the faint scent of lilies. She lifted her shirt to her nose and smelled deep. The scent carried her back.

It was Mother's Day. She was six years old, making her mother breakfast in bed without her father supervising. She buttered the toast, poured the orange juice without spilling a drop, and even shared some of her beloved Cinnamon Toast Crunch cereal. The last touch was two pink lilies in a tall glass. They were her mother's favorite.

One by one, she moved each of the items from the counter to a tray she'd set on the carpeted area of the room. When the tray was full, she carefully slid it down the hall to her parents' bedroom and crept silently inside. Both her parents were still sleeping, and the sun was just rising outside, bathing the room in soft blue light.

"Happy mommy's day!" she shouted.

Her parents jolted and sat up in bed.

Her mother turned bleary eyes to Jane, then smiled wide. "What's this?"

"I made you breakfast!" Jane said proudly.

Wraith smiled, remembering the nervous look her parents had exchanged, though she didn't understand it at the time.

"Yes, you did!" her mother said and sat up. "Thank you, sweetheart, that's very nice."

Wraith watched her mother mouth silent words. In answer, the tray lifted from the ground, drifted through the air, and settled on her mother's lap. Her mother looked at the bowl of cereal, then at Jane, eyebrows raised. "I get Cinnamon Toast Crunch?"

Jane nodded and smiled. "It's a special occasion."

Her parents laughed.

"Come here, Janey," her father said.

She went to him and he pulled her up into the bed, setting her between her parents. Her mom bent down and kissed her forehead. "You even brought me flowers."

"They're your favorite," Jane said proudly.

Her mother's smile tugged at Wraith's heart.

"Yes, they are," her mother said. "But you, my angel, are sweeter than any flower."

"I love you, Mommy," Jane said.

Her mother turned and gave Jane a hug.

Wraith could almost feel her mother's arms around her. Almost.

"What about me?" her father asked.

"You have to wait for daddy's day," Jane said seriously.

Her parents laughed, and so did Wraith.

The memory faded and Wraith found herself on the cold bathroom floor, her knees drawn up to her chest and crying. She didn't let herself wallow—well, not for long. She could practically hear Shadow telling her to get up. Her friend would be right. Wraith wasn't that little girl anymore. Truth was, she wasn't sad. That was the first complete, lucid memory of her parents. Her real parents. She held it tight, then tucked it away into her heart, where she could pull it out whenever she needed—and, likely, she would need it.

She got to her feet, turned on the faucet, and picked up the toothbrush.

Once she was dressed, Wraith stepped back into the bedroom and found a tray of food sitting at the dressing table. She looked the food over: perfectly sliced and decoratively arranged fruit, a large blueberry muffin, some cheese slices, and a bottle of water. She wasn't much of a fruit eater, but she also knew not to turn away free food, especially when you're starving. A couple of minutes later, the food was gone and she'd sucked down half the bottle of water in a series of large gulps. Time on the street taught you to eat fast when you got food. Someone was always watching, ready to take it from you.

She slung her bag over her head, grabbed the bottle of water, and stepped out of the palatial room.

CHAPTER THIRTY-SEVEN

Dante drew in a deep breath as he looked around the expansive library, his eyes moving from the polished hardwood floor to the bookshelves, so high a ladder was need to reach the highest. He looked over the spines of the books and thought of the great care that had been taken collecting each, and their history, the one not on their pages. The door opened and he turned, smiling when Caitlin and Edward walked in.

"Thanks for seeing me before you left," Dante said. "I wanted to say I'm sorry. It wasn't right for me to keep things from you. I won't do it again."

Caitlin shrugged. "I know it came from a good place." She gave him a wry smile. "But if you try that again, I'll kick your well-toned butt."

Dante laughed. "I'm touched you noticed."

"Excuse me," Edward said, "spell-wielding fiancé right here."

Caitlin wrapped her arm around him and kissed him slowly. At the kiss's end, she nuzzled her cheek to his chest. Then she dropped her arm and grabbed his backside.

Edward jumped and turned a shade of pink.

"Save it for the wedding night," Faolan said as he entered the room.

"Speaking of which," Caitlin said, turning a level gaze to Dante.

"I'll be there, I promise," Dante said.

Edward opened his mouth.

"Not for the wedding night," Dante said, "just for the wedding."

"And the reception, of course," Faolan said as he approached, then turned to Caitlin. "Sorry to interrupt, but we're ready to go when you are."

"There's something else we need to discuss, if you don't mind," Dante said.

Caitlin gave him a questioning look.

"It won't take long, I promise," Dante said.

Edward glanced at Dante, then at Caitlin. "I'll get Fiona and meet you outside," Edward said and kissed Caitlin's cheek.

When Faolan had escorted Edward out and closed the door, the library was silent. Dante's gaze drifted out the large windows to the truly enormous backyard. Some of the kids they'd spirited from the cells were playing, and it warmed his heart to see them getting a chance to be kids, even if only for a moment.

"It's amazing how easily they can slip back into

being kids," Caitlin said. "But I think there's going to be a lot of nightmares for a long time to come."

"But right now they get to be kids," Dante said. "It's not much, but it's something."

"What happens to them now?" Caitlin asked.

Dante looked at her. She was staring at the playing kids too, a smile on her lips that could only be called motherly.

"There's still too much dust to settle in Seattle," Dante said. "We can't let them go back."

"You'll send them back to the streets?" Caitlin asked.

"I won't be sending them anywhere. I don't want them back on the streets, but some of them, maybe a lot of them, would balk at going back into the system. I don't blame them, all things considered. We'll try to find homes for them, but I can't promise how success-ful that will be. What I can promise you is that I'm not going to abandon them."

Caitlin shook her head. "I didn't mean to imply that." She turned and looked out the window again, this time her smile was bittersweet. "It's just, well, sad; all those kids with no place to go and so unwilling to trust."

"The people who were supposed to help them were the ones who handed them over to be tortured and killed," Dante said. "I don't know what we can do for them, but Brigid and I will make sure they have a place to go. I can't, I won't, force them to do anything. The last thing I want is for them to run."

"I know you'll do the right thing," Caitlin said and took his hand, giving it a squeeze. "You always do."

Dante turned to her, fighting back tears but smiling. He drew his hand from his pocket and away from the leather box he'd been turning in his fingertips. Was it the right thing to break the final promise to a friend?

"Are you okay?" Caitlin asked.

Dante drew in a breath, smiled, and squeezed her hand. "I am."

Caitlin looked as if she was going to press him, but she didn't, for which Dante was grateful. They both turned back to the window, neither saying anything for a long while.

"You need to be vigilant," Dante finally said.

He could feel Caitlin look at him, but he just kept watching the kids play.

"I don't know what the Order has planned now," he continued. "They're beaten but not destroyed. And they've shown an interest in mortal wizards."

"Eddy," Caitlin said, turning to watch him walk across the grass with Fiona. "You're worried they'll come after Eddy."

Dante nodded. "They focused on children this time, but that might not always be the case. I don't believe it was a coincidence that someone started watching your house." He turned to Caitlin and saw the look of fierce defiance on her face. He couldn't help but smile.

"They'll have to come through me to get him," she said, stating it as simple fact.

"First, they have to come through me, and several others," Dante said.

Caitlin turned to him and nodded.

"I meant it when I said I won't keep things from you," Dante said. "When you get back, have Edward see what he can find in that library of his. I don't know if he'll find anything, but that's a good place to start."

"After the wedding," Caitlin said as she turned back and watched Fiona playing with some of the other kids.

"Of course," Dante said.

They stood in silence for a long moment, just watching the children play.

"They're waiting," Dante said. "You better go."

Caitlin looked at him again. "You sure there was nothing else?"

"It can wait," Dante said. "Now go ahead. I'll follow in a few days, after I take care of some loose ends."

"Okay," Caitlin said and gave him a hug, her face not even reaching his chest.

Dante smiled, hugged her back, and kissed the top of her head.

"You didn't strain your back reaching all the way down here, did you?" she asked.

"Maybe a little."

She stepped back and smiled at him, but it softened. "It can wait?"

"It can."

"Okay," Caitlin said. "See you in Boston." She stood, turned, and left the room.

"LOST?"

Wraith jumped and turned to find Brigid standing in the hallway. Even just standing there, she was elegant and beautiful, but carried an air of strength that Wraith found inspiring.

"Sorry. Didn't mean to scare you," Brigid said.

"Are all elves as quiet as you?" Wraith asked.

"Pretty much," Brigid said with a smile. "So, need some help navigating this place?"

In point of fact, Wraith had been wandering hallways for the better part of fifteen minutes now. She knew without a doubt she'd gone down the same path at least four times, but she couldn't figure out how that happened. All around her the information of the place was in constant flux, shifting and changing.

"Um, yes," Wraith said.

Brigid smiled and Wraith felt at ease.

"Come with me, dear."

Wraith followed, and they made a couple of turns Wraith was sure weren't there before. Her confusion must've shown on her face.

"You're not imagining it," Brigid said. "The layout of the house changes."

Wraith blinked. "It what?"

"It changes," Brigid said. "This house was originally a convent in Ireland. I had it brought over stone by stone."

Wraith thought she almost looked wistful.

"It was built for the nuns by the magi," Brigid said.

"They were a collection of wizards. Part of the protection they built into this place is that the layout changes around you, unless you live here of course."

Wraith looked around, and now she could see the quantum information wasn't really changing. Rather, it was splitting apart and joining other pieces to form new formulae. It was, well, brilliant! The wizards who—

"Wait, did you say wizards?" Wraith said, having stopped dead in her tracks.

Brigid turned and nodded.

"Where are they now?" Wraith asked. "I mean, are the wizards still around?"

Brigid's smile faded. "Sadly, no. I'm afraid they were decimated centuries ago. A few survived and took refuge with the Dawn Court while the Taleth-Sidhe went to face the Order."

"Seanán?" Wraith asked.

Brigid smiled. "Exactly right."

"He won, right?" Wraith asked.

Brigid smiled, but not much. "Eventually. But that's a story for another time." Brigid resumed walking and Wraith followed.

"What happened to the survivors?" Wraith asked.

Brigid laughed. "I said, it was for another time."

Wraith let out a sigh.

"I'll tell you that there was one. After the fighting was done, he fell in love, got married, and had children," Brigid said. "His son wasn't born with the touch of the craft. However, his son's son was."

"Where is he?" Wraith asked.

Brigid smiled. "Planning a wedding, and taking care of a very special little girl."

Wraith furrowed her brow and was about to ask another question, but figured she'd pushed enough. So instead she just said, "Thank you."

"You're welcome," Brigid said.

They walked in silence after that, and Wraith was glad when they came to some stairs. At least it was progress. But that led to more hallways. Finally, they rounded a corner and came to a pair of large oaken doors. Brigid opened them into a large room. Okay, it was a huge room. Two walls were floor-to-ceiling windows, and it let in the morning sunlight. There were several chairs around a fireplace, and even more scattered throughout the room, along with six sofas that looked like they should've been in a museum.

"He's waiting for you," Brigid said and nodded to one of the chairs.

Even from behind, Wraith recognized Dante.

"Thanks, again," Wraith said.

"Can I ask what you plan to do?" Brigid asked.

"Keep some promises," Wraith said. "I also want to make sure no more kids get taken. The Order is still out there. We might've hurt them, but they're not done for. I'm going to correct that."

Brigid smiled. "Good for you." She handed Wraith a card.

"What's this?" Wraith asked, looking it over. On it was an address and a phone number.

"If you plan to stay in the area, I hope you'll come to me if you need anything," Brigid said. "Food, clothes, money, advice, or just a safe place to sleep."

Wraith narrowed her eyes. "Not to sound ungrateful—"

"But why?" Brigid asked.

Wraith nodded.

"Whatsoever you do for one of the least of these, you did for me," Brigid said.

Wraith blinked and opened her mouth, then closed it. After a moment, her brain began working. "A Christian elf?"

Brigid smiled. "Let's just say, there is truth everywhere if you look for it. I offer you my help because you might need it, and I have it give."

Wraith handed the card back.

Brigid's smile faded.

"I don't need the card," Wraith said and tapped her head. "I've got it here."

Brigid's smile returned. "I do hope to see you again Jane Essex, Wraith, rememberer of the forgotten."

Wraith smiled at the moniker. "You will, I promise."

"Good," Brigid said, then kissed each of Wraith's cheeks. "Until then."

As she turned and left, Wraith thought of all those forgotten kids. Maybe that would be a good starting place to look for the allies her parents told her to find.

Wraith turned and stepped further into the room, looking around. She'd never seen anything like it before. It was beautiful, but it made her afraid to touch anything.

Dante stood and smiled at her, but there was the ghost of something else behind it. She couldn't help but feel as if she was intruding on something very private.

"How are you feeling?" he asked, offering her a chair.

After a moment's hesitation, she sat, carefully, and shrugged. "Clean, and not hungry."

Dante sat across from her, chuckled and smiled. "That isn't what I meant."

Wraith nodded. "Different, but better, I think. I don't know. I feel numb inside, like the pain and grief in my heart is too much to feel." She let out a sigh and felt a twinge in her heart. "I miss my friends. But I'm remembering things, and I don't feel like I'm going to explode. So that's something, I guess."

Dante nodded and somehow she knew he could relate, at least to the pain. He wore a mask of confidence and surety. Actually, it was probably sincere, but she could see in his eyes that he'd known pain that could compare to her own. Living as long as he had, it could probably dwarf hers.

Guilt and regret began seeping into her from her broken heart and the next words were out of her mouth before she could think to stop them. "I broke my promises to them. I failed them, my friends, and all those other kids. I should've been able to save them, but I couldn't."

"No, child, you didn't fail anyone," Dante said. "Believe me, I understand. It's a hard thing to break promises to your friends." He drew in a slow breath and shook his head. "But sometimes it can't be helped. Of course, that doesn't make it any easier to live with."

Wraith shook her head. "No, it really doesn't."

"Are you okay?" Dante asked.

Wraith shrugged. "Not really, but—"

"I'm sorry," Dante said. "It was a stupid question."

"I think I should go," she said.

Dante looked at her. "Right now?"

Wraith stood. "Yes, I'm sorry."

Dante stood as well. "Don't apologize. Before you go, the others would like to talk to you."

"Geek, Con, and Sprout?" Wraith asked.

Dante nodded.

Wraith considered saying no, but the thought of seeing Sprout won out.

"Okay."

Dante led her out of the room and back into the maddening hallways. Thankfully, it was only a couple of turns before they came to a set of French doors that opened onto the backyard. Actually, it was more like a small forest walled in by hedgerows. They stepped outside, and she marveled at the colors. The green of the grass and leaves on the trees were vivid. Likewise, the wildflowers were almost bursting with color, and so fragrant she could smell them from where she stood. It was all completely wild, and utterly beautiful because of it. Something inside her sang at the intricate formulae that made up the trees and all the life around her. She closed her eyes, drew in a deep breath, and felt the warmth of the sun on her face. Somewhere in her heart, Shadow was smiling. And somewhere, SK was saying he was hungry and Fritz was elbowing him in the ribs. She smiled and laughed, but just a little.

"This way," Dante said.

Wraith opened her eyes and followed him around the house. The old gray stones that made it told Wraith that Brigid hadn't been exaggerating about the age of it. She was so lost in studying the house that she didn't notice Dante had stopped walking. She bumped into him, though he didn't budge. She opened her mouth to apologize, but her words froze in her throat.

A large marble rotunda that could've come from ancient Rome stood in the distance. Inside was a table where Con, Geek, and Sprout sat playing a board game and laughing. Con's arm was in a cast, Sprout had a bandage on her forehead, but they were smiling. Wraith's heart ached as she looked on, but the image of Ovation's death made her turn away.

"I don't know if I can do this," Wraith said. "How can I tell them about Ovation?"

"They don't remember anything, including him," Dante said.

Wraith looked at him. "What?"

Dante shook his head, still looking at the trio. "They don't remember anything from the last month or so. Neither Brigid nor I can find any physical explanation."

"You're saying someone messed with their heads?" Wraith asked. "But why?"

"I don't know," Dante said. "There's a lot that's happened I can't explain, but I'm going to find out."

Wraith felt sadness burst from her heart, and her knees nearly gave way as a sob overtook her.

Dante caught her and drew her close, holding her up. "What is it?"

"I'm the only one who will remember him," she said. "And it's all my fault. All of it."

Dante turned and looked at her, lifting her chin. "It wasn't you, it was the Order," he said. "They did this. They are to blame, not you."

"But if it weren't for me—"

"Then it would've been someone else," Dante said. "This is not your fault, Wraith. Don't you dare take any of the blame that rightfully belongs to them. Not one bit. Do you hear me?"

Wraith nodded and in that moment, she knew with rare clarity exactly what she was going to do and how she would do it. "You're going to help the fifties, right? All of them I mean."

Dante shifted, clearly surprised by the question. "Those who want it, of course. Some of those we saved decided to stay here. Others preferred being on their own, but they'll never be turned away again if they come looking for help. I'm making sure no one ever is again."

Wraith nodded, then looked at the three she still considered her friends but to whom she was now a stranger. "I want to talk to them."

Before Dante could answer, Wraith began walking to the rotunda. She was tired of feeling weak and afraid too. She didn't feel that way now. She felt strong, and in control of her own destiny.

Dante was quick to catch up to her, and when they neared the rotunda, Con turned and spotted them. Soon Geek and Sprout noticed him looking and they turned as well.

"Con," Dante said and nodded at the Candy Land game on the table. "Who's winning?"

"I am!" Sprout said and smiled brightly.

"As usual," Geek said with a smile.

Con looked from Wraith to Dante. "Is this her, then?" His accent was still there, but it was softer somehow, less theatrical, more natural sounding.

"This is Wraith," Dante said.

Geek eyed her. "You do seem familiar." He narrowed his eyes, clearly digging for the source of the familiarity.

Wraith felt sympathetic pains for him, especially when he came up with nothing and shook his head in defeat.

"I explained the situation to them," Dante said. "I thought they deserved to know."

"Too right. We did, mate," Con said and shook his head. "Can't say I much like the idea of having a great heap of my memories go missing."

Wraith nodded. "I can relate."

"Thank you," Geek said and offered his hand, "for helping them, and for saving me."

Wraith turned to him, took his hand, and shook it. "You don't have to thank me. In fact," she reached into her bag and pulled out the Dr. Strange shirt, neatly folded. "I'm pretty sure this is yours."

Geek smiled and shook his head. "No, it was. It's yours now. I want you to have it. I don't really have much, but it was my favorite." He smiled more, and it was the same smile he'd had when he'd compared her to Nightcrawler. "From what I hear, it suits you."

Wraith smiled despite herself, and was going to insist he take it back. But when she looked at Geek, she could see it would be pointless to argue. Instead, she tucked the shirt back into her bag.

"Thank you," she said. "I love it."

Before Wraith could react, Sprout had climbed over Con, threw her arms around Wraith's neck, and hugged her tight.

"Thank you for saving me and my big brother and our friend," Sprout said.

Wraith glanced at Geek, who just chuckled and shook his head.

"Would you like to be my big sister?" Sprout asked.

Tears threatened to break loose, so Wraith hugged the little girl back, stroking her hair and saying softly, "I'd like that very much."

After a long moment, Sprout let go and smiled at Wraith. "I always wanted a big sister."

Wraith mussed her hair. "And I always wanted a little sister, so it works out." She turned to Con. "How would you like a chance to make sure nothing like this ever happens again, to anyone?"

"Whatever it is, love, I'm in," Con said with a fierce smile on his face.

"Me too," said Geek.

Dante looked at her expectantly.

"You're less likely to kick a pup if it has teeth," she said.

"Brilliant, let's do it!" Con said.

Wraith nodded at his cast. "Soon. You need to heal. All of you." She turned to Dante. "I have some things to take care of. Can—?"

"I don't think Brigid would let them leave before giving them a clean bill of health," Dante said.

"She's really nice," Sprout said.

Wraith kissed the little girl's cheek. "She sure is."

Sprout beamed, then looked at Wraith. "What do you have to do?"

Wraith glanced at Dante. "I have some promises to keep," she said. "And one to break," she told to herself.

"Do you need a ride somewhere?" Dante asked.

Wraith shook her head. "No, I just need a door."

Wraith stared at the closed door and frame around it. Focusing, she began building the equation in her head. As it wove together in her head, matching numbers and symbols drifted into place. Reaching into the darkness of her mind, back into the church, she careful pulled together the memories she had. It wasn't about an address; it was about connection. It was the sounds she remembered first: the hum of car tires on the street outside, the rustling of the leaves on the big tree outside her bedroom window, the birds singing. As she reached deeper, more memories began to surface. She could hear the sound of her parents talking, the creaks and sounds of a lived-in house.

Then came the smells; her mother's perfume first, and it carried her deeper. Soon she could smell oil, gasoline, and metal—the garage. That scent faded and she smelled, well, nothing. A brief panic ran through her, but she kept her focus. Then she realized there was a smell, and it was just so familiar, it hid perfectly in the background. It was the background. All the smells and sounds blended together forming a near whole. Before long, she could feel the soft carpet on her bare feet, and sinking into the plush couch wrapped in her favorite blanket. When the scents and sounds had built an image so vivid she could see it, she opened her eyes, reached out, and touched the doorknob. The moment her fingers touched the cool metal, the last of the numbers drifted into place and probability became a certainty.

She held her breath, opened the door and stepped through.

Sadness crashed over her like a rogue wave, and a held breath came out in a shuddering sob.

CHAPTER THIRTY-EIGHT

She stood in the entryway of what she knew was her house, had been her home. It wasn't even an empty shell now; there were empty beer cans and cheap liquor bottles all over the filthy carpet. Holes were burned where cigarette butts had been dropped and had smoldered. She turned slowly, looking around as a child's desire to come home began quietly dying. The walls had been torn open so the copper wiring could be stolen. The hollowing grief turned to burning anger as she looked over the graffiti on the walls. She wasn't angry with the kids and homeless that had used the house as shelter, she was angry at herself. Memories of squatting in abandoned homes churned through her head. Those had once been someone else's home, and she'd shown no more respect for it than anyone did this place. Karma was a master of poetic justice.

She drew in a breath and pushed away the regret,

grief, and anger that threatened to drag her into darkness. If she let it, she'd never get out again. So she stepped forward, over the trash and debris, through what had been the living room. But those demons of pain are persistent; and while she was lacking memories, this place was filled with them. She wept, quietly, when she saw the spot where the Christmas tree had gone every year.

She kept walking, past the dining room where her mother had made sure they always ate dinner together. Glancing into the kitchen, she saw the refrigerator, and tried to ignore the visions of paintings and report cards that had once hung there with pride.

Knowing it was a losing battle, she let the grief in. It was going to have lots of company anyway. And she did the only thing she could: she looked past the broken windows, torn open walls, and instead drew each memory into her heart, capturing it so she could take it with her. Memories were all that was left here.

"My inheritance," she said and laughed ruefully.

Turning away from the kitchen, she walked down the hallway. Unconsciously, she stepped over a spot on the floor that she knew would creak and wake her parents.

"If only," she said to herself.

She passed the bathroom, not daring to look inside, and continued on to her parents' room. The door was missing. A glance inside turned her stomach. More detritus, including used condoms, covered the dingy floor. Out of the corner of her eye, she saw the lingering fragments of a ward on the doorframe, now dead and useless. Clenching her jaw, she stepped inside, careful to step around the disgusting remnants of youthful lust.

The room felt both larger and smaller at the same time. Even empty and torn apart, she still felt that odd sense of invasion kids feel going into their parents' room when their parents aren't there. Once she reached the center, she turned, scanning the room.

"A secret place," she said to herself, repeating her mother's words. The floor was carpeted, so it couldn't be a loose floorboard. The closet doors were broken and hanging useless. Holes ranging from fist-sized to more than a foot in diameter covered the walls.

Hopelessness welled up from her heart.

"There's no way anything could've stayed hidden here," she said to the empty room.

A thought came to her. She drew the goggles from her bag and slipped them over her head. Adjusting the lenses, she shifted the scene. Faint traces of strong emotions drifted like motes of dust in the air. The walls and ceiling were crisscrossed with wisps of faded magic.

She didn't see anything.

After ten minutes, she finally gave up and pushed the goggles back onto her head. Happily, she left the room and the desecration of her parents' most sacred and private place behind. She was about to turn to leave, when, without meaning to, she turned toward her room. The door was closed, and though it had some holes and dents from where someone had kicked it repeatedly, it also still bore dozens of stickers.

Without her telling them to, her feet carried her there until she was looking over the door that, to her, read like the history of her childhood. Her very young years were represented by unicorns, flowers, and pixies. All were faded and old. The newer ones were almost entirely bumper stickers. The oldest were jokes relating to inside fantasy jokes.

"One sticker, to rule them all," she read aloud and chuckled.

The newest of all were math or science jokes.

"'The speed of light: not just a good idea, it's the law,'" she read.

Wraith appreciated the irony, considering how she'd gotten here. When she'd looked over every sticker several times, she couldn't avoid it anymore. She reached out and ran her fingers over the letters across the middle of the door. Someone had started to peel them away, but years had practically bound them to the wood, and the vandal had apparently given up at removing the word *Room*, leaving only the adhesive residue to tell what had been there. *Janey's* was still intact though. She ignored the rather unflattering note someone wrote with a Sharpie below it.

Drawing in a slow breath, she pushed the door open and stepped in. As she did, she felt a faint tension slide over her. She blinked and looked around. Her room was practically untouched. Turning back to the door, she could see the lingering wards woven into the doorframe. She touched the smooth wood, tracing over the equation that was still strong. That didn't make sense. Why would the wards in this room still be intact, but not in any others? The answer came to her almost immediately. Her parents would've placed the most powerful and most lasting wards to protect what mattered most to them.

She studied the ward, realizing it was a connection to her parents. It was elegant in its efficiency and effectiveness. It wouldn't explode, or set the intruder on fire. It would nudge the person to go somewhere else, a whisper that nothing of importance was in here. Deeper still, she could see that if someone was set on entering, once inside, a nagging fear would fill them. It would be a like a splinter in the mind, and the only way to remove it would be to leave. Wraith tried to imagine the willpower the people who'd taken the furniture from here must've had.

She found herself smiling with pride. Her parents hadn't been slouches— they'd been real, honest–to–goodness wizards.

Her eyes drifted down the inside of the doorframe and she saw lines drawn in intervals; the one starting at maybe three feet from the floor was marked with a *2*.

Her fingertips touched the black mark. "I guess I was always tall."

She followed the lines up with progressing ages, jumping two or three inches every year. The last three lines were spaced better than four inches apart. She stared at the last line, *15*, just above eye level. Her eyes closed, and she leaned her head against the doorframe, letting a few tears fall to the carpet.

Her mother's voice drifted through the years and she could almost feel her gentle touch wiping tears away.

*"**S**weetie, I know you loved Mr. Cuddles," her mother said, "but he wouldn't want you to cry; he'd want you to remember all the good times you had with him, and how lucky you were."*

"Lucky?" Jane asked, the shoebox-turned-hamster-coffin held tight in her small hands.

Her mother smiled and nodded, wiping the tears away. "Out of all the little girls in the world, Mr. Cuddles was your friend. That's pretty special, don't you think? Almost like magic."

Wraith smiled the smile of that little girl, and her mother's comforting words wrapped around her like a warm cloak. She stood up straight, drew in a breath, and turned from the doorframe, then she stopped.

"Almost like magic," she said, casting the words out like a net, hoping to ensnare a memory she knew was there but could quite see.

Pieces were all that came at first: doing geometry homework, struggling to figure it out. She held fast to that memory, closing her eyes to focus more intently. Slowly, it expanded in her mind.

"Didn't your teacher tell you about pi?" her father asked.

Jane shrugged.

Her father smiled, scooted his chair closer to hers, and pointed to the math problem. "It's a magic number," he said writing it out.

"Magic?" Jane asked, dubious.

Her father looked at her seriously, continuing past the tenth digit. "Oh yes. It goes on forever, and never, ever repeats with any kind of pattern."

Jane thought about that and furrowed her brow. "But that's not possible."

Her father smiled. "Why?"

"If it goes on forever, it has to eventually repeat," she said. "Even if the pattern was a trillion places, it would have to repeat. Just by ever deceasing probability."

Her father smiled at her. "Except its magic, so it can defy the standard models of probability."

Jane rolled her eyes. "Dad, I'm nine and a half," she said. "I know there's no such thing as magic."

He smiled more. "Oh, don't be so sure about what you know. Before Einstein, everyone knew that time was constant."

Jane considered that. "I suppose, but—"

"Magic is just a term we use to describe something we can't explain with our current understanding," her father said.

Jane considered that too, and nodded slowly. "I guess that makes sense."

He leaned in close. "There's another reason I know it's a magic number," he said.

"How?"

"Look at the first three numbers," her mother said as she came up from behind and set a glass of milk on the table.

Jane did, but didn't see anything.

"It's your birthday," she said and kissed Jane's cheek. "March fourteenth."

Jane smiled, then realized she was smiling and forced it back. That of course made her smile more. "Does that mean I can do magic?" she asked, trying to put some skepticism in her voice.

Her parents shared a smile, obviously seeing past the ruse.

Wraith held to that memory for a long time before tucking it away in her heart for safekeeping, letting it fill her with warmth and comfort. She smiled, soaking in the simple joy of just knowing her birthday.

She opened her eyes and looked around the room. Could that be another reason why the wards here were so strong? It made sense. If you were going to hide something, what better place than somewhere you had built to protect that which was most precious to you.

"A secret place," she said to herself, scanning more slowly.

After a moment, she sighed in exasperation with herself and lowered the goggles over her eyes. She made a few minor adjustments to the lenses and then the tendrils of magic that wove over the room came into glowing clarity. She stopped and stared in utter amazement. It was beautiful. Thousands of individual lines, some white, others gold, blue, green, purple, red—every color imaginable, wove together all around the room. Each pulsed with something akin to, well, a pulse, a heartbeat. Her gaze moved to the closet, and it seemed that the threads grew brighter there.

She opened the door and was washed over with memories of hiding there as a child, door closed and sure no one would ever find her there; as if the spot she occupied was outside normal space. That's when she saw the lines of glowing power that squared off one corner, the same corner she'd always chosen. She reached out and touched a filament of magic. It thrummed like a guitar string, resonating with the others until the whole room seemed to hum in a clear and perfect tone.

Along the middle of the back wall, a line of numbers appeared in shimmering script: zero through nine. Her heart raced with excitement and she was smiling broader than she had in recent memory. Reaching out slowly, and carefully, she touched the three.

The number grew brighter and a new tone, lower in pitch, filled the room. She could almost see the wave form on the threads of power, its frequency slowing.

She touched the one. The amplitude increased, but the frequency slowed; the tone grew louder, but lower in pitch.

She touched the four. The vibration in the magic around her grew higher in pitch and more powerful still.

Moving faster she pressed one number after another: 3.14159265358979

Upon touching the sixteenth digit, the previous— well, *sounds* was the only word she could think of, even though she wasn't really hearing them—began to play together. The "music" it created washed over Wraith and filled her with awe. It was beautiful, like the sound of the entire universe resonating. It was also incredibly familiar. Then it dawned on her. It was Beethoven's Moonlight Sonata, her mother's favorite song. Wraith closed her eyes, remembering her mother playing it on the piano and teaching her to play it. Then she remembered the wizard, and her promise to him.

"No more broken promises," she whispered to herself.

When she opened her eyes, the square in the corner of the closet had changed. The wall itself didn't disappear, but Wraith could see beyond it, into a space outside of space. Inside, she saw something glowing bright in shades of white and blue. She reached in, her hands passing through the matter of the drywall as if it didn't exist, and touched something smooth. She drew out two . . . somethings, rectangular and completely covered in a dense weave of magic lines. It took her a moment to realize they were books, but with the goggles on she couldn't see their material form under the intense magic in them. Her heart raced and she ran her hands over them reverently, then stepped out of the closet. Around her, the music faded into silence, and she could see the wards over the room began to dim slowly. It occurred to her that the wards must've been set up to stay until someone found the books.

She pushed the goggles up and the world now looked as if it was painted in muted grays—crude shadows of the beautiful light she'd just seen. Dimly, she thought of Plato and his Allegory of the Cave. Maybe he was on to something.

Pushing that thought aside, she focused on the two books in her hand. They were bound in old leather, dark and worn, but well cared for. There were no titles, not even embossing left behind from gold leaf that had worn away. She didn't know how, but she knew the bottom one was her father's and the top one her mother's.

She opened her mother's book slowly, holding her breath.

It came out in a slow, whisper. "Wow."

EPILOGUE

Private Bobby Collins smelled the familiar scent of antiseptic and heard the beeping of machines. Being in the hospital was a good thing. It meant he wasn't dead, which hadn't been a certainty when things went down. He tried to move and instantly regretted it. He let out a grunt of pain.

"Easy, soldier," a man said.

Collins opened his eyes and saw the commanding officer of the Legion of Solomon, *his* commanding officer, standing over him, stone-faced as ever. The man, simply called One, was in his early forties, but they'd been a hard forty. His face wore lines that showed every mile, and his brown hair was peppered with gray that was just as earned. He wasn't tall, or built like a linebacker, but he was made of military-grade steel and could take apart half a dozen men years his junior.

"How bad is it, sir?" Collins asked.

One reached out and pressed a button on a machine. A moment later, Collins felt the sharp edges of his pain dull and a faint euphoria fill him.

"Bad enough to need morphine," Collins said, his words a little slurred.

"You got burned up good, son," One said. "I honestly don't know whether to give you a medal or kick your ass."

"Sir, if it's the latter, may I request a deferral."

One chuckled. "You're going to be fine, Private Collins. Or should I call you Ovation? You've been using that name for a while now."

Collins drew in a breath, not too deep. "No, sir. He was killed by the Theurgic Order. The body, or rather a body, was burned beyond recognition."

"Who was he?" One asked. "Did he have any family?"

"No, sir," Collins said. "He was a street kid. Some poor slinger with the bad luck to be a suitable doppelganger for me." Collins shook his head. "He wasn't supposed to die in there, sir."

"What happened?"

Collins went over the events. The plan had been for him to observe and direct from the cover of his version of invisibility. Not that he'd really been invisible; he'd just manipulated everyone into overlooking him. It was a trick that had saved his bacon a number of times in Afghanistan, and got him noticed by the Legion in the first place. Safely hidden in plain sight, he was supposed to weave the complicated illusion. After seeing the illusionary execution, Wraith would then take out the Order. With that done, she'd go to release the captives, or take Geek and teleport out. Once clear, Collins would collect the unconscious double, set the charm to change one of the Order members into his corpse, and get clear. He hadn't expected the place to turn into a scene from hell. The only reason he hadn't suffocated or been killed himself was thanks to the charms he'd been carrying.

Collins shook his head. "It wasn't a normal fire, sir. Not even a normal magical fire. I couldn't keep it away from the kid, and I couldn't let him get up and run, or go and grab him without—"

"Without sacrificing the mission," One said.

Collins nodded

"Well, it's probably not much comfort," One said, "but that one boy's death saved countless others. That operation had killed hundreds of kids that we know of, and sent dozens more into the world with power they couldn't control. Thankfully, none the likes of the asset."

Collins nodded, but didn't look up.

"I told you it wasn't going to be much comfort," One said.

"Yes, sir."

"You did good, private," One said. "I'll admit I wasn't sure you could pull it off, but you did. This was a tough mission, but you got it done."

"Thank you, sir." Collins thought back to how it all

had played out. Manipulating two changelings and a wizard hadn't been easy, but he'd managed. He was impressed how well his mental magic had worked. All he had to do was tweak some memories, and insert himself to create a shared past. Of course, he also had to make sure they didn't remember anything from the last few weeks. After that, he'd only needed to nudge them every once in a while to say or do what was needed to push Wraith in the right direction—the one that had led to her going after the Order. It would've been easier to just get inside Wraith's head, but he couldn't risk it. Those phantoms of hers would've tipped her off. Collins knew he was just lucky that she'd decided to go to the market alone, which had given him a chance to set the scene.

His stomach turned when he thought back to all that had required. He'd made sure he hadn't hurt Con or Sprout too badly, just enough to make it look like the Order had kicked the door in, fought, and then fled with Geek and himself. That still meant he hurt a little girl. That made him the kind of guy whose ass he'd kick, if given the chance. Then he thought of Wraith again. She was a sweet kid, and he genuinely felt for her, but it wasn't any different than a kid with a bomb strapped to her. He did what he had to do to make sure an Order cell was destroyed. As One had said—How many kids wouldn't be tortured and killed now? No, Collins didn't have to like what he did, he just had to do it.

"I know that look," One said. "I've seen it in the

mirror a couple of times, but it looks especially bad on someone your age."

Collins didn't say anything, and he didn't look at One.

"It wasn't pretty," One said. "Lives were lost, including a few good FBI agents—"

"What?"

One nodded. "The team that was sent into to investigate had the security clearance to know about us and our work," One said. "The Order managed to get a mole on that team. She killed her partners."

"What happened to her?" Collins asked.

"Her body turned up with a single tap to the head," One said. "I can't prove it, but I'm sure the faeries did it."

"The Order are like roaches," One said. "They get in everywhere. That means we have to use methods that don't always sit well with our consciences. But that's a good sign."

"Sir?"

"It means you're still a human being," One said. "But you're also a soldier. You don't get the luxury of regret or guilt. That's my job."

Collins nodded.

"You should know that our surveillance of the Order stronghold reported back that all the captured kids got out, including that one from your group. What's his name?"

"Dustin, sir," Collins said. "Went by Geek. He was half troll."

One shook his head. "This just gets more and more

bizarre. Anyway, the point is, it looks like the only casualties were your double and that Order cell. Put a substantial dent in their operation too. Based on the body count, they're going to need one hell of a recruitment drive to recoup those numbers, and that will take time."

"And then?"

"Then we hit them again," One said. "And again, and again, until they're gone."

"Will they ever be gone, sir? I mean, all of them?"

"Our job is to fight the enemy until there is no more enemy." One handed Collins a cup of water with a straw. "Some good is getting done too. We're having a lot of success undoing what they did to those mortal kids, removing the souls bound to them. I know it's not much, but it's something."

Collins drank.

"I don't know if this is a war I'll ever see the end of," One said and set the cup aside when Collins was done. "But it's a war that needs fighting. Most of the country has no idea what's going on around them— and don't want to know, including some on Capitol Hill who fund this unit. We don't feel it's in our best interest to trust the security of our nation, and our species, to the faeries. We've advised the secretary of defense; both he and the president agree. As such, we've been given the green light to begin recruiting others."

Collins nodded. One was right. This was a fight humanity needed to fight for itself, and he was glad that more were going to be given the chance to help.

He turned to look at his CO, opened his mouth, then closed it and looked away.

"Speak freely, soldier," One said. "You've earned that much at least."

Collins swallowed. "What about, Wra—the asset, sir?"

One eyed him for a moment. "She was carried out by the lead elf, the regent. She was unconscious, but appeared alive with no obvious injuries. We have no report on her whereabouts or condition at this time. I'm not proud of the fact that we had to resort to manipulating a troubled child to eliminate this cell, but she was the only one with the power to pull it off." One nodded at Collins. "You just rest and heal, son. Let me worry about her."

"Yes, sir."

"Two is taking care of you. You'll have a few more scars when this is done, but he expects you to make a full recovery." One pulled something out of his pocket and set it on Collins's chest.

Collins reached to take it and realized for the first time that his arms and hands were covered in bandages. He ignored them and took up the patch. It was a Seal of Solomon: two overlapping triangles—the symbol that would eventually be known as the Star of David—within two circles, the space between which was filled with Syriac writing. And there was a "4" in the middle of the star. It was the Legion's command-unit patch, and only worn by seven members: the most powerful wizards who made up "the circle." Collins, as support, was technically just on loan from his unit and still normal Army.

"We lost a good man in this operation," One said. "He'll be missed, but the team is a man short now. You'll be the youngest to ever join the circle, but I think you're up to it. Interested?"

Collins nodded. "Yes, sir. Thank you."

One smiled. "Okay, I'll check in on you again soon." One saluted. "At ease, Four. Welcome to the circle."

"Thank you, sir." Collins returned the salute, or as close as he could manage in his condition. When One left the room, Collins looked over the patch and smiled, as much as he could. He let out a breath and said a silent prayer and apology to his double. Collins hated that he hadn't even known the kid's real name.

Collins shook his head, set the patch on his chest, hit the button for more morphine, and closed his eyes. He didn't want to think about it anymore. He didn't look himself over either. He didn't want to see how bad off he was.

Of course, he didn't want to see the look on Wraith's face when she saw him getting his throat cut either, but he did. He probably would for a long time to come.

Before slipping off into a morphine-enhanced sleep, Collins heard voices outside his room.

"Were you able to get inside?" One asked.

"No, sir." It was someone Collins didn't recognize. "The house has wards on a level we've never seen before."

"All our reports said he was a mediocre talent at best," One said. "Is the intelligence bad?"

"I don't know, but they did spot the observation team. It could be the faeries."

"I don't like how close he is with the faeries," One said. "We may have to take a more direct approach and speak to the good Dr. Huntington directly."

"Yes, sir."

ACKNOWLEDGMENTS

I want to thank everyone who has supported and inspired me as this book has developed. I've learned that writing a book might be a solitary feat, but finishing a book is anything but. Thanks to the Knights for their constant support and encouragement: Kenda, Mike, Dustin, Kristin, Casey, and Geoff. To my friend Samn (I amn), thanks for the inspiration. To Ned and Ed, "SPOON!!!" Thanks to my mom and Neil for your support and for all the copies you've bought and given away. To Margaret, my agent, thanks for being such a great agent and sounding board. To my publicist, Caitlin, I really appreciate your enthusiasm and hard work. Thank you again to Rebecca, my editor, and everyone at HarperCollins (Caro, Jessie, Pam, and David) for your dedication and excitement with this book and for making me feel like a real author. To my HarperVoyager Impulse colleagues, I so appreciate having a support group. You all have been great through this. Last, but certainly not least, my deepest thanks and undying gratitude to the American Faerie Tale fans.